By Christopher Dow

Fiction

Effigy
> Book I: Stroud
> Book II: Oakdale

The Books of Bob
> Devil of a Time
> Jumping Jehovah

The Clay Guthrie Mysteries
> The Dead Detective
> Landscape with Beast
> The Texas Troll Unlimited
> Darkness Insatiable

Roadkill
The Werewolf and Tide, and Other Compulsions

Nonfiction

Lord of the Loincloth (nonfiction novel)
Book of Curiosities: Adventures in the Paranormal
Occasional Pilgrimage: Essays on Film, Literature, and Other Matters
Living the Story: The Meandering, True, and Sometimes Strange
> Adventures of an Unknown Writer
>> Vol. I: Growing Up Takes a Long Time
>> Vol. II: Growing Old Takes Longer

Martial Arts

The Wellspring: An Inquiry into the Nature of Chi
Circling the Square: Observations on the Dynamics of Tai Chi Chuan
Elements of Power: Essays on the Art and Practice of Tai Chi Chuan
Alchemy of Breath: An Introduction to Chi Kung
Leaves on the Wind: A Survey of Martial Arts Literature (Vol. I–VI)

Poetry

City of Dreams
The Trip Out
Texas White Line Fever
Networks
A Dilapidation of Machinery
Puzzle Pieces: Selected Poems

Editor

The Abby Stone: The Poetry of Bartholo Dias
The Best of Phosphene
The Best of Dialog

The Dead Detective

The Dead Detective

Christopher Dow

Phosphene Publishing Company
Temple, Texas

The Dead Detective
© 2008 by Christopher Dow
ISBN: 0-9796968-3-6
ISBN 13: 978-0-9796968-3-1

Published by:
Phosphene Publishing Company
Temple, Texas, U.S.A.
phosphenepublishing.com

2.1

For Sydney and Mariko

The past is the only dead thing that smells sweet.

—Edward Thomas

The Dead Detective

Prologue

"SHIT, IT'S COLD." ART DURWARD cradled his shotgun and blew into his hands. "Right, Clay?"

When Guthrie didn't respond, Durward stared at him and repeated, "Right, Clay?"

"Yeah."

Durward watched Guthrie for a moment, then pulled his eyes away. He leaned forward and peered around the bushes at the decrepit bungalow next door. The streetlight half a block away threw just enough illumination over the front yard to show it hadn't been mowed in months. Junk and trash in the tall grass made dark, unidentifiable mounds that were threatening in the low light. The front door lay shadowed within a shallow porch.

"Damn stupid perps. If I was in there, I'd know I was surrounded."

"If you don't shut up, Art, he's gonna hear your big mouth."

Durward glared at Guthrie, nose wrinkling and brow clouding.

"Fuck you," he said. "You're not a detective yet. Until next week, you're just another grunt like us."

"Keep it down," snapped Murphy, the third member of the group.

"All I did was ask my partner a simple question." Durward's voice took on a peeved tone. "That okay with you, Murph?"

Murphy just looked away in the stiff silence. After a moment, Durward's face cleared.

"Sorry, Clay," he said. "I just never seen you like this."

Guthrie remained remote and made a desultory show of checking over his shotgun.

Durward glanced contemplatively into the night and blew out a heavy breath that hung for a clouded moment around his face.

"Shit, it's cold," he said to no one in particular.

At that moment, a crackly voice muttered from the officers' com sets, "Ready unit one?"

"One ready," Murphy replied.

"Okay," came the response. "We go in two minutes."

"Think he's in there?" asked Murphy as the team leader queried the other units.

"If he isn't, I hope the poor sap we bust in on doesn't drop dead with surprise," Durward said.

Then silence fell as they readied their weapons, and themselves, for the tense moments to come.

"In five," came the voice over their com sets. "Four, three, two, one, go!"

The three cops came around the bushes at a dead run, heading straight for the front door. Two other cops loped from the house opposite, and Guthrie knew that even more were heading for the back door. He also saw that he and Art would get to the door first.

Then they were there. As Durward raised his heavy, polished black boot to kick in the door, Guthrie heard a faint, metallic snicking noise, like ball bearings clicking together. It had to be....

The sound was obliterated as Durward's boot slammed into the door, next to the lock, splintering the frail frame. The door burst inward, and Durward, Guthrie crowding close behind, rushed inside. Guthrie's eyes took in the scene instantly though he seemed disconnected from it all—the man in his underwear, the glazed animosity in his eyes, the machine gun turning, Art leveling his shotgun. Guthrie swung his own shotgun upward, took a step.

Suddenly Art was stumbling, off balance and unable to defend himself, and the sounds of his shuffling feet and surprised grunt were swallowed by a roar so loud and long and insistent that it became a physical force slamming repeatedly against Guthrie, hurtling him to the floor. His numbed chest couldn't seem to take in a breath, and his hip was burning, burning. He blinked to clear the hot tears from his eyes, only the wetness was too thick for tears. Tears were not clots of gray grease soaked in crimson.

Art was stretched out next to Guthrie. The first half of the burst from the machine gun had taken him full in the face, and he was nearly headless. But that didn't keep his body from jerking spasmodically. The toe of his polished black boot kicked rhythmically against Guthrie's leg, and each touch jolted pain through Guthrie's hip and thigh. In the startling silence that lay in the wake of the roar, a portion of the crimson-shadowed world moved closer until it loomed over Guthrie and became the darkest shadow of all. Protruding from its center was the barrel of a gun, metal encircling final emptiness, and the emptiness was an eye, and it was looking for him.

Guthrie instinctively raised his hand and jerked his trigger finger, and another roar blasted a hole in the silence. He didn't even feel the shotgun's recoil throw the weapon sideways out of his grip. All he knew, or cared, was that the empty eye lost sight of him as the shadowed presence behind it fell away. That was all that mattered—that the shadow and its empty eye were gone.

No, something else mattered, but he couldn't remember what, only that it, too, was gone.

Then a second shadow hovered over him, but this one didn't have an empty eye. It leaned close and laid concerned hands on his chest.

"Clay. Are you with me?" It was Murphy.

In the background someone was moaning. Art...? No, Art no longer had a mouth. It couldn't be Art.

"I fell, Murph." His voice sounded feeble in his own ears.

"Jeez," Murphy said. "Hold still." He looked up and bellowed, "Officers down! Get an ambulance!"

Other officers crowded around while Murphy stripped off Guthrie's coat and Kevlar vest.

"Listen Clay. Your leg's been hit. I can't tell how bad, but the vest ate the rest of the slugs. You're gonna be okay. You hear me, Clay? You're gonna be okay."

Guthrie heard, but he was drifting, and the words were swallowed by distance.

He didn't believe them, anyway.

1

HE NOTICED THE MAN'S EYES first. They were a gray that seemed about as organic as steel, and their gaze was just as adamant. And he was packing heat—Guthrie sensed the gravity of it even before he saw the discreet bulge beneath the jacket of the contemporary, well-cut suit.

Guthrie wondered if Alice had hired him. The thought came unbidden because death lurked in those cold eyes, and she was about the only person who hated him that much. Of course, there were the criminals he'd helped put away during his time as a cop, but he didn't think any of them would bother tracking him down. All that had been more than two years ago, anyway.

The eyes quickly scanned Guthrie, and he knew the look. He'd just given it himself. It wasn't judgmental or critical of Guthrie's casual attire—it was only to see if he was armed. One glance told all. It's hard to conceal a gun under a T-shirt.

The cold eyes turned back to Guthrie's face, and Guthrie suddenly felt naked. Naked enough that he almost shut the door on the man. It was his house, dammit, though the man's look made it clear that possession was only a relative proposition. Suddenly, Guthrie wished he *was* armed and that the gun was in his hand and aimed at the man's chest.

"Yes?" Guthrie asked.

"Your name Clay Guthrie?"

Guthrie considered. The man was about forty-five, a little taller than Guthrie's own average height, and his hair was jet black. Those opaque eyes bored out over an aquiline nose. He stood there with a lean, deadly grace that suggested intense training, experience, and self-assurance. He was the consummate professional in manner and tone. Not the slightest hint of personal opinion, not the slightest threat, just the simple question.

Guthrie hadn't the faintest idea of what a man like this would want with him, but if he wanted Guthrie dead, Guthrie figured he'd be that way already. Besides, if he said no, the man would be back.

"I'm Guthrie."

"My name is Corbin Ingram. I work for Benjamin Egan. Mr. Egan is head of Rampart Security Systems."

Guthrie nodded. "I've heard of it."

"Mr. Egan would like to talk to you about a job."

"A job? With Rampart?"

"A job for Mr. Egan."

Guthrie considered again. Rampart was one of the largest security companies in the city. Every cop knew of it, some moonlighted for it, and a few had permanently joined its payroll. Its primary business was providing building security, from a single night watchman on lowly warehouse duty to major security for office buildings and industrial parks. Guthrie had fleetingly thought about applying there himself when he'd gotten out of the hospital. He could limp through a warehouse as well as anybody. Rampart supplied everything from closed-circuit television surveillance to bomb-proof limousines to bodyguards who would take a bullet for a client.

Or presumably, Guthrie focused on Ingram, deliver one.

Before this man with the impassive face and steel eyes showed up at his door, Guthrie had spent the morning mulling a slow breakfast and a slower book detailing the construction of electronic bugging devices, all the while fighting the urge to switch on the TV. But at this time of day, programming was limited to talk shows, soap operas, and reruns of fossilized series sandwiched between commercials for lawyers, trade schools, and psychic hotlines, so he'd doggedly kept at the book until Ingram's unexpected knock saved him from an in-depth discussion of the relative merits of various types of directional microphones.

The day, in other words, was slow. As slow and dull and numb as the day before and the day before that and, presumably, as tomorrow would be. He had to do something—he couldn't just sit here on his ass waiting to get fat and old. He was only thirty-three, and watching the wallpaper yellow could take a long, long time.

"What kind of job?"

"Mr. Egan will have to explain that."

"I might as well tell you now that I'm not interested in being a security guard."

"Mr. Egan doesn't personally interview security personnel."

So there it was. An offer to tempt him from his lethargy. The only question was, was it real? No. Two questions. Why him? A job for someone the caliber of Benjamin Egan was pretty rarefied air. Not that Guthrie couldn't use the work. His house was falling apart, and his disability pension could barely support his basic expenses. In short, he needed a shot in the economic arm.

That was what he told himself, but he knew there was more. More, even, than getting away from the TV and the book. He had to get out and do something, anything, to get away from himself, because locked up in this lonely house with his memories for one more day was more than he could take, especially since he couldn't take a drink. He'd held off drinking since the shooting, but he knew that couldn't last indefinitely.

"When did he have in mind?"

"Right now."

"Okay. Give me the address, and I'll be along in a few minutes."

"Mr. Egan asked that we drive you."

Ingram nodded toward the midnight blue Mercedes that Guthrie couldn't help but notice parked in the driveway behind his brown Honda Civic. The driver, a man of about thirty with close-cropped blond hair and, judging from the thickness of his neck, plenty of muscle, sat in the driver's seat watching the transaction on the porch. At least Guthrie supposed he was watching. His face was turned in their direction, but his eyes were covered by mirrored sunglasses.

Guthrie shrugged. Ingram hadn't asked Guthrie if he wanted to be driven, but no matter.

"I'll be right back."

Leaving the door open, he went to the bedroom, changed his clothes, and put on a tie and a sports jacket. The spring day was pleasant but might grow chillier later. Besides, Egan probably expected those, at the very least. In a couple of minutes, Guthrie was back on the porch, locking the door.

Ingram ushered him to the car and opened the door to let him in the front next to the blond man, who was, indeed, as beefy as his neck implied. As Guthrie got in, Ingram contrived to brush up against him, and Guthrie wondered if the man was disappointed Guthrie hadn't donned a gun as well as a tie. If he was, he didn't show it but closed the door and slid into the seat behind Guthrie. The blond man put the car in gear and backed out of the driveway.

Taking in the plushness of the Mercedes, Guthrie had to admit that he was a little embarrassed at the condition of his house, which probably was worth considerably less than the car. It was a sixty-year-old frame cottage sporting its fourth or fifth roof—Guthrie found it a little hard to count the layers of that much crumbling sediment.

He'd meant to fix it up. That's why he and Alice had bought it. They'd planned to fix it up as soon as he made detective. Maybe even add a second story to make room for kids. But since the shooting, he hadn't had the money or the energy. Besides, with Alice gone, what was the point? The place had all the amenities—central air in the winter, central heat in the summer—and it seemed best to let it follow its own inclinations to slowly subside into the black gumbo clay that is Houston's constantly-shifting excuse for bedrock.

He shrugged mentally. It was about all the home he needed now. More than enough if it just had a new roof. In the back were a couple of bedrooms, one of which he restlessly used for the purpose implied. The second served as a den, filled with a desk, computer, book shelves, and an old sofa. The backyard was separated from the front by a six-foot wooden fence whose primary reason for existence was to mask the ruin of his separated two-car garage, where he kept his washer and dryer and little else of value because the roof leaked like a sieve. In a climate like Houston's, where winter is a rainy season and semitropical deluges punctuate the rest of the year, things living in his garage had to be certified to one hundred meters or they'd better keep out. Behind the garage and the big, overgrown backyard was a thirty-year-old brick apartment complex whose cheap construction guaranteed many years of futile attempts at upkeep. The complex's parking lot adjoined Guthrie's backyard, from which it was separated by another wooden fence.

The blond bull didn't seem to notice Guthrie's decrepit house. In fact, he didn't seem to notice Guthrie, but Guthrie was all too aware that the man's deliberate disregard was as penetrating as the gaze of Ingram's ball-bearing eyes on the back of his head. Guthrie found himself tensing, and he forced himself to relax, but not too slowly. These men could read his every move and gesture, and he didn't want to seem either aggressive or weak.

They're just delivery boys, Guthrie reminded himself. Tough, high-priced, and dangerous delivery boys, but none of that mattered just as long as they got him to Benjamin Egan and this job.

As the blond steered through Guthrie's southeast-side neighborhood toward the traffic circle where Broadway and Park Place meet under the Gulf Freeway, Guthrie concentrated on the scenery, such as it was. Usually he was driving when he passed along these streets, and he didn't often get a chance to take a good look at his own neighborhood.

It was just as ugly as the last time he'd bothered to check it out—more houses as run-down as his own and, at the traffic circle, a small cadre of lowlife derelicts and homeless who eked out scanty livings by selling newspapers or flowers, washing windshields, or more likely, simply begging. It seemed there was one at every corner every day, just like it was the office and they were on the job, which was harassing anyone unlucky enough to get caught by a red light and making them feel rich and guilty just for owning a damn car. Personally, Guthrie was sick of the whole lot of them. It was like running a gauntlet just to go to the grocery store. He wished he was still a cop so he could bust them all. Hell, he *had* busted some of them.

The blond didn't run the gauntlet but sheered off onto the inbound Gulf Freeway feeder, heading toward downtown. In seconds the Mercedes was up to speed on the freeway, and it quickly passed the interchange for Loop 610, which rings downtown at a radius of about seven miles. After fifteen minutes at a steady five miles-per-hour above the speed limit, they'd circled downtown, exited at Memorial Drive, and were headed west toward Memorial Park. The blond kept to Memorial Drive all the way through the park and, soon after, crossed under the West Loop. Guthrie was vaguely gratified to see that although he was on the opposite side of town, economically as well as physically, even these intersections had bums selling newspapers, flowers, and windshield washes. Or just begging. Looked like things were bad all over.

Tough, Guthrie half-sneered as he turned away from the window. He managed to maintain, didn't he? It was marginal at best, maybe, but at least he gave enough of a damn about himself that he wasn't drunk and on the street. He had something, even if he wasn't sure exactly what it was, that kept him from joining the bums on the corner. He wasn't like that, he promised himself. Not that low. Never that low.

Fuck 'em, he snarled silently to mute the thoughts he dared not think. If they'd given up, that was their get-out, so fuck 'em.

Just past the Loop, the driver wheeled the Mercedes into a long curving private street that wove its way among several high-rise office buildings. Guthrie knew the place. It was called Bayou Towers, and the rent wasn't cheap. The blond pulled up in front of one of the buildings, and Ingram got out. Guthrie followed. It seemed like the appropriate thing to do.

The Mercedes slid off as Ingram led Guthrie inside. An elevator took them to the twenty-fourth floor. The offices of Rampart Security occupied the entire level, but Ingram steered Guthrie away from the main reception desk and down a side hall to a nondescript door that he unlocked with a keycard. They went down a second, shorter hall. About half way to the end, Ingram pushed open another unmarked door and ushered Guthrie through.

Guthrie found himself in a spacious office lined with darkly elegant shelves filled with old books and bookshelf knickknacks that could only be termed artifacts. The way he'd come in seemed like the office's second, or back, door.

"Mr. Egan will be with you in a few minutes," Ingram said flatly, then he left through the primary door, which shut soundlessly behind him.

The leather-upholstered furniture smelled of polish. The desk was a very dark, densely grained wood topped with green marble. In front of the desk was a guest chair, and behind it was a wide plate glass window through which could be seen a grand view of downtown, the spires a little hazy with distance, humidity, and smog.

Guthrie sat down to wait, but he didn't sit for long. For some reason, he felt exposed near the window, and the glare from the plate glass quickly began to hurt his eyes and give him a headache. He got up, blinking back hot spots, and retreated across the plush carpet to the cooler area of the room where the dark bookshelves lined the wall.

Running his eyes over the titles, he saw that the shelves held an astonishing collection ranging literature, philosophy, science, and mathematics. The single unifying factor was that all the books appeared to be old and, probably, rare. Guthrie didn't doubt a substantial number of first editions rubbed covers with reprints no less venerable. He wanted to take one of the books down and look at the title page, but an uncomfortable feeling of being watched kept his hands immobile.

Trying to act nonchalant, he surveyed the room. No cameras were obvious, but then this was the office of the head of Rampart. No security device *would* be obvious. He saw only the desk and chair and glaring window.

The sensation of being observed persisted, though he tried to put it out of his mind. Maybe it was some sort of test to see how he reacted to stress. If he ignored it, it would go away. He turned deliberately to study the fine old leather spines, but the headache begun by the glare abruptly flared so sharply that he grabbed his forehead with his left hand and steadied himself against the shelves with his right. For several long moments, he breathed heavily as the pain throbbed through his brain. Then, just as suddenly as it began, the headache stopped.

He straightened and let go of the shelves. What the hell had that been? Visions of embolisms and tumors crowded his thoughts, but he quickly forced them down. If he was sick, he'd just have to deal with it later.

He rubbed his head again, then quickly lowered his hand as a measured voice sounded from behind him.

"Mr. Guthrie. Thank you for coming. I'm Ben Egan."

2

GUTHRIE TRIED NOT TO ACT startled as he turned to look at the man who had so silently entered the room behind him. Benjamin Egan was about Guthrie's height and thin on the edge of gaunt. Light brown hair graying at the temples put him in his fifties, though he moved like a man ten years younger as he came across the room. Egan's face was an impenetrable mask, but his sharp, dark eyes hinted that something ruthless lurked beneath the carefully cultivated veneer. Well, why not? Egan didn't get the bucks to buy a room full of rare books and prop them up with archaeological kitsch like this by being happy-go-lucky.

Egan went around the marble-topped desk and settled into his chair. Guthrie sat, too, noticing that the glare from the plate glass behind Egan went a long way toward obscuring the man's features. Egan tented his hands and stared at Guthrie over the fingertips.

The wait went on just long enough to make Guthrie edgy. At last, Egan lowered his hands and said, "I've done a little checking on you. I hope you don't mind."

He didn't seem to care if Guthrie minded or not as he slid a file folder from the top of a short stack, opened it, and perused the contents.

"Let's see, you were a cop for about ten years."

"That's right."

"A tough business. Lawbreakers are bad enough. They curse and spit, and sometimes it comes to violence. But even the people who scream law and order sweat and get indignant when some cop pulls them over for speeding."

"I wouldn't have thought that the head of a ritzy security company would know what it's like being a street cop."

Guthrie meant it to sound bantering, but it came out edgy. Even though Egan had entered the room, Guthrie's neck still prickled as if unseen eyes watched him, and it was making him ill at ease. At least the headache had subsided.

Egan laughed. It wasn't loud or long, only unsettling, as if his mask had cracked enough to let out just the appropriate amount of ruthless humor before snapping shut again like a trap.

"Believe me, I know. I haven't always run this company. I've done everything from foot patrol at night to busting burglars to dealing with the problems of men under my command. Your record says that you were a good cop. You had high marks from your superiors, and you were smart. On your way to detective. Then you were shot."

Egan selected a sheet of paper from the file, deliberately holding it high enough to let light from the window show through and long enough for the letterhead to register on Guthrie's consciousness. It was from a major credit reporting agency.

"You've been out of work since."

"Why the interest?" Anger edged into Guthrie. He didn't appreciate the way Egan liked to twist the knife after he stuck it in.

"Purely professional, I assure you. My business is collecting and utilizing capable men."

"Are you offering me a job with Rampart?"

"Before we discuss that, let's talk about your problem."

"Problem?" Guthrie nearly burst out laughing, but it would have been embittered laughter, and he didn't want to give Egan that much hold on him. "You want to point to something specific?"

Egan shook his head.

"You'd like to think your problem is something like debt, boredom, injury, or divorce. But I know men, and there's something underneath it all that's eating at you. Your problems all began when you were shot. You were on your way up, then came the shooting, and here you are—on the way down. What happened?"

"You've got all the facts there." Guthrie gestured at the dossier, wishing he could get his hands on it to see just what Egan did know.

"I have facts, yes. But there are truths that lie deeper than facts."

"And what do those truths tell you?"

"I think people bother you. You don't trust them. That often indicates a man who doesn't trust himself."

"My wife runs out on me after I get shot protecting our community from a drug-crazed criminal and watching my partner of four years get killed—doesn't that qualify me for a little mistrust?"

"It wasn't much of a homecoming, was it?" Egan almost sounded sympathetic. "You'd been in the hospital less than a week when the duty nurse heard you and your wife arguing. After that, she stopped coming to see you, and when you went home, she was gone. Must have been a long recuperation."

Guthrie didn't know that the argument had been overheard much less made its way into any report. But he wasn't thinking of that. He was wondering if the depression began when Alice left, though he knew it hadn't. Her departure merely had carved him out inside, and he hadn't felt anything after but emptiness. The depression filled the vacancy later, at the assembly, when the chief of police pinned the badge of heroism on his chest in front of the rest of the force and the media with their bright lights. It flooded in the instant the thunderous applause broke through to him and he looked down and saw the crutches and felt the terrible knowledge that his hip would work fine under most circumstances, but his days as a functioning cop were finished.

"What's the point, Mr. Egan?"

"The point is simple. If a man is going to work for me, I have to know what he's made of."

"And your file tells you that?"

"No," Egan admitted. "If you were that simple to read, you wouldn't be here. I need men I can trust to think for themselves. But I also need to understand them. You don't click for me, and I want to know why. There's something missing." He tapped the report. "Something that's holding you back from the kind of success you might enjoy."

"I've got what I need."

"Hardly. And not what you want, either. You're bitter, which says more than the facts in this dossier ever could. You've got intelligence and guts, but it takes more than those to achieve success. It even takes more than luck."

"What's it take?" Guthrie was genuinely curious.

"Cooperation. Oh, yes," Egan went on, seeing the dismissive look fill Guthrie's eyes. "Cooperation. These days a man's got to have allies, and the stronger the allies the better. Cooperation is like a marriage. It takes two lesser parts and welds them into a more-powerful whole." He adjusted one of his cuffs. "But then, I forget that's not the case in your experience."

"Don't get too personal."

Guthrie guessed Egan was trying to rattle him. He didn't know why, unless Egan wanted to see how far he could push before Guthrie pushed back. Probably just the kind of man he was. Must be the same reason he'd sent two deadly men on a boy's errand. His eyes bored into Guthrie like he was drilling for deep insight, but maybe it was just a test hole. Guthrie put on his best poker face.

"All right. But I still wonder what made your wife leave. Do you drink?"

"No."

"Nothing. Not even at parties?"

"No. And I don't go to parties."

"But you did drink. Too much."

"I don't like people digging into my business."

"Strange words from a man whose profession was digging into other people's business," Egan said without a trace of mirth. "But perhaps appropriate. Who better to understand how well or ill the facts of a dossier reveal the inner person? Maybe you do have the qualities I'm looking for." Egan again leaned back in his chair and smiled disarmingly. Guthrie couldn't tell if he'd passed Egan's test or if the guy had just gotten bored.

"Let's get back to cooperation," Egan said. "I simply meant that an alliance, be it marriage or a business partnership, must produce a gestalt sufficiently vital to energize the individuals involved and bring rewards not otherwise available. Like what goes on between partners on a beat. You depend on each other for your well-being, and the two of you depend on the rest of the police department to back you up. Now, though," Egan held out his hands, palms up, "you are without any of those elements that formerly allowed you to unite with your fellow man—your partner is dead, the police force no longer wants you, and your wife left you."

"I'm listening."

"The world is different than it's ever been before," Egan said. "The day of the rugged individualist is over. Now we face what I call the black hole theory of economics. Just as the universe has numerous gravitational objects called black holes that are gradually sucking all known matter into themselves, so too does the world have economic entities that are steadily subsuming all smaller enterprises."

"And it's either become your own black hole or be swallowed by another, is that it?"

"Resources are no longer free for the taking. They are quickly being collected, and collections require more management than a single person can bring to bear. These days, no matter what your field, it's either join an organization or join the bums on the street."

"And your organization is the right one for me?"

"Possibly. Rampart presently handles security, and we've done quite well in that arena, but I want to expand."

"You want a bigger collection."

Egan smiled.

"I'm thinking of opening an investigative division."

"You want to hire me as a detective?"

"You've correctly made your first deduction. How does the title senior investigator sound?"

"Like too much for a shot-up patrol cop."

Egan's chuckle held a sardonic ring.

"I may doubt your ability to market yourself, but I would never malign your intelligence or professional qualifications. Or your courage. This," he tapped the dossier, "attests to all of those. Besides, it's what you were trained to do. You'd passed the qualifying tests. If you hadn't been shot, you'd be a police investigator right now, and we wouldn't be having this conversation. I'm simply giving you a chance to get back into the profession." He tented his fingers and stared over their tips at Guthrie. "Interested?"

"Mind if I sleep on it?"

"Perhaps a test case would tell us both if you're up to the standards I hope to set with my investigative division."

"What might this test case be?"

"Some clients have recently lost a valuable antique. Burglary. Since Rampart was responsible for their security, I also want to be responsible for recovering their property. I'm offering you the opportunity to make the recovery, and your success will be a passing score on your entry exam, so to speak."

"What do you get out of it?"

"It's not what I get, Guthrie. It's what I keep. I keep my reputation. Rampart is well known. Trusted. I can't have that trust besmirched by anyone, particularly a common thief. It's bad for business."

"And bad for insurance rates."

"That, too."

"I suppose you haven't reported the theft to the police."

"It's not necessary to bring them in on this yet. Not until you've had a chance to prove your abilities. Perhaps the job will even whet your appetite for the kind of work you might do for Rampart."

"Like I said, I'm not sure about that aspect," Guthrie reminded Egan. "How does that affect the deal?"

Egan shrugged.

"My clients' property must be recovered in any event. I'm offering you the case. We can talk about the rest when you've recovered the property. If you don't," he shrugged again, "then it's all moot. Until then, we'll treat this strictly as a one-time arrangement. I'll offer you $500 a day plus expenses, with two full weeks' pay in advance, whether or not you succeed in recovering the property."

"Pretty generous. What's to keep me from sitting on my laurels and riding out the two weeks?"

Egan again uttered that sardonic laugh.

"Just asking the question means you wouldn't." Egan's eyes narrowed. "And I think you need the work more than the money. But as an extra incentive, I'll pay an additional twenty thousand upon successful completion." He didn't blink when he said it.

"That must be one heck of an antique," Guthrie said. "What is it?"

"I'll let the Harveys—the owners—tell you about that. My only concern is finding a man to take the job of recovering it."

"Sounds like a no-lose deal."

Egan's outward calm didn't alter a bit, but suddenly the humor blunting the edge of his ruthlessness vanished from his eyes, leaving naked, glittering blades. For the first time, Guthrie wondered if Egan kept a gun concealed in one of the drawers of his massive desk.

"I could lose," Egan replied.

"All right," Guthrie said. "I'll take the case as a one-shot deal. The rest is on the back burner with no guarantees."

"There are never any guarantees," Egan said, reaching for a desk drawer. Guthrie tensed, then caught himself and relaxed as Egan withdrew an envelope instead of a gun and slid it across the marble desktop. Inside was a thick bundle of crisp $100 bills and a slip of paper bearing a pair of names, an address, and a phone number. Guthrie was trying to surreptitiously count the money while pretending to read the paper when he became aware that someone was standing behind and to the right of his chair.

It was Ingram.

Guthrie hadn't even heard the door open.

"Ingram will see to it that you get home," Egan said. "I'll call the Harveys and tell them to expect you in about an hour."

Ingram escorted Guthrie through the office's back door, to the ground floor, and out of the building to the same curb where the Mercedes had deposited them forty minutes earlier. The Mercedes wasn't there, but a pastel green Chevy sedan was. On the side, white lettering spelled out *Rampart Security Systems*, and above the words was a shield-shaped logo framing a large letter "R" wrought in medieval-style script.

The driver standing by the door was not the bull-necked blond but an Hispanic who was almost as bulky. He had a clipped mustache beneath a large hatchet of a nose, and behind it all, a heavy, pockmarked face.

"Cuchilla will drive you home," Ingram said as the Mexican opened the door. Guthrie slid into the front seat, and Ingram handed him a card on which was printed a single phone number. "Use this number when reporting to Mr. Egan."

Guthrie took the card, then Cuchilla closed the door, went around to the driver's side, got in, and started the engine. Ingram watched until the car was out of sight.

Cuchilla didn't say a single word all the way to Guthrie's house, not even to ask directions.

3

GUTHRIE STEERED INTO RIVER OAKS, land of luxuriant plutocrats, domain of Houston's ultra-wealthy, home of the Harveys. It was an embarrassment simply driving his six-year-old Honda through the neighborhood. Usually, the closest peons ever got to River Oaks was during the annual spring flower festival euphemistically known as the Azalea Trail, when the public was allowed to tour the opulent grounds around the homes and ogle well-tended gardens of spring flowers, particularly azalea bushes heavy with pink and white blossoms.

Guthrie would have said he stayed out of River Oaks because the gigantic homes depressed him, but the simple fact of the matter was he'd never been invited. Without an invitation there was just no reason for him, or anyone like him, to linger. And he wasn't masochistic enough to like sightseeing in a neighborhood where the homes probably cost more to maintain annually than Guthrie would make in his lifetime. So normally he stayed away, but today he'd been invited.

The Harveys' house sat on a curving street several blocks off River Oaks Boulevard. Apparently they weren't traditionalists; the modern architecture of the two-story house was completely devoid of the colonial and plantation influences prevalent among many of the neighboring homes. Guthrie liked the way the layout made the house seem a lot less pretentious than its neighbors without sacrificing its sense of style and substantiality.

He swung into the driveway arcing across the wide front yard from the left. The drive opened into a modest parking area before disappearing behind tall, motorized wooden gates at the right side of the house. Guthrie parked next to the only car present—a powder-blue Jaguar—and went up to the front door.

The butler who answered was a short, middle-aged man with dull gray hair and a suit of identical color.

"My name is Guthrie. I believe the Harveys are expecting me."

"Won't you come in?"

Guthrie obliged and, a few moments later, found himself in a huge living room, talking to the victims themselves.

"Ben Egan tells us you can help find an object that was stolen from us, Mr. Guthrie," said Carla Harvey. Her black hair was cut in a short, stylish bob, accentuating her longish neck and the angular planes of her face. The hair didn't look dyed.

Guthrie, once accustomed to giving people the cop look, decided to try for the opposite effect, and he put on his best expression of receptive professionalism. At least he hoped his face conveyed that message. If it didn't, if Guthrie let any of his real feelings into his expression, it might say something that might make her and her husband, Lloyd, kick Guthrie right out of their house in a huff and a hurry. Guthrie certainly didn't want that, though judging by Carla's cool demeanor she'd never be huffed, and she'd never ever be in any particular sort of hurry.

Guthrie's receptive professionalism also took in the Faberge watch circling Carla's wrist and the fur wrap draping her chicly unclad, somewhat square shoulders. The fur looked like it had once actually warmed a swarm of little varmints instead of being exuded from some chemical process, but Guthrie didn't know enough about fur to be able to tell for sure.

Lloyd was no ditch digger, either. An inch or so over six feet, he wore one of those modern, ultra-cut two-piece suits costing a lot more than the three-piece jobs most plebeian businessmen wear. The Rolex, with little diamonds instead of numerals, contrasted nicely with Carla's timepiece, yet complemented it at the same time, saying, yeah, we have different tastes, but both are the best.

"Mr. Egan mentioned an antique."

"A bronze sculpture," she answered.

"A sculpture? You mean a statue?"

"A life-size bronze head," she clarified. "A bust."

"It is a very rare and expensive antique," Lloyd lounged back and put in, unnecessarily Guthrie thought. Egan wasn't paying seven grand with the promise of twenty more to hunt down a plaster casting. Besides, these people didn't look like they owned anything that wasn't rare and expensive.

Lloyd crossed his right ankle over his left thigh, giving Guthrie a good gander at his western boots. They seemed to be made of some sort of snake skin. Boa, or maybe python. Some kind of big constrictor that insinuates itself around its prey and squeezes and squeezes until there's not a bone left to allow upright movement. Lloyd probably liked to see things crawl. His curly brown hair was as precisely coifed as Carla's. Most likely he spent almost as much as she did to keep it that way. The two of them were of indeterminate age, anywhere from a seasoned forty-five to a preserved sixty.

Was he being too harsh? After all, he'd just met them, and so far Carla had done 90 percent of the talking. That didn't make him like her any better than her husband, but there was an unpleasant arrogance about Lloyd that was pronounced enough without words. Maybe it was the too-relaxed way Lloyd lounged there, self-assurance oozing out of his skin like uncontrived sweat from the brow of a pro wrestler.

If confidence was a quality Carla shared equally with Lloyd, her poise exuded class in inverse proportion to the tackiness of his endangered-species boots. Guthrie took in the tight restraint of her shoulders and figured her sophistication was probably as brittle as fine crystal. If shattered it would send one sharp sliver leaping right up to give a good, vindictive slice. But considering the smooth way she drew a slender, dark brown cigarette from her gold cigarette case, she maintained an ability that all the king's horses and all the king's men didn't. She'd be able to put it back together again before walking away.

As Carla placed the cigarette between her tastefully mauve lips, Guthrie noticed that the filter was wrapped with lavender paper. Next out was a jeweled lighter, and its brief flare touched life to the cigarette's tip. She returned the lighter to her handbag and blew smoke into the room. It was an expensive cigarette, but it smelled no better to Guthrie than the smoke from any other. Aw, hell, it was her house. Let her pollute it if she wanted.

Guthrie may not have liked the Harveys on first sight for being wealthy—make that stinking rich—but at least he understood the feeling. It was a matter of simple jealousy. The divide between their circumstances and his intensified his awareness of his own financial quagmire. And their self-assurance only highlighted the helpless slide into despair he'd been experiencing since he'd been shot and Alice deserted him.

Besides, even if he had misgivings about his clients, Guthrie was working, and that alone was a pleasant change from brooding on the spaces of his empty house, its doors closed on the irrevocable past. For the first time since he left the hospital, he actually felt alive and mentally clear. He almost cracked a smile, but beneath the euphoria, he sensed that usually people came to a detective with problems that were too cheap and sleazy for public scrutiny. The smile died unborn, and now Guthrie found himself wondering what would be cheap and sleazy about this case. But he shook off the thought. It wasn't cheap, at least. Egan was paying him well, a fact that bought the Harveys some leeway.

That brought to mind the fat envelope of cash Egan had given Guthrie. The past two years had taught him to do with progressively less—though he sometimes wondered how progress could be so debasing—and he didn't need a lot. The money in the envelope, alone, would go a long way toward paying his debts, and the promise of more gave him hope that an ease of financial distress would erase his despair. He wasn't about to let petty jealousies stand in the way—he'd take the cash, even if it came from people who shouldn't be asking him to find property that shouldn't be missing.

And, despite it all, Guthrie actually was interested and curious. After the shooting, his life had taken on a toneless quality, a uniformity of rote daily activities blending seamlessly into weeks and months of ennui. He spent most of his time trying not to think, not to remember. Difficult as that was. His mind was the type that had to digest something, and if nothing else was available, it chewed on itself. And he couldn't allow that. So there was just the waiting emptiness that had to remain empty.

But now, like a miracle, there was something to consume that was outside himself, something that failed to click into its proper place, and his mind ached to swarm over it like a starfish over a clam, trying to get at the tender meat inside. And maybe at the pearl whose secret presence would make it all worth while.

That's what made Guthrie interested. What made him curious was that cheap and sleazy now appeared rare and valuable, and these rich folks had given him a case that should have gone to a higher power.

"Mr. Egan said you haven't spoken to the police."

Guthrie was forced to give them credit. They had their stuff down pat and didn't bother glancing at each other. Lloyd just lounged back, sliding the right constrictor boot from his thigh to cross the other boot, ankle to ankle, and watched Guthrie from beneath eyelids that might have been made of the same material. Carla inhaled her expensive smoke and polluted the air some more.

"We have no desire to press criminal charges," she said. "We simply want our property returned with as little fuss as possible."

Maybe we're back to cheap and sleazy, Guthrie mused. Why did everyone seem like they wanted to conceal the theft? But what could be so cheap and sleazy about a statue of a head? He could only surmise the Harveys might have engaged in a little hanky-panky in acquiring it. A lot of antiques in the hands of private collectors rightfully belong to someone else. Some are stolen from galleries, museums, or private owners. Others are torn from countries raped of their cultural heritages by conquistadors, tomb robbers, and scavengers grubbing for anything and everything but integrity. Even churches are not immune to indignities. Hundreds of priceless objects and artifacts disappear yearly from alters to find their ways into the hands of collectors whose yen for rarity and beauty exceeds their scruples.

Even if he decided for the moment to give these folks the benefit of the doubt and let this sculpted head be rare and valuable and let it be their legitimate property, the matter, somehow, still rang false.

"Tell me the circumstances surrounding the burglary."

"It occurred on Saturday," Carla said. "We went to a dinner party that evening. The bust was in its case before we left and was gone when we returned."

"Any idea who the thief might be?"

"None whatsoever."

"Who knew about the sculpture?" For some reason, it made Guthrie uneasy to think he might soon be searching for a missing head.

"Anyone who has visited our home might have seen it." This from Lloyd. "We made no secret of its existence."

"How about this dinner party you went to. Who was there?"

"Is that relevant?" Lloyd asked, and Guthrie shrugged.

"Probably not, but I'd like to know anyway."

"A group of friends and business associates," Carla said. "Here, you might want to look at this."

She slid a manila envelope from a nearby end table and passed it to Guthrie, who shook out the contents. The envelope contained a deed of ownership for an antique bronze bust, referred to as "Katib of Jashyari," sold to the Harveys three years earlier by Radcliffe Antiquaries. Included was a physical description and history, a photocopy of the deed, and four color eight-by-tens. Guthrie ignored the description and history for the moment and concentrated on the photos.

The shots showed a man's head cast in bronze. A light green patina had invaded the grooves and creases, but otherwise the dark metal shone with a dull, polished sheen. The background against which it stood was a muted light gray. One shot was of the front, one of the back, and the last two from each side. The head was sturdily mounted on a base of rough black stone, as if the stone was dark clothing draping a suggestion of clavicle and chest.

Marble, Guthrie surmised, and a glance at the description showed he was right. The total weight was just over twelve pounds.

He turned his attention to the face and saw a man of early old age who appeared to be Middle Eastern. He was handsome in an ascetic sort of way and wore a neatly trimmed full beard.

"It certainly is an interesting likeness," Guthrie commented. Neither Lloyd nor Carla replied, aloud, but a glance passed between them the significance of which escaped Guthrie. He wasn't about to let ignorance stop him. "His name was Katib?"

"The name is inscribed on the base," Carla replied. "It might be the name of the subject, or it might be the sculptor. Jashyari was a city-state in what is now Persia."

"Was he a king?"

"We don't know," Lloyd replied. "But he must have been a great man in his time."

Figures. Nothing plebeian for the Harveys. But the sculpture's expression stopped Guthrie right there, confuting such a facile association. The man's face, particularly around the eyes, bore clear signs of a natural intelligence and determination tempered by a benevolent graciousness, and maybe even wisdom. This man may have been born to wealth and power, but he did not despise the beggar for his poverty or the cripple for his pain.

The eyes themselves were as striking as the expression infusing the features surrounding them. The orbs were dull white, the irises a rich, lucent brown, and the pupils so black they seemed to absorb light. Ivory eyes, the description told him, topaz irises, and pupils of black jasper. Rich eyes, he reflected, though he knew their intrigue lay not in the expense of their materials but in the wealth of disconsolate eloquence artfully wrought in their stare.

How old was this thing? He searched for a date in the supporting documentation, and when he found it, his mind went as cold as the metal face in the photos.

"According to this description, the head is more than a thousand years old." Guthrie spoke as blandly as he could because now he was smelling a stink riper than cheap and sleazy. He was smelling scam. He wondered how much this sculpture was insured for, and he also wondered if they really expected him to actually recover it.

"Museum quality," Carla replied, just as blandly. "Quite remarkable, isn't it?"

"It seems to be in good shape considering its age. No dents or even much discoloration, from what I can tell."

"It is a rare antiquity, but it has never been an archaeological artifact," Lloyd supplied. "It was never lost and buried but instead has been in the possession of an unbroken succession of owners."

Guthrie could accept that if the provenance bore out, and he could verify that with Radcliffe Antiquaries.

"Okay. Assuming I find out who took it, just how far do you expect me to go to get it back?"

"You're the detective," Lloyd said. "Ben brought you into this for your expertise."

Guthrie couldn't tell if he was being sarcastic, humoring Guthrie, or just plain serious. Or maybe Egan had failed to inform the Harveys that Guthrie was just a shot-up ex-cop playing at being a detective and probably way out of his league. Then again, no one would have had to say anything to them about which league each of them was in.

"Ben hired you to recover our property," Carla said before Guthrie could respond to Lloyd. "How you go about it is your business. I assure you, Lloyd and I desire no adverse repercussions from illegal activities by you or anyone else. Please use your best judgment."

Guthrie twisted his professional blankness into what he hoped was a professional smile.

"Fair enough, Mrs. Harvey. May I look around the house?"

"Inspect the scene of the crime?" Lloyd asked, and he reached languidly for a button set discreetly beneath the edge of the end table beside his chair. That was it. Languid Lloyd. Except it was the kind of languor that still reminded Guthrie of the boots. Constrictor. The question was, was it the languor preceding a meal or that which came after? A moment later the butler came in.

"Carla and I have a prior engagement," Lloyd said to Guthrie as everyone rose. "Alton, please see to it that Mr. Guthrie has everything he needs."

"Very good, sir."

Carla retrieved the original deed from Guthrie and said, "You may keep the rest of the packet for your investigation."

Guthrie nodded and shook Lloyd's hand. Lloyd didn't allow his palm to come into contact when shaking. Such a grip always made Guthrie suspicious, like the person was trying to conceal something.

Carla also extended her hand. Guthrie took it, but she surprised him by flipping his hand with a smooth, practiced motion. Guthrie didn't react, but even if he had, she had time enough to give his palm a good once-over. Nothing about her face changed, but he got the impression that a satisfied smile spread under her skin. He wasn't sure he liked that any more than Lloyd's shifty grip.

"Your lifeline is broken in several places."

"I'd have thought once would be enough," Guthrie replied, thinking of the ache in his hip.

"Indeed," Carla raised her eyes to his. "You should take care of yourself, Mr. Guthrie." She dropped his hand.

"Still want me to take the case?"

As she gazed into his eyes, the hidden smile broke the surface, but somehow it didn't seem the same. Now it belonged on the face of a finishing school instructor.

"Certainly, Mr. Guthrie. Please call us if you have further questions."

Then they were gone. Guthrie turned to Alton.

"Shall we inspect the scene of the crime, Alton?" he asked.

"Very well, sir," the butler replied dryly.

As he followed Alton through the house, Guthrie wondered what magic it was that, for him, never failed to produce the cheap and sleazy out of a silk top hat.

4

"WHO DISCOVERED THE BUST WAS missing?"

"Mr. Harvey," Alton replied. "He and Mrs. Harvey were quite upset."

"Where was it kept?"

"In a locked cabinet in the study. We are on our way there now."

As Alton led Guthrie toward the back of the house, Guthrie found himself staring openly. The art on the walls would have been perfectly at home in the modernist galleries at the Museum of Fine Arts, or better still, in the Menil Collection. Picasso, Monet, Klee, and Ernst were some of the more prominent names on the canvases. At last, Alton ushered Guthrie into the study. A spacious backyard bordered with colorful flower beds showed through wide windows.

"The cabinet is there." Alton pointed to a span of shelves and cabinetry built into one of the interior walls.

The particular unit Alton indicated was a cubicle large enough to comfortably hold the head, fronted with a glass door. The compartment was just the right height off the floor that, had the head been present, it would have directly faced Guthrie.

The door was fastened by a high-grade double combination lock. Guthrie stepped closer, checking for jimmy marks, but the wood was unmarred. Whoever had opened the cabinet had to have done it the right way.

"Can we open this?"

"Certainly, sir." Alton produced a paper on which two sets of four numbers were written. "Mr. Harvey anticipated that you might wish to do so." He moved toward the cabinet, but Guthrie stopped him.

"Mind if I do it?"

"Mr. Harvey instructed me to accord you every courtesy." Alton handed over the paper. "You must turn the top dial first."

Guthrie glanced at the top set of numbers and turned the appropriate dial. The lock's action was smooth as a butterfly's kiss. Guthrie knew next to nothing about locks, but it struck him that it would take a good safecracker to get past this one. Or someone with the combination.

As soon as he'd spun the correct combinations on both dials and twisted the handle to open the door, he saw that a thief could have jimmied all night on this cabinet and been unsuccessful. Beneath the dark hardwood veneer lay an inch of steel. He rapped around the inside of the case, and except for the glass, it was all as strong as a safe.

Then he amended his observation of the relative vulnerability of the glass. It may have been the most transparent part of the cabinet, but it was thick and heavy and probably nearly bullet-proof. A small explosion or a hell of a lot of heat might get through it, but little else would.

Curiously, a light mesh of wire lay sandwiched in the glass. The wire looked reddish, as if it might be copper. Or gold.

He suddenly realized that the case was not only a safe but a Faraday cage as well. What the hell was that for?

"Was the door left open after the theft?" he asked.

"I'm not certain," Alton answered with polished precision.

Guthrie gave the cabinet one last inspection. There, at the bottom lower right, where it would be obscured when the door was closed, a discreet engraved logo bore the name Vulcan Armor Inc.

"Anything else taken?" he asked as he straightened and closed the door.

"Not that I am aware."

Guthrie thought of the Picasso and the other paintings. Hell, on the wall right across the room was a van Gogh just the right size to tuck under an arm. It hung there like a ripe apple just begging to be picked.

"That's odd, isn't it?"

"Perhaps, sir. I am not privy to the workings of the criminal mind."

Curious. The average person couldn't get into this safe without the combination. It would take a professional safecracker, but a pro wouldn't take only a single, awkward, and hard-to-fence item, no matter how valuable, and leave other incredible treasures just hanging around on the walls.

Not unless he'd come for just that one thing. The possibility struck Guthrie that the thief might have been working in collusion with someone who wanted only the head. One of the dinner guests at the party the Harveys had attended? It made sense. A dinner guest would know that the Harveys were out for several hours. Being a so-called friend of the Harveys, he or she might even have been able to provide a map of the layout. The thief would have opportunity and plenty of time to complete his work. But still, why take the bust and nothing else?

Guthrie handed the paper with the combinations to Alton. "The Harveys will want to have the locks reset."

"Undoubtedly."

Guthrie gestured toward the windows.

"Could anyone have gotten into the house through these?"

"It would be obvious if they had," Alton replied. "The windows in this room are hermetically sealed and cannot be opened."

"Any other way into the house beside the doors?"

"There are ways, I suppose, for a determined person to get inside," Alton conceded. "Mr. Harvey and I looked carefully, but we found no indication of forced entry."

"How many on the domestic staff?"

"There are two besides myself. Deborah is the housekeeper and Edna is the chef."

"Were you here that night?"

"No. We had the night off."

"Is that usual?"

"It is. The Harveys either go out every Saturday night or they entertain, and we are off."

"Even when they entertain?"

"Yes. Edna leaves a buffet on the dining room table, and we clean up on Sunday."

"Pretty generous of them," Guthrie said.

"The Harveys are quite liberal."

I'll bet, Guthrie thought. "So no one was home?"

"That's correct. Deborah and I attended the theater, and Edna visited a friend."

"I'd like to talk to them." Alton led the way, and as Guthrie followed, he asked, "The house is protected with a Rampart Security burglar alarm system?"

"Certainly. Window detectors and motion sensors throughout the house. We always set it if no one is home, and according to Rampart Security, it has not been tampered with."

Alton took Guthrie to a spacious, modern kitchen, where the odor of baking bread filled bright air. He introduced Guthrie to Edna, a trim, attractive blonde of around forty-five wearing a colorful apron. She was perched on a stool, reading *Gourmet* magazine.

"Could you give me the address and phone number of the person the Harveys visited that night?" Guthrie asked Alton.

"I'm not sure I should...."

"Of course you should. Mr. Harvey said to provide me with whatever I need, and I need to know where the Harveys went and who they were with."

"Very well, sir." Alton's face was deadpan. "They attended dinner at Ms. Barbara Sidell's."

"I'll need her address and phone."

"Very good, sir." The butler sounded like he was beginning to choke on the word "sir." He glided out of the room.

"Nice kitchen," Guthrie commented. "That bread smells delicious."

"Thank you." Edna smiled, but she didn't offer him a sample.

Guthrie strolled toward the back door and stared through the inset window at the expanse of driveway behind the wooden fence. He asked if Edna had seen anything unusual the night of the theft.

She told him she hadn't, but she'd left about seven to meet a friend for dinner.

"Did you set the burglar alarm before you left?"

"Yes. I'm sure I did. I remember. Anyway, it was still set when the Harveys came home."

Alton returned with another woman who looked the same age as Edna and about twenty pounds heavier. Alton introduced her as Deborah. Apparently she was Alton's wife. Guthrie went through the questions with Deborah, but like the others, she'd noticed nothing out of the ordinary. She and Alton had left shortly after six, about an hour after the Harveys departed.

"Did the Harveys have any guests that day? Friends or business associates, maybe?"

"None," Alton answered.

"How about service people? Anybody come to fix anything? Any deliveries?"

"There was one," Edna said. "From the liquor store. That was around noon."

Too early, Guthrie thought. The Harveys would have missed the sculpture if it had been taken during the day.

"None later? Closer to the time you left?"

Her brow wrinkled.

"I...I don't think so."

Though she sounded tentative, Guthrie was about to let it go when Deborah interrupted.

"But there was, Edna. Don't you remember? The man from the liquor store came back. I saw him drive up just as Alton and I left."

"He did?" An expression of puzzlement settled over Edna's features, and she shook her head. "But that would have been too late."

"I'm certain it was him," Deborah insisted.

Guthrie looked at Alton, who said, "I know the man she means, but I don't remember seeing him that evening."

"I'm sure I saw him," Deborah said, but now she didn't sound so sure. "At least, I recognized the van."

"You don't remember a second delivery from the liquor store?" Guthrie pressed. Edna rubbed her forehead.

"Come to think of it, I guess there was. I was so rushed, I must have forgotten about it."

"You said it was too late for a delivery."

"I suppose so," Edna said, frowning. "To tell the truth, I barely remember, almost like a dream. But yes, I remember now. He did come back. He said he made a mistake and delivered the wrong order the first time, and he was going to lose his job if he didn't correct it. He's such a nice man, and I couldn't refuse. He brought the right order with him, in a carton, but I was too busy to deal with it. He said he'd go to the wine cellar and change out the bottles himself."

"You have a wine cellar?"

"Not really a cellar," Alton said. "Would you care to see?"

"I would."

Alton exited the kitchen. As Guthrie and the women followed, he asked Edna, "Did you mention anything to the delivery man about everyone going out for the evening?"

"I might have," she said a trifle guiltily. "I was in such a hurry to get ready."

"How about when he was here earlier?"

"I don't know. I don't think I would have."

The wine cellar was a small, cool room situated behind the kitchen, off a hall leading deeper into the house.

"What's down there?" Guthrie wanted to know.

"That's where the three of us live," Deborah said.

"Any access into the rest of the house from your quarters?"

"There is a doorway into the main hall," Alton told him.

"How long was the delivery man in the wine cellar?" Guthrie asked Edna.

"I'm not certain." She frowned. "I was so busy. It didn't seem long, not more than a few minutes."

"Did he take anything with him when he left?"

"He had the wrong order in the carton."

"Can you describe him?"

"Yes, he's been here a number of times. He's about your age, but a little taller, and his hair is darker. And I think he eats right."

"Why do you say that?"

"He always looks so healthy."

"Sounds like you're familiar with him."

Edna blushed through her frown. "He's attractive and well built. And he always has something nice to say."

"What's the name of the liquor store he delivers for?"

"Armin's," Alton told him. "We always buy from Armin's. It's in River Oaks Plaza."

"Do you think the delivery man is the thief, Mr. Guthrie?" asked Edna, her face twisted with anguish. "Goodness, I hate to think I was responsible."

"It's possible," Guthrie shrugged, "but not especially likely. He's the regular delivery man, and you say he was only out of sight for a few minutes. That wouldn't have been long enough. Besides, why would a delivery man steal something so difficult to get at when other valuables are more readily available? I don't think you have anything to worry about. I'll check on him, but I'm more inclined to think we're dealing with a professional burglar." He glanced around at them. "Thanks for your help."

"Ms. Sidell's phone number and address," Alton said, handing a folded slip of paper to Guthrie.

"Thanks. Any idea who else might have been at the dinner party?"

"As I was not in attendance, that would be pure speculation on my part. Perhaps Ms. Sidell can enlighten you."

"Yes. Well, thank you all. I'll be going, now."

"The door is this way," Alton gestured.

"I'll go out the back, if it's all right. I want to check the grounds."

Alton nodded, took Guthrie through the kitchen, and let him out onto the driveway.

Guthrie walked around toward the rear of the house, not sure what he was looking for. What he found a spacious, well-tended lawn surrounded by a brick wall mostly concealed behind shrubbery. The back of the house was partly masked by a glassed-in conservatory the enclosed the back door. He strolled across a flagstone patio and tried the conservatory door. It wasn't locked, but had it been, he could have gotten through it using his Swiss Army knife and not made any noise in the process. The back door was another matter, solid, well seated, and fastened by an expensive lock without an external keyhole. It would be a tough door to get past without leaving marks, and Guthrie's inspection revealed none.

He returned to the side of the house and let himself out of the gate. As he did, he saw Alton watching him from an upstairs window. Ignoring the butler, Guthrie went to his car and, in a few moments, was on the street, heading for River Oaks Plaza.

5

River Oaks Plaza caters primarily to the wealthy of River Oaks and the white-collar wannabe professionals from Montrose and the Heights. The building that housed Armin's Liquors was perfectly indicative of the upscale but diverse nature of the establishments inhabiting these four blocks of West Gray between Shepherd and Waugh. Cohabiting the building with Armin's were a gourmet restaurant, a largish specialty furnishings store, a shoe store, a shop selling African and South American handicrafts, and a fancy ladies' underwear boutique.

Armin's was tucked between the last two. As Guthrie headed toward the door, he passed a pair of young African-American women in jeans and dark T-shirts who were standing in front of the boutique, called Cypria, pointing and giggling. After a glance, Guthrie was inclined to join in, but somehow the third-world handicrafts in the window beyond Armin's sobered him. The price paid to the original artisans who supplied the handicrafts shop was probably as skimpy as the lingerie displayed in Cypria's window.

He tried to shake off the bitterness. Was the cash he'd hidden at home before departing for the Harveys' making him feel just a little guilty? More likely, it was the fact that he was about to enter a liquor store. He hadn't been in one since the shooting, and the thought of all that booze inside suddenly made his mouth go dry.

Guthrie didn't drink anymore. He couldn't afford to for practical considerations, not to mention financial ones. There was a time he could remember all too well, when he'd poured large quantities of nasty-tasting liquid down his throat and liked it. Actually, some of it he didn't remember too well, but he must have liked it since he'd indulged frequently on duty as well as off. These days, he could admit that his intake of liquor just prior to the shooting probably contributed significantly to the tragedy that followed. He hadn't been drunk, exactly—the heightened tension had leveled any alcohol-induced euphoria he might have felt—but he'd certainly indulged. And if, as he squatted there in the cold and dark, waiting for the raid and contemplating its outcome, he'd expected euphoria afterwards, he hadn't counted on a hipful of lead to bring it down quite so fast. Or permanently.

When he finally woke up to the fact as he lay in the hospital and emerged from the pain killers' haze that alcohol no longer ruled him, he thought for a time that he might be able to reconnect with Alice on some sort of fundamental level. And for a few days, it seemed he was right. She visited regularly, the dutiful wife, concerned and considerate, with the specter of grief pulling at the corners of her eyes. But it turned out, ironically, that his boozing had been the glue that held them together, for it had kept him complacently blind and uncommunicative. Kept his bitterness at bay and out of his mouth.

The interlude, if it had ever been more than a figment of his imagination, lasted only until the day of Art's funeral. She returned to the hospital afterwards, a black hat covering her dark hair, and he knew she was on edge. Knew that he should keep his mouth under control no matter how he felt. God, he wished he'd had a drink then to shut him up. To close him up. Maybe she wouldn't have had a chance to peer into the gaping emotional wound that pained him more than his physical one. But no, he'd had to open his mouth.

"I hope they managed to bury all of him."

The words emerged too easily. He tried to tell himself it was just brutal cop humor, the result of seeing too much scum, too many dead and dying. Hell, he could have said it to Art. Art would have understood and would have laughed.

"That's a shitty thing to say." Alice's upper lip twisted in contempt. "He was your friend."

"It's not like he gives a damn about that now," Guthrie retorted. "If he ever did."

"I don't know what happened to you, Clay," she said, turning to the window, nervously fingering the strap of her purse. "You used to love life. You played music, you...."

"I'm a fucking cripple," he snarled. "That's what happened to me."

"That's not what I mean, and you know it. When we first got married, I thought...."

"Did you?"

She half turned, a dangerous brightness in her eyes.

He should have backed off, said something like, "I don't think either of us thought much about the future back then." He had the chance, but no, he had to push it, had to turn his inner wound into a weapon that would wound her, too.

So he said, "You always let your pussy do your thinking for you."

She staggered. And the dangerous brightness of her eyes blurred behind an icy, appraising stare that, in turn, flared into horror that wanted to be disgust.

"Clay. My God." She stepped toward the bed, knuckles white on the strap of her purse. "I knew you were sick, but I never imagined...."

And then she was gone as utterly as if she'd never been.

But she had been. He could remember her all too clearly. And that memory almost drove him back to the bottle when he got out of the hospital and discovered she'd packed up and left. But for some reason, it hadn't. He'd dried out in the hospital, but more important, he'd sobered up. Maybe facing the truth of Alice's departure finally put the fear of God and liquor into him. He hadn't had a drink since. It was the only good thing to come out of it all.

Taking a breath, he went into Armin's.

The decor inside was definitely nicer than the homely places he'd once frequented, but that was par for the area. When he walked up to the counter, the young, slender, sandy-haired clerk asked if Guthrie needed any help.

"Is the manager in?"

"Yes, he is. May I tell him what it's about?"

"No."

The young man gave the appearance of obsessive neatness, but the eyes he turned on Guthrie were raw, tired, and touched with meanness. But apparently they saw a cop, and curiosity mixed with fear edged in behind the malice.

"I'll get him." He disappeared through a door into the back and returned in less than a minute. "Mr. Dobbs will be right out."

Sure enough, a moment was all it took for a short, pudgy man with a serious face to emerge from the back.

"I'm Tim Dobbs." He didn't offer his hand. "How may I help you?"

"I'd like to know about a liquor delivery you made to Lloyd and Carla Harvey on Saturday."

"I'm afraid I can't divulge information about customers," Dobbs said.

"I didn't ask about the Harveys," Guthrie pointed out. "I've been hired to investigate the theft of a valuable antique from the Harveys' home. It would be in your best interest to answer a few questions, Mr. Dobbs."

"Can you verify your employment with the Harveys?" Dobbs looked like he hoped Guthrie couldn't.

"A phone call should do it," Guthrie said. "I'm sure you know Alton, the Harvey's butler."

Dobbs disappeared, and Guthrie turned on the clerk.

"Been here long?"

"Four years."

"Do you make deliveries?"

"No," the clerk said, appearing thoughtful despite his bloodshot eyes. "And don't ask me who does, because I won't say anything unless Mr. Dobbs says its okay."

"Probably wise if you want to keep your job another four years," Guthrie said.

Dobbs returned.

"I'll do what I can to help," he said.

"How about the liquor delivery? Was one made?"

"Would you mind coming to the office?" Dobbs waved a hand toward the back. The clerk showed a disappointed expression.

"Lead on," Guthrie said and trailed the pudgy man to a small, neat office behind the stockroom. While Guthrie sat, Dobbs scrolled through a ledger on his monitor.

"Yes," he said. "A case of French wine. White. The order was placed on Saturday morning, and we delivered by noon."

"Was there a problem with the order?"

"Problem? What sort of problem?"

"Did your delivery man take the wrong order?"

"I don't think that would be possible," Dobbs said, frowning. "We are particularly careful, especially with good clients like the Harveys."

"So your delivery man didn't have to return later in the afternoon or early evening to correct a misdelivery? About six."

"I am unaware of it if he did. He shouldn't have. We stop delivering at five on Saturdays." Dobbs frowned again. "Did he?"

"Who makes your deliveries?"

"We use a couple of men. Delivery people aren't very reliable, you know. I believe Mark was working Saturday."

"Mark?"

"Mark Batten."

"What does he look like?"

"He's tall and well built. Dark hair. Mid to late thirties. Handsome, I'd say."

"Caucasian?"

"Yes. Of course."

"Is he due in today?"

"I'm not sure. Wait a moment." Dobbs pushed a button on an intercom, and the clerk's tinny acknowledgment came over the speaker. "Please come back here, Tony," Dobbs said, and when Tony arrived, he asked, "Is Mark delivering today?"

"He's supposed to, but he hasn't showed up yet."

"Like I said," Dobbs shrugged helplessly. "Those kind of people are unreliable."

"But he did go off duty at five?" Guthrie asked.

"Tony was here on Saturday, weren't you, Tony?" Dobbs seemed relieved to pass on some of the responsibility.

"That's right," Tony said. "Mark left at five."

"Did he say where he was going or what he might do?"

"If he did, I don't remember," Tony shrugged.

"Did he take the delivery van?"

"I didn't notice. We keep it parked out back, and I don't go out there much."

"If he took it," said Dobbs, "he shouldn't have. We're not insured for private...."

"Do you have his phone number?" Guthrie interrupted.

"I'm not sure I should give it to you," Dobbs replied. "After all, this isn't an official investi...."

"The Harveys consider it completely official. For your information, your delivery man approached the Harveys' cook around six on Saturday evening, claiming to have misdelivered the order he brought earlier in the day. That puts him on the premises around the time of the theft. And he was driving your van. I don't think the

Harveys will take it kindly if you withhold information. They might even think you're involved."

"Please." Dobbs held up his hands and vehemently shook his head. "I assure you, I knew nothing of this situation before you came in. I'm only too happy to help the Harveys."

While the manager fingered through the Rolodex near his phone, Guthrie glanced at Tony. The clerk seemed to be enjoying his boss's discomfort. Dobbs found the card he was searching for, pulled it out of the Rolodex, and handed it to Guthrie.

"That's his number and address."

Guthrie pulled out his phone and punched in the number. After three rings, a droning recorded voice began to list the times the features would begin, for today, Monday, April 11, at the Edwards Cinema at Greenway Plaza. He disconnected.

"Mark must like movies," he commented.

"What?" Dobbs was perplexed.

"You ever call this number?"

"No. There was never any reason to. Mark has only been with us a few months, and he was never tardy or absent." Dobbs shook his head sadly. "I can't believe it. I hope the Harveys don't blame me. I didn't know Mark was like that. He seemed intelligent and educated. Not like a thief at all."

"But like a delivery man?" Dobbs just looked helpless, so Guthrie said to Tony, "What about you? Notice anything about Mark?"

"He's a bit odd at times."

"Odd how?"

"I don't know," the clerk shrugged. "Like he's spooked by something. And he's superstitious. But I don't really know much about him. As Mr. Dobbs says, he hasn't been here long."

"What kind of car does he drive?"

"He has one of those sport-utility vehicles," Tony said. "A Lexus. It's silver gray."

"You must pay your delivery drivers well," Guthrie said to Dobbs.

"What? Not really. Minimum wage."

"Pretty expensive car for a minimum-wage earner, isn't it?"

"I suppose so. I never thought about it."

"All right, Mr. Dobbs," Guthrie soothed. "I'm sure you're as victimized by this situation as the Harveys. But let me know if Mark comes in or if you remember anything else." He wrote down his phone number and gave it to the manager.

"I will," Dobbs said, his expression more pitiful than before.

Guthrie left Armin's and drove immediately to the West Alabama address Mark Batten had given Dobbs. When he got there, he sincerely doubted that the dry cleaners he found had ever been occupied by Mark Batten.

By now, it was late afternoon, and as he headed home, Guthrie got caught in rush hour traffic. What was normally a fifteen-minute jaunt turned into forty minutes of aggressive hell. Even so, at first he was feeling pretty good. Mark Batten was his man. He had to be. Guthrie only had to find the guy, and he'd be home free with the location of the head.

At least he hoped so. Guthrie would have preferred that Batten was working on his own, but that was unlikely given the obscurity of the sculpture, the difficulty in obtaining it, and the fact that nothing else was taken. Probably Batten was hired by one of the dinner guests who now had the head in his or her possession. Batten was a good starting point, though, and Guthrie figured he could shake Batten up or shake him down to find out where the sculpture was.

But Guthrie's contentment soon soured. At first glance, the case was a straightforward one of stolen property, but a few less obvious things bothered Guthrie, like Egan's apparent desire to keep the whole affair under wraps and a fee that seemed to Guthrie to be way too hefty, although certainly Egan wasn't pinching pennies to come up with it. And that whole business about the case being a test of Guthrie's skill.... If Guthrie wasn't so pensive, he'd have laughed aloud at the absurdity.

And there were the Harveys themselves, people whose personal strangeness went beyond having wealthy friends who might stoop to larceny to acquire their antique sculpture. On the surface they were overtly ostentatious and underneath subtly crafty. But then, who was Guthrie to judge the folkways of the filthy rich? He had a hard enough time paying his bills without useless speculation on what it would be like to never have to worry.

What did worry Guthrie, though, was the hint of violence lurking in the deadly expertise of Ingram and the beefy blond driver. Guthrie wasn't particularly afraid of trouble; he'd seen his share in ten years on the force. But he didn't plan on falling prey to it, either, and Ingram and the blond meant the kind of trouble Guthrie preferred to avoid because it was the kind he couldn't win or walk away from.

The more Guthrie thought about the case, the less he liked it. Except for one thing—he was back in the game, and the seven grand retainer was no absurdity, even if the pretext seemed to be. He snorted appreciatively. Being a detective didn't seem much different than being a cop, which he always figured was a fool who willingly dug bare-handed through a bucket of garbage in search of a razor blade. It was dirty, dangerous work and left a bad odor. Not to mention wounds that rewarded success as well as failure. And he wasn't thinking of his bum leg. He was thinking of all those little daily slices that left scars in places he never dreamed could be hurt. Like the scars left by his partner's death and his wife's desertion....

Damn Egan for dredging that up. At least he hadn't homed in on the real crux of the matter despite the fact that he'd been brutally honest and enjoyed Guthrie's every wincing minute.

Thinking of Egan sitting there in his plush office, perusing Guthrie's dossier and inferring the truth of a man from a gaggle of words, brought Guthrie's blood to a sudden boil. Fuck him, he thought, seeing himself sitting on the envelope of cash and letting Egan sweat out the fact that he'd failed to recover the Harveys' property. That'd really piss him.

But Guthrie couldn't do that. There was the matter of the twenty thousand promised on successful completion. That was a new roof and plumbing, and maybe a trip out of town, too. Besides, just the thought of spending another afternoon in that damn house, drowning his thoughts with the TV, was enough to eradicate any idea of not trying to complete the job. Hell, he'd wanted to be a detective, anyway, and now the chance had dropped into his lap. Considering it might be his only chance, he couldn't afford to mess it up.

Finally, he reached the traffic circle, congratulating himself on arriving in one piece, and a few minutes later, he pulled into his driveway and hurried into the house.

Inside, he found a directory, checked it, then picked up the phone.

"Vulcan Armor," said a receptionist's voice.

Her perkiness grated on his nerves. Not only was it too late in the day to sound that happy, what could be so damn fulfilling about answering the phone at a safe manufacturing company?

"I'd like some information on your company," he said, managing to keep his voice level.

"Would you like me to connect you with one of our sales staff?"

"That's not necessary. Do you have any brochures? Maybe an annual report?"

"I'd be happy to send those out to you, Mr....?"

Guthrie gave his name and address then hung up.

He was getting hungry, but there was one last thing to do before he ate. In the den, he took out the envelope Egan had given him and spread its contents on the desk.

The money looked good, lying there. It felt good. Hell, it smelled good. It might not make up for a ruined life, but at least it was a way to prolong it more comfortably.

Eventually, he gathered up the cash, hid it, and made himself some dinner.

6

AFTER BREAKFAST, GUTHRIE CARRIED HIS coffee into the den and turned on his computer. For about six months after the shooting, he'd been on short-term disability and so, technically, remained a member of the police department. That bureaucratic fine point meant that his password to the Houston Police Department records databases remained active, and he'd seized the moment to establish a secondary password that would allow him access once he officially went off the roles. He felt no guilt. The department had been his life and his future, and he couldn't bear to be so suddenly expunged from it. And with Alice gone, he'd needed the extended psychological connection with the department more than ever.

At first, he spent a lot of time listening to a police scanner and digging through the databases—activities that not only filled the empty time but made him feel connected to something. In a few months, he learned more about the database than he ever had as an active officer. He could even connect with federal law enforcement files. But by the time he'd become thoroughly versed in its nuances, all his fantasies of still being a cop had been crushed beneath the weight of the doctor's final report on the condition of his hip. That report seemed to completely sever all hope of reconnection with the department. Listening to the scanner and searching the databases quickly became painful reminders rather than solace, so he quit. Better to accept the inevitable, just as he'd come to accept the permanence of Alice's absence.

Now, a year after he'd last used it, he prayed that his bootleg password still worked. He keyed it in, and luckily, miraculously, he found himself once again in the familiar electronic portrait gallery of humankind at its most contemptible and corrupt.

Thank goodness for bureaucracies, he thought.

Quickly, feeling like a kid sneaking through a house where he shouldn't be, he ran a check on the name Mark Batten.

The search produced nothing. No arrests, no driver's license, no automobile records, no address, no phone, no nothing. He did a search on Lexus SUVs, but none were registered to anyone named Batten. He printed out the list, but the several thousand names were daunting. If he had a squad, they could conceivably track down and question every owner, but all he had was himself and no real authority. He tossed the list aside, not knowing whether to be upset or intrigued—he felt a little of both.

He shut down the computer and contemplated his next move. If he couldn't get some background on the thief, he'd have to settle on some background on the stolen item. Taking one last sip of coffee and grimacing at its tepid bitterness, he headed for the door. His destination was Radcliffe Antiquaries, the place the Harveys had purchased the sculpture.

Radcliffe Antiquaries was located in a curious building on Main Street, half way between downtown and the Texas Medical Center. The building was composed of several adjacent two-story structures, but only an architect or a wrecking crew could have ascertained the exact number. Two-thirds of a century back, most of the block had been uniformly refinished with a white facade that married Arabian architecture to Art Deco sensibilities.

Guthrie had noticed the building often. It was a product of Houston's early twentieth-century growth—in its heyday, probably equivalent to the suburban malls of the present. Now the lower-floor storefronts were occupied by an art gallery and three antique dealers and the second-story offices by lawyers probably in dire need of clients. Guthrie had been in a few cheap law offices, but an antique dealer was a rare experience.

Radcliffe was about mid-block. Guthrie parked by the curb on the nearest side street and walked around the corner to the front door. A tiny bell tinkled as he entered the cool restraint of the shop's interior.

At first, Guthrie thought he was alone. Despite the incredible clutter of antiques, the shop bore an ambiance of vacancy, as if everyone had gone out for lunch at the same time, accidentally leaving the door unlocked. Then one of the antiques at the back unfolded from behind a gigantic roll-top desk made of dark, highly polished wood.

The mobile antique was a white-haired old man. It was a toss-up which was more ancient, him or the desk. In any case, the desk had proved the more durable. The man, small and wizened, walked with a sort of shuffle that wasn't exactly mincing or halting but as if he didn't have full range of motion in his hips. Guthrie could sympathize.

As the old man toddled up, Guthrie resisted the impulse to peer closely to see if he might be wearing a patina of dust over his impeccably conservative brown suit. But no, he wouldn't be. Nothing in the shop was dusty, as if dust could not abide here, even though the task of dusting the place looked to be too monumental for the old man to undertake.

The old man's small eyes, as dark and polished as the desk, searched Guthrie like a cop frisking a prisoner. There wasn't a trace of geriatric hobble in those quick, bright orbs. Guthrie suspected the old guy was checking him for money rather than a weapon or illicit merchandise. Evidently he didn't find any, for his manner, while remaining polite, subtly hinted that the delivery entrance was around back.

"May I help you?"

Guthrie was surprised. He'd expected to hear a brittle wheeze reminiscent of a dry, cracked clarinet reed, but the voice was low, rich, and mellow, like that of a disc jockey at a classical music station. Maybe proximity to classical stuff like old music and period furniture did that to you.

"I'm investigating the theft of an antique," Guthrie said.

The old man's eyes widened slightly, not in indignation or fear, just in mild surprise.

"Are you with the police?"

"No. I've been hired to recover the property."

"My," the old man said. "A private detective. What a surprise. You're the first one I've met."

When the old man referred to him as a detective, Guthrie felt a little jolt followed by a warm surge. What was it? Purpose, he decided. It felt like purpose.

"Do you think I might have stolen it?"

"What?" Guthrie's sense of purpose took a bump and almost slid off the road. "You?"

"Well, certainly. I have quite a lot of them." The old man waved around the room. "I love antiques."

"I can tell. Looks like quite a collection."

The white head leaned forward conspiratorially and the mellow tones dropped in register. "To tell the truth, I can barely bring myself to part with one. I simply hate to sell them. Gives me an excuse to charge extra."

He straightened and chuckled, and Guthrie smiled politely.

"No, Mr. Radcliffe, I didn't...."

"Mason, young man. William Mason."

"Sorry, Mr. Mason. Is Mr. Radcliffe here?"

Mason's mellow chuckle came again.

"My dear young man, if Mr. Radcliffe were present, I'm afraid we would have to sell him as a relic. Or perhaps as scrap. He's been dead for, let me see, nearly twenty-five years. But he built this business, and when I took over, I kept the venerable name."

"I see. So you're the owner."

"Lock, stock, and barrel."

"Then maybe you can help me."

"I confess," Mason said, a sly twinkle in his eye. "I'm the one who stole your antique."

"You?"

"Yes. And I've got it hidden here somewhere. Would you like to know where?"

"That I would."

"If you could give me a hint what type of antique it is, perhaps...."

"I can do better than that." Guthrie handed him frontal photo of the sculpture. Before taking it, Mason removed a spidery pair of wire-rimmed spectacles from his inner jacket pocket and perched them on his face where they looked like cobwebs clouding an old bust. He accepted the photo then, and as his eyes focused on it, they grew larger than the lens magnification warranted.

"This is the Katib." All his playfulness vanished instantly. Unless Guthrie was mistaken, what replaced it was fear, though Mason kept it well concealed behind his antique experience.

"Katib of Jashyari." Guthrie gave him the photocopy of the deed. "Is this authentic?"

The dark eyes darted over the paper for a moment, then Mason laid the deed and photo on a small round table with three carved legs ending in claws holding two-inch glass balls. Eyes still dancing, he wrung his hands.

"This is terrible," he muttered.

Guthrie took the statement as an affirmative answer.

"The Harveys agree with you, Mr. Mason."

"I don't know what I can do. I helped them acquire it, but that was the last of it, I assure you. I haven't heard of it since. What I said before...about having what you're looking for. I was simply jesting."

"I don't doubt you," Guthrie soothed, wondering what had rattled the old fellow. "I just came here for a little background information."

"Oh." Mason still fidgeted, but the rapid movement of his eyes slowed to a reasonable rate.

"Would you like to sit down?" Guthrie asked, playing host.

"Yes, please."

Guthrie tried to assist Mason into the nearest chair, an ornately carved curving wooden frame with a tapestry cushion for a seat, but the old man demurred.

"Not this one. It's a Hepplewhite. Too valuable to sit on. At my desk, please."

Guthrie got him into the big leather chair, where Mason appeared to gain strength from the desk's bulk and myriad, mysterious compartments.

"Please sit, Mr. Guthrie. What do you want to know?"

"Is this one safe?" Guthrie indicated a worn desk chair that didn't appear to be a day over fifty. At Mason's nod, Guthrie sat.

"You're taking this pretty hard, Mr. Mason."

"It's just dreadful. As I told you before, my antiques are like my children. It's difficult enough to part with one, but to have one stolen, it is like...like...."

"A violation?" Guthrie supplied.

"Exactly." Mason nodded vigorously with a movement that made his acquiescence seem too calculated. "It is a violation."

"You said you helped the Harveys acquire the sculpture. You didn't sell it to them?"

"A piece like the Katib is far beyond my financial means," Mason said. "If I sold all of this," he waved around the room, "at top dollar, I still could not afford the Katib."

"Isn't Radcliffe Antiquaries listed on the deed as seller?"

"A mere formality. The Harveys are valued clients, and when they heard the Katib was on the market, they approached me to act as their agent in the transaction. The actual transfer of the property was between the Harveys and the seller."

"Who was the seller?"

"Actually, the seller wishes to remain anonymous. That is why my firm's name is on the deed. I don't think...."

Guthrie waved off Mason's protest. "The seller's name isn't important. So all you did was handle the transfer of title, and you never actually saw the sculpture in the flesh, so to speak?"

"That is correct, although more than paperwork was involved. I also researched the Katib's provenance."

"Is it really as old as the description says?"

"Probably older. Metalworking technique and stylistic values date it as seventh or eighth century, but historically I was able to trace it only two centuries prior to the beginning of the Crusades. At that time, it was in the collection of the monarchy of a minor city state located in the Seljuk Dominions." When Mason saw Guthrie's expression of incomprehension, he added, "In present day Turkey. During the Third Crusade, at the end of the twelfth century, it was acquired by a Scotsman named Kendal Donn, who accompanied Richard Lionheart to the Middle East."

"That's a nice piece of detective work."

"Why, thank you." Mason smiled for the first time since he'd seen the photograph. "But it wasn't mine. I employ a talented researcher who pieced together the history from records in the Middle East and in the Vatican archives."

"Are there any antique dealers who might buy such a sculpture?"

"Unlikely."

"You sound pretty positive. It's old and valuable."

"Those same qualities also make it practically unsellable. In the first place, no reputable dealer would handle such a piece without authenticated documentation of ownership."

"There are always disreputable dealers."

"Alas, you are correct." Mason gave a helpless shrug. "What is one to do in a world such as this? But I think there is an equally important reason why most dealers wouldn't handle the Katib. It is not well-known. Demand for it would come from a select few. Most antiquarians would take it to be old and valuable, but not the extreme rarity it actually is."

"So the thief wouldn't be able to fence it to just anybody. It'd have to be a dealer who knew the piece itself."

"Yes. And I can probably name all of them off the top of my head. There can't be more than half a dozen in the world."

"You think the thief stole the bust for a personal collection?"

"Another collector? Yes, it is possible." Mason paused thoughtfully, and his little dark eyes lifted to bore into Guthrie's. "Far more plausible than his having stolen it to sell to a random buyer."

"That might make it very difficult to recover," Guthrie pointed out. "But I've considered it."

"Whatever the possibilities, Mr. Guthrie, you must recover the Katib and return it to its rightful owners."

Mason's intensity surprised Guthrie.

"I was hired to find it, and I will." Guthrie paused, deciding he could be as calculating as the old man, or at least try. "If the thief is dealing with a collector, would you have any idea who that might be?"

"Impossible to say," Mason demurred. "I may know dealers, but I can't be aware of all potential collectors."

"Of course," Guthrie replied. He stood. "If you do hear anything through the...ah...."

"The collectors' grapevine," Mason supplied with a wry twist to his lips.

"The grapevine. Naturally. You'll let me know?"

"I will be attentive—though, since the piece has been stolen, I doubt its sale will be publicly mentioned."

"Any little hint might help."

"I will pursue the matter and let you know immediately should I hear anything useful." The old man looked quizzically at Guthrie. "Was there anything else?"

He looked like he wanted to close up shop and hide away for the rest of the day.

"I guess that's about it." Guthrie rose and retrieved the photo and photocopy of the deed from the small round table. "Oh, yeah, this researcher you employed. Can you tell me who that was?"

"Why do you ask?" The eyes, still nervous but now sharper than ever, came to a dead stop on Guthrie.

"In your business, I'm sure you check out everything, right? Provenance, special markings, damage and repairs, and such?"

"Of course."

"Same reason. You need to know every detail about your antiques, and I need to know every detail about a case."

"It was John Travis. I use him often because he's quite meticulous and knowledgeable. In fact, he's a professor of both anthropology and art history at the University of Houston."

"Interesting combination."

"Indeed." Suddenly the old man's eyes bugged slightly, and he clawed out and caught Guthrie's arm.

"You'll tell them, won't you? The Harveys? Tell them I had nothing to do with it."

"I'll tell them. And I'll let you know as soon as I've recovered the head."

"Yes, please." The old man dropped Guthrie's arm and slumped in his ancient leather chair like an old cushion whose stuffing has long since given out.

"Thanks for your time, Mr. Mason."

The old man nodded, and his birdlike eyes followed Guthrie until he'd left the shop.

Outside, Guthrie headed toward his car, hearing the door lock behind him. As he rounded the corner at the end of the block, he was so lost in thought that he nearly bumped into a pair of black girls in their late teens. Guthrie apologized, and they giggled and flashed dark, twinkling eyes at him before disappearing around the building.

Guthrie went on to his car, but his pace slowed. Something nagged at him, but he couldn't quite put his finger on it. He shrugged. Must be the puzzling way the old man had reacted to the news that the sculpture had been stolen. Whatever it was, Guthrie put the feeling on hold as he got into his car and steered out onto Fannin. The University of Houston was his next stop. The way people were reacting to the sculpture's loss made him more curious than ever, and he wanted to talk to John Travis, the professor who'd researched it for Mason.

7

FIFTEEN MINUTES LATER, GUTHRIE FOUND a visitor's spot at the University of Houston. He was familiar with the campus, having graduated from UH himself. Twelve years hadn't changed the place much. Even in his day, almost every plot of ground that could be built on held a building, but now he saw that the campus had subsumed several adjacent blocks. He thought he remembered which of the buildings housed the social sciences, but before he went there, he paid a visit to the student bookstore, where he looked through a course catalog. The courses next to the name Travis indicated a heavy leaning toward the art and archaeology of the Middle East.

Guthrie left the bookstore and walked across campus, feeling out of place among all the hurrying young people. He found the anthropology department and approached the secretary, a middle-aged black woman who gave him a smile as he approached her desk.

"Could you tell me if John Travis is in today?"

"Dr. Travis?" She looked surprised. "No. He's not in all semester. He's on sabbatical."

"Is he in town, do you think?"

"I don't know. He might be. I haven't seen him, but someone was picking up his mail until last week. Let me check with Dr. Gibson." She lifted the phone, punched a button, and said, "This is Sharon. There's a gentleman out here asking for Dr. Travis. Do you know if he's in town?" She listened a moment then hung up.

"That was our department chair. He says he thinks Dr. Travis is in town, but he's not sure. Dr. Travis's sabbatical included some time in the Middle East for research."

"May I speak with Dr. Gibson for a few moments?"

"I'll ask." She called again, made the request, and hung up.

"He's right down that hall," she nodded. "Fourth door on the left."

"Thanks."

The door to Gibson's office was open. Guthrie knocked on the frame, and the burly, brown-bearded man behind the desk looked up and gestured to a chair.

"Come in. You're the fellow looking for John? What can I help you with?"

"My name is Clay Guthrie. I've been hired to do some research on an artifact that may be Middle Eastern in origin. I understand that Dr. Travis is an expert in that area, and I hoped that he might be able to help me."

"You certainly came to see the right man," Gibson said. "If it's Middle Eastern, John can identify it. Too bad he's not here. He's due back at the end of the summer."

"I see. And you don't know if he's in town?"

"Sorry," Gibson shook his head. "He might be, or he could be in the Middle East. I think I heard him mention something about being out of town some, but I don't know exactly when."

"Is there anybody who might?"

"Maybe someone in the art history department. John has a dual appointment. Fact is, we're lucky to have him. We're not exactly a top-tier school, though our department's pretty good. He could go anywhere, even the Ivy League schools."

"What keeps him here, then?"

"Personally, I think it's because of the art and artifact trade. What with all the money in Houston, there's a good bit of it. That's how John made his mark, you know, fighting the illegal trade in looted artifacts."

"What does he do, work with the museums?"

"Not much the museums can do," Gibson shrugged. "Actually, sometimes they're the culprits. John mostly does a lot of independent appraisal work. That allows him to keep tabs on the different types of artifacts going through the private antiquities market. That's the real indicator of the illegal trade. In fact, that's what he's doing on his sabbatical—working on a book on art and artifacts plundered from the Middle East."

"Do you know what dealers he works with? Maybe they can get in touch with him."

"We never discussed it. Mind if I see what you're asking about?"

Guthrie produced the photo of the sculpture and passed it over.

"Middle Eastern, you say? Yes, I suppose it is, though it's a bit unusual. How old is it?"

"That's part of what I'm trying to find out. Maybe from the time of the Crusades or a little before."

"That narrows it down to only half a millennium," Gibson chuckled. "Well, I can't say. I'm a cultural anthropologist, not a physical one, and my area's South America." He handed the photo back to Guthrie. "As I said, John's your man for this kind of thing, but since he's not here, you might check with Martina Flores in art history. She's worked with John, and she's an expert in that area and general period. Maybe she in touch with him."

Guthrie thanked Gibson and left his office. On his way past the receptionist, he paused.

"Do you have a faculty directory?"

She handed one over, and as he thumbed through it, she asked, "Looking up Dr. Travis?"

"Yeah, I thought I might call him at home."

"You can forget that, then," she said, gesturing to the directory.

"His number's not listed?"

"Not anymore. He had it taken out last year."

"Why?"

"I guess he was getting too many calls."

"How's that?"

"Women grad students," she clarified.

"They like him, huh?"

"Hubba-hubba." She did a quick twist in her chair, and her breasts shook.

"But not you?"

She rolled her eyes and gave a playful snort. "He's got a lot of animal magnetism, I'll grant. But let's be realistic. I'm not a good-looking grad student who isn't interested in anything permanent except an archaeological site."

"There's a lot to be said for stability," Guthrie said, returning the directory.

"Too bad there aren't more who think that," she said. "Here." She flipped through a Rolodex, scribbled an address and phone number on a note pad, and passed the paper to Guthrie.

"Could you tell me how to get to the art and art history department?"

She pulled a photocopy of a campus map from a drawer, circled the building he was looking for, and gave it to him.

Thanking her, he left and headed toward the building she'd indicated. Dr. Flores was in class, so he waited near her office until she was done. She was a slender brunette of medium height with the kind of looks that would last through middle age.

"I wonder if I might have a few moments, Dr. Flores," Guthrie said as she unlocked her door.

"Are you a student?" she asked, barely glancing at him. The trace of accent he heard in her voice indicated her native language had been Spanish.

"No. I've been hired to do some research on an artifact. I understand John Travis knows something about it, and I'm trying to get in touch with him."

Flores quickly entered her office and busied herself with putting down her books and notes and switching on her computer.

"What makes you think I know anything about where John is?"

"I'm just checking with his colleagues. Dr. Gibson in anthropology said your field was similar to Dr. Travis's. I thought he might have said something to you."

"Look," she said, staring at Guthrie for the first time. "I haven't even seen John since last summer. I heard he's on sabbatical, but aside from that, I haven't the faintest idea of where he is. Nor do I care."

"Sounds like you must have at one point."

"And what business is that of yours?"

"None at all."

"That's right. Now, if you'll excuse me...."

"Mind if I ask you for a quick professional assessment?"

"Regarding?"

"This." Guthrie handed her the photo of the sculpture.

"Where did you get this?"

"From the owners. Ever see it before?"

"I've seen the photo but never the real piece. John was researching it for one of his clients. Is this the piece you're researching?"

"Yes."

"I thought John already did that."

"So I've been told. I was just trying to get any background that might be missing from his report. Did Dr. Travis ever mention anything about it?"

"Not really." She shrugged, but Guthrie could sense interest in her stance. "He did a lot of research, and I didn't always know much about what he was working on."

"I'd have thought you'd be interested professionally."

"Yes…."

"Yes?"

"John used to share his work, but toward the end…."

"So you were close at one time?"

"Why do you keep asking that?" She sounded peeved, but weary, too, as if was a well-worn topic.

"I guess I can't help it. You're an art historian, so you ask questions about art. I'm a detective, so my job is to ask questions about people."

She considered this for a moment then grudgingly said, "John and I were close for a while. But that ended eighteen months ago. About the time he was researching this," she handed the photo back to Guthrie. "We haven't talked since. Now, if you'll excuse me, I have work to do."

"Thanks," he said. But his mood was pensive as he left the building. His early breaks were all crumbling, and aside from discovering that John Travis had probably broken off a relationship with Flores for a series of flings with graduate students, he hadn't found out much. Certainly nothing relevant to the case, and he was quickly running out of options. He still needed to meet with the other party guests, but he wanted to wind up his background search on the sculpture before he tackled a separate line of inquiry. A drive out to Travis's house might find him home. Guthrie could ask his questions and move on.

Since it was nearly noon, however, he decided to grab a bite to eat before he left campus. Just for old time's sake, he walked to the University Center and went through the cafeteria line. The food looked like it hadn't changed any more than the campus had, so he paid for a small pizza and a cup of coffee, settled at a table, and ate.

As he finished his meal and sat there ruminating, something kept niggling at his thoughts, but it wasn't sudden revelation. It was subdued laughter that rose from behind him. The laughter wasn't loud, but he had an itchy feeling it was directed at him. He glanced around and saw two young black women several tables away. They weren't looking at Guthrie, but he had the strong impression they had been the second before he'd turned. He shrugged off their mirth. Who the hell knows that went on in the minds of college kids? He certainly didn't. He could barely remember what was on his own mind at that age. Probably college girls. He chuckled to himself.

The girls got up and headed toward the exit. Guthrie watched them as they did, and just before they went outside, they glanced back at him. At that instant, Guthrie realized what had been bugging him. He'd seen them before. Twice—once outside Armin's and again when he'd left Radcliffe Antiquaries. Seeing them a third time in fewer days was a little too coincidental, especially since each time had been miles apart, and most definitely since they'd apparently been observing him. He surged to his feet and hurried after them.

As Guthrie went through the exit and down the steps in front of the building, he saw the girls jogging up to a campus shuttle bus.

"Hey!" he yelled. "Wait!"

The shorter girl glanced at Guthrie then poked her companion and whispered to her. They quickly boarded the bus.

Guthrie stopped running as the doors closed and the bus pulled away from the curb. The girls sat down in the seat at the rear of the bus and waved merrily at Guthrie through the back window.

Guthrie considered chasing them down but shrugged it off. Even if he caught the bus, what was he going to do—accost two young women in public?

Instead, he headed for the visitor's lot. If the girls were following him, he'd have another chance to corner them. For now, he thought he'd head on over to John Travis's house on the outside chance the antiquities expert was home and might be able to tell him more about the bust. Maybe he could explain why its theft made William Mason so nervous.

8

TRAVIS LIVED IN BELLAIRE, ON South Rice Boulevard. Guthrie couldn't say much for the neighborhood—it wasn't bad, it just wasn't a terribly inviting place to live. South Rice was a main drag, and small businesses strung the west side of this stretch between Fournace and Bissonnet. Along the east side sat post-World War II houses. The fact that the houses fronted for a residential neighborhood didn't make them a spiritual part of the middle class ethos that lay behind them. These houses were a buffer zone and, like any such area, prone to oddities of character.

One of the houses had been converted into a mini-church for a Christian splinter sect, or so Guthrie gathered from the sign. He'd always wondered how these little churches survived. The congregation couldn't have surpassed fifty. What kept it financially solvent? And what kept it going on more esoteric levels? Strong beliefs, he guessed. Not much else could. Still, the place was of architecturally sound brick construction with an attractive if simple front design, and the grounds were clean. Something substantial, no matter how modest, maintained its solvency.

Guthrie drove past the church, looking for Travis's house, but for some reason, he missed it, so he drove around the block to make another pass. He went by the church again, slowed, and glanced at the houses, trying to see addresses.

He was just about at the right number when a sudden blare snapped his attention to the road. Instinctively jerking the wheel, he veered back into his own lane just in time to avoid a head-on collision with an on-coming pickup.

Swearing and shaken, he steered the Honda into the next drive on his right—a small parking lot in front of a defunct convenience store sitting between a bar and a glass company. The bar was open, and the way his hands were shaking, he sure could use something to calm his nerves.

Then he caught himself. What the hell was he thinking? And what the hell had that fiasco in the street been? He was a pretty good driver—they'd taught him chase and evasion tactics at the academy—and he didn't think he'd taken his eyes off the road long enough to wander into the oncoming lane.

But apparently he had.

He sat there for several minutes, telling himself that it was nothing, calming his jangled nerves. Finally he got out, took a deep breath, and stared across South Rice. The house that had to belong to Travis was a couple of houses back the way he'd come, right about where he'd almost collided with the pickup.

The place was shaded by five huge oaks and masked by a thick, dense, unkempt hedge half again as tall as Guthrie. No wonder he'd missed the address on his first pass. About all that was visible from this angle was part of the roof, so he walked to the far edge of the bar's lot, directly across the street from the house. Even from here, he could only see part of the house through the gap in the hedge where the driveway entered the front left corner of the lot, rolled close by the left side of the house, and ended at a detached two-car garage.

The house, itself—what he could see of it from his vantage— was beet-colored brick with wood trim painted an equally dismal red. The driveway was empty, but he couldn't say the same for the garage. With the big double roll-up door down, an elephant could have been hiding inside. But a door that size wouldn't invite lifting and closing each time Travis came home. Most likely the garage and the house were as vacant as the drive.

Well, he'd have to try, anyway. He waited for a couple of clumps of traffic to pass then quickly trotted across South Rice. But when he reached the sidewalk in front of the hedge, he stopped, suddenly overwhelmed by the impression that something was terribly wrong. He actually caught himself taking a step backwards and sniffing the air, as if he expected to taste the stench of death coming from a disgusting tangle wedged in the shrubbery. All that actually touched his nostrils, though, was the tang of exhaust from the traffic on the street, so he shook off the thoughts, took the half-dozen steps to the driveway, and peered into the front yard around the last bush. The yard wasn't much—a space little more than the width of the house and only twenty-five or thirty feet deep, stubbled with stingy, yellowish grass.

Up close, the house was peculiar in a way that hadn't been apparent from across the street. He hated to attach the word ominous to anything that wasn't a weapon or the desire to use one, so the disturbing quality remained undefined, particularly since there was nothing notable about the house itself. Like many of its neighbors, it was one of those designs called modern in the fifties. It still looked good, if you liked those kinds of looks. Better maintained than Guthrie's place, though he thought his homier since a cold and gloomy feel seemed to cloud this property. Probably because of the old oaks overshadowing the yard and the dense hedge crowding in.

He stared at the house for a long time, reluctant, for some reason, to approach. Decay tickled his nostrils again, and he sniffed the air, hoping to get some direction. Was it coming from the hedge? Maybe he was wrong—all he smelled now was the odor of car exhaust.

He studied the hedge. Its thick, bushy height was definitely there to maintain the privacy of the house, and the feeling was reinforced by the partially opened horizontal louvers of heavy wood masking the building's front windows, giving them the same hooded stare he remembered seeing in the eyes of the more dangerous street criminals he'd dealt with.

And the longer he looked, the more that privacy demanded consideration. Guthrie shuffled his feet, hesitant and apprehensive. The place was obviously occupied by a shy, reclusive individual. A picture of John Travis began to form in Guthrie's mind—rumpled hair, stooped shoulders, glasses, tweed. Hush Puppies. Why was Guthrie here, anyway? To ask a few silly questions? Unimportant questions, really. Questions whose answers couldn't really aid Guthrie's search. And the man was on sabbatical. He was engaged in important work that affected the integrity of the entire art world. Could Guthrie or any decent person actually justify disturbing the privacy of such an important man for something so trivial as Guthrie's errand?

Privacy, Guthrie had to remind himself sternly, was a relative matter. As a cop, he'd seen often enough that personal privacy sometimes had to give way for the greater good. Someone had swiped the Harveys' property—valuable property—and Guthrie had been hired to return it. If the investigation forced him to ask a few essentially innocent questions of persons peripheral to the case, so be it.

With a shock, Guthrie realized he was rationalizing that the Harveys' personal good was equivalent to the greater good that once gave Guthrie cachet to question just about anybody. My, how money can alter perspectives, he thought. Seven grand, and old Guthrie is replacing protest songs with paeans of praise. At that rate, the remaining twenty thousand would have him voting the Harveys, and Egan, into office. The absurdity of the thought jolted a humorless laugh from his throat.

That and the knowledge that he wasn't all that decent.

But in truth, was he really convinced that this Travis fellow had any information of value to the investigation? The documentation the Harveys had provided told him all he needed to know, and Travis was simply a loose end to be tied and forgotten. A pointless loose end. In fact, it struck Guthrie, questioning Travis wasn't proper procedure. Not proper procedure, at all.

He rubbed his suddenly sweaty palms against his pants. His throat was dry and chest constricted, making breathing shallow. What the hell was he doing here?

Guthrie shook his head again, this time like a man coming out of a drugged stupor. He had something to do, that's what. A job. The house, remember? Supposed to go up and ask a few questions. Yeah, that's right. Knock on the door and meet John Travis. So what the hell are you doing standing here at the end of the driveway like a rodent mesmerized by a viper?

Guthrie squeezed his eyes tight, took mental hold of himself, and tried to sweep the cobwebs off his synapses. Just how long had he been standing here, debating with himself?

He didn't know that any more than he knew the reason he'd gotten into a murky and convoluted philosophical argument with himself about the propriety of asking Travis a few questions about the history of the sculpture. He only knew that he'd been hired to find the head, and if that required he ask a few questions, that's what he was going to do, even if it meant violating the privacy of a man he didn't know—a busy and important man at that—just because he was, himself, ignorant and unable to bring any kind of true intelligence to the problems he faced. And lacking true intelligence, he had only a certain cleverness to divert himself. In fact, wasn't diversion what this trip was all about? It was, after all, a pretend investigation. All pretend. Just as he was a pretend investigator meandering around the city following easy leads that would ultimately take him nowhere and reveal nothing rather than bring him face-to-face with the truth that he couldn't find Mark Batten and probably never would. The whole premise for talking to Travis was worse than pointless—it was entirely misdirected, ill conceived, and senseless.

Damn! he thought. Talk about senseless! What's wrong with you, you fool? Shut the blather, and get your ass up to that front door!

Guthrie used the same mental technique he'd learned as a cop when he'd encountered dangerous situations. Though the doubts and fears crowding his mind numbed his legs, he smothered them with dogged determination, focused on the house, and willed his leaden feet forward. The mental tension was so intense that passing through the driveway gap was like pushing bodily through the hedge itself. Tendrils of invisible branches clung to his mind, raking it with guilt and hesitation. After what seemed like a lot longer than it probably was, he stumbled across the beggarly grass to the front door.

Once there he didn't feel a hell of a lot better. The sensation of raking tendrils vanished as soon as he entered the yard, but the creeping itch that replaced it was worse. He felt eyes observing him through the cracks between the louvers, eyes radiating meanness and hatred from beneath partly closed lids.

Travis must be inside, watching, Guthrie told himself, but the realization did nothing to suppress the images that shambled out of the closets of his memory. He saw himself mounting another porch in a different time, and he wasn't alone. Art Durward was with him, and both of them were breathing heavily as adrenaline pounded through their brains.

With an effort, Guthrie dragged himself back to the present. To the real and tangible. A door was in front of him, located in the recesses of a little walled porch. He only had to take a step and reach out and knock. Simple movements, but the porch was so small, so enclosed, so dark. Gasping was the only way to breathe. He wasn't normally claustrophobic, but he knew if the recess possessed an exterior door, or even a screen, he'd never be able to make himself go inside. But it didn't, so, skin crawling, he took the single step up with feet that had to have roots pulled from the cement walk.

The door was painted the same color as the rest of the trim, a red dark as dried blood. Guthrie dropped his eyes as he lifted a heavy, clumsy hand to knock. The smooth paint rasped his knuckles like pumice on baby flesh.

For a moment after he knocked, while he rubbed pain from his knuckles, there was a dead silence. Then he heard a faint but sharp noise all the more ominous and startling for the silence preceding it. The noise could have been anything, really. Just the wind creaking a branch or the house settling. That's what he thought later. Right now, though, his mind reeled as shadows darkened the present with the memory of the clicking metallic sound that came from behind another closed door. That metallic sound that had served as both warning and signal.

He'd heard that sound just as Art slammed through the door, and its echo in his memory drowned the sound of the frame splintering as the door burst inward. Then Guthrie was following Art inside, seeing the man in his underwear, seeing the machine gun, seeing Art bringing up the barrel of his own weapon. Suddenly Art was stumbling, falling, and the confused sound he made as he fell was obliterated by the machine gun's blast. And Guthrie fell, too, slammed and hurtled to the floor, chest aching so much he couldn't breathe, hip on fire with a burning that smoldered yet in his soul. His eyes were filled with hot tears of pain, but the tears were gray clots that spread blood across his vision when he tried to wipe them away.

The only thing that that had saved Guthrie as the crimson-tinged shadow rose in front of him and cast its empty, searching eye in his direction was the spasmodic kicking of Art's boot against his leg, each touch sending shocks of pain through his ruined hip and jarring him back to reality. All he saw was that eye, searching, and Guthrie, panic wheeling through him, jerked up his own weapon and pulled the trigger again and again, not realizing that the recoil of the first blast had thrown the shotgun from his hand, only knowing that he had to kill that eye because it had seen him, knew him, and was searching....

Guthrie, suddenly and without thought, found himself out in the yard, crouched over a pool of steaming vomit, blood pounding achingly through his head, extremities vibrating with adrenaline.

He wasn't sure how he'd gotten there, though he must have leapt there in a single bound. He tried to stop shaking, but he felt trapped between the hedge and the house and, at the same time, completely exposed and vulnerable in the middle of the small yard.

And the vomit, pizza an hour earlier, looked too much like bloody brains.

One thing kept flashing in his mind with inexorable urgency— get the hell away from this house and forget the whole damn thing. It wasn't just a want, it was a need, brutal and intense. Emptiness was searching him out where he stood, and he had to find safety before it shed its final fiery sight.

There was no time to do anything but uproot himself from where he crouched and trudge toward the driveway gap. Through it he saw the street and, across that, the bar and boarded-up convenience store. Traffic bustled down the pavement. Everything out there was bathed in warm sunlight. More than ever this murky, hedged-in yard was as dismal, claustrophobic, and unfriendly as the inside of a violated tomb at dusk. The sunlight outside meant safety from the dark emptiness of remembering. Out there was peace and the light of blessed forgetfulness.

He took only a couple of steps before he found himself passing through the gap in the hedge. Instead of the clinging sensation, this time it was as if he were a nasty bit of gristle spit out toward the all-too-close street. He stumbled to a stop at the curb just as a Nissan sedan snarled past, horn blaring. The wind of its passage stung his eyes with road grit, and he blinked painfully as tears welled.

He lifted a hand to wipe them away but was suddenly afraid his hand would come away dripping clotted crimson. He heard a moan but couldn't tell if it came from the traffic or the wind in the trees shading the house.

Or from his own lips.

A panicked, blinking glance up and down the street showed there was enough time to get to his car if he was quick. He was.

Not until he was behind the wheel of the Honda, with the engine purring and the transmission in first, did he look across the street at Travis's house.

Surprisingly enough, it appeared normal. Normal as hell.

9

BY THE TIME GUTHRIE REACHED THE traffic circle at Broadway and Park Place, his hands had quit shaking, but he was feeling pretty disgusted with the whole situation. Disgusted with himself, really. He could only hope that Travis hadn't been watching through the louvered windows to see him stooped over his own puke in the front yard.

What the hell was wrong with him? Now was not the time for an emotional breakdown. He didn't need old memories, especially those particular memories, to lurch into his mind as he stood on the threshold of, if not success, then some semblance of recovery.

But Guthrie knew what was wrong. He was floundering. If he hadn't realized it before, it was clear now. He'd been floundering since the shooting and the flat reality it had introduced into his life. Floundering through currents that kept sucking him under. Now, ahead, he could see an island onto which he could drag his tired carcass, at least for a time. The island was the relatively small but very real pile of money Egan promised for a successful conclusion, and all he needed to do to rest on it was get hold of Mark Batten. Why was such a simple task becoming so troublesome? He almost found it possible to believe in a personal demon who repeatedly led him to the brink then maliciously held him back just as he was about to fly.

As he sat there, brooding and waiting for the light to change from red to green, he glanced at the bum on the corner. The man was as much a fixture of the traffic circle as the signs and signal lights. Guthrie had observed him there for at least three years. The guy was big and hulking and dressed in filthy clothes. His face and neck, where they were exposed around the edges of the dirty yellow-gray hair and beard, were blistered deep red by the sun. He carried a sign that read, "Will work for food," but his puffy features, crimson eyes, and sloppy stagger proclaimed more loudly "Will beg for alcohol."

Is that me? Guthrie wondered. Am I only one low step up but just as pitiful?

It was a bleak thought that the only things separating Guthrie from the bum were abstinence from alcohol and a disability pension that allowed him to tread water enough to keep his head above the surface. Class, he admitted, was as much a matter of perspective as anything. His own simple lifestyle would make this man as jealous of Guthrie as Guthrie was of the people he was working for. All it had taken was a couple of days of close proximity with Egan, the Harveys, and their toadies to bring to the surface the nastiness of Guthrie's personal mixture of desire, envy, disappointment, and guilt. The jealousy was an acrimonious undercurrent only barely discernible to himself, but it carried him to the deeper, treacherous waters of intimidation, where he'd become enthralled by his own pitiful self-image.

And it always came back to that, though he no longer was sure just when the problems had started. He used to pretend they'd begun with the bullet that shattered his hip and police career or while he lay in the hospital, brooding on the empty house he knew he'd find when he returned home. But he knew his problems had been with him longer than that—long enough that they'd festered into a sore no doctor could cure during the long months of his convalescence as he lay in that silent house, that empty home, wishing that the crippling bullet had killed him as surely as it's fellows had killed Art. And lying there, he could only be thankful there hadn't been any second story or children to occupy it.

But that had been the last thing he'd been thankful about for a long time. Until Ingram had knocked on his door and taken him to Ben Egan. In the final analysis, he knew it wasn't the money Egan offered that kept his future just a little brighter and less sunburned than that of the bum on the corner. He now had work. The occupation he'd wanted.

The preoccupation.

No. He wasn't like the bum. He couldn't be, couldn't let that happen. Wouldn't. He had this case, and he would make it work for him, make it pay off with more than the money Egan offered. He didn't know how or what the currency would be. Self-respect? Fortitude? Knowledge? Whatever it was, he was going to find it no matter how deeply it lay hidden.

The light turned green, and as he edged into the traffic circle, past the bum, it occurred to him that he'd have to be extra careful. He wasn't superstitious, but he'd learned long ago to trust his instincts, and those instincts told him to be as wary of the people with whom he was dealing as he was of his own failings.

A couple of minutes later, he was home, and he made sure the doors were locked before he took a long, hot shower to wash off the stink of fear that lingered from his breakdown in Travis's yard.

When he was done, he toweled dry, dressed, and for a time, sat at his desk reading and rereading the background material on the head. And looking at the photos and the fascinating countenance they depicted.

At about five, his rumbling stomach forced him into the kitchen. He was starved, particularly since he hadn't, in effect, had lunch. He baked a chicken, steamed a pot of vegetables, then carried a plateful to the dining room table.

Dinner was not a particularly happy time for Guthrie. He was a decent cook, at least at the eight or ten dishes he rotated through every couple of weeks. Eating alone was another matter. Guthrie read at meals instead of having conversation, a habit that had done more to alienate him from polite small talk than anything else. Tonight, before he sat down to eat, he retrieved the book on electronic surveillance that he'd been reading for several days.

He was only a couple of bites into the book when a knock sounded on his front door. He opened it with some trepidation, expecting to see Ingram and the beefy blond driver. Instead, he saw an older, lean black man with a short bush of white hair.

"Cut your yard, mister?"

Out in the driveway sat a battered two-tone green Ford pickup with a couple of lawnmower handles jutting from the bed. Crude block letters painted on the door read, "Terry Lawn Service."

"No, thanks," Guthrie said automatically. Normally he cut his own grass since he couldn't afford to hire out the task, and he still wasn't used to the fact that he had several grand stashed in the bedroom. But the cash wouldn't last forever.

"I'll do a real good job for ya'," the old man said before Guthrie could close the door. "You can ask your neighbor down the street. Mr. Prentice. Maybe you know him."

He gave a big, confident, engaging grin, flashing teeth as snowy as his hair. Guthrie felt himself weakening, but the old guy looked at least seventy. Guthrie saw himself agreeing and the man keeling over before the yard was half done.

"I don't think I do," Guthrie said. "Anyway, I cut it myself." He patted his stomach. "Got to get some exercise somehow."

"I sure could use the work," the old man said. He looked pretty pitiful, though beneath that, Guthrie sensed pride and determination. Must have taken a lot of that to keep the old guy going this long.

But Guthrie was thinking of something else, too. He was remembering his thoughts earlier on what separated him from the bum on the corner. A good part of it was enough pride and determination not to let himself sink that low. Maybe it was the same with this old guy. Guthrie might not have much sympathy for the bum because the bum had given up, but he could for this man because, like Guthrie, he was still floundering enough to keep his head above water.

Even so, Guthrie couldn't bring himself to set him to work. The idea of hiring a lackey, and an old black man at that, to do menial labor struck a little too close to home at the moment, now that he was Egan and the Harveys' lackey, doing their dirty work. But he admired the old man, and he wanted to do something for him.

"Listen," he said. "I can't let you do my lawn right now. But I was just eating dinner, and I'd be happy if you'd join me."

"Why you want to do that?" The old man shied back a bit, suspicion in his eyes.

How could Guthrie explain without sounding condescending or like a plain fool?

"Let's just say I could use the company," he said. "I haven't eaten dinner with anyone in a couple of years."

"Coupl'a years? You ain't got no family? No friends?"

"I guess not."

"Sad to hear that." The old man took a tentative sniff. "What you cookin'?"

"Baked chicken and vegetables. Just came out of the oven."

"Sure smells good." The old man looked suspicious again. "You sure this ain't no charity? I don't want no charity."

"If it's charity, it's for me," Guthrie said. "Really. Please, come in." Guthrie held open the door, and the old man came inside. He may have looked seventy, but Guthrie noticed that his back was straight and his step firm. His years of hard work had produced some rewards, if not wealth.

Guthrie ushered him over to the table, went to the kitchen and fixed a plate, and brought it into to the dining room.

"What would you like to drink?"

"You have any Chinese tea?"

"Chinese tea?" Guthrie chuckled. "I'm not much of a tea drinker. I don't even have Lipton."

"A glass of water'd be fine."

Guthrie got it and set it by the old man's plate, noticing that the old man hadn't begun eating though at this time of day, he must have been hungry.

"Go ahead," he said, sitting down at his own plate. "You didn't ave to wait for me."

"Sure I did," the old man replied. "You're having me for company. Be rude of me to start without you."

Guthrie nodded. "Well, let's dig in. I'm starving."

And they did, wordlessly, until they were finished. Even though they didn't speak, having the old man eat with him was somehow comforting to Guthrie.

"Ah," Guthrie said at last. "That feels better."

"Yeah," the old man said. "I've always noticed that feeling better always makes you feel better." He peered at Guthrie, then shook his head. "You don't really look like you feel better."

"What do you mean?" Guthrie demanded a bit sharply. To cover the reaction, he patted his stomach and forced a smile. "Good food is the soul of contentment. Somebody said that, I think."

"'Soul is not synonymous with stomach,'" the old man replied. "Thomas Carlyle said that."

"Wasn't he a writer?"

"Scottish essayist and novelist. About a hundred and fifty years ago."

"You read him?" Guthrie tried to keep his astonishment off his face.

"When you're as old as I am, you've done a lot of things. And what is it that you do, young feller?"

"I guess I'm a detective. For the moment, at least."

"You guess? A person ought to know who they are."

"I was a cop, but a couple of years ago I got shot. I haven't done much since."

"You must have been severely injured."

"Lost my hip. It's artificial, now. Doesn't bother me much, but it hurts some when the weather changes or I'm on my feet a lot."

"They say a lame man's been touched by the gods."

"If that's so, I'd just as soon have been left alone. Being touched by the gods hurts some."

"I imagine it does. You were saying you're a detective for the moment. What does that mean?"

Guthrie wondered at a suddenly overwhelming urge to confide in this total stranger. The old man was far more intelligent than he seemed at first, and Guthrie knew he should be suspicious, but the old guy obviously had no stake in anything relating to Guthrie. He was just some old yard man who, for whatever reason, had been unable to rise above the social constraints faced by black people everywhere. Guthrie needed a sounding board, and the old man was intelligent enough to understand the serious dilemmas Guthrie faced.

But Guthrie knew it was more than that. Deprived of real human contact for too long, he yearned to talk, yearned for a sympathetic ear and some semblance of intimacy. And the old man seemed receptive, even if he was simply listening politely because Guthrie had fed him.

But what could Guthrie say, really?

"Well," he started, "I've been offered a job as a detective with this security company, and I'm trying to solve a case to prove myself."

"How you like it so far?"

"Don't know." Guthrie thought a moment. "It's kind of like being a lookout who wears stilts so he can see ahead, only to discover that everybody is slogging through a swamp. So instead of being on top, the fellow on stilts sinks deeper than the rest."

"It's always like that when you're trying to see past the veil of mystery. You going to take the job?"

"I don't know. I can do this one gig and still keep my head up, but I can't say too much for my employer. I don't think I'd like drawing a steady paycheck from him. But I like the work. It's real, not some abstract puzzle."

"Yes," the old man nodded, his gaze distant. "We all need something to become absorbed in. Something to help us forget." He drew himself back to the present. "So, what is this test case of yours?"

"I'm looking for stolen property. A sculpture."

"Must be valuable."

"So say the owners. A River Oaks couple. They're rich as hell and just about as nasty."

"You think that because they're rich they're bad." The old man shrugged. "If they're bad, maybe it's just because they're bad."

"Bad because they're bad?" Guthrie laughed. "Is that the opposite of feeling better makes you feel better?"

"No. It's the same thing."

Guthrie sighed, knowing the old man was right and realizing it was impossible to lay blame for his problems at the steps of the rich. They had to have as much diversity of character and ethical fiber as any other group, economic or cultural. Plenty of people attained wealth through talent, hard work, and perseverance. Maybe that's what really bothered Guthrie—it wasn't the wealthy who kept him down. They didn't need to. He'd done a crackerjack job of that all on his own by not possessing the guts and ability to make a success of the opportunities life granted. Then he'd compounded it all with complacency, self-indulgence, and self-pity. And irredeemable mistakes.

"Having any success tracing the thief?"

"I thought I was close yesterday," Guthrie said. "Now, I'm not so sure."

"What's the problem? Can't find him?"

"Not yet. I've got a name, but not much else. And the name's probably phony. There are still a couple of leads to follow, but they're mostly for background information. And I can't seem to get anywhere with those either."

Guthrie paused, not wanting to remember this afternoon's desperate, irrational fear, knowing that he could not open up about it to this stranger because he could not open himself to it. But he'd said this much, and he could only stumble on, hoping to minimize the incident.

"I went to follow one today, but I had some kind of breakdown." He shook his head, trying to clear out the reminder of his weakness. "Forget it. It's not important."

"Maybe it's not you," the old man said.

Guthrie gave a snort.

"Oh, it's me, all right. Call it bad memories."

"I know about those," the old man said. "You've got to be careful not to build up too many of them because the older you get, the more they prey on your mind."

"I wish I could go back and change things," Guthrie confessed.

"It's hard enough to change something about the present," the old man said. "But let me tell you what's even more difficult. And dangerous. Transforming oneself."

"I can see the difficult part, but why dangerous?"

"Some transformations are reversible. You can muddy water, but if you let it sit long enough, the mud sinks back to the bottom. Some are irreversible, though, such as turning ingredients into prepared food. If you don't do it right, you don't get cake, you get a mess. It's the same with turning facts to solutions or changing ignorance to knowing. Before considering an irreversible transformation, one should ponder the ramifications, even if one cannot always predict the outcome or consequences."

"I don't think that's entirely possible. Not unless you could tell the future."

"I'm sure there are precious few of us who can do that." The old man was thoughtful for a moment, then he stood, picked up his plate and glass, and headed for the kitchen.

Guthrie gathered up his own dishes and followed. As he set them on the counter by the sink, the old man pulled out a business card and tucked it behind a refrigerator magnet.

"Just in case you need some lawn work in the future," he said.

Guthrie glanced at the card. Below the words "Terry Lawn Service" was a phone number, and above them was a symbol that looked a little like a pair of hieroglyphs.

"What's that?" Guthrie pointed to the symbol.

"It's an ancient African word for good luck." The old man gave a self-deprecating smile. "I'm a little superstitious." He turned and headed for the door.

Guthrie snapped on the porch light as the old man went out into the early evening.

"I can't figure out why a man like you is mowing lawns."

"Have to do something," the old man replied with a smile. "And I'm too old to do anything else. Besides, I get to meet interesting folks like private detectives and such."

"Which am I?" Guthrie asked. "A detective or such?"

"We'll see after you transform." The old man chuckled then said, "Thanks for dinner, Mr. Guthrie," and headed toward his truck.

Guthrie watched while the old man got into the pickup and started it. He half expected the old rattletrap to take thirty seconds of cranking to start, but the engine caught immediately and settled into a throaty purr. The old man backed onto the street, and in a moment his taillights disappeared around the corner.

It wasn't until then, as Guthrie was shutting the door, that he wondered how the old man had known his name.

10

IN THE MORNING, GUTHRIE DECIDED to go back to Travis's house. It wasn't something he really wanted to do—the memories he'd dredged up there weren't ones he cared to dwell on—but he knew he had to go. Maybe it was a sense of pride or to prove his guts were still intact. Or maybe it was a matter of twenty grand. Each was reason enough not to let himself get spooked by the past or any place he might inadvertently associate with traumatic events. Besides, Travis was a loose end that needed to be tied, and since Guthrie couldn't find Mark Batten, he might as well take care of this knot. Taking a deep breath, he headed toward Bellaire.

Today, he was too early for the bar to be open, otherwise he might have actually broken down and stopped in for a bracer. Instead, he parked in front of the defunct convenience store, got out of the car, and stared at the dark red house crouching behind the unkempt hedge.

The cheery morning light barely penetrated the canopy of huge oaks, and Guthrie stood there for five minutes before he finally gave up looking for a reason not to go over there and walk boldly up to the front door. The light traffic down the block wouldn't even give him the excuse of having to wait for the next pack of cars to roll past, so he gathered himself and trotted over to the sidewalk in front of the hedge.

By the time Guthrie got to it, he was absolutely certain something lay dead in the thick foliage, though he couldn't actually smell anything definite. Probably he was just catching a near-subliminal hint of odor clinging to the desiccated flesh and drying bones of a skeleton belonging to some neighborhood pet who'd made the mistake of wandering onto South Rice only to be tossed in a writhing, broken arc across the sidewalk, into the ragged and suffocating grasp of this bushy boundary.

The image stayed with Guthrie because a similar fate befell Alice's cat, Carrie, about six months before the shooting. Carrie was missing for a couple of days before Alice found her body in the thick row of cannas that bordered the driveway. She'd obviously been hit by a car and crawled into the cannas, one of her favorite haunts, to die.

Guthrie got the shovel and buried Carrie in the back yard while Alice tearfully watched. Afterwards, her grief stayed longer than Guthrie thought necessary, but he did his best to ignore it. She'd owned the cat longer than she'd been with him, and it was surrogate for the child the marriage had failed to produce.

But as the weeks passed into months, he witnessed Alice's sorrow transmute into an aloof reserve, and finally into open hostility. He'd arrived home drunk one night, and everything came to a head. His drinking meant more to him than she did, she said. He was married to the bottle, not her. She could put up with the uncertainties and dangers of his job but not his alcoholism or the meanness that came with it.

And he couldn't forget the other denunciations Alice threw in his face. He didn't love her at all, he just wanted to possess her. He'd let his power as a policeman taint his life, and she'd become little more than a live-in maid and cook and target for his outbursts of abuse. That wasn't her idea of marriage. She wasn't just some street person he could bully into easy submission, and if that was what he wanted from her, he could go to hell. She wanted love, and if he wouldn't—or couldn't—give it to her, she'd find someone who would.

Then came the most damning accusation of all. He couldn't stand the thought that her attention might be occupied by anything else, even a helpless pet, so Guthrie had killed Carrie. He'd deliberately run her over in the driveway and callously thrown her body into the cannas.

Guthrie unsuccessfully argued his innocence. He admitted he might have neglected Alice, but she was blowing everything all out of proportion. He was as sorry as she about Carrie. How could she think he'd be so deliberately cruel? But Alice was too convinced otherwise to hear what he said. After the outburst, her hostility turned to frigid indifference. She began sleeping on the sofa, and their marriage became a partnership in name only until she disappeared after the shooting.

Staring at the hedge, Guthrie wondered how it would be to die, like Carrie, trapped in a muffled green world of barbed branches and tiny creatures with prior, if equally short-lived tenure. Would he feel the tickle and minutely rending pinch of scavenger ants feeding subterranean metropolises? The hedge was an entire world hiding only three yards from people sublimely oblivious behind the rolled-up glass and air-conditioned hiss of the metal coffins ferrying them from the treachery of brittle home lives to the wasteland of commercial competition.

He felt complete affinity with the quiet cool of the bush, just as he'd at first found the solitude of the empty home he returned to after his release from the hospital agreeable and somehow right. Alice was gone, and with her had gone something precious and irreplaceable. He didn't know where or why, or even what. It simply had vanished into the flux of a deserted future, and he knew it only by its absence in the rooms they'd called home.

He'd quit caring about making headway. Why bother advancing into absence? Better to just hold his ground and not lose what little remained. And the same feeling was here in this peaceful shade, where he no longer had to worry about life and its headlong rush. Life, like the fast traffic at his back, lost meaning, as if any sense it might once have made now diminished as rapidly as the vehicles that passed him once and then were gone forever. The calm of isolation and fathomless contemplation was a far better and painless place. In the green gloom, even the toxic tang of exhaust would be purified, promising a deeper sense of immaculate distillation.

The hedge was thick, dense, its branches tightly interwoven in harmonious solidarity. He parted them with both hands, not wishing to disturb the peace and fraternity of the dead within this shrubbery hermitage, desiring no more than a glimpse of the sacred relics. He wanted only peace and approbation. He longed only for the proximity of inviolable sanctity.

Miraculously, thick as they were, the leaves and branches parted before his fingers like living waters, revealing the shrine of a perfect hollow sagely and completely ensconced within a verdant paradise. Here there were no barbs or prying eyes, no belching petrochemical fumes. Here, where he could so comfortably nestle and contemplate the microcosm until it opened into realms of mysterious depths and stunning beauty, was a place destined from the first word that vibrated the universe into being to hold his spirit and the crude, unnecessary flesh that bound it.

Moving to the place was a warm welcoming. Truth was no fickle spouse, but a living environment whose branches urged him inside with gentle touch and rustling mirth. Happiness, security, warmth, repletion, and never, never to be alone.

He felt a disturbing presence behind him like the pressure of necessity urging him forward. His mind told him his backsides were exposed to the world outside the hedge, and all he needed for total security was to wriggle in just a little farther. He groped deeper as a sound of squeaky leather and stiff formality rose up at his rear. The sound was totally alien to the warm and gentle rustle of the brush, but at the same time familiar, jostling buried memories and raising blind panic. He had to get away from that sound. He had to go completely into the green world where that sound and its imperatives and memories could not penetrate. Where he would be safe.

As he wormed his way deeper into the hedge, words called to him, but they belonged to a world that no longer possessed purpose and were without meaning or consequence. He saw a branch strong enough to use for leverage within reach, and he stretched toward it. Just as his fingertips brushed dust from the fine bark, he felt rough fumblings at his back.

Then horror happened. Strong hands gripped his belt, and he was hauled, gasping, out of paradise.

He cried out as twigs and branches raked like barbs across his flesh and jerked tangles of hair from his scalp. But the ultimate horror was that the scar that had covered his hatred for Alice also tore away, spilling acid serum across his mind, burning away all possibility of peace or detachment. It was all her fault. All the shit he'd gone through and done and suffered could be laid at her door. She'd brought evil upon him, and now he was immersed in its grip.

But he had no time to do more than absorb the stunning pain as he stumbled back from the hedge and slammed into a cop. The cop grunted from the impact, and his partner hurried around the end of the Bellaire PD cruiser parked by the curb, its flashers going. She stopped a couple of paces away, hand resting on the butt of her service pistol.

But in a moment, both cops could tell Guthrie was disoriented rather than dangerous.

"You live here?" asked the cop who'd stolen Guthrie from a heaven that was beginning to look suspiciously like hell the more Guthrie's senses returned. Guthrie admitted he didn't, and the cop asked why he was crawling through the bushes.

The bushes. Yeah, Guthrie thought. Crawling through the bushes. The plain old, green old bushes.

Guthrie caught hold of the hysteria before it could more than choke a grunt from his throat.

"Cat." He managed to change the second choke into a word. "My cat."

"Your cat?"

"Yes. Someone said they saw my cat get hit by a car along here the other day. I was looking for it. I thought it might have been thrown into these...bushes."

"Did you see it in there?" asked the second cop.

"No, officer. I didn't."

"Couple of days ago, you say?" she asked.

Guthrie nodded, and the first cop lifted a judicious nose and sniffed the air.

"I don't smell anything. Couple of days in this weather, you should be able to track it pretty easy if it was here."

"Yes, officer. You're probably right."

"Maybe your cat was still alive," ventured the second cop. "Maybe after it got hit it crawled off somewhere else."

"That must have been what happened," Guthrie agreed.

"Your cat's not here," said the first cop. "Just move along."

"Good idea," Guthrie said. "And thanks."

He said the last word with real feeling, but neither of the cops told him he was welcome. They just watched him hurry across South Rice, get into his car, and pull out of the parking lot.

Guthrie left Bellaire, uneasiness riding his shoulder like a little demon. He didn't quite know what to think about what had happened to him. He didn't want to think about it. For several minutes, he headed blindly along the West Loop, driving a good deal slower than usual and wishing he still did drink so he could get down with his habit and forget forever about visiting John Travis.

He'd swung around onto the South Loop before his thoughts and feelings caught up with him, like attenuated elastic snapping into its normal shape. Exiting the freeway, he pulled into the nether end of a Sam's Club parking lot and switched off the engine. The whirring reverberation of the automatic cooling fan switching on and off harmonized with the constant undulating rush from the freeway, and both sounded sympathetic notes to his own confusion. At last the fan was quiet.

Guthrie's inability to approach Travis's house was worse than frustrating. Far worse. The unexpected anxiety attacks jeopardized his work, and as barren as it was, this case was the only straw he had to cling to. He wracked his brain but couldn't divine what stopped him short of his goal. He felt exactly the same as he always did. At least he thought he did. But obviously something was wrong for him to suddenly become so fatally apathetic. Or ethically paranoid.

Ethically paranoid! Did working for Egan and the Harveys mean he must now engage in the kind of double-talk they might mouth? Hell no. Call it like it was. Call it scared shitless about some dark but unmanifested danger. Call all yesterday's worry about the correctness of his actions a sham masking the rotten core of his fear and today's miscarriage a willingness to die rather than face that fear.

But of what was he afraid? Danger? The unknown? Or was it the danger of knowing that had driven him onto a highway that went in circles and then into this parking lot for the wholesale anonymous?

Guthrie stared at himself in the rearview mirror, saw disheveled hair, sallow skin, and pinched corners around his eyes. He could admit he'd never been exactly the most stable sort, but he couldn't remember ever totally losing himself like he had at Travis's house.

Perhaps he hadn't fully shaken the trance he'd fallen into standing there outside the hedge, but the idea that something otherworldly was happening crossed his mind. It made sense, he shuddered, envisioning himself sitting inside the hedge, thoroughly enjoying the limited scenery and not seeing the end approaching. Or worse, seeing and happily anticipating. He wondered if he would have ever come to his senses, maybe after his body was too debilitated from thirst and starvation to crawl or move or cry out to the indifferent traffic rushing by not ten feet away that a human being, trapped in the tangles, was dying like an animal.

Touching the several shallow scratches scoring his cheeks and temples, he remembered the clutching leaves and branches and wondered if his beard, sprouting after days of imprisonment, would have entwined with the branches in sympathetic kinship. Would the ghost of his personality have fused with the shade of the lurking house as well?

He rubbed his forehead with the heels of his hands as if trying to erase the thought. He might be able to trust his intuition, but he couldn't allow himself to fall prey to some fantasy excuse to justify his own personal failure. It was me, Guthrie told himself. Me, myself, and I.

But that thought, though more rational, was all the more terrible. Like those stories of demonic possession. If you accept the supernatural explanation and ascribe the vile and insane behavior of the possessed to a demon spawned in Hell, that was frightening enough, for it says there are those among us who can be physically and psychically invaded by an external evil force. But if you subscribe to the rationalist, materialist viewpoint and say this behavior is merely a kind of dangerous psychological aberration, doesn't that, in a way, make things scarier? The supernaturalist claims an occasional innocent can be invaded, but the materialist says any one of us can go psychotic for no good reason.

Though God knows, Guthrie thought, I have reason enough.

Guthrie could tell what he was trying to do with all this intellectualization about manifest evil and psychological bugaboos. He was trying to avoid the actual issue of his own apparent deterioration, which was, itself, a mask to disguise the face of fear he saw when he stared in the rearview mirror and tried to think of anything but those memories he had tried so assiduously to bury.

Maybe, he thought, it will all go away if I don't think and don't go out looking for answers. I'll just sit on the money and....

But he knew that no amount of money could buy silence for his memories. Only the preoccupation of work could dull those, even if they would never fully abandoned him.

At the moment, though, he felt too exhausted to deal with any of it. He needed food to calm and energize him. He started the car, drove down the feeder until he found a cluster of restaurants near Reliant Stadium and went into one and ordered. The wait for the food in the cool restaurant, nearly empty at this early hour but filled with practical bustle as the wait staff prepared for the noon rush, went a long way toward settling his nerves. After the meal and two cups of coffee, he felt ready to get some solid work behind him and prove he was still a viable, functioning member of society.

He wasn't about to return to Travis's, though. Not today, at least. Perhaps tomorrow he'd go back there and see what he could see. But not right now.

There was one lead he still could follow, however—the other dinner guests. And what better place to start than with Barbara Sidell, the woman who'd hosted the dinner party? Guthrie dug out her address and saw that she lived just a short jaunt around the Loop, back toward the Galleria. He went out to his car, U-turned under the freeway, and headed that way. He avoided looking across Bellaire as he passed.

11

BARBARA SIDELL DIDN'T LIVE IN River Oaks, but her exclusive hotel address wasn't any comedown. The hotel was called the Spindletop—an appropriate enough name if you're old Texas rich, Guthrie thought. If you're old Texas poor, you'll just have to stay in Motel 6 while you're in town.

The Spindletop was just outside the West Loop, not a mile from Benjamin Egan's high-rise offices. Guthrie found the guest garage, wheeled his Honda into a space between a Cadillac and a Buick, then headed for the lobby elevator. While he strolled through the lobby, searching for the elevators to the upper floors, he tried to ignore the posh that scintillated from the colorful abstract paintings and tasteful landscapes on the walls and echoed off every polished surface before being soaked up by the thick carpeting. The Spindletop was exclusive enough that Guthrie felt as out of place as a Bora Boran in an Arabian Knights Temple.

When he found the elevators, he punched the up button and glanced around. The expansive lobby was pretty quiet. A couple stood at the reservation desk talking to the clerk, and in the lounge area, a pair of men in dark business suits sat in plush armchairs, conversing with each other. The car came, and Guthrie stood back to let a couple and a single man exit before he got in. He pressed the button for the eighth floor and, as the doors were deciding that it was safe to close, glanced into the lobby.

The couple who'd gotten off the elevator were ambling toward the front doors and the valet parking, but the man was striding purposefully toward the two men in the lounge area. And he glanced back over his shoulder at Guthrie.

By the time that fact registered on Guthrie, the elevator doors made up their mind and slid shut, barely giving Guthrie a chance to fix the man's face in his memory. He was older—maybe sixty—tall, distinguished, and graying. His features were oddly small on his face, giving him a severe look accentuated by the tense set of his jaw. While the car cruised up to Barbara Sidell's floor, Guthrie contemplated the man and the look of barely veiled animosity that had been plain on his face. The guy didn't seem like house security, not with the expensive suit he was wearing. Besides, his stride and bearing reeked authority of a different sort than cop. Guthrie supposed he'd just have to chalk up the man's glare to Guthrie's natty attire.

On the eighth floor, he found Sidell's door and rang the bell. Just after his second ring, the door opened.

"Hello, Mr. Guthrie. Won't you come in?"

Weren't those spider's words?

A predatory air hung about the extraordinarily beautiful woman, an air that belied her petite stature, casual manner, and friendly smile. Maybe the smile was a little too demure not to be wicked. The top of her long, blonde hair only came up to Guthrie's chin, and the rest of it was gathered into a thick rope plaited down the back of her slender neck. She held out her hand, and Guthrie noted the delicate, almost bony wrist and the long, naturally colored but exquisitely manicured nails.

As he shook with her, she let the touch linger in a way that drew him into the room. The door shut behind him with a quiet, solid thump.

She was probably the most intoxicatingly beautiful woman Guthrie had ever been this close to. And the white, almost sheer silk shift she was only half-wearing did little to hamper the effect. It nearly disappeared against her pale skin and was so thin it not only revealed all her exquisite curves but the fact that nothing lay between the silk and those curves to clutter the smooth lines. She appeared to be in her early thirties.

"You know who I am?" Guthrie tried hard to keep from stammering, and he succeeded. Barely.

"Why certainly. Carla told me all about the missing bust. She said they'd retained a private investigator to find the thief."

Word traveled fast for something supposed to be confidential.

Past the entry was a large living room faced on the opposite wall with wide glass opening over the woods behind the hotel. The apartment was high enough for Guthrie to clearly see across the treetops. It was an expensive view, with the expanse of Memorial Park in the near distance and the towers of downtown beyond. The furnishings were low, intimate, and well-cushioned. She led him to a wide sofa, the rope of her hair rolling sinuously between shoulder blades bared by the low-cut back of the shift. The hair wasn't the only thing rolling.

As he sat down she asked, "Can I get you a drink?"

"No, thanks."

"Ahhh."

The syllable was drawn out breathily, and Guthrie wasn't sure what it meant, but he didn't ponder long. His attention was caught by the painting dominating the wall directly across the room.

The painting was a life-size and rather explicit reclining nude—a portrait, if he wasn't mistaken, of his hostess. It was the kind of art that demanded extensive perusal, and as she swayed across the room to a sumptuous armchair directly beneath the painting, he noticed the artist hadn't had to resort to pictorial augmentation to portray her flatteringly. Guthrie deliberately steered his eyes towards her as she sat. He didn't want to appear too curious. Sidell crossed her legs and stared intently at him.

"I've never met a private detective before," she said. "What's it like?"

"Boring," Guthrie said, unwilling to admit that he was new to the business. But he reminded himself that he had worked a lot of investigations as a cop. "You spend all day asking different people the same questions, then you spend all night watching the bushes grow in front of someone's house."

Her laugh was a trilling little brook.

"And now you're here to ask me some of your questions?"

"If you don't mind."

She rose and undulated across the floor to the sofa. If the portrait was alluring, the real thing standing over him was maddening. Her nipples strained against the thin fabric, and the smooth lines where the silk fell from her hips beckoned with sheer concealment.

"Have you asked these questions before?"

"Some."

"Good. I like a man with experience. After that, are you going to wait outside and watch the bushes grow?"

"If I remember correctly, there aren't any bushes in your hallway."

"No, there aren't."

Guthrie couldn't say much to that, so he tried changing the uncomfortable direction the conversation was taking.

"Mind if I ask you those questions, Ms. Sidell?"

She glided onto the sofa to his right with a movement as smooth and subtle as the material of her gown. She slid her left hand onto the sofa back behind his neck, draped her right forearm over her perfect hip so that her fingers brushed the inside of her thigh, and twisted a little to face him. The action did interesting things to her cleavage.

"If we must talk about that stuffy old head, you'll have to call me Barbara."

"Okay, Barbara." It came out heavy, and he felt like an idiot, but there was nothing to do except blunder on. "I understand the Harveys were guests here the night the sculpture was taken."

"Yes. Hmmm. A dinner party." She smiled. "We rotate as hosts. Last week was my turn."

"So, it was a regular affair."

"Affairs are never regular," she crooned. "Especially those of long standing."

Guthrie could have kicked himself. He went on, trying to be more cautious with his vocabulary. "And next week it's the Harveys' turn?"

"Next week?" Again she gave her trilling little laugh, and this time it lingered, almost like a song. Guthrie was reminded that Alice used to sing while she did her housework. The memory startled him, but what was more surprising was that he missed Alice's wordless tunes more than he'd realized because he'd always associated them with her contentment.

He brought himself back to the present just as Sidell moved her head, her earrings catching his eye. They were parallelograms of red enamel, about an inch to a side, each containing an elaborate curvilinear tracing of gold filigree like a delicate, glittering net. Glittering. Almost scintillating. Almost....

He blinked.

"No, Carla and Lloyd were the week before. Next week is Martin Hastings. After that it's Ben's turn, then Carla and Lloyd again." Her sentence was finished, but her voice carried a lilting melody past the period.

He blinked again. Something was wrong with his eyes. They seemed filmy, like he'd just awakened and everything still had a haziness that diffused and softened harsh outlines.

"About what time did the guests arrive?"

"That's a curious question."

"Why so?"

"It almost seems like you suspect one of us."

"Not at all. I'm just trying to get a feel for the background."

Damn!

"Of course, Clay." Wry humor tickled the corners of her mouth, and she reached over and touched him briefly on his knee. "Everyone was here by seven."

He didn't remember giving her his first name, but it must have come to her along with his last name and the reason for his visit. She was doing that singing thing again, almost sub-audibly but openly, without demurral, as if she didn't care if he thought it was normal or not. He didn't, but he wasn't sure he cared, either. Her touch made the matter recede into insignificance along with the pain he'd been carrying with him since the shooting. He looked at her face, but highlights caught like drops of starlight in the satiny gold folds of her earrings held his gaze for a long moment. Dimly he was aware that she was caressing the back of his neck with her left hand.

She's toying with you, Guthrie told himself, but he found it difficult to hear the words much less comprehend their meaning. If her simple touch could take away the pain, then what ecstasies awaited a more consummate caress? And it had been a long time since he'd heard a woman sing contentedly in his ear....

The scintillations continued to hold his eyes, and her hair glowed like a golden halo in the light streaming through the windows. Her shift was a shimmering, living tissue of lustrous longing as her breasts rose and fell with her breath. Her moist green eyes were like springs of unfathomable depth, and the slow blink of the eyelids that covered them was a gesture toward the deeper pool of her lips. Her lips.... Her voice....

Guthrie fumbled in his jacket pocket for the photo of the missing sculpture, pulling away from her touch at his neck. He wasn't really thinking about what he was doing, he just knew he had to distract her, and the photo was all he had to work with. He passed it to her, and as she took it with her right hand, she quickly pulled her left hand down off the back of the sofa and tucked it beneath her left thigh.

There was something about the way she did it that made him itch, if for no other reason than it was the first thing she'd done that seemed awkward and unnatural. Sure, reaching across with her right hand to take the photo had revealed a generous portion of cleavage, which he figured was intended, but the way she was leaning toward him already served that purpose. And the speed with which she tucked her left hand beneath her thigh made it seem as if she was hiding something. He'd seen similar gestures used too often to conceal a weapon or contraband. Whatever she was hiding wasn't a gun or a knife, but it was something she didn't want him to see, and he started looking for it. Not obviously, but carefully, and the focus did him good, taking his mind off her body and her soothing voice and the way she was using both against him.

"Yes, I know this silly little man," she said. "Carla and Lloyd are quite attached to him."

She handed the photo back with the same awkwardness, keeping her left hand beneath her thigh, and he was certain now that she had something under there.

"You don't seem to think much of it."

"I'm not partial to cold, intellectual men. I prefer someone with a warmer temperament. Someone a little more dangerous." She bent close, and he was uncomfortably aware of her left nipple less than an inch from his arm.

He leaned away from her while he replaced the photo in his jacket pocket, and she glanced down briefly, as if to measure the distance between her nipple and his arm and gauge his zone of discomfort. As he settled back, she smiled, blinked her eyes, and leaned closer, deliberately pressing her breast against his bicep in punishment for asking her to take it away.

"Tell me, Clay, what does a man like you do when he's not chasing criminals?"

She kept close enough for her beast to remain touching him, but he could ignore it now. In her moment of inattention, while he replaced the photo and when she thought he wouldn't possibly peruse areas of her body other than her breasts, he discovered what she was hiding.

It was her left thumb. She'd kept it tucked discreetly beneath the edge of her leg, but when he leaned back, he caught a glimpse of it. One glimpse was enough. It was as ugly a thumb as he'd ever seen —grossly spatulate with a coarse, tumorous knuckle and a discolored, misshapen nail, thick and horny. His skin crawled as he realized that she'd been caressing his neck with it.

At first thought, he could see why she went to all the trouble to hide it. Everyone has flaws, even women who step right out of magazines devoted to the cult of beauty, but this was a bit much for a woman who looked like her. That made him wonder why she hadn't resorted to cosmetic surgery. She could have afforded an entire body lift if she wanted one. Not that she needed it.

But as awareness of the thumb and her determined effort to conceal it from him seeped thought his consciousness, the more the wrongness didn't stop with a display of simple vanity. She'd taken pains to hide a relatively trivial fact, and that made her dishonest. And she was revealing parts of herself she shouldn't. That made her dangerous.

All the seductive atmosphere around Barbara Sidell seemed like a mist she exuded to mask the one terrible defect to her beauty. The deceit diminished her even more than the defect. Suddenly she was a little Lolita holding age at bay with prurient innuendo and Oil of Olay. The lust inflating Guthrie ever since she'd opened the door evaporated, leaving only the faintest miasma to remind him that where there are mists, often there is a bog.

Guthrie knew charged emotions are far more difficult to conceal than charged ideas. He had no difficulty, or so he believed, concealing his thoughts from the Harveys, but he didn't think a poker face would keep Sidell from sensing that her seduction, whatever its purpose, had soured.

Quickly, he got to his feet, though the smooth drag of her flesh on his arm made the act difficult.

"Unfortunately," he said, "There are so many criminals out there, I don't have much time for anything else." Guthrie hoped his words didn't sound as desperate as he felt.

"I see." She stood, also, and followed him to the door.

"By the way," he said, pausing on the threshold. "You mentioned that one of the other guests was Martin Hastings. Would you mind giving me his address?"

She did, from memory, without the slightest hesitation.

"And there was someone named Ben," Guthrie pressed. "That would be Ben Egan?"

"Of course." Her expression was of open curiosity, but her eyes showed an acid dissatisfaction. "Ben Egan."

"Thank you for your time, Ms. Sidell."

"No trouble at all, Mr. Guthrie." She didn't bother offering to shake good-bye, and he noticed she kept her left hand casually hidden behind her hip. "I hope you find what you're looking for. Come back and see me if you need anything. Anything."

Guthrie headed toward the elevators. Exactly when the apartment door closed behind him, he wasn't sure. A minute later, he rode down to the lobby and, in another, took the elevators to the parking garage. As he descended, he was all too aware of the trickle of nervous sweat leaking from his armpits. He gave a nervous grimace as he again thought about Sidell stroking his neck with her hideous thumb.

Thank God he'd gotten out of there in one piece, he thought as the elevator doors opened and he emerged into the cement cavern where he'd parked his car.

A man stepped in quickly from the side and tried to grab Guthrie's arm with one hand and punch him with the other. But ten years as a cop had taught Guthrie his fair share of dirty fighting. Knocking the groping hand aside, he slammed the heel of his palm into the man's face, felt a crunch, and had the momentary satisfaction of seeing the man stumble back, clutching a nose spewing blood. The guy was one of the two men he'd seen earlier in the lobby.

Guthrie spun, and found himself facing the second man. This one held a gun.

Suddenly something hard slammed against the back of his head, and he went down, ears ringing and vision whirling. A kick to his ribs sent him sprawling.

"That's enough."

Painfully, Guthrie rolled over to see who'd given the command, and the two strong-arm men hauled him to his feet. It was the older man who'd gotten off the elevator.

"I'm going to tell you this one time only," the man said. "You will drop this case, or you will die."

He nodded to the man Guthrie had hit, and the man slugged Guthrie in the gut three hard times, leaving bloody fist prints on Guthrie's shirt. The other man let go, and Guthrie sagged to the pavement.

"I hope I've made myself clear," the boss man said, then he and his goons turned and entered the elevator, leaving Guthrie to struggle to his feet and stagger to his car.

12

GUTHRIE WANTED TO GO HOME, but despite his bruises, he couldn't afford to waste the remainder of the afternoon. There was still Martin Hastings to question, so Guthrie drove toward the Memorial area address Sidell had given him.

Hastings didn't live in one of the sprawling modern ranch-style homes that made up a lot of Memorial. From the look of his medium-size brick house, which shared a street with other closely spaced medium-size brick houses, each in a postage stamp yard, Hastings wasn't as ostentatious as most of the other dinner party guests.

Guthrie emerged from his car, buttoned his jacket to conceal the bloody fist prints, and walked up to the front door. After his fifth ring, it was obvious that Hastings wasn't home, so Guthrie returned to his car and headed for his own.

When he got there, he was feeling wiped out. It had been one hell of a day. His first destination was the bathroom, where he checked his rib cage then smeared some muscle rub into his bruised flesh.

Afterward, he checked his mail to see if the material from Vulcan had arrived, but all he found were bills and junk mail. The junk went into the trash unopened, and luckily, he could dispose of the bills nearly as easily. He drove to his bank and deposited ten of the $100 bills Egan had given him, then he went home and wrote out some checks and left again to drop them off at the post office.

When he got home, his stomach was growling, so he went to the kitchen and put some of the leftovers from the night before into the microwave. After he ate, he sat down in front of the TV, intending to immerse himself in something that might take his mind off everything that had been happening to him the last few days.

The next thing he knew, he jerked awake, startled, he thought, by some noise. But all around him the house was silent. It must have been in his dream, some hazy image of menace now fading quickly into his subconscious. His watch read just after midnight.

Sighing, he heaved himself off the sofa and went to the bathroom to brush his teeth. When he came out of the bathroom and returned to the living room to turn off the TV and the light, he was brought up short by the sight of a man perched casually on the arm of the sofa.

He was Eastern, probably Chinese, about Guthrie's own age, and a little smaller in size. The blandly impassive, no-nonsense expression on his face wasn't particularly threatening, but Guthrie took less than two seconds to ponder that fact before he snatched up a table lamp, jerked out its cord, and threw it at the guy.

With effortless grace, the man rose and sidestepped the missile. As the lamp crashed against the wall, Guthrie whirled and took a step toward the hall. He'd meant to distract the man long enough to retreat to the bedroom and get to his .38, but the man's movements were like lightning. And impeccably timed. Guthrie felt a nudge on his side, neither painful nor violent, but enough to send him off balance. Another nudge sent him into a spinning tumble.

Then the guy was back, and his control was masterful as he grabbed Guthrie's arm and pulled. Guthrie's face stopped a good foot closer to the rug than either of his hands. The man hoisted Guthrie upright, and Guthrie tried to reward his kindness with a knee in the groin then a punch to the face. The intruder flowed more smoothly, and once more Guthrie headed for a fall.

He caught Guthrie again, and Guthrie slugged him in the gut. Or tried to. Guthrie's fist touched its target but couldn't find any substance to impact against. It was like punching a feather pillow. The elbow Guthrie jabbed at the man's grinning teeth suddenly found itself air-borne, and Guthrie toppled again.

This time, after the man caught Guthrie, he was through being as polite as before. Instead of hoisting Guthrie to his feet, he eased him down onto the floor and stepped back. Guthrie rolled over, panting, and stared up at him. The man perused Guthrie as calmly as an expert cook appraises fresh fish in the market.

"You're a pretty good street fighter," the man lied in a voice devoid of accent. "But I'm better." This time he was considerably more truthful.

He hadn't hurt Guthrie yet, despite ample opportunity. That was encouraging. Guthrie got slowly to his feet, showing as little antagonism as possible.

"You're better," he agreed. He wondered if he could get to the gun then shrugged off the idea as absurd. "Very much better."

"Come with me." The man didn't say it like it was an order, only like he meant it.

"Can I get my jacket? It's in the bedroom closet."

"I'll get the jacket." While the man was gone, Guthrie turned off the TV. A moment later, the man was back, amazingly with the right jacket. Guthrie put it on and followed him though the back door. Guthrie started to head for the gate to the driveway, but the man touched his shoulder. In the dark, Guthrie could only see the outline of his head as he shook it.

"Not that way. There are men watching your house." He turned and led Guthrie down the narrow passage between Guthrie's ramshackle garage and the fence separating the back yard from the neighbors. He stopped about twenty feet past the end of the garage. On the other side of this section of fence lay the apartment complex parking lot.

"We'll go over here."

They climbed the fence and dropped into the lot, and Guthrie's new friend went up to a dark gray Mercury sedan that beeped when he punched a button on his key fob. He slid behind the wheel and motioned Guthrie toward the passenger seat. He didn't appear to be particularly concerned that Guthrie might try anything rash—like running.

Guthrie didn't feel that foolish. He got in, wondering where they were going. The driver snaked through the neighborhood to the Gulf Freeway, headed inbound, then took the interchange to the Southwest Freeway. At this hour, there were few cars on the road, but the driver kept to the speed limit. At the West Loop, he turned south for a mile or so before exiting onto Bellaire Boulevard and continuing west. Out this way, beyond the City of Bellaire, lay suburbs, including Houston's principal Chinese community, which had overlaid the typical American strip malls and neighborhoods with a colorful flavor and signs bearing ideograms as often as script.

Several miles after turning off the freeway, just past an intersection marked by a large water tower, Guthrie's escort steered the Mercury into the parking lot of a large shopping center. A supermarket dominated the east end, and strung out from that was an array of stores typical to large shopping centers: pharmacy, furniture rental, dollar store, and a few others. Everything was closed at this late hour, and the parking lot was empty of all but a couple of derelict cars.

When the driver finished negotiating the parking lot, he swung the Mercury around the west end of the center, which housed a washateria, and entered a thirty-foot-wide service alley that lay between the back of the building and a high wooden fence. That worried Guthrie, but he tried to reassure himself that, had the man intended to harm him, he would have done it already, back at Guthrie's house.

Lit by streetlights placed at irregular intervals on electrical service poles, the alley was a hundred and fifty feet long, at least, and dead-ended at the rear side wall of the supermarket. It was strewn with seven or eight dumpsters, some against the shopping center's back wall and some against the fence, beyond which Guthrie could see little aside from a few trees and open space. Whatever was there, it was too open to be a neighborhood. The driver went almost to the end of the alley and stopped the car near the back wall.

"Please get out, Mr. Guthrie."

The alley was pretty clean, considering, but the streetlights did less to illuminate it than cast a pall of dismal anticipation. The uniform dull brown of the alley's cement-block walls and metal doors provided little encouragement. As good a place to die as any, Guthrie thought. Or as bad. He prepared himself for the worst by letting his knees knock together almost imperceptibly. Then the driver pointed toward a door in the supermarket wall.

Guthrie hadn't noticed the door as they'd driven up and parked, though he didn't see how he could have missed it. It was about ten feet from one of the brown metal doors and, since it was painted a bright red, should have been clearly visible in the headlights as they'd approached.

As Guthrie neared, he could see that the door was probably wood beneath its glossy red coloring because the surface was carved in a bas-relief. The design was composed mostly of straight lines, and except for the half-dozen squiggles near the bottom, it looked a bit like a very simple child's maze. There was something fascinating about the scheme, a visual quality that intrigued and drew the attention and awareness. But there was a repellent quality as well, as if the convolutions, despite their simplicity, were a snare into which he could fall and become lost if he stared too long. Almost instinctively, Guthrie shied away.

"That say something?" he asked, more rhetorically than realistically expecting an answer. To his surprise, the driver gave him one.

"It's the Old Master's Talisman. It prevents evil spirits from entering and facilitates the cure of epidemics."

"Looks Chinese," Guthrie commented encouragingly, but without answering, the driver opened the door and ushered Guthrie through. The door closed, snipping off sight of the dark alley.

Guthrie blinked. Nothing could have been more removed from the dismal aspect of a murky, angular, and grimy service alley than the warm glow, soft contours, and potpourri of odd and enchanting smells residing behind that door. The difference was so drastic that he felt a dizzying sense of dislocation as he entered. A dark and ancient wooden counter divided the largish room, and in the wall behind the counter was an open doorway obscured by a curtain of carved wooden beads.

"Wait here," said the driver as he went around the end of the counter and through the door. The curtain gave barely a rustle as he disappeared, leaving Guthrie alone to peruse the rest of the room.

The place was worth studying. Except for the gaps of the doors, all four walls were completely lined from floor to ceiling with wooden shelves as dark and ancient as the counter, and covering the shelves were bottles and jars of many sizes and styles. Most of them were old and hand-blown, and Mason wasn't embossed on any of them. None of the jars bore labels, and the contents varied considerably—this one held dried flowers, that one an orange powder, and another what appeared to be some sort of ugly fungus.

It went on like that. Desiccated vegetable matter, colored powders, random nastiness, and smatterings of indefinable chunks and crumbles. When Guthrie reached the counter, he glanced over the top at the worktable hunkered behind it. The tabletop was neatly arrayed with mortar and pestle, various measuring spoons and scoops, ceramic mixing bowls, and a metal balance scale that seemed to be the only modern thing in the place. Even the floor was out of place—not the expected cement slab but a random network of wooden parquet so worn, particularly in front of the counter, that Guthrie had to conclude it must be as old as the rest of the fittings in the room. And a lot older than the shopping center.

Someone had gone to a lot of trouble to make this place appear so authentically old that it really was authentic. And what the hell was it doing hiding behind an ornate red door in the wall of a plain alley behind a shopping center? Guthrie didn't know, but he guessed this place must be some kind of apothecary shop.

"This way."

Guthrie hadn't even heard the curtains click, but there was the driver, holding back the strands of beads so Guthrie could pass. Guthrie went around the counter. The curtained doorway opened into a cozy reception area, but no one was present to take advantage of the well-used furniture. Guthrie noticed the worn parquet floor was still with them, appearing no newer. A single doorway, hung with another beaded curtain, was set in the far wall, and they went through into a short but crooked hallway flanked by what seemed to be exam rooms. The crookedness seemed to ensure complete privacy between the exam rooms. The corridor ended in a heavy wooden door.

Past that were living quarters. Though Guthrie didn't see much of them, they looked to be less quaintly antiquated than the apothecary shop.

He was taken to a large, brightly lit kitchen complete with dining table made of some reddish, light-grained wood and motioned to sit, which he did with some reluctance because of the view he saw out of the window. Sunlight poured through the opening, and if his abbreviated glimpse of a widening rocky ravine that opened onto gently rolling, dry countryside meant anything at all, Guthrie badly needed glasses, a psychiatrist, or both. When he entered this place, hadn't it been the dead of night in an alley behind a Houston shopping center?

But he wasn't allowed to contemplate the impossible view before two young black women entered. He stared at them, knowing it wasn't glasses he needed, though he still might require that psychiatrist, for he recognized them instantly as the girls he'd chased the day before.

"Ah, my shadows," he said, and they regarded him with amusement. "Want to tell me what's going on?" Guthrie asked the driver.

"You are here to meet someone who is presently engaged but who will soon become available." The driver joined Guthrie at the table as the girls brought over a teapot and four handleless cups.

"Tea?" asked the older one. "It's spiced oolong."

"Okay," Guthrie replied then took a sip of the fragrant liquid she poured for him. "That," he gestured in the direction of the room they'd first entered, "is some kind of apothecary shop?"

"You might call it that," the driver nodded. "I'm Li Wu, and this is Cindy," he pointed to the older girl, "and Mary."

"You fight pretty good," Guthrie said to Wu. "Some kind of martial art?"

"Li is a master of tai chi chuan," said Cindy.

"And my shadows? What do you do?"

"They shadow," Wu chuckled. The girls followed, and despite himself, Guthrie joined in. Then he sobered.

"What about this person we're waiting for. Who is he, and what does he want?"

"It's best to let Master Tereba speak his own desires," Wu replied.

"He'll tell you his wishes when he arrives."

Guthrie couldn't imagine that Li Wu needed to call anybody master, considering his superlative martial arts skills.

Guthrie was bursting with questions, but the trio's friendly but tight-lipped silence told him he would just have to wait for this Master Tereba. So they just sat and sipped their tea. After the second cup, Guthrie, feeling as restless as he was curious, rose and went to the window.

Sure enough, his eyes hadn't deceived him. The bright countryside looked a bit like some of the more rugged parts of West Texas, though a little less arid. He noticed that there weren't any cacti, and the plants he could see didn't look familiar.

"I don't understand," he said after a few moments, feeling strangely removed from his own emotions. He looked at Wu.

"We don't understand, either," Wu told him with an apologetic smile.

"But where are we?" Guthrie asked. Wu didn't answer. Instead, his eyes focused on something behind Guthrie.

"We are in my home, Mr. Guthrie."

Guthrie jumped and spun. He could have sworn that the door behind him was too far away for anyone to have entered and covered the distance so rapidly and quietly.

"Mr. Guthrie," Wu said with a slight bow, "meet Master Tereba."

Guthrie found himself staring into the face of the old black yardman he'd invited to dinner the night before.

13

"THANK YOU FOR COMING," TEREBA said. "I hope you haven't been inconvenienced."

"Li Wu was insistent but very polite," Guthrie assured him.

"It is not appropriate to use a hatchet to swat a fly on the head of a friend."

"I can go along with that," Guthrie said.

The wiry old man smiled, motioned for Guthrie to sit, then took a seat across the table. For some reason, he looked older than he had the night before. No, Guthrie amended, it was more that he exuded age.

"Would you like some tea?" the old man asked.

"I've had some, thanks. I'd just like to know what's going on. I'm not trying to rush you, or anything, but you did bring me here for a reason."

"I've experienced many cultures." The old man stroked his chin and smiled. "I am not offended by your desire to get right to the point. Sometimes, speed is the best policy. I had Wu bring you because I'm interested in the case you're on."

"The case I'm on?"

Tereba smiled, and as he did, his eyes opened into bottomless black pits. They weren't antagonistic, but Guthrie certainly didn't want to fall into them. "You suggested we not beat around the bush," the old man reminded him. "We are, I believe, discussing the bronze bust stolen from the Harveys. You mentioned it to me last night."

"I didn't mention the Harveys or that it was a bronze bust. What do you know about it?"

"More than anyone else can, Mr. Guthrie. Let's say that the sculpture once belonged to my family."

"Funny, it doesn't look African."

"Nor does it bear much resemblance to the Harveys."

"Fair enough," Guthrie conceded.

"It was appropriated under unfortunate circumstances many centuries ago."

"A thousand years?" Guthrie was skeptical.

"Give or take a year or two," Tereba said in a tone that seemed sincere. "I wish to have it back in my possession. It is, in fact, vitally important that the bust be returned to me."

"I'd like to oblige," Guthrie said, and he meant it because, for some foolish reason, he actually believed Tereba. But he also meant it when he said, "Unfortunately, I have an agreement with the current rightful owners."

"You have an agreement with Ben Egan."

"Egan is paying me."

The wizened features took on a look of what appeared to be genuine concern touched with disappointment.

"Does money mean so much?"

The immeasurable eyes bored into Guthrie with incredible intensity, and Guthrie flinched.

"When money is scarce, you go for what you can get," he replied. "But a contract is more than money, Mr. Tereba. Egan may be paying me, but I represent the Harveys since it's their property that's been stolen."

"Duty and honor?"

"I've got precious little of either of those left, so call it what you like. The truth is, before Egan came along, I had nothing and was sinking fast. But now I've got this case, and it looks like my only chance to get some kind of meaning back into my life."

At Guthrie's words, a cloud seemed to cross Tereba's eyes, dulling the intensity of their gaze, though their attention on Guthrie didn't waver.

"Yes," the old man said in a voice that barely concealed pain. "This sculpture is my key as well as yours. I need it as badly as you, and for much the same reason. I, too, know what it is like to lose oneself."

The depth of Tereba's tone as much as the meaning of the words sent a shock through Guthrie. He realized at some primal level that the old man had spoken truly, and that he had revealed something of himself to Guthrie in that instant of rapport. The revelation made Guthrie like the old man more than he already did, but it didn't make him any less wary. Tereba was the most enigmatic turn this perplexing case had yet taken.

"What's so important about this sculpture?" Guthrie asked. "And don't give me that line about it being a family heirloom. No one traces a stolen object for that long unless the object has very special significance beyond its monetary or historic value. I could see someone tracking Christ's chalice or King Arthur's sword, but why the head?"

"Objects like the ones you mention have intrinsic value that cannot be measured in terms of economics or scholarship. They are repositories of a power that can have a potent impact on human beings and the course of historical events. Like a battery, such objects have a charge, though you would not be able to register it on scientific instruments. Only one instrument is sensitive enough to be affected by such a power."

"What's that?"

"The human psyche."

Guthrie leaned back in his chair and studied Tereba. The old man returned the stare, expression deadly serious. He didn't appear to be insane, and the other three in the room obviously deferred to him. But psychic power?

"The sculpture is one of these charged objects? A psychic battery?"

Tereba nodded, and Guthrie decided to continue humoring him.

"Tell me, Mr. Tereba. What would you do with the head if you had it?"

"Like batteries, charged objects have polarity, positive and negative, but unlike batteries, they manifest only a single pole, at least on this plane of existence. That pole can be the positive one or it can be the negative. Objects like the Grail or Excalibur emit positive polarity, but some objects, like the bust, are not so beneficial."

Guthrie thought of Egan, the Harveys, and their friends and could readily believe they'd get a kick out of negative energy. And William Mason certainly was spooked by the head, or rather, by its loss. But that didn't mean Guthrie believed Tereba's assertion that some kind of mysterious power actually resided in the sculpture.

"You still haven't answered my question. What would you do if you had it?"

"You wish to know if I would use it to perpetrate evil?"

Tereba's black eyes flashed from their unknown depths. They were scary eyes. Yeah, Guthrie liked him a lot but suddenly feared him more. He didn't know why, since the old man had yet to say or do anything to make Guthrie actively apprehensive. Though he appeared lithe, he was old, and Guthrie could probably snap him in half like a stick. If he could get past the old man's gaze. Whatever was in that stare, just a little was all it took to cow Guthrie. But even cowed, Guthrie couldn't knuckle under completely.

"I'm not trying to insult you, Mr. Tereba. I'm just trying to get to the bottom of this case, and I'd like to arrive with my skin intact."

"Your case is finished," the old man said, a note of defeat in his voice. "You must have concluded, as we did, that Prentice has the sculpture back in his possession."

"I don't know anyone named Prentice."

"He's the leader of Zeroth," Wu said.

"Zeroth?"

"The group," Wu clarified. "The Harveys, Egan, Hastings, and Sidell."

"I thought the head belonged to the Harveys."

"Zeroth and everything about it belongs to Prentice. That includes the head. The Harveys and the others are just lackeys."

"Is Prentice a tall, distinguished-looking gentleman accompanied by a couple of thugs? Somebody like that roughed me up and threatened to kill me if I didn't get off the case."

"We're not sure what he looks like," Wu said. "But he generally doesn't operate that way."

"He doesn't have to," Tereba amplified.

"Besides," Guthrie pointed out, "if this Prentice wants the head, why hire me then try to scare me off? And if he already has it back, all he has to do is have Egan fire me. Egan hasn't, so the head's still missing. And I've learned a few interesting facts the last couple of days."

Guthrie dangled the bait, and Tereba bit.

"I'd be very interested to hear about them." The way the old man smiled made Guthrie unsure about just which of them was on the rod-and-reel end of the line.

"I've been inside the Harveys' house. The thief passed up what must be millions in art to target the sculpture. And it was in a tough safe to crack—armored and with double locks—that was undamaged. That means the thief was either a real pro or an amateur with the combinations. I'm betting on the latter, because a pro wouldn't have passed up the art. Want me to go on?"

"Please continue." Was that a glint of understanding behind the old man's curiosity? And beyond that a flicker of hope?

"Okay. The theft occurred when the Harveys were out for a regular dinner party—with this Zeroth group, as a matter of fact. And the servants were out also, so whoever arranged it must be familiar with the Harveys' schedule. And their house."

"You think another member of Zeroth stole the sculpture?"

"According to what I've heard from them and you, not many other people would know about it," Guthrie said. "But I don't think any of them were personally involved in the actual theft."

"An accomplice?" Tereba asked, and he glanced at Wu, who raised his eyebrows and nodded. Tereba turned back to Guthrie.

"Do you know the identity of this accomplice? Is he the man who lives on South Rice Boulevard?"

"It must be him, Grandfather," Cindy said. "He's got a watch-dog guarding his house. Mary and I couldn't even get close."

Guthrie didn't remember any dog at Travis's, but then he hadn't been terribly observant on his two visits. He shook his head.

"The man on South Rice is just a loose end—an art historian who did research on the sculpture. The guy I'm looking for posed as a delivery driver to gain entry to the Harveys' house."

"You know who he is?"

"I've got a name, a description, and a vehicle. I'm working on the rest."

"It seems I may have underestimated your instincts," Tereba said earnestly. "But you must realize that this situation is far more grave than you can imagine. If you do retrieve the sculpture, you must bring it to me before you return it to the Harveys."

"Look," Guthrie replied. "You've got to remember, I was hired to return the head to the Harveys. You say the head used to belong to your family, and maybe it did, but so what? Manhattan belonged to the Indians. The Harveys have title to the sculpture now. If I get hold of it and give it to someone else, I've become the thief. I'm giving it back to them if I find it."

"True," agreed the old man. "You were hired to perform a task, and I understand that you must fulfill that task or you will be in their debt. That wouldn't be good for you. I'll do nothing to endanger your arrangement with Egan or the Harveys. Please bring the head to me, anyway. I simply wish to examine it, to hold it for a few minutes. Perhaps I can, how shall I put it, discharge the battery. Afterward, you'll be free to return it to the Harveys."

"What's to prevent you and your kung fu expert here from just taking it away from me and keeping it?"

The old man's expression of injured innocence seemed real enough, though Guthrie was certain he could have looked any way he wished.

"The sculpture is of interest to me only because of the power it carries. Once the power is gone, I will have no further use for the object. Besides," Tereba asked, "have I treated you shabbily so far?"

"I'll consider it," Guthrie told him, though privately he doubted that he'd comply.

"He'll look inside," Cindy said.

"As he must," Tereba nodded.

"And the watchdog must be there for a reason," Wu put in. "He needs to get past it."

"Yes," Tereba said reflectively, staring at Guthrie as if he were a slab of cold meat. "He needs protection. But I think that Mr. Guthrie is somewhat protected already by his own predicament."

"My predicament? I don't see how this case...."

"Come now. Surely you know I'm not talking about the case but about the darkness within you."

"Egan told me something like that," Guthrie muttered. "Said I had a problem."

"Egan is a perceptive man, if you consider awareness of an apple's skin to be knowledge of the fruit's essence."

"So what's my problem?"

"Do you mind if I examine you?"

Without waiting for an answer, the old man rose smoothly, came around the table, and peered deeply into Guthrie's eyes. His pupils were unusually large and deep, and looking into them made Guthrie uncomfortable, but after a moment, the old man shifted his gaze. He took up Guthrie's hand and felt his pulse. Then he let go and began passing his palms around Guthrie's torso, about six inches away.

This lasted for about a minute, during which Guthrie wondered nervously if the old man was finally exhibiting his madness. But Wu and the girls watched the procedure with quiet, confident interest, so Guthrie sat still and submitted. When the old man finished, he exchanged a significant look with Wu.

"What was that all about?" Guthrie asked.

"I understand now why they chose you."

"Zeroth, you mean? Yeah, well that's not so hard to see. I'm a low-rent sucker desperate enough to take anything that's offered."

"Don't mistake the symptoms for the disease," Tereba said. "I'm afraid you are dangerously ill."

"I'm fine," Guthrie said.

"Not so, Mr. Guthrie. You appear to be in good health, and your hip is doing nicely, though I'm sure you will always experience intermittent pain. But the darkness within you blocks the flow of your spirit. If there were a physical cause, I could perhaps do something about it, but it is something deeper and far more crucial— something medicines cannot touch."

"I promise I'll see a psychiatrist when this is all over."

"Psychiatry can't help you, I'm afraid. Your vital spirit has been eclipsed, and the flow of your mana is sluggish and practically immobile. Soon it will stop altogether." Tereba smiled sadly. "You are an empty man, Mr. Guthrie. That is why your memories echo around inside you so readily."

"Everyone has memories," Guthrie said a little more quickly than he intended.

"A moment ago, I said that the skin is not the essence of the fruit. Did you ponder what might be the true essence?"

"The fruit itself, obviously."

Tereba gave a minute shake of his head.

"The seed. Without it, fruit is nothing but temporarily organized earth that decays all too readily. The seed that allows the fruit to propagate and persevere through time is the fruit's love of living. You, Mr. Guthrie, have lost that seed."

"Meaning what?"

"If you look honestly enough, you will see for yourself that you have gone dead inside."

"Pardon me, Mr. Tereba,"Guthrie bristled, "but that's bullshit."

"Is it? Why, then, did Egan hire you of all people? Does it make sense to you?"

"He had some rigamarole line," Guthrie admitted, "but I guess it did sound fishy."

"Zeroth chose you precisely because they are aware of your true condition. You are disposable because you already have disposed of yourself, and that makes you useful to them in this particular endeavor. They think it will protect you from the power of the bust long enough for you to return it to them. But it makes you useful to me, as well."

Guthrie snorted derisively.

"Nobody in their right mind would believe a word you're saying."

"A terminal cancer patient can deny he is ill, but his disease will kill him nonetheless. Life is motion. He who remains still is buried by the sands of time, and your spirit has quit moving. You are an empty husk—you just don't realize it." The old man peered at him. "Or perhaps you do. Perhaps that is why Egan's words bothered you. Inside, you know that all you have left is your skin."

Guthrie wanted to protest that he was as whole as anybody, but the words halted half formed. He had lost too much to doubt the essence of Tereba's words even if he could deny their literal substance. But if he wasn't whole, he certainly wasn't a dead, empty husk, either, as the old man claimed. Damaged, yes, wounded and dispirited, but very much alive. How could he hurt so much if he wasn't?

In a bravura show, he held out his arm and pinched it.

"Ouch," he said, dropping the arm. "I think I just proved you wrong. Dead men don't feel."

"You are persistent, aren't you?" the old man said. "An admirable trait. I hope it serves you well. But it does not alter the facts, even if your skin seems to have remained rather sensitive." He smiled. "And since you still have your skin, we must do what we can to protect it. We'll have to trust that your emptiness will do the rest."

Tereba nodded to Wu, who began to move toward Guthrie like a feline stalking its prey.

"Wait a minute!" Guthrie shoved back his chair and stood, feeling trapped behind the table. "I thought you said you wouldn't swat a friend with a hatchet."

"Please give us credit for a little more sophistication than that," the old man said, opening his hands and stepping toward Guthrie.

They all were closing in on Guthrie, now. He knew he'd never get by Wu, but he couldn't let himself go down without a struggle. The old man or the girls would be easier to bowl over, but despite the threat, Guthrie couldn't see himself hurting them. Instead, he up-ended the table, flinging it in Wu's direction, and tried to dash to the door that led back to the apothecary shop.

He made it about half-way across the kitchen before Wu had him immobilized in the middle of the floor, hog-tied in an arm lock that was painful only when he tried to wriggle free.

"I can't get the sculpture if you kill me," Guthrie ground out as Tereba and the girls bent over him.

"I'm sorry, Mr. Guthrie, but I really must. If you are not dead, you will not be able to retrieve the bust unharmed. Besides, you have already killed yourself." Tereba's face took on a stony serious-ness. "And I'll tell you this: I'd give *my* life for it. And believe me, I've lived long enough to have developed a real attachment to it. As for your life, I'd sooner save it than let it go, but I must have the sculpture. You bring it to me, and I'll do what I can to help you restore yourself."

"And if I don't bring it to you?"

Tereba shrugged. "One way or another, it will be all over for you."

"You're worse than those bastards I'm working for."

"I'm offering you a way to truly live again. Please consider any discomforts you endure in the meantime as therapy necessary for your cure."

The old man smiled, and he bent close and reached out to Guthrie, who writhed in Wu's arm lock.

"Hold still, young man," Tereba said, smile turning slightly ex-asperated. "If all that remains of your life is your skin, we must take care to preserve it. Don't force us to damage it in the process."

The fingers of his left hand, surprisingly strong, dug into Guthrie's neck as his right palm pressed against Guthrie's abdomen, right below his navel. He suddenly twisted the palm, and it felt like something inside of Guthrie wrenched loose and twisted away. The light in the room grew dim then faded entirely.

14

THE LIGHT SHINING IN GUTHRIE'S eyes lied. It said the day out there, just past the window, was bright, cheery, and warm. Knowing better, he groaned and rolled over. He was in his own bed, in his own bedroom, but aside from that, nothing seemed right. When he stretched, his limbs were numb, as if the muscles were strung together with leaden wires. He felt terrible.

No, not terrible. Empty.

Guthrie lay there, trying to piece together what had happened the night before—the fight with Wu, the ride to the shopping center, the ancient apothecary shop, the kitchen windows with bright sunshine illuminating a desert gorge....

Shut up, he told himself. I'm not empty. I just had a bad dream. Just a dream.

He sat up and swung his feet off the bed, noticing that he was stripped to his underwear and T-shirt, but suddenly his middle went flaccid, emanating a humming chill, and vertigo insisted he return to a prone position. He managed to collapse backward instead of onto the floor, his feet dangling over the side of the bed. They seemed much too far away to worry about, so he left them there.

Gradually, the vertigo subsided, but after a few moments, he felt an itching just below his navel. He reached down to scratch, and his fingers encountered a light, crinkly resistance. Groaning, he dragged himself back onto his pillow, pulled up his shirt, and tugged down the waistband of his underwear. Just below his navel, a three-inch-square patch of gauze was taped to his skin. He peeled off the bandage, and beneath was a tattoo, starkly black against his pale skin. He couldn't see it too well from this angle, but it appeared to be eight little stick men with flat instead of round heads who surrounded a quartered square that trailed a pair of wavy lines.

It was a minor maiming, to be sure, but done without Guthrie's knowledge or consent. Guthrie recalled the contrast between Tereba's bemused smile and the unfathomable mystery of his infinite eyes. Somehow, the memory made him feel colder, and the humming chill sent another shiver through him. He pressed the gauze back into place, thinking that if he went back to sleep, he'd wake as if none of it had happened.

His phone was on the bedside table, and he hadn't noticed it until now, but now it rang. The caller ID read "Unknown," and he wondered if he dared answer. But he had to—he might as well be a puppet the way everyone was pulling his strings.

"It's Cindy," said a voice. "You're awake."

Guthrie was in no mood for pleasantries.

"What do you want?"

"Grandfather sends his apologies. He wants you to know that he didn't intend for you to be frightened last night. He hopes you're feeling well."

"Not as well as I did before I met him," Guthrie groused.

"But no worse, either," Cindy said.

"That remains to be seen."

"He hopes you'll heed what he said. It'll be best for you."

"I'll be the judge of what's best for me, and you can tell him I have no intention of doing anything he wants."

"But you must...."

"Coercion and lies aren't the best way to earn trust," Guthrie said harshly. "He bullied me, and besides, I don't believe a damn thing he said. In fact, I don't even believe he's your grandfather."

"Well," Cindy admitted, "he's not. He's older than that. But we are related to him."

"How?"

"You wouldn't believe me if I told you."

"My point, exactly. And another thing: What's this tattoo he put on my stomach? He marked my body without my permission."

"He's only protecting you from danger."

"If he wants to protect me, tell him to keep away," Guthrie said. But he was curious. "What's it mean?"

"I don't know," she said coolly.

"Come on," Guthrie insisted. "You know something."

"Grandfather instructed me not to…."

"Look, it's my life on the line here. If the old man expects me to do his dirty work, I deserve to know the facts and what the dangers are."

"But you just said you weren't going to do his dirty work." It was Cindy's turn to sound sarcastic.

"We're talking about his expectation and what I need to know to fulfill that expectation, not my intentions."

"There is no danger from the tattoo," Cindy said, speaking tersely as if to a recalcitrant child. "It's a mystical Chinese symbol called the Talisman of the Armor of Earth. It depicts a kuei, a spirit that is part of the soul. The kuei is surrounded by eight characters for Heaven. The kuei can come into contact with ghosts, demons, or other evil and remain unpolluted. It also represents a man who has not been properly buried."

"Couldn't he have found a better place to put it?"

"It's over your power center," she said, as if that explained everything. "The talisman has some advantages. You'll find that the watchdog at the house on Rice Boulevard won't be able to notice you anymore. It probably won't help with the Ravens, though."

"The Ravens?"

"You've met them. Ingram and Stanton."

"Stanton's a big blond guy?"

"Yes."

"Why do you call them the Ravens?"

"I don't know. It's just what they're called," she said. "Come to the shop when you find the sculpture, and Grandfather will make everything all right."

With that, she hung up.

Guthrie put the phone on the beside table, rolled out of the bed, and stood up with a groan. The vertigo had abated, but sudden shivers tremored his body, though it couldn't have been cold in the room. The sensation was akin to the first day of a bad cold, when the histamines hadn't kicked in yet and nothing was aching, but his head felt just the slightest bit woozy, and his limbs tingled with a sort of hyped-up energy that seemed more nervous than muscular.

He stumbled into the bathroom, stripped, and got under the steaming spray from the shower head. The water was hot as hell, and at first, Guthrie's skin felt like it was going to slough off. But as the heat suffused though him, it loosened the leaden wires and made him feel more pliable. Warmth spread from his gut, bringing a tingling to his fingers and toes. Even if he didn't feel quite right when he finally got out, he felt a whole lot better. Feeling better makes you feel bet....

Shut up, he told himself. Don't think about him.

But he couldn't help himself. Dead, the old man had said. Dead and empty inside.

Bullshit, he thought. These people may be using him, but they wouldn't want to hurt him, at least not until he'd fulfilled his task. A broken tool is useless.

Even so, he couldn't help but remember the sudden splitting headache that had come over him in Egan's office. Headaches, vertigo, anxiety attacks, paranoia. Hell, several times during the last few days, he'd practically hallucinated, especially at Travis's house.

But he wasn't sick, he told himself. Not sick. It's only anxiety and stress. It'll get better. Just give it a little time.

He toweled dry and went into the bedroom to dress. After that, he ate a bowl of cereal then poured a cup of coffee and sat on the living room sofa, contemplating what to do next.

The problem was, there weren't a lot of choices since there'd never been much to go on to begin with. Even if the man who'd used the name Mark Batten was actually the thief, that information had led to a dead end. And apparently, Guthrie couldn't even do something simple like check out John Travis without suffering some kind of anxiety attack.

Still, at this point, Batten was his single viable lead, so Guthrie dug out the only item that could possibly take him anywhere—the lengthy list of Lexus SUV owners. Almost absently, he began reading.

Boredom almost caused him to miss the name nearly at the bottom of the list. John Travis owned a silver Lexus RX.

Guthrie switched on his computer and connected to police records. A few minutes of searching showed that there wasn't much to find on Travis. He was about as straight a citizen as you could imagine. He didn't even have a single traffic citation.

But there was that one remarkable fact—the silver Lexus.

Hell, Guthrie thought. There were a lot of those things on Houston's streets—just look at the list. Then again, maybe not. If both Batten and Travis drove Ford Explorers, that could easily be pure coincidence, but a Lexus of the same color was far less of one.

Guthrie realized that the car wasn't the only point of similarity. Both men were involved with the sculpture at some level, and Guthrie couldn't find Travis any more than he could find Batten. And come to think of it, the secretary in the anthropology department had noted how attractive Batten was to women, and Edna, the Harveys' chef, had said the same thing.

The connections were pretty loose, Guthrie knew, but they were there, and they were all he had.

Steeling himself for another encounter with his sordid past, he headed for his car. Dead or not, he was about to pay another visit to John Travis's house.

15

FOR THE THIRD TIME IN as many days, Guthrie trotted across South Rice to the sidewalk in front of the hedge surrounding Travis's house. Considering the questionable track record of his two previous visits, he figured he wouldn't even make the curb this time, but he did. The hedge greeted him by remaining coldly impassive, for which he thanked the powers that be. Even so, he kept to the edge of the sidewalk farthest from the foliage as he padded toward the driveway.

He expected trouble there, too—some other ugliness from his past to blow its foul breath over him. But it was as if the disturbing experiences of the other visits were some sort of obscure waking nightmare that was rapidly fading into the background welter of memory's noise. He passed through the gap in the hedge like nothing was there but a gap in the hedge. After everything, the normalcy of it was almost unsettling.

As he trod the sparse yellowish grass to the front door, a weight of apprehension lifted from his shoulders. The virus of fear and confusion afflicting him must have passed from his system; he was back in form. He took the step into the entryway without a falter and rapped soundly on the door. No one answered, which was what he expected since there wasn't a Lexus SUV parked next to the house.

He moseyed down the driveway. There were no exterior shutters on the windows along the side of the house, but all were curtained. That bothered him, because he wanted to get a peek inside to see if the watchdog the girls had mentioned might be there. If it was, it hadn't noticed him yet because it wasn't barking.

About halfway down, he passed a side door, and when he turned the corner to the backyard, a screened-in porch loomed around the back door. This, being hidden from the street, was ideal for his purposes. Using his Swiss Army knife, he slit the screen next to the frame, unhooked the catch, and let himself into the porch. The back door yielded after a few moments of prying with the large screwdriver he'd brought for just that purpose, and he paused at the threshold, waiting the appearance of growl and bared fang. But none came. Travis must have taken the dog with him, Guthrie thought as he entered the gloomy cool of a room that might have been a bedroom but now held office furniture.

A desk and computer table were arranged along one wall, six legal-sized filing cabinets stood against another, and the remaining two walls were occupied by floor-to-ceiling shelves loaded with books. Ignoring the office for the moment, he made a quick but thorough search of the rest of the house: kitchen, dining room, living room, main bath, master bedroom, and second bedroom.

The master bedroom contained an old, ornate wrought iron bed and an antique armoire, but aside from these two pieces, the rest of the furniture in the house was of the generically impersonal sort available in any discount furniture outlet.

But if the furniture was prosaic, the collection of stuff in the living room wasn't. The place was like a museum of things not old enough to qualify as true antiques but old enough to be of some worth and interest. A dozen obsolete film cameras were arranged on a long shelf on one wall in the living room, a Les Paul Gibson guitar in a Plexiglas case hung like an artwork on another, and a signed Norman Rockwell print graced a third. Under the guitar squatted an old Seeburg jukebox in nearly mint condition, fully loaded with 45s from the '50s and '60s. Sitting around were a mint-condition metal Coca-Cola ice chest at least as old as Guthrie, a hand-cranked phonograph a good deal older, and a pair of pre-World War II Zenith radios sporting big dials and station pointers long enough to qualify as daggers. Below the camera shelf, a glass-front display cabinet held a variety of knickknacks and kitsch, none of recent vintage.

Travis was obviously a collector of art and artifacts, but from all appearances, he specialized in early- to mid-twentieth-century Americana. Guthrie wasn't sure what he'd expected, but considering Travis's professional expertise, it seemed odd that nothing present remotely resembled the Middle Eastern in style or the medieval in age. But then, if Travis did own really old or valuable artifacts, he certainly wouldn't be foolish enough to leave them lying around in the living room, particularly if they'd been stolen.

Guthrie returned to the bedroom and rummaged unsuccessfully through closets and drawers—anything large enough to hold the head. All he found in the former were clothes, some vintage, and a baseball bat and glove, and all that occupied the latter were underwear, socks, T-shirts, and sweaters. The kitchen yielded only food, utensils, and pots and pans. There were no dirty dishes.

Guthrie went back to the office, the one room he hadn't searched yet, and was immediately drawn to the bookshelves. Guthrie considered himself an eclectic reader, and a couple of minutes in front of the shelves was enough to learn that Travis was, as well. Most of the books were nonfiction, and given Travis's background in anthropology and art, Guthrie could see a strong slant in those directions. Fifteen minutes of browsing revealed a lot of books Guthrie thought he'd like to read if he could find, or afford, them but absolutely nothing germane to his investigation except an album of photographs.

As Guthrie shuffled through the pages, Travis wasn't hard to pick out. Most of the recent shots showed a dark-haired man in his late 30s, athletic and handsome, though not overly rugged. There were pictures of Travis playing baseball, Travis at the beach, Travis on mountaintops, Travis in the city, Travis at archaeological sites, and Travis at parties. A number of the earlier ones were taken with Martina Flores, his former girlfriend from the university. From what Guthrie could tell, the singular unifying theme was the snotty, self-satisfied expression that always showed on the man's face. Maybe it was the supercilious expression that grated on Guthrie, or maybe it was the rapid turnover of young women who showed up in most of the more recent shots. All were attractive, and invariably they were looking adoringly at Travis while he smirked at the camera.

The secretary at the university said Travis had animal magnetism, but hell, did the bastard have to flaunt it? The photo book was more a catalog of acquisitions than an album of memories. Guthrie wrinkled his nose, pocketed a photo from one of the last few pages, then put the book back on the shelf.

Next, he checked the wooden desk. It held the usual assortment of office supplies like paper, envelopes, and pens. The deep file drawer contained current personal bills, none of which revealed much except that Travis paid on time and that his bank account, while modestly cushioned, wasn't especially enviable, probably due to the house note, the payment on that Lexus, and all of his extracurricular travel with his lady friends.

That left the bank of filing cabinets. They weren't locked, and Guthrie began flipping through their contents. Most of the drawers held various papers one might expect of a university professor. Except one. That contained Travis's financial records for the past couple of years. Interesting, Guthrie thought. Looked like Travis hadn't bothered to file his income tax this last year. Pretty sloppy for someone who seemed so neat and organized.

Guthrie was about to shut the drawer when a word on one of the tabs caught his eye.

Vulcan.

The file was tucked in the back of the drawer, and when he pulled it out and opened it, he saw a bundle of paycheck stubs lying against the manila. Paychecks issued by Vulcan Armor to someone named Brad Adams for a period beginning last spring and ending two weeks ago. The figures on the checks showed that someone named Brad Adams was pulling down ninety-five grand a year.

Could Travis be Adams? If not, why did he have the check stubs? If he was, what would an anthropologist be doing moonlighting under an assumed name at a company that manufactured safes?

The answer lay beneath the check stubs on a folded slip of paper that looked as if it had been hastily crumpled then smoothed out. Guthrie unfolded the paper and saw two lines of four numbers. He couldn't be positive, but he thought he recognized them as the combinations to the Harveys' double-lock safe.

Guthrie put the file folder back in the drawer and saw that the next folder was labeled "Armin's." It contained a handful of checks —uncashed—made out to Mark Batten.

Travis had been a busy boy for someone who was supposed to be on sabbatical.

The discovery, though, threw a kink into Guthrie's speculations that the thief had used inside information from one of the dinner guests. Travis's guilt was staring Guthrie in the face, but if Travis had worked for both Vulcan and Armin's under assumed names, it looked like he might have pulled the job on his own. He was obviously a clever and knowledgeable fellow. He knew about the head, he'd scoped out the owners, and he'd pulled off the job. But if he was working solo, that still left Guthrie wondering why he'd been threatened off the case by the man in Barbara Sidell's parking garage.

Guthrie blinked as a sudden rage born of frustration and resentment heated his vision, and he whacked his palm against the filing cabinet.

Damn bastard, Guthrie thought, rubbing the sting from his hand. First can't find him, then can't get into his house, now can't even speculate about him without it getting all twisted. Why the hell'd the bastard have to make the job harder than it already was? There was no answer, but that didn't moderate Guthrie's anger.

He stuffed the files back into the drawer and slammed it closed. Then he found the phone book, looked up Vulcan's number, and punched it in on the phone that sat on the desk.

"I'd like to speak to Brad Adams, please," he told the too perky receptionist voice that answered on the second ring.

"One moment, please." A Muzak version of Led Zeppelin's "Stairway to Heaven" replaced the voice, and Guthrie waited, wincing at a good song done wrong.

"This is Brad Adams's office," a man's voice said, and not a moment too soon. "May I help you?"

"Mr. Adams?"

"No. Mr. Adams isn't here."

"Do you expect him back soon?"

"I'm not sure when he'll be back. Is there something I can help you with?"

"Not really. I need to talk to Mr. Adams personally. Any idea where he is?"

"I'm not certain. Who did you say you were?"

"I'm Bill Osmond," Guthrie said, picking a name from a book spine on the shelves. I'm a real estate broker. Mr. Adams asked me to look into the purchase of a piece of property, and I'm calling to let him know I found the ideal lot."

"I see."

Did he?

"Is there a number where he can be reached?"

"Not that I know of. Who did you say you were, again?"

"I'll try back later." Guthrie cradled the phone.

Interesting, he mused. If Guthrie was a judge of anything, his years on patrol had taught him to read between a person's words, and what the man on the phone hadn't said spoke a lot. Especially that the people at Vulcan were suspicious of Travis—or Adams, as they knew him—and that they didn't know where he was any more than Guthrie did.

Somewhere inside himself, Guthrie could feel a spark of admiration for Travis, but it was submersed in a deepening animosity. Surely Travis, as Batten, had stolen the sculpture, but why? He already had everything he needed. Damn! He had everything Guthrie wanted—absorbing work, a nice house, adoring girlfriends, a steady income, the admiration of his colleagues. Most of all, he had direction and purpose. He even had spare cash for nice things, frivolous things. How the hell much did he squander on travel, on his pseudo antiques, or on those women in the photos? More, probably, than Guthrie could ever hope to spare. But no, none of that was enough. Now he had to have the sculpture, too. He had to steal it and drag Guthrie into a quagmire that had, at first, looked like escape, but now seemed more confounding than the paralysis of the past two years.

Certainly more dangerous.

Well, fuck you, Travis, Guthrie thought as he left the house and returned to his car. Fuck you and the boat you rode in on.

Guthrie sat for a couple of minutes in his car, staring at the house crouching behind the hedge, wondering what the hell was going on, not just with the investigation, but with himself. Apparently the anxiety attacks of the previous two days had vanished. He gave thanks for that, but not for the fact that their residue seemed to have left a depression that only elevated itself through an expression of ungrounded hostility for the man he was hunting. It bothered Guthrie that he was losing what little objectivity he had, but at the same time, he couldn't seem to prevent himself from inflaming his own ire.

And the hell of it was, the more he learned, the less sense things made. That wasn't right. A detective was supposed to understand more as he progressed, not less.

For the first time in his life Guthrie seriously considered professional counseling, but the idea quickly vanished. Even if he could afford the cost, he couldn't afford the scrutiny. With a sigh, he realized he would have to find his own therapy by finding Travis and the head. At least he now had something concrete to go on. All it would take was a bit of confirmation.

He twisted the key in the ignition and buzzed off toward Armin's Liquors.

As he drove, he thought about why Travis might have stolen the head. Travis was a collector, to be sure, though the period and style of his personal collection were way out of sync with ancient artifacts. But it could be that Travis's twentieth-century Americana was simply a surrogate for the truly rare artifacts that he dealt with professionally. They were artifacts he could afford. It must have irked him to know that people like the Harveys, who didn't have a fraction of his understanding, were the ones who accumulated the real antiques, leaving the surrogate of pop-culture kitsch to the real experts like himself. Maybe that realization had finally made the man snap, had finally given him his fill of just looking at and researching ancient artifacts. Maybe he'd decided he had to have one of his own, any way he could get it.

But Guthrie's mind kept coming back to the man in Barbara Sidell's parking garage and his threat to kill Guthrie if he didn't lay off the case. That threw a wrench into any speculation that Travis had stolen the bust for himself and gave validity to Guthrie's original assumption that Travis had stolen the sculpture for a third party, most likely one of the dinner guests. Sure, he could have taken it just to sell. He knew its rarity and value, and considering his professional background and interest in the illicit trade in artifacts, he must be tapped into the collector's grapevine, to use William Mason's euphemistic phrase. But Mason said the sculpture would be hard to sell, and if Travis's only motive was money, what about all the Harveys' art? He could have snatched any of it just as easily as the head —easier—and made millions more—enough to buy his own collection of genuinely old artifacts.

So there was still something Guthrie wasn't seeing, something that made the head important in a way that went beyond money. Was Tereba right? Was the sculpture some sort of psychic battery?

Guthrie shook his head. That was beyond him, and he didn't believe it, anyway. To Guthrie, nothing mattered except recovering the head, and the only part of all this speculation that remained germane was the fact that Travis was the thief. And that left three possibilities. The first was that Travis had hidden the sculpture in his house where Guthrie hadn't been able to find it. The second was that he had it with him or had hidden it somewhere else. And third, maybe he'd already gotten rid of it to someone else.

It looked like the only way Guthrie was going to get the answers was to catch up with Travis. Damn it, he groused to himself. That meant a stakeout. There was nothing else left to do.

But maybe there was. Guthrie was increasingly disturbed by the fact that everyone seemed to know more about what was going on than he did, and that wasn't right. Wasn't he the detective? Wasn't he the one who was supposed to find the answers? He thought about going to the Harveys and questioning them, but he knew that would be a waste of time. They'd told him just about all they were going to.

And the attempt might prove worse than futile. The man in Sidell's parking garage had already threatened him, and Egan's thugs —the Ravens—wouldn't hesitate a second if their boss ordered Guthrie disposed of. The situation was dangerous, and the Harveys were close to the eye of the storm. Asking questions of them might inadvertently bring Guthrie into the less than charmed circle of Zeroth's enemies, and that was a place Guthrie wanted to avoid.

Guthrie needed time to think. He wanted to get out all the info, spread it across his desk, and go through it once again, because right now he wasn't seeing past the obvious.

He wheeled the Honda into a parking space in front of Armin's Liquors and went inside. The clerk, Tony, was behind the counter, and he grew suddenly alert as he recognized Guthrie.

"Do you want to talk to Mr. Dobbs?" he asked. His face seemed a bit more gaunt than when Guthrie had last seen him, but his eyes weren't as raw.

"Not necessarily." Guthrie pulled out the picture of John Travis. "Do you recognize this man?"

"That's Mark," Tony said after a quick glance. "Did you find him?"

"Not yet, but I'm working on it."

"You must be, if you've got his picture. Who's the woman?"

Guthrie shrugged just as Dobbs came through the door from the back.

"Oh. Mr. Guthrie, isn't it? Have you found Mark?" Guthrie held up the photo, and Dobbs peered at it.

"That's him. Have you caught him?"

"I'm in the process of catching him."

"You know something funny?" Dobbs said.

"What's that?"

"After you left, I started thinking that you might be able to trace him from his bank, so I called our bookkeeper to see what bank endorsed his paychecks. He never cashed any of them. Now, why would anybody work and not get paid?"

"He got paid, don't you think?"

Dobbs's eyes widened as that sank in.

"Oh. Yes." His expression of mortification was a wonder to behold. "The Harveys don't think I had anything to do with it do they?"

"Have they bought any liquor from you since I was last in?"

"Why, yes. Just yesterday. Another case of wine and some Scotch."

"I think it's safe to say you're in the clear as far as the Harveys go."

"Yes. Yes." He shook his head with concern that probably was more for his own skin than anything the Harveys had lost. "It's terrible about the theft."

"Yes, terrible," Guthrie said, pocketing the photo. He left Armin's, returned to his car, and drove home. When he arrived, he was surprised to see a powder-blue Jaguar parked in his driveway.

Whether he wanted to talk to them or not, the Harveys had come calling.

16

AS HE PARKED NEXT TO the Jag, Guthrie cringed at the contrast between the Harveys' mansion and his ramshackle bungalow, then shrugged it off. They probably expected no more of him, just as he expected no less of them.

"Hello, Mrs. Harvey. Mr. Harvey," he said as they all emerged from their vehicles.

"We want a word with you, Guthrie." Lloyd said.

"Watch out for that fire ant bed, Mr. Harvey."

Give Lloyd credit. He didn't jump in panic, though he did quickly glance down and step extra wide over the mound.

"Been meaning to take care of that, but I haven't had the time."

"Hard on the case?" This was from Carla. Her veiled tone didn't sound particularly sarcastic, but Guthrie thought it did contain just a bit of seething anger.

"I have been," Guthrie said as they mounted the porch. "Come on in." He dug the mail out of the mail box and ushered them into the house. Inside the living room, he tossed the mail onto the coffee table and gestured toward the sofa. "Have a seat."

Carla played the opening gambit.

"You questioned Barbara Sidell and Martin Hastings about the theft."

"Correction. Hastings wasn't home."

"Don't quibble, Guthrie," Lloyd said. "You went to his house, and that's what counts."

"I thought you wanted me to recover the statue," Guthrie said, not bothering to ask how they knew he'd gone to visit Hastings. "Even if I had hard physical evidence in this case, which I don't, I'd have to interview potential witnesses and suspects."

Anger flashed in Lloyd's eyes. "You weren't hired to cast aspersions on our friends."

"Pardon me," Guthrie said, repressing his own ire but not the urge to needle Lloyd. "I thought I was."

Lloyd started to sputter, but Carla laid a hand on his arm then stared at Guthrie. Guthrie didn't like the look that flickered through her eyes. It placed him right back under the rock he'd crawled from beneath to enter their lives. But what really hurt was the disappointment that chased the contempt.

"I suspect everyone except me," he attempted to amplify. "I'm the only one I'm sure didn't take the sculpture."

"And what makes you think our friends might have?" Carla asked.

"Motive," Guthrie said. "And opportunity. The foundations of all cases not involving random elements. The thief is someone who knew about the bust, and he or she must have also known that Saturday night would be an opportune time. That limits the field, and the dinner guests are logical suspects."

"But why couldn't it be a random thief?"

"A lot of reasons—Picasso, Matisse, Miró, and Ernst, just to name a few." Guthrie shrugged. "A simple burglar would have taken your art and left the sculpture. That means the thief was after just the head."

"Well," she said, sitting back, an encouraging expression suffusing her features. "That seems logical. Doesn't it, Lloyd?"

Lloyd grunted, obviously unswayed. Or mollified.

"Do you suspect one of our friends?" She lit one of her expensive cigarettes and began to fill the room with common smoke.

"Not necessarily," Guthrie said, passing her a coaster to use as an ashtray. "Actually, I've got a lead on someone else."

"The liquor delivery man?" Carla asked. "Alton said you questioned Edna about him."

"I don't see the relevance...," Lloyd began, but Guthrie cut him off.

"Did Alton mention that the delivery man made an unscheduled delivery early Saturday evening? And while he was there, he was out of sight long enough to do the job. And he left your house carrying a cardboard box big enough to hold the bust."

"That's pretty flimsy," Lloyd's sarcasm indicated he hadn't quite recovered his constrictor cool. "The box could just as well hold wine."

"The manager of Armin's knows nothing about the late delivery," Guthrie said, doing his best to give Lloyd the benefit of the doubt. "The delivery man hasn't shown up for work since the day of the theft, he was hired under a fictitious name, and he gave a false address and phone number." Guthrie shrugged. "That looks suspicious to me."

"But if you know nothing about this man, how can you find out if he is the one who took the bust?" Carla asked.

"I didn't say I knew nothing," Guthrie pointed out. "I've found out who he really is, and I'm in the process of tracking him down."

"Who is he?" Trust Lloyd to get right to the meat of the matter.

"I'm not ready to say, he may not....

"Look, Guthrie," Lloyd snapped. "We're paying you a substantial sum of money. You work for us. When we ask you a direct question, you give a direct answer."

"Mr. Egan is paying me," Guthrie reminded Lloyd, looking him right in the eye. "If I do find any answers, how I arrive at them may not be simple or necessarily desirable to elucidate, and I'm not going to try. Nor am I going to openly accuse anyone until I'm positive they're guilty and I have the evidence to back it up. If you don't like it, I'll be happy to refund Mr. Egan's retainer minus expenses incurred to date."

"Your case is shaky," Lloyd said, "unless you can prove this delivery man is some kind of professional safecracker."

"He doesn't need to be. He was temporarily employed by the company that constructed the armored cabinet where you kept the bust. And I know for a fact that he somehow obtained copies of the safe's combinations."

Carla stiffened ever so slightly and exchanged a look with Lloyd that Guthrie couldn't read.

"Please, Mr. Guthrie," she said, turning back to Guthrie. "We said for you to use your own discretion. We want you to go on with the case." It was nice hearing the words, though Guthrie figured they stuck in her craw.

"Fine. I'll stick with it and get your head back."

Lloyd asked in the most civil tone he'd yet used with Guthrie, "Do you think you can locate this man?"

"Don't worry. It shouldn't take long."

"You must find out if he has the bust or if he's disposed of it."
Carla's voice was so brittle that it seemed as if she might crack.

"I will."

That elicited a small smile from Carla, showing her aplomb had returned. Even Lloyd finally seemed appeased.

"One important reminder, Guthrie," Lloyd told him. "When you find the head, be certain to bring it to us immediately. Within the hour. You must not hesitate."

"When I lay my hands on it, you'll be the first to know."

Carla stood up, smoothed her skirt, and strode to the door, Lloyd trailing. Guthrie watched them go down the steps toward their car, and a moment later the Jag disappeared around the corner.

Guthrie lingered on the porch for a few seconds, scanning his street. The Harveys showing up on his doorstep unannounced made him suspicious. They weren't the sort to waste their time driving across town to see Guthrie if they weren't sure he was home, and it was even less conceivable that they would wait around for him to come home if he wasn't there. But they might have received a call that Guthrie was on his way.

Hadn't Wu said that men were watching his house? Egan had no shortage of men who could follow Guthrie and make that call. Besides, how else could the Harveys have known Guthrie had gone to Hastings's house?

The street was clear, but that didn't mean anything. Guthrie didn't associate with his neighbors, nor did he know all their cars by sight.

He went back inside, sat on the sofa, and checked the mail he'd tossed onto the coffee table. Among the bills and pointless credit card come-ons was a large white envelope bearing the Vulcan logo. It was the packet of information he'd requested. Guthrie flipped through the material, starting with the big four-color brochure. The company manufactured and installed security systems, safes, armored and fire-proof filing cabinets, burglar bars and storm shutters, and even armored cars.

The promo material didn't contain anything of much use to Guthrie, but the corporate report did. The introductory message from Vulcan's CEO was accompanied by a portrait of the man whose goons had beat up Guthrie in Barbara Sidell's parking garage. And his name was Martin Hastings. Presumably Hastings hadn't been home when Guthrie'd gone to his house because he and his goons were having a drink to celebrate roughing up Guthrie.

Surprise, surprise. No wonder Carla and Lloyd had reacted to the news that Travis worked for Vulcan. Guthrie had thought they were simply shocked at Vulcan's shoddy security, but surely they knew their business associate and fellow party goer was boss there. And now Guthrie had to ask himself why they hadn't revealed that fact.

But why clutter things more than they already were, especially since the sequence of events was finally making sense? Hastings knew about the head and could provide access for his accomplice, Travis. The thief's assignment must have come right from Vulcan's top man, and it certainly gave Hastings a motive to threaten Guthrie off the case. It also would explain the paychecks—they were Travis's payoff meted out over time in a quasi-legal manner. And the phony name? Guthrie wasn't sure. Probably it was a double blind to protect Travis's identity and to eliminate any connection with Hastings. And it would keep Travis's IRS records in line with his salary as a university professor. Guthrie was willing to bet that somewhere in the city was a bank account in the name of Brad Adams to which Travis held the pin number.

The man on the phone at Vulcan—who could well have been Hastings himself—had been suspicious, and that could only mean one thing: Travis must have reneged on the deal with Hastings and dropped out of sight with the head.

Guthrie was tired. He was tired of the Harveys, their friends, and the run-around. He was tired of fighting for answers from the very people who should be eager to supply them. And most of all, he was tired of being tired.

But he was relieved, too. At last something in this case had broken open, and it was time for a few answers. He'd linked Travis with Hastings, and since he wasn't having a hell of a lot of luck tracking down Travis, he might as well try Hastings again. Hell, he couldn't do worse than he had with Travis. Besides, it looked like Travis was simply a flunky, and Hastings was the top dog. That gave Guthrie just the excuse he needed to pay the man another visit—say, early in the morning before Hastings had a chance to leave for the office or attach himself to his goons.

Right now, though, Guthrie was beat and feeling pretty lousy. His guts ached and felt tingly all at the same time, and he didn't think it was due to the stressful encounter with the Harveys. Maybe it was hunger. He went to the kitchen to see what there was to eat.

When he opened the fridge, he almost puked at the smell of the last of the leftover baked chicken, even though it was only a couple of days old. Suppressing a gag, he threw the food, dish and all, into the garbage. He considered going out for something, but nothing he could think of sounded appealing, so he rummaged in the fruit drawer. One squishy, discolored peach brought up more gorge, and he quickly shut the drawer. The vegetable bin held little more promise, but there was some lettuce, the remainder of a bag of carrots, and one tomato.

He made a quick salad and ate it without dressing, but it didn't fill him or make him feel any better. His guts churned a little and ached all the more. He went into the living room, where he tumbled, exhausted, onto the sofa. He tried to quiet the roils in his mind and gut by watching a movie on TV. It almost worked. At last, he stumbled into the bedroom and fell onto the bed. It was still early, but he wanted to get up early.

No, what he really wanted was out, but that now seemed impossible. Now, the only way out was through.

That night, he tossed between tangled sheets. He didn't remember dreaming that he cried clotted crimson tears.

17

GUTHRIE WOKE BEFORE DAWN. HE could tell he hadn't had enough sleep, but as soon as he was conscious, he knew he had to get up. Time to confront Martin Hastings. Maybe he'd repay Vulcan's distinguished CEO in kind for the way his thugs had knocked Guthrie around.

Then again, maybe not, Guthrie thought as he rose and felt the emptiness in his gut. Remembering how little he'd eaten the day before, he ate a big bowl of cereal, though he had to force himself to finish it. Then he took a hot shower, which made him loosen up somewhat. He'd already opened his car when he remembered Hastings's goons and the death threat. He doubted that they lived in the house with Hastings—it wasn't big enough—but he went back inside and got his .38 from the bedroom closet, anyway. Back in the car, he put the gun in the glove compartment before pulling out of the driveway.

In a few minutes, he was on the Gulf Freeway, creeping inbound with the early morning rush hour traffic. As soon as he passed the Loop interchange, he shifted lanes as frequently as he could, keeping as sharp an eye on his rearview mirrors as he did on the road ahead. Sure enough, there it was. His tail. It was a pastel green Chevy compact looking almost too generic, like it was part of a fleet. Although it wasn't marked, Guthrie recognized the color and could easily imagine a white Rampart logo emblazoned on its doors.

He took the downtown exit and soon snaked between the tall buildings. With all the traffic, one-way streets, and traffic signals, he didn't have much trouble losing the tail. Afterward, a quick couple of turns led him onto Memorial Drive, which took him west.

As Guthrie pulled up in front of Hastings's house about twenty minutes later, he noticed that one of the doors of the attached two-car garage was up and that both stalls were filled. Someone was home and probably getting ready to leave for work.

He stuck the .38 into his belt behind his back, went to the front door, and rang the bell. After three tries without response, he left the front porch, walked over to the open garage, and peered inside. Parked in the stall farthest from the house was a canary yellow 1955 Thunderbird convertible that looked like it had just come off the assembly line. The stall directly in front of Guthrie held a late model gray Mercedes. Its driver door was open, and a shiny lump lay on the pavement beneath the door sill.

The lump was a key ring looping eight or so keys. After a quick glance around, Guthrie entered the garage and bent to pick up the keys, but he stopped when he a small smear of drying blood on the sill of the car door. Straightening, Guthrie peered into the car. Nothing seemed out of place except that single smear and the keys. Then he glanced across the garage floor toward the door leading to the house. A dozen or more scatters of blood trailed along the cement. The door was open, and a partial hand print in scarlet marred the white paint of the frame about three feet from the floor.

Guthrie pulled out the .38 and eased through the door. Beyond was a utility room, and the blood there was thick enough that the heavier spatters were not yet dry. Careful not to step in the blood, Guthrie made his way into the house. It looked like someone ahead of him hadn't been so careful. Almost all of the spatters were smeared, as if someone had swiped a mop through them in both directions.

Guthrie worked his way across the modern kitchen, where the spatters thickened into small puddles. A bloodstained drawer pulled completely from the cabinet lay on the floor, cutlery and utensils scattered across the green and white terrazzo tiles.

The widening trail of blood led into the dining room, where the table was shoved back and chairs lay overturned. Next to one of the chairs, Guthrie found a large carving knife, its wooden handle bearing a bloody hand print, its blade impaling the body of a large rat. Four more sliced-up dead rats lay nearby, one severed nearly in half.

Swallowing thickly, Guthrie forced himself to follow the blood across the hall into the living room.

There was nothing living in it. The pile of gore staining the center of the white carpet was eloquent on that point.

Guthrie had seen bad things during his years as a cop, but never worse. Never. As he edged closer, staring hard in the dim light filtering through the drawn curtains, he realized it was so bad it took on an almost clinical cast.

There really wasn't much left of Martin Hastings, if that was who this had been. What lay on the bloodstained carpet was a raw, red-stained skeleton picked clean of ninety percent of the parts that made bones a living, breathing human.

Several more rat bodies lay near the hall door, and the peripheries of the blood smear on the carpet showed tiny red footprints. Guthrie bent over to examine them, when a faint twitter jerked him upright.

Panic pounding in his skull, he swung around, seeking small, furry assailants. The dim light let him see quick shapes darting along the baseboards before the twitter sounded again and he realized the shapes were tricks of shadow and his imagination. He breathed heavily and relaxed a little. The sound was only a bird outside the window, calling to its fellows.

Guthrie didn't feel so clinical that he could stay in the room any longer than was necessary to get a thorough look. He returned to the kitchen, only now noticing the tiny red paw marks he'd missed seeing because he'd been looking for human prints. There were thousands of them—so numerous in places they looked like smears themselves. Pulling out his cell phone, he called 911. After he hung up, he went back out through the garage to his car. He replaced the pistol in the glove compartment and waited for the police to arrive.

They did a lot faster than they would have in his own neighborhood. At first, there were just two of them. Guthrie told them there was a body inside and where to find it, though he wasn't sure that the remains actually qualified as a body.

"You might want to wait," Guthrie warned, but one of them went inside to check while the other stayed outside to keep an eye on Guthrie. The one who went in came out in less than two minutes, face pallid.

"What is it, Ryan?" asked the other.

"I don't think I can say," Ryan told him in a strained voice, then turned to Guthrie. "You touch anything in there?"

"No," Guthrie said.

"Let me see your identification."

Guthrie gave him his driver's license.

Ryan looked it over, looked Guthrie over, then looked at the license again. His hand was trembling.

"We'd better wait for the lieutenant," he said. He kept the license.

"Here he is," said Ryan's companion a minute and a half later as three more police cars arrived almost simultaneously. By now several of the neighbors were watching discreetly from their yards and windows. No unruly crowds elbowing for a gander in this neighborhood.

"What were you doing here?" the lieutenant asked as soon as he'd seen what was inside and set the investigation in motion. His name was Upton. He was black, balding, and a little taller and ten years older than Guthrie. His shrewd eyes didn't show much of a reaction at the state of the body.

"I'm investigating a case of stolen property," Guthrie said. "Martin Hastings was a possible witness, so I came here to ask him a few questions."

"Who are you working for?"

"My clients wish to remain anonymous."

"Don't give me any crap, Guthrie. Nothing is confidential in a homicide investigation."

"I saw the body, too, lieutenant," Guthrie said evenly. "Didn't look like any homicide I ever saw."

"I suppose you've had a lot of experience with murder, being a peeper and all." Upton's tone wasn't exactly a sneer, but it was pretty close.

"I saw enough while I was on the force," Guthrie told him flatly. That got Upton's attention.

"You were on the force, eh? Why'd you quit?" He was ready for Guthrie to be a coward, or maybe crooked and caught.

"Disability. I took a bullet in the hip. Happened about two years ago."

"Yeah," Upton said after a pause. "Guthrie. I remember. Your partner was killed, and you killed the perp. Drug raid, wasn't it?"

"That's right."

Upton's hard expression didn't change, but suddenly he was Guthrie's friend. He didn't say so, but he didn't have to. Guthrie could see it in his eyes. Guthrie had been a comrade and almost given the ultimate sacrifice. As far as Upton was concerned, Guthrie was still in uniform.

"You're private now, eh? How's business?" He sounded like he was considering that line of work himself.

"I'm not sure," Guthrie admitted. "I'm just getting started."

"So, you're working a stolen property case?"

"Yeah. Somebody swiped a small antique. The owners don't want to make a big deal about it, they just want it back." He eyed Upton and gave a slight grin. "And I'm still not telling you who they are. They're rich, though. River Oaks rich."

"Swank." Upton wrinkled his nose. "They think this guy is the one who took their knickknack?"

"Not that I know of," Guthrie said. "Looks like it was a delivery man. But Hastings was with the owners, and I just wanted to clear all the bases." He glanced towards the house. "I don't guess he'll be telling me anything, now."

"If that guy in there is Hastings," Upton pointed out.

"If that in there is a guy," Guthrie echoed, and Upton gave a snort of laughter.

"We'll know soon enough. Okay, give your statement to the officer over there, then you can go. But make yourself available if we need you, hear?"

Guthrie thanked Upton then went over and told the officer how he'd come to discover the body. He was feeling pretty drained by the time he finished, and he ached all over from post-adrenaline fatigue. And the day was only half over.

After he left, he drove far enough to get out of the neighborhood then pulled into a parking lot and punched in the Harveys' number. Alton answered.

"This is Guthrie. May I speak to one of the Harveys?"

"Do you have some good news for us, Mr. Guthrie?" Carla Harvey asked as soon as she came on the line.

"Depends on how much you liked Martin Hastings."

"Martin?"

"There's no easy way to break the news of death, Mrs. Harvey."

"Martin is dead?" She didn't sound as if the news hit a soft spot.

"He is. I found his body when I went to talk to him this morning."

"Was...," she began then paused as if debating the wisdom of asking. "Was he murdered?"

Why should he be murdered? Guthrie wondered. More people die of heart attacks.

"The police don't know," he told her. "He may have been, but the condition of the body made it impossible to tell."

"What happened?"

"From all appearances, he was eaten by rats."

"Oh."

That was all. Twenty hardened police officers were shocked and mystified, and all Carla Harvey had to say was that single syllable.

"I'll be going now," Guthrie told her.

"Yes. Thank you for your call."

She hung up, and so did Guthrie. He sat there for a few moments, totally at a loss and almost doubting the reality of the last couple of hours.

He needed answers, yet every stone he upturned revealed only more questions. The Harveys weren't talking, and certainly neither was Hastings. There was the old man, though. Tereba. He needed something from Guthrie, and he obviously knew a lot more than he'd revealed. If he wanted, or expected, Guthrie to succeed, he should be willing to part with some information that would help Guthrie achieve their mutual goal.

But that meant that Guthrie would have to look him up, and Guthrie wasn't sure he wanted to be anywhere near Tereba. As scary as the old guy was, though, he was probably the closest thing to a friend that Guthrie had right now, and he was the only person involved in this mess likely to tell Guthrie anything useful.

Guthrie drove toward the shopping center where Wu had taken him. He had no trouble locating the place—the water tower was an infallible landmark. Pulling around back, he drove past the dumpsters to the end of the alley, looking for the quaint red door in the far wall.

There was no carved red door.

He returned to the front of the shopping center and examined it. There was absolutely no doubt in his mind that this was the correct place. Wu had made no effort to conceal his destination when he'd brought Guthrie here only forty-eight hours ago, and Guthrie easily recognized his surroundings.

Just to be sure, Guthrie drove up Bellaire, searching. A quarter of a mile west, he found another shopping center, and though he knew it wasn't the right one, he drove behind it anyway, just to convince himself. The convincing didn't take long, so he returned to the shopping center he was positive Wu had taken him to and pulled around back and down the alley. No red door.

He parked, walked to the metal door closest to the approximate location he remembered being occupied by the carved red door, and tried the knob. It turned, and he opened the door. Inside was a large warehouse space full of cartons of food and other grocery products stacked on pallets and large metal carts. A couple of workers in stained green aprons turned to stare at him. The warehouse was wide enough that had there been a red door it would have opened into this same space.

Guthrie closed the door, perplexed. He knew he was at the correct location, yet it could not be the right place. He walked to his car, telling himself something was wrong, all the while knowing the wrongness must be in himself.

But wrong or not, Guthrie couldn't let go. He drove around front, parked, and went into the store. He had to do some shopping, anyway. While he filled a tote basket with fruits and vegetables, which were, considering the way he felt, the only things that looked palatable, he examined his surroundings. By the time he'd finished and returned to his car, he had to admit that the store was, plain and simple, just a grocery store.

So he went home. There was nothing else to do, even though his mind was churning with confusion.

While he put up the groceries, he noticed the card that Tereba had stuck to the refrigerator door. Munching an apple, he went into his den, sat at the desk, pulled out his phone, and tried the number. The line was answered after several rings by a young female voice.

"Cindy?"

"Mary."

"This is Guthrie."

"Of course."

"I came by for a visit, but I must have gone to the wrong place."

"You went to the right place," Mary said.

"But the red door wasn't there. Did someone paint it?"

"No. It just isn't there right now."

"Not there? What's that mean?"

"It's somewhere else." He could hear the shrug in her voice. Guthrie's brow wrinkled, and he shook his head.

"You mean someone removed it?"

"Something like that."

"But I didn't see the door that was put up in its place."

"There is no door in its place," she said. "There is only a wall. Look, you'll just have to trust Master Tereba. The door will be there when you need it."

"But if it's not there, how...?"

"Have faith, Mr. Guthrie. Goodbye." The phone clicked.

Guthrie laid his phone on the desk and settled back in his chair. For a long time, he just sat there, staring at the blank computer screen, mulling over Carla's response, the vanishing door, the case's bewildering complications, and most of all, his own tremendous ignorance and apparently growing insanity.

Around five, the phone rang.

"This is Corbin Ingram." The man's voice was as cold as his eyes. "I work for Mr. Benton Egan."

"I remember."

"Mr. Egan would like to see you."

"When?"

"Now."

"I wouldn't have thought that Mr. Egan worked this late."

"Mr. Egan is always working."

"Look, it's been a long day...."

"Mr. Egan insists."

In other words, Guthrie realized, come voluntarily or have the Ravens come for him.

"The same place you brought me the last time?"

"Mr. Egan is at home. He would prefer to meet you there." Ingram gave Guthrie the address.

18

EGAN LIVED LESS THAN A mile from the Harveys. Guthrie found the house easily enough. It was on a winding lane that swung down a gentle incline into an area heavily shaded with ancient spreading oaks. The quiet cool and heavy hedges masking the homes here were a far cry from the nakedly sunlit yards of the mansions of the Harveys and their neighbors. An eight-foot brick wall lurked behind Egan's hedge, and the entrance to his narrow asphalt driveway was a mechanically operated wrought-iron gate, now open. A call box affixed to the wall suggested Guthrie announce himself, but he ignored it as he steered into the drive. The open gate was invitation enough, and the pair of surveillance cameras set in metal housings high on the wall on either side of the gate indicated that a call would have belabored the obvious, anyway.

Once past the gate, he cruised down a long drive that curved across grounds as large as a good-sized city park, toward a house that seemed impossibly far away. The tract was so thickly arched with oaks that the earth lost even a dappling of the late afternoon sunlight. The light diminished so dramatically, in fact, that even its quality seemed altered, and Guthrie had to resist the temptation to switch on his headlights.

As he neared the house, the pavement dipped noticeably, and he surmised Egan's property must back up to Buffalo Bayou. Only in close proximity to one of the half-dozen bayous lacing the city does the coastal prairie upon which Houston sits assume any texture. Buffalo Bayou, the city's major watercourse, winds in from the western suburbs, slides between River Oaks and huge, wooded Memorial Park, skirts the north side of downtown, then becomes the Houston Ship Channel before emptying into Galveston Bay forty miles to the southeast.

Here, though, west of downtown, with River Oaks on one side and Memorial Park on the other, Buffalo Bayou was as scenic as it ever got, and about as close to its pristine condition as it would ever be again. Early in their marriage, Guthrie and Alice used to walk Memorial Park's numerous trails when the weather wasn't too hot or the ground too wet. They liked to hike all the way down to the bayou, where the trees and thick underbrush grew close to the edge of the muddy banks. The stream, typically sluggish and murky green in dry weather, would swell to a dangerously turbulent, muddy flood during Houston's frequent torrential downpours.

The closer Guthrie approached the house, the more he felt the water-borne coolness in the air beneath the oaks. He bet there was a hell of a mosquito problem around here in the summer, but that wouldn't matter in the house, where even dust mites would fear to tread.

He parked the Honda behind Ingram's midnight-blue Mercedes, which in turn was behind a silver Porsche and a brand-new pastel green Chevy cargo van. The familiar white shield and medieval "R" of the Rampart logo was painted on the van's doors, just above the letters that spelled out the company name for those not in the know.

Guthrie got out and approached the front door, but he didn't have a chance to ring the bell. The door opened abruptly as he stepped into the entryway, and he found himself stabbed by Ingram's gray eyes, which seemed even less organic than before.

Stanton, the blond bull who'd driven the midnight-blue Mercedes, stood in the hall. He was dressed, like Ingram, in a simple dark suit, and his cropped hair looked almost white beneath the hall light. The first time Guthrie had seen him, he'd been sitting behind the wheel of the Mercedes. Now that he was standing, Guthrie could tell he was shorter than Ingram by several inches but outweighed him by fifty pounds of beef that more than made up for the lost height. Stanton's hands were casually grasped behind his back, and Guthrie would've bet a pistol was gripped in one of them. He tried not to act too interested in either of the guards or the Picasso lithograph on the entryway's wall.

"This way," Ingram said.

Leaving Stanton at the door, Ingram led Guthrie through the house. In his casual clothes, Guthrie felt like a cartoon character let loose on the pages of *Architectural Digest*. He wondered if Egan wore business attire even when lounging around watching TV. He'd have to in order to feel at home. That's what bugged Guthrie about a house like this. It would look really great on the pages of some glossy architectural magazine, but it would be impossible to live in comfortably. He couldn't imagine a recliner chair existing here, or even a hassock on which to prop tired dogs after a weary day. Maybe there were no weary days in this house.

After what seemed like a hundred yards, Ingram ushered Guthrie into a spacious office. The office didn't look exactly like Egan's office at work, but it was close enough that even a mediocre interior decorator would have had no trouble determining Egan's taste.

Egan didn't bother to get up from behind the big mahogany desk. Sure enough, he was wearing a suit.

"Have a seat," he said as Ingram made a silent exit.

Egan watched Guthrie take the chair in front of the desk but didn't give him time to get comfortable.

"You haven't reported to me, Guthrie."

"I've been busy."

"Very. You seem to be raising a bit of dust with this case."

"House cleaning tends to do that," Guthrie replied.

"The question is, have you removed any of the dust, or are you simply redistributing it and clouding the air in the process?"

"The Harveys dropped by last night to ask the same question. I told them I was making progress. They didn't tell you?"

Egan's expression didn't change, but a definite chill came into the air. Guthrie didn't think it was from the air conditioning.

"I'd prefer you report your findings to me rather than the Harveys. I am the one footing the bill."

"They cornered me. I didn't want to be impolite."

Egan snorted.

"I hardly think they'd have noticed," he said. "Or cared if they had."

"I'm not so sure. Lloyd's pretty practiced at it."

Egan's chuckle sounded almost human.

"He is, at that. But then so are most people in his line of business. That's the irony."

"What is his line of business?"

"They didn't tell you? No, I suppose they wouldn't. They're that kind of people."

"You didn't tell me, either."

At Guthrie's jibe, Egan leaned back in his chair, a cool expression smoothing his brow.

"Public relations and advertising, Guthrie. That's the Harveys' line of business." His voice held more than a trace of a sneer.

"You don't like advertising and PR?"

Egan stared for a long moment before answering. Whatever he was thinking didn't show through his hard exterior.

"I am not a fan of the Harveys' trade, and I avoid it whenever possible. Look around, Guthrie. You won't find a television. Television is an instrument which removes one from the immediacy of reality. It is also the prime tool of people like the Harveys. I prefer a more direct approach to life. Advertising and PR are so inherently devious and unprincipled. Like the law. In each, truth is perception rather than fact, expediency instead of a universal value."

"You don't believe in the law?"

Egan laughed again, and this time it rang more pleasantly.

"I make my living by it," he said, "But I trust the laws of nature more. They are so much more definite and inarguable. The claws of a tiger need no hype to convince one of their efficiency, nor can they be regulated, bought, or cheated."

"Something's gonna get you, eventually," Guthrie said. "The jungle itself if nothing else. Aren't you wondering what made me suspicious of the dinner guests?"

"Did the Harveys imply that they suspect one of the dinner guests?" Egan didn't seem surprised at Guthrie's sudden change in tack, but his quiet question in return contained a piercing quality that nearly made Guthrie wince.

"Not at all. I implied it, and when I did, they stressed the improbability that any of the guests might have been involved in any way."

"And yet you are suspicious enough to make inquiries on your own."

"On your behalf," Guthrie reminded him.

"Perhaps I should terminate your contract."

"I don't think you want to do that. You paid me for two weeks' work up front, and I've only been on the job half that. Besides, there's my detecting test." Guthrie showed some teeth of his own. "You wouldn't want me to fail because you didn't give me sufficient time."

"Yes." Egan smiled thinly. "That. But even if I do terminate your employment, you haven't lost anything."

"I'll have lost my finder's fee," Guthrie said. "And you'll have lost the head. What a pity. I was just about to recover it, too."

Egan didn't speak, but merely leaned back, tented his hands in front of him, and waited.

"Let's get back to the dinner party," Guthrie said. "That's when the sculpture was taken."

"It was an excellent time, with everyone out of the house," Egan agreed.

"And who would have known that everyone would be gone? Let's see." Guthrie counted off on his fingers. "There were the victims themselves. And Barbara Sidell. I've talked to her, and she was pretty revealing, though not about the theft." Egan chuckled at that, and Guthrie went on. "And you were there, of course. And we can't forget Martin Hastings. But then, he's not saying too much these days."

"I heard about Martin. Most unfortunate."

"That's putting it euphemistically."

"You discovered the body. He was killed by some sort of animal, wasn't he?"

"By several hundred, I'd say," Guthrie replied, remembering all too clearly the raw skeleton on the blood-stained white carpet. "You know, I find it curious that I mentioned to the Harveys that the thief might have worked for the company that built their safe, and the next morning Hastings is dead."

"Why should that be curious?"

"Hastings was CEO of Vulcan, wasn't he?"

"You have been raising a cloud of dust. Or is it a smoke screen?"

"Were you ever interested in acquiring the sculpture for yourself?"

Egan carefully perused Guthrie then leaned forward and said, "That took some nerve. Maybe that's what I see in you. You came into my office looking like a raggedy house cat, but underneath I sensed a tiger."

"So you aren't interested in the head?"

"Certainly rare and interesting, but I'm afraid not to my taste. I prefer paintings." The expensive knickknacks on the surrounding bookshelves shouted *liar*. Guthrie didn't let it show he'd heard, but maybe Egan had, for he went on with a too-casual wave of his hand, "I really haven't much personal interest in art aside from the fact it lends a certain character to life. Bare walls are tedious." He shrugged. "And art is a good investment." The deadly smile cracked his face once more. "If it is acquired legally."

"The lack of legality obviously doesn't bother some people. Besides, someone out there is interested in owning the head."

Egan's eyes sharpened.

"Others have inquired into your investigation?"

Oh, shit, Guthrie winced. He didn't want to drag Tereba's name into the conversation.

"I mean the thief. And the person he stole the head for."

"Why do you suspect he didn't just steal the head for himself?"

"The rest of the Harveys' art was untouched, though far more accessible."

"Yes." Egan nodded thoughtfully. "I see what you mean. And Martin? You suspect him?"

"Could be. But he didn't pull off the theft."

"Another man? The elusive Mark. Batten?"

"If you knew that, why did you hire me?"

"I didn't know until you found out. But really, Guthrie. If you think you can find it now, you must be dreaming. I've followed your progress, even if you haven't bothered reporting in. You think it was this delivery man? Batten? Perhaps, but that trail's gone stone cold."

"Let's call it lukewarm."

"You've located him?" For once, there was a gleam of real interest in Egan's eyes. Or was the interest feral?

"Not yet," Guthrie admitted, "But I know how to find him. I should have him cornered in a day or two."

"It would be much simpler if you just told me."

"Might be," Guthrie said. "But aside from the fact that I don't yet know his exact whereabouts, what about my extra fee for recovery?"

"All right," Egan conceded. "If you can find it, you'll have earned the fee. But one thing, Guthrie. After you locate the head, bring it to me immediately."

"What about the Harveys?"

"The Harveys will get what's theirs. I'll see to that." Egan certainly looked like he meant it. "Good-bye, Guthrie."

"Good-bye," Guthrie said. He rose and opened the door, when Egan stopped him.

"By the way, Guthrie. Have you talked to Barbara?"

"Sidell? Not since the other day. Why?"

"Apparently she received a phone call early yesterday evening, after which she went out hurriedly and never came back."

"You think I made the call?"

"I think not."

"Who, then?"

Egan shrugged. "Who can say?"

Guthrie went into the hall. It was empty as he started back toward the front entrance, but he walked only twenty paces before Ingram slid around the corner ahead. He waited for Guthrie to reach him then, with a smooth stride, led Guthrie to the entryway. Stanton was still there. Guthrie expected him to open the door to release Guthrie from the stifling atmosphere in the house, but the big man didn't do that, Instead, he edged Guthrie up against the wall.

"I think he knows more than he's telling," Stanton growled, apparently to Ingram, though he stared directly and belligerently at Guthrie. His eyes were like dim, deep pools without ripples to disturb the view of a large, writhing shadow lurking near their common bottom.

"I don't think Mr. Egan would appreciate...."

"Mr. Egan isn't concerned with your welfare, dick," Ingram spat, grabbing Guthrie's upper arm in an iron grip. "He hired you for a job. I'm just here to remind you that I'm not as polite as he is. You do what you're told, or we'll make certain you never do anything else."

He squeezed Guthrie's arm hard, expertly digging his thumb into the space between Guthrie's muscles, deep into the nerves. It should have hurt like hell, but suddenly the tingling vibration that had been in Guthrie's gut for the last couple of days flared, twanging leaden tones through his torso and limbs. As Ingram twisted, all Guthrie felt was a dull buzzing less painful than a heartache on a distant wind. For once, Ingram's steely eyes showed something more lively than blankness and quick death. They bore puzzlement that Guthrie wasn't crouching in sudden pain, and in that moment, his grip loosened just enough for Guthrie to wrench out of it.

As he pulled free, Stanton's thick fingers reached up with unexpected quickness and fastened around his neck. Guthrie found himself shoved up against the wall, and breathing suddenly became almost impossible. The blond leaned close.

"I eat a punk shit like you for breakfast and still come away hungry."

"You should brush your teeth more often, then," Guthrie managed to squeeze out of his constricted throat.

The shadow at the bottom of the blond's eyes writhed, muddying the water. The hand around Guthrie's throat constricted, and the other whipped up and cuffed Guthrie across the face, once, twice, three....

"That's enough."

Guthrie's vision cleared enough for him to see Egan step into the entryway. Stanton reluctantly released Guthrie, who gasped and managed to sag against the wall instead of slumping to the floor.

"I hope we're clear on who's in charge," Egan said. "Bring the sculpture to me the moment you find it."

Ingram opened the door, and Stanton shoved Guthrie through.

"Remember, Guthrie," Egan said. "The price of success is a fat paycheck. The price of failure is...well, let's just say it's Mr. Stanton here." He indicated the blond.

Guthrie had no reply, and Stanton shut the door.

Guthrie got in the Honda and drove off. Even though the Ravens were back at Egan's house, behind the closed door, Guthrie could feel their eyes on his back all the way to the gate. And maybe a little beyond.

19

GUTHRIE ROSE THE NEXT MORNING, squeezed a pitcher of fresh orange juice, poured himself a glassful, and took a swallow. Carrying the glass into his study, he sat down at his computer. He'd been threatened, bullied, overwhelmed, and even seduced, and he was tired of all the games, right across the board, from Egan's abusive power to the Harveys' manipulative chic, from Hastings' threats to Sidell's contagious seductions. The whole lot of them exuded the kind of nastiness Guthrie associated with a bundle of snakes, entwined and coldly repellent. It was time he investigated them as well as investigating for them.

He opened his connection to police records and began running checks on everyone associated with the case. By the time he'd finished with local, state, and federal records, plus a look at company financial statements and corporate reports he found on the internet, it was nearly dinnertime, and he'd come up with a hell of a lot worse than motor vehicle violations. While he ate, he thought over what he'd discovered.

As Egan had mentioned, Lloyd and Carla Harvey owned an advertising and public relations firm. Harvey Communications was one of the largest in the city. Or the state. They even handled national and international accounts. The latter were mostly European, but a few hailed from Asia and Africa.

Their ages surprised Guthrie—Lloyd and Carla were a little more well-preserved than he'd given them credit for. That made him even more wary than he already was. Age confers experience, and for people like the Harveys, experience added deception and danger to the equation. They'd been married nearly thirty years. Neither had been born to wealth, apparently, but they'd been mighty busy accumulating it. Although most of their careers had been spent in the employ of others, about twelve years ago, they'd bought out a local company called Jandl Public Relations, renamed the firm Harvey Communications, and quickly garnered several major local accounts. Since then business had boomed.

"Bad," Guthrie muttered as he spread Ben Egan's info across the desk. Egan was a heavy hitter who'd gotten his start as an Army Ranger. After four stints in the service, two as an MP, he seemed to have simply drifted into security work, hiring on as a bodyguard for a small Houston-based security company. Six years of field work led inexplicably to a partnership in the firm. Four years later, at the sudden but not untimely death of his senior partner, the partnership blossomed into full ownership. He changed the name to Rampart Security and, as of this year, had a decade and hundreds of millions of dollars in contracts under his belt.

Egan was dangerous, no doubt about it. And so were the Ravens. Corbin Ingram had been with Egan almost from the beginning of Egan's reign as sole ruler of his domain, serving as Egan's personal aide and chief enforcer. He was fifteen years younger than his boss, and probably fifteen times as deadly, in a personal context, at least. Military training, marksmanship, martial arts—a well-rounded trio to which one might plausibly add murder, particularly considering the several blank years in his military record following his participation in actions in the Middle East.

Murder not only was plausible for Craig Stanton, it was an established fact. Guthrie quickly recognized the face in the mug shot, but Stanton had put on a lot of solid muscle since his single arrest five years earlier. He'd been an Ohio boy who, on attaining his majority, gravitated to a neo-Nazi outfit that quickly realized the youth's repressed potential. Four years of paramilitary training in central Idaho taught him the tools of the trade. At last, perhaps to prove to himself the efficacy of his training, or maybe just unable to suppress a boyish urge for a good time, he practiced his skills on a black couple who were headed from Yellowstone National Park to Vancouver. Stanton was smart enough to finish the job without any witnesses but dumb enough to try to use the victims' Visa card at an ATM machine.

He claimed he found the wallet and was acquitted for lack of evidence, but that marked the end of his paramilitary career. Apparently afraid he might blab about their installation and organization, the neo-Nazis sent a five-man hit squad after him. How he hooked up with Ingram wasn't clear, but the five men were later discovered shot to hell and back in a deserted farmhouse in Oklahoma, while Stanton found a perfect alibi in Ingram, who claimed Stanton was in Houston at the time of the massacre.

Guthrie still didn't know why the girls had called them the Ravens, and the report didn't mention the word, but he was beginning to get the picture. Birds of death.

Barbara Sidell's dossier aptly demonstrated the flip-flop characteristics possessed by this bunch. She was as rich as Egan or the Harveys, but her wealth didn't come from death and destruction or from institutionalized scamming. It came from pulchritude. Why wasn't Guthrie surprised? She owned a major interest in a clothing manufacturing company and was sole owner of a small, exclusive chain of fashionable clothing stores catering to well-to-do women. She also operated a string of boutiques offering clothing those well-to-do women wouldn't be caught dead in. Outside their own bedrooms, that is. If Fredericks of Hollywood smacked of trash, and Victoria's Secret was upscale, Sidell's Cypria was exclusive enough most people probably had never heard of it. Guthrie hadn't.

But wait a minute. Maybe he had. The name did sound familiar. He picked at the edges of the vague memory, but in the end couldn't recall. He gave up and turned back to the dossier, only to see that she also owned Armin's Liquors. But there was an even greater puzzler.

Sidell was a three-time loser on convictions for prostitution.

A woman who had Sidell's kind of money didn't need to charge, and Guthrie's personal experience indicated she was willing enough to give it away if it suited her ends. Or, to be more accurate, her price hadn't involved cash. But after Guthrie checked her financial records he saw the convictions were all eight to ten years before, prior to the start of her successful businesses.

Guthrie knew Sidell must have been broke at the time of the arrests because she'd resorted to a public defender in all three cases, and he couldn't help but question how a down-and-out hooker had begun a multimillion dollar clothing operation without capital. It would be a tough business to break into even if one found substantial financial backing. Further reading revealed a fourth arrest resulting in acquittal, and that time, she'd had her own lawyer. Obviously she'd begun to accumulate funds of some sort. Or maybe she'd lucked into a sugar daddy.

Guthrie took a long gander at the mug shots that accompanied her sheet and noted that the years had been kind to her in more ways than financially. She looked ten years older in the photos. Probably she'd had plastic surgery since her ship had come in, which made him wonder why she'd done nothing about that ugly thumb of hers. The thought made him glance at her fingerprints. What would a print of that thumb look like? Oddly, it looked as normal as the rest of the prints.

Then there was the late Martin Hastings. If not cut from the same cloth as Egan, Hastings had come from the same loom. It seemed that his involvement in Vulcan Armor was more hobby than serious enterprise. He'd made his real money as a munitions supplier whose peripheral involvement in illicit arms deals in trouble spots around the world were just the warp of his weave. Hastings's company supplied weapons to various right-wing organizations and armies around the world. Guthrie wondered if that included neo-Nazi paramilitary training camps in Idaho. There also were hints that he equipped private armies in Brazil who ensured that native tribes wouldn't complain about attrition of their areas of rain forest by making certain there were no natives left to complain.

If some money possessed a bad odor, Hastings was a rich dead skunk. The financial sheet showed his ties to Egan were closer than ideological. The two were partners in a chemical company that manufactured explosives, and Egan was a major shareholder in Vulcan.

Wait, he thought, something jogging his memory. He returned to his desk and went back to the Vulcan annual report, where something caught his eye. It was the logo discreetly printed on the back—Harvey Communications. Guthrie pulled out the file on the Harveys' company, scanned the extensive client list, and saw that Harvey Communications handled not only Vulcan's advertising and PR but also that of the companies owned by Sidell and, surprise, Egan and Hastings. So much for Egan's protestations of mistrust for the Harveys and their line of business.

A tangled web, Guthrie sighed, as he stared at the small mountain of paper that had accumulated on his desk. He leaned back in his chair, and closed his eyes. He'd thought it might be useful to know a little about his employers, but all this was more than he'd bargained for, and none of it made him feel any more secure.

The one thing Guthrie did know for sure was that this case was stickier than simply recovering a missing art object. If only a part of what he'd learned from Tereba and other sources was true, he could forget any recovery fee. The reality was that he had to find the sculpture simply to protect himself. To survive. It was as simple as that. And to accomplish that vital goal, he needed to put aside everything but the task at hand and he had to play it ultra straight, in particular with Egan, if he didn't want to find the Ravens tap, tap, tapping at his door some dark and dreary night.

There are worse things than ravens, though, he thought, remembering Hastings and the thousands of tiny red footprints.

Guthrie had started with a few questions, and the list had multiplied geometrically, transforming a simple case of retrieval into a fight for survival. And worse than his need to know the answers was that he was curious. Maybe deadly curious, which made it seem all the more like he was rushing headlong in the dark toward a precipice he knew lay just a few steps ahead.

But what could he do? He was naturally curious. That's what always made him want to be a detective, what made him become a cop and ask questions and dig dirt. He wanted answers. Guthrie wasn't going to pretend to analyze his own reasons for wanting those answers or give some song and dance about the search for truth and justice. Probably the real answers had nothing to do with those vaunted concepts. But whatever the reasons might be, damn it, Guthrie was a detective. He had to be because he'd lived through two empty years of creeping decay and nothing was left but the curiosity. Nothing was important except the curiosity.

But where had that curiosity left him?

Not much of anywhere, he realized. All he had was Travis's apparently uninhabited house, some odd impressions, some revealing dossiers, and not much else. He'd been in the house, and it was empty; the impressions had taken him nowhere; and the dossiers, while revealing on one level, were ciphers on another. Questions piled on top of questions, and it seemed he had no way to find any of the answers he needed, nowhere to turn. Nowhere but the pile of dossiers. So he picked through the pile and looked again. And looked some more.

What did these people have in common beyond financial connections? Those weren't, in themselves, overtly suspicious. Lloyd and Carla had said the party guests were business associates. Even so, instinct told Guthrie the connections went deeper than financial ties and weekly attendance at one of their homes every Saturday night. After all, you don't spend that much time around people who aren't your friends, and the party guests certainly didn't seem to like each other all that much. Even Egan admitted as much. So, if there was a more powerful connection, it must matter since it wasn't apparent on the surface.

What was that name Tereba had called the group?

Zeroth.

Guthrie started looking. The first reference he found was in the lineage of ownership of Radcliffe Antiquaries. William Mason had told Guthrie that he'd bought the shop from Radcliffe, but that wasn't strictly true. He'd bought it from a closely-held financial investments corporation called Zeroth Holdings, Inc. And, oddly enough, Radcliffe himself had bought the firm from Zeroth in 1965. Prior to that, the shop had been called Pearce Fine Arts and Antiques, and a Ronald Pearce had acquired it from a company called Zeroth Title Company in 1956. That was as far back as Guthrie could trace the ownership of Mason's shop to Zeroth, but already the name was cropping up.

He went back to the Harveys' records and, sure enough, after a bit of probing, he learned that when they'd bought Jandl Public Relations and turned it into Harvey Communications, Zeroth Holdings had been the intermediary and maybe even had capitalized the venture.

Guthrie checked the phone books, but Zeroth wasn't listed, so he turned back to the computer. By midnight, he'd connected with databases and government records, and he finally thought he was on the track of something. Not only were Sidell and the Harveys represented by Zeroth Holdings, so were Egan and Hastings. The company headquarters was in a building downtown.

An Avery Prentice was listed as chairman and CEO. Guthrie remembered the name from his conversations with Tereba. Apparently Prentice had founded the company in 1955. Pearce Fine Arts had been his first acquisition. In addition to the companies Guthrie already knew about, Zeroth's holdings ranged from real estate and construction to energy, medical supplies, and shipping and trucking. It seemed there wasn't a pie Zeroth didn't have its collective fingers in.

Guthrie shook his head, stared at the myriad papers strewing his desk, and groaned. Did corruption always have to involve the wealthy and powerful? The answer came just as quickly. As a street cop, Guthrie had seen plenty of gutter-level corruption. It ran the gamut of theft, rape, murder, drug addiction, and child and spousal abuse to perversions Guthrie wasn't comfortable contemplating. It left ugly legacies, shattered lives, and wounds that would never heal, but there was a certain comfort knowing that only rarely did low-level corruption reach beyond a limited radius of influence. The immediate victims suffered, and so did their families and friends, but they could be numbered. Guthrie couldn't excuse the acts or forget the victims, but at least he could understand. There was something human about the dirt in the street, something born of passion and thwarted desire, of need and deprivation.

He supposed, though, that he could also comprehend the cold calculation of Zeroth as it methodically and ruthlessly utilized the resources of the many companies it owned to increase its holdings and power. It was, as Egan termed it, the black hole theory of economics in action. There no longer was room for small stakes; the world was being portioned out among big players with ample resources and carefully chosen allies. Big players played big games. That was why an organization like Zeroth made perfect sense. There was safety in numbers, and strength, and there were a lot more hands available to take in and manipulate the swag. More power. Why would they settle for less?

Oddly, Zeroth's size made its predilection for secrecy all the more puzzling. How can one acquire that much and still remain unknown? Or at least unrecognized. And why would it need enforcement of the caliber of Egan and his Ravens? The answer was simple enough. A particular Zeroth tactic was capitalizing on the weakness of small companies struggling to find niches in the gaps left by the large corporations. In decades past, organized crime would have used threats and violence to eat up small businesses in its path; in the new corporate age, Zeroth, with the same ends in mind, had adopted similar methods. There had been investigations into swindle, extortion, pressured buyouts, and political corruption, but none of it had ever been tied to the parent company. It seemed that Zeroth's low-key approach and its diversity—spread as it was among six individuals—managed to diffuse any pointed scrutiny, and the investigations had never resulted in charges being filed. Like the mobs, Zeroth wielded political influence as well as a heavy hand, but unlike the mobsters, its members fastidiously paid their taxes.

Guthrie had learned about Zeroth only because Tereba had put him on the track, and he didn't think that anyone not deliberately pointed in the right direction could ever connect the people involved with their various nefarious schemes. But thanks to Tereba's hint, Guthrie knew, and while that knowledge didn't make him feel any safer, it did give him some leverage.

But he still didn't know why the sculpture mattered so much. Why was a financial management company like Zeroth so interested in it and anxious to get it back? What secret powerful enough to sway a hidden empire could lurk behind those immobile features and striking eyes? Tereba called the head a psychic battery, but for Guthrie, that was less an answer than it was another question that he couldn't answer.

A far more likely scenario occurred to Guthrie. Though stealing the sculpture may have been Travis's objective, perhaps recovering the sculpture was incidental to Zeroth. Maybe it was really Travis's head they were after. Whether or not Hastings had put Travis up to the theft, Travis had infiltrated Zeroth deeply enough to have enabled him to steal something it valued. He might have discovered even more, as Guthrie had. That made Travis dangerous to them, and they'd want him disposed of. And there couldn't be a better method than hiring some poor slob nobody would miss to track him down. Once Guthrie found Travis, the Ravens would come for both of them. It made perfect sense. Guthrie was a disposable napkin being used to wipe up a spill.

At last, he switched off his computer, but for a long time, he just sat there, staring at the blank screen. Somehow it was comforting, knowing that all those dancing, shimmering, confounding pixels were at rest. Finally acknowledging that was what he needed himself, he went to the bedroom, undressed, and lay down. But tired as he was, sleep didn't come easily. His day of digging on Zeroth had made Guthrie feel like an insignificant pest crawling the impenetrable hide of a beast whose true dimensions were too large to discover.

He needed more than a map to find the borders of Zeroth. He needed an atlas.

20

THE NEXT DAY WAS SUNDAY, but Guthrie couldn't afford to rest. Not that he didn't want to stay in bed. He'd slept fitfully, his dreams filled with massive, dark architecture inhabited by the memory of smoke. He didn't want to believe Tereba's claim that he was a walking dead man, but he strongly suspected that someone—maybe the old man himself—had done something to him that was taking him in small but implacable steps toward death. There had been that terrible wrenching inside when Tereba had twisted his palm into his guts. Or maybe the old man had poisoned that tea Guthrie'd drunk. He certainly had the means with all those herbs in the apothecary shop.

The slightly vibrating aching in his guts constantly suffused his body and strung his nerves, and and he felt like crap. His appetite had dwindled to almost nothing, and he'd lost the slight paunch he'd carried just a week earlier. The clothes he wore no longer smelled of body odor; they just got dirty like old rags left outdoors. And though the weather was balmy, he was perpetually cold. But the chill he felt did not bring a shiver, for it seemed to emanate from his own bones.

Because a hot bath did relieve some of the symptoms, he began to envision himself a cold-blooded reptile whose metabolism and mobility depended as much on external heat sources as on anything within. But the heat he absorbed dissipated all too quickly, leaving him numb and heavy, as if the final dregs of mortality that survived the spirit's departure consciously sought a return to the soil.

He wasn't stiff or clumsy, and for that he was thankful—at least rigor mortis was polite enough to wait for consciousness to vacate. Nor had he lost his strength or stamina, and he seemed to have become somewhat impervious to pain. But mostly he just felt nebulous and attenuated, as if his connections to tangible reality were wisps of dissipating mists. If he reached out mentally to grasp them and use them to draw in his fading sense of self, the wisps merely dissolved between the fingers of his thought and were gone, leaving him even more dissociated.

When life has erected impossible odds against a person, at least he can slink back into a safe and familiar place and pretend that, for once, the odds have magically tilted in his favor. For Guthrie, ironically, that meant going back to where he'd had the most trouble—Travis's house —because that was where he'd also had the most success.

Guthrie grabbed an apple and headed for the door. In a few minutes, he was on the freeway, driving toward Bellaire. He had his tail again, or another car just like it. This driver, though, was more sophisticated. Guthrie only managed to lose him by spending an extra half hour on surface roads weaving in and out of traffic and taking obscure shortcuts he'd learned as a cop.

Finally, the pastel green Chevy on his tail vanished. At least Guthrie thought it did, though as he steered with greater purpose toward Travis's house, he had an itchy sensation that he was still being watched. But maybe it was just the nagging of his bad hip. It was twitching like it always did when a change in the weather was imminent—his personal barometer, infallible and always present. The weather on the radio corroborated the testimony of his hip, predicting thunderstorms.

He arrived without spotting anyone following, so he was feeling pretty comfortable as he pulled into the parking lot of the bar across South Rice from Travis's and parked where he could see down the driveway. He switched off the car, hunkered down in the seat, and stared at the dull red house crouching beneath the huge oaks. Travis had to come home sooner or later.

Didn't he?

Not long after Guthrie began watching, a man strolled down the sidewalk, and his footsteps quickened as he passed the hedge. The change was almost too subtle for Guthrie to catch, but he was scrutinizing the place and everything about it extra carefully, remembering the jolting fear he'd felt the first time he'd approached the house and the numb terror with which he'd escaped it the second time. Did the man realize he'd sped up, or had he rationalized his accelerated pace?

Soon afterwards, two boys on bicycles steered their vehicles off the sidewalk, into the street, at the driveway of the house just before Travis's, then back onto the sidewalk one house beyond. Playful antics or obscure response? The mail carrier came. She visibly balked and took a deep breath before hurrying through the driveway gap. Was she apprehensive or just tired from her rounds? She reappeared a moment later, walking fast. Was she was running late or just running?

Possibly, Guthrie thought. Something—the heavy hedge, the looming oaks, the house itself—appeared to have a strange effect on everyone. He thought about what he'd experienced on his first two visits to the house and had to admit it had been real and agonizingly personal. But had it been realistic? It wasn't as if the negative memories engendered by the attacks were such fresh wounds that they could easily be peeled open in all their gory glory. Those things happened two years ago or more. Sure they still hurt, but the pain was a dull ache now, not flaring agony.

The longer he sat and studied the house and witnessed the subtle but unmistakable reactions of everyone who went by it, the more it seemed that the house somehow created anxiety. Maybe it worked on everyone like it had on him, by magnifying fears and sorrows already present. He didn't know. Nor did he want to admit that, without a doubt, the whole yard felt like it contained an invisible caged beast. But it did. At last Mary and Cindy's assertion that Travis had a watchdog made sense. Something in there certainly had bit hard into Guthrie during his first two visits, just as it nipped at the heels of anyone who came close.

Guthrie recalled the Old Master's Talisman carved into Tereba's red door. Was that how such things worked—a curious drawing on the door bringing a protective force to live around the house and safeguard it from those who would do the owner ill? Guthrie wondered if the thing in Travis's yard possessed a form that he just couldn't see or if it was an amorphous aura squatting over the property like a miasmic fog. He wasn't sure he wanted to know, especially because he bore a similar talisman tattooed into his flesh.

One thing he did know, though, crazy or not, was that he could no longer deny that something beyond his ken was going on. He still couldn't accept all of Tereba's claims at face value, but the inexplicable things that had been happening to him had no rational explanation.

He thought back to Tereba's undeniable authority and power, Barbara Sidell's overpowering sexual magnetism, and a man attacked and eaten alive by rats. Nor could he shake the itchy feeling that he was constantly watched, even after he'd shaken the Rampart tails. And now, his own eyes had seen evidence that his experiences in Travis's yard were not simply personal aberrations.

His hand moved to his belt buckle as he thought of the talisman on the skin beneath. It was strong enough to protect him against the watchdog, but he couldn't shake the dismal thought that the invisible beast in Travis's yard was nothing compared to Zeroth. Even Tereba dared not confront the organization directly but was using Guthrie as his pawn. The trouble was, Guthrie was totally outclassed and outmaneuvered. And ashamed. Ashamed at the answer to the question: Why him? It wasn't pleasant to contemplate that he was cheap and sleazy enough; that he was dumb and expendable hurt more.

But not so dumb he hadn't discovered the existence of John Travis. Egan might have people on the payroll who could run Travis to ground and retrieve the sculpture. People willing to be more efficiently brutal than Guthrie. But not anyone who would ask the right questions or follow up the odd-ball lead tossed in his lap. For that they needed a detective, no matter how inexperienced, no matter how cheap and sleazy. Without Guthrie, no one aside from Martin Hastings would have known that Travis existed.

That fact might not have meant much to the rest of the world, but it gave Guthrie a sense of validation. The detective badge he'd so coveted while on the force would never be his, but discovery truly was in his blood. The realization brought a ray of hope—maybe he wasn't all that expendable, either.

Just as obviously, though, Zeroth hadn't expected him to ask the kinds of questions he was asking or make the connections he'd made. He'd been hired to find stolen property, not dig into the machinations of an exclusive and corrupt financial organization. Guthrie wasn't qualified to judge or understand all the implications of what he'd discovered. Hell, he couldn't even see all the implications. What he'd seen was a looming shadow, and nothing more—an intangible presence that not only permeated but ravished everything it touched.

Oh, Jesus, he thought. A conspiracy theory. I've become a conspiracy theorist! Was paranoia next? But like the fellow said, being paranoid doesn't mean they aren't out to get you. Aren't there conspiracies out there in the bright, lovely world? Real conspiracies big and small? Conspiracies to end relationships, to defraud, to commit robbery and murder. Conspiracies to gain political advantage and accumulate wealth, power, and control. Maybe a detective had to be a conspiracy theorist because the conspiracies really are out there waiting to be exposed. But Zeroth was a conspiracy a bit larger than Guthrie bargained for, and it might not unravel easily. In fact, the way things were going, Guthrie might grab onto this one wriggling thread that he believed could unravel the fabric of Zeroth, only to find that it was a strand of spider's web ensnaring him instead.

That image jolted Guthrie unpleasantly back to the present. He stared at the hedge across the street, vividly recalling how it had made slow death in the tangles so enticingly comfortable, so inevitably pure. He remembered Egan's job offer that promised Guthrie a secure niche in Zeroth. And he thought of Lloyd Harvey's boots made from the kind of snake that wrapped its victim in loose coils before squeezing out its life.

That was when he saw a silver Lexus pull into the driveway.

Guthrie blinked in disbelief as the SUV stopped just past the side door. A man got out and hurried into the house. Guthrie glanced at the photo he'd pilfered. It was unmistakably John Travis.

"You bastard," Guthrie snarled. He realized that he hadn't actually expected Travis to show. Instead, he'd come here to sit by the banks of the familiar in order to slip out of the stream of events that had so quickly become a flood. But the current refused to let him go. It still tugged his feet toward new territories downstream. He'd better get those feet moving before it was too late and he was sucked under. Better to kick out for shore, even if it was only a barren island inhabited by a thief.

21

AS GUTHRIE HURRIED ACROSS THE street, an exhilarating shock took hold of his nerves, and he felt like he was flying before the flood. He went to the same entrance Travis had used. From his previous visit to the house, he knew it led into the kitchen. Easing open the door, he slipped inside.

Travis wasn't in the room. Jumbled food half-filled a cardboard box on a counter, and cabinet doors hung awry. It appeared that Travis was in a hurry to pack and get out. Guthrie could hear him moving around in the bedroom, opening drawers and shuffling around in the closet. He went in that direction, padding down the short hallway to the "T" where it split to go to the two bedrooms. Peeking around the corner, he jerked his head back just as a flash of brown, swishing wickedly, crushed the drywall where his face had been.

Travis jumped around the corner, a baseball bat gripped in his hands, and came at Guthrie. He wasn't swinging the bat wildly or making any unnecessary moves in the confined hallway, and Guthrie backed away, keeping his distance. He wished he'd brought the .38 out of the car, but he hadn't.

"Wait a minute, Travis," Guthrie said as he backed into the kitchen. "Put that thing down. I just want to talk." He thought about trying to escape through the kitchen door, but he'd closed it, and in the seconds required to get it open, Travis would have ample opportunity to lay him out. Instead, Guthrie backed across the kitchen toward the dining room.

As Travis came into the brighter light of the kitchen, Guthrie began to think he might have some sort of chance to get out of this situation intact. He could tell it was Travis, but time or events had not been kind. The man facing Guthrie across the bat looked terrible—gaunt, pallid, and lifeless.

"Come on, Travis. I just want to talk."

But Travis wasn't in a talkative mood. The dining room left plenty of room to swing the weapon, and he came on fast.

Guthrie may not have been a kung fu expert like Wu, but what he knew stood him in good stead. He jumped away from Travis's two opening swings and ducked and swerved two more. By now, they'd waltzed through the dining room, and Guthrie retreated into the middle of the living room. Travis must have been getting frustrated or desperate because his next swing came overhand.

It was just the kind of move Guthrie was waiting for. He sidestepped to the left, grabbed Travis's moving right wrist with his right hand, slammed his left palm against Travis's extended upper arm, then pivoted sharply to the right. Travis lost his balance, swung around with the turn in a wide arc, and spun away when Guthrie let go at the end of the pivot.

To give Travis credit, he didn't drop the bat as he flailed wildly toward the armchair in his path and tumbled over it. But he was forced to let go when Guthrie ground a foot on his wrist and slugged him on the jaw. Before Travis could do more than gasp and open his eyes, Guthrie whipped a pair of handcuffs from his hip pocket, snapped them on the gaunt man's bony wrists, then straightened and stepped back.

"Don't get up," Guthrie warned as Travis rolled over and stared up at him. The man hadn't shaved in days, and the sour odor said he hadn't bathed, either.

"How'd you get in here?" Travis asked.

"You mean past the thing you have guarding your house?" Guthrie laughed. "Seems it likes its meat still alive."

Guthrie meant it as a joke, but Travis obviously didn't get it.

"Who are you?" he asked, but Guthrie had a question of his own.

"Where's the sculpture, Travis?"

"What sculpture?"

"The one you stole from Lloyd and Carla Harvey."

"What makes you think I did that?"

"People say the strangest things to a man they think is dead. Martin Hastings hired you to steal the sculpture for him. You do remember Martin Hastings, your boss at Vulcan Armor?"

Travis clammed up and averted his eyes. Guthrie picked up the bat and prodded him with it.

"Talk, you fuck. I may be dying, and if I am, you're the cause. I know you have the head, and I'm taking it back to the Harveys."

"He doesn't want to go back to the Harveys." Travis's voice was almost a whisper.

"What?"

"Fuck you."

Anger rose in Guthrie like gorge. He'd been pushed, coerced, and threatened. Maybe he'd even been killed. He'd had about as much as he could take, and it was all because of this greedy asshole on the floor in front of him. Now it was time for a little payback.

In a voice turned harsh, he said, "I'm getting it. The only question is what it costs you. How much of this place do I have to smash up before you start talking?" He raised the bat and threatened the Seeburg jukebox.

"You're a fool," Travis said. "You don't understand anything."

Guthrie just wanted to shake up Travis, to shock him into admission and revelation. But the man's expression of callous indifference made something break loose inside Guthrie like an awning ripped loose by a powerful wind and sent flapping across the terrain of his mind to wrap itself blindingly around the core of his reason. Guthrie couldn't really blame Travis's expression, but damn if he couldn't lay blame at his door. Guthrie had been dragged into this mess because of this bastard. It was all his fault. To hell if there were other factors raging inside Guthrie's own breast, things like frustration and fear mixed with ample portions of self-contempt and guilt. Right now, all Guthrie could feel was the desperation of a cornered animal thrashing toward the slightest hope of life.

When he took the first swing at the Seeburg, he thought he had control, thought he would only shatter the glass dome, and that would be enough. But this case and his circumstances had brought him to a point where self-control was an image without substance, an ideal unable to produce phenomenon. He had responsibility but no power, accountability but no authority, and necessity without hope.

As the blow shot cracked lightning across the glass dome, Guthrie's own brittle temper split. Black despair flooded through his mind, swirling with currents of rage, loathing, vindictiveness, and terror, washing everything rational from him. The bat in his hands was like a scepter of power, and Guthrie swung again and again, smashing at the Seeburg.

Smashing. Smashing....

For a timeless, almost ineffable span of pure consciousness he was aware of nothing but his oneness with the bat, the shattering of glass and plastic, the satisfying feel of thin metal bending under impact, and the exhilarating play of muscles charged with adrenaline. In his inner darkness, he rejoiced in the only power he now possessed, or that possessed him—power over another.

Gradually, light returned to Guthrie's mind, bringing with it awareness of sensations and images. The pounding of his own heart echoing inside him now that his rage was expended. The bat chipped and gouged in his white-knuckled hands. Travis on the floor beside a cheap, overturned armchair, lit by a wedge of afternoon light that edged between the heavy wooden shutters. A room filled with the material leavings of a twentieth century that had fled swiftly and clumsily into the twenty-first.

The Seeburg dead on the floor, weeping black tears for the shattered memories of music that would never play again.

Just as Guthrie was dead.

As the rage drained out of him, leaving emptiness, he knew it was true. He could feel his still-agitated heart pounding in his chest, but there was no reassurance in its gradually slowing thump. Some unknown but vital element of his being had vanished, leaving hollowness at his core. He'd managed to camouflage the symptoms from himself beneath a cloak of bitterness that repelled examination, but he'd instinctively known that he could not mask them from the world, so he'd hidden himself away in his crumbling house with his crumbling memories—little more than an automaton habituated to vacant and gradually ceasing motions.

He knew it was true because, in some indefinable way, he felt different than he once had, though apparently he'd paid so little attention to how that had been that he now found he was unable to describe it. But he remembered enough to know he did feel different.... No, it was, he had to admit, that he no longer felt. He claimed, even to himself, that he did, but he knew it wasn't true. Love and joy and hope had fled, leaving the dregs of hatred, longing, and despair, and even those were sere and brittle within him, stirred by the slightest breeze but ready to crumble entirely. Even what he'd thought of as pain was merely depleted exhaustion filled with the dust of pretense.

But if this hollowness was death, did life really have such little meaning that the spirit could depart so easily, leaving only a residue of absence and yet allow the flesh to remain malleable? Was life so infinitely delicate?

He shook his head. That was beyond him, but there was something that he still retained, even if he was dead. His frustrated desperation remained potently alive. He couldn't beat it to death with a bat any more effectively than he could a rain storm.

Brutally repressing the unnamed shame that wanted to well up from his gut, Guthrie turned on Travis, mangled bat in hands, muscles quaking with adrenaline.

"Talk, you mother fucker, or you're next."

Even Guthrie's shimmering fury could not mask the fact that Travis's dispassion had outlasted the destruction of the jukebox. Worse, the threat of death brought an odd light of desire to the man's face. It was the first expression of real feeling Guthrie had seen there.

"Yes." Travis said the word with total conviction. "I'm next."

He was prostrate, but he could lash out with his feet, and he did, catching Guthrie sharply on the shin. Bloating with rage, Guthrie raised the bat and stepped in.

Travis, eyes quivering with self-pity and longing, hissed, "Yes. Now. Yes."

The perverse appeal for death halted Guthrie before he could swing the bat. He stumbled back, panting, as Travis writhed on the floor.

"Do it! Do it! Please!"

Suddenly sickened by his own insanity and confounded by Travis's hunger for death, no matter how brutal, Guthrie threw the bat aside.

Travis burst into whimpering sobs, and Guthrie stood there, looking down at him, mind awash in confusion. What was this mad hatred for Travis? He didn't even know the man, but there it was, as naked and raw as the trembling in his limbs. Guthrie could thrash Travis all he wanted, wreak his home, abuse and humiliate him, and maybe even beat him to death, but none of it would provide one ounce of solution to the conundrum that Guthrie now realized twisted inside him like a Gordian knot of the soul.

Travis wasn't at fault for Guthrie's condition any more than Guthrie was at fault for the plight of the bum on the corner near his house. Yet Guthrie had transferred the rage of his frustrations to Travis just as he'd transferred his fear and guilt to the bum.

Guthrie couldn't let it go on. Lifting his arm, he brushed the spit flecking his lips onto his sleeve then hauled the still-whimpering Travis to the bedroom and cuffed him to the iron bed.

After a while, Travis's cries subsided, though he made no effort to wipe the tears from his eyes and cheeks. He just stared up at Guthrie, stoicism replacing the outburst of emotion.

"You look like shit, Travis. I look around this place and I wonder what's happened. You had it solid. I envied you. You were an interesting guy, you had things worth having. Hell, you had a life, man! Now look at you. When was the last time you had a bath and a good meal? You see yourself in the mirror lately?"

Travis burst into a gale of sardonic laughter that subsided as quickly and bitterly as it began.

"What do you know about any of it?" Travis said, so quietly Guthrie could barely hear him.

"Not much," Guthrie admitted. "But that doesn't mean I don't feel sorry for you."

"And you want to help me."

"I want the head."

"Tough luck. It's not here, and I'm not telling you a damn thing about it."

"You'll tell me."

"Not even if you torture me, kill me. Why don't you just leave? Unlock these," he rattled the cuffs, "and turn your back."

"Not a chance."

"Leave me alone. You can't do anything for me, and you can't do anything to me. I'm not giving you the bust. It's my only salvation."

"Look." Guthrie brushed his hair off his forehead and stared down at the man on the bed. "You're not thinking clearly. Something's got you screwed up. If I didn't know you better, I'd say you were strung out."

"You know me? Ha!" The laugh sounded like a cat spitting. "How the hell do you know me?"

"I know you're not really what I'm seeing here. Something's gone wrong."

Travis turned his face to the wall and made no reply.

"Come on, man, let me help you. We'll take the sculpture to the Harveys and...."

"Forget it."

"I'll share my reward money with you. Fifty-fifty. There's plenty for both of us."

The sardonic laugh barked out again, startling the air in the room.

"I have eternity in my grasp and you want me to sell it for an ounce of gold? Don't be a fool."

"I can't comprehend eternity, Travis. I told you before I was dead, and it's true. Let's just say I've been poisoned, and there's someone who'll give me the antidote if I bring the sculpture to him. If I don't, there's no hope for me."

"I'd trade your life for my eternity, any day."

"I'll remember you said that," Guthrie promised. "All right. I'll just have to find it on my own."

A brief search of Travis's pockets revealed a ring of keys. In addition to the house, office, and car keys, there was a pair of new-looking padlock keys.

The garage! Of course. The only place Guthrie hadn't looked.

Travis said nothing as Guthrie hurried out of the room. In seconds Guthrie emerged outside and went over to the garage. Sure enough, there was a padlock on it, though the lock didn't look especially new.

Guthrie bent over the lock, trying to fit one of the keys into it, but his trembling hands fumbled and couldn't make the key work.

He stopped, took a deep breath, and tried again. Just as he realized that the key wasn't going to fit no matter how steady his hands, a shadow loomed up behind him, wielding a baseball bat. Guthrie had just enough time to wonder how Travis had freed himself before the bat wiped away the question with a slash of darkness.

22

GUTHRIE WOKE UP WOOZY AND disoriented. He didn't know how long he'd been out, but it must have been a long while because night had crept over the city, leaving the driveway in darkness. Amazingly, he'd lain on the pavement in sight of the street for half the afternoon, and nobody had noticed. Chalk up one more to the power of Travis's watchdog.

He sat up, fighting a wave of dizziness and nausea, and touched the back of his head. A long lump oozed stickiness onto his fingers, and a stiff thickening along his shoulder explained why the bat hadn't crushed his skull. As he crouched to his feet, something jangled to the pavement. He had to go to his hands and knees to gropingly discover it was his handcuffs, his keys dangling from the lock. He stood again, and a few staggering moments brought him to the side door of the house. It was wide open.

Flipping the wall switch sent a sudden flare of light blasting into his eyes. A steady throb was spreading from the lump into the rest of his head. Cool water from the tap in the bathroom washed most of the blood out of his hair and soothed the pain if it didn't eliminate it. He helped himself to the aspirin bottle, wincing at his injured shoulder but thankful that it wasn't broken, then checked his watch. Just after eleven o'clock. Travis was long gone.

Guthrie went through the house. Travis had gotten loose by forcing apart the weaker rungs of the bedstead. The dresser drawers and closet were in disarray, and the box of food was gone from the kitchen. It looked like Travis planned to be away from home for a while.

But Guthrie did find something of interest. In the living room, a considerable pile of unopened mail lay in a drift beneath the mail slot.

More because it offered the excuse to sit down than out of any real expectations he'd discover anything useful, he scooped up the envelopes, took them to the sofa, and began sorting through them.

Among the junk mail, mail order catalogs, sweepstakes come-ons, and bills, was a receipt from a real estate management company for rental on an industrial office–warehouse space. The receipt was dated a week earlier.

The city map in Guthrie's car gave him a fix on the location— less than two miles from Travis's home—and he drove toward it. The area was filled with light industrial and service companies interspersed with deteriorating apartment complexes and a few ramshackle frame houses marking the vestiges of the old neighborhood that once had been the sole occupant of the area.

The address Guthrie sought was in the last building of an old three-row office–warehouse complex. Inside it would have a cold, damp, cement slab floor, a single rickety office in front of the warehouse space, and a dingy toilet at the back. Probably the roof leaked. The office window, set in the wall next to the rusty metal door, was sealed with plywood. On the other side of the office door, a roll-up door provided access to the warehouse space. The whole place was decrepit, and the asphalt parking lot was pitted, littered, and dirty. A rusty, eight-foot chain link fence at the end of the buildings separated them from an overgrown empty lot.

There was absolutely nothing to recommend the place except, presumably, a low price and a landlord who probably didn't care what went on inside as long as the rent was paid. But the vacant tableau of the adjacent warehouses indicated potential tenants thought even those weren't sufficient inducements. Only two other spaces on the row were occupied—a carpenter was three doors down from Travis on the same side, and an auto repair shop was almost exactly opposite. Both businesses were closed for the night.

Travis's Lexus was parked in front of his door.

Guthrie didn't want Travis to hear his car and get spooked, so he eased up to the end of the row, parked, and walked across the rough asphalt toward Travis's space. The night was unusually warm and close, and Guthrie limped, his hip giving him a dull variation of those sharp twinges it always did just before a front swept in from the north. The predicted bad weather wasn't far off.

Guthrie checked the Lexus. The driver's door was unlocked—a careless act for such a nice vehicle parked in a questionable location like this. It was as if Travis didn't care. Or maybe he was just preparing for a quick retreat.

We'll see about that, Guthrie thought. He trotted back to his own car, where he grabbed the red steering wheel lock-bar he kept on the floor of the back seat. In a moment, he was back at the Lexus, locking the bar in place. Chuckling hurt his head, but he did it anyway. He turned from the car to the building, massaging his sore shoulder.

Decrepit or not, Travis's place appeared tight, from the plywood over the window to the heavy-duty padlock on the roll-up door. An empty padlock hasp was fastened to the personnel door—an obvious necessity since the built-in lock was old and flimsy.

Guthrie carefully pushed open the flap covering the mail slot and peered inside. A dim light emanating through a half-closed door to the warehouse space at the back revealed a slice of the small front office, empty, dusty, and silent.

Closing the flap, Guthrie put a cautious hand on the doorknob. The slightest sound on a still night like this would immediately convey his presence to anyone inside. The door was locked, but the old lock yielded easily to Guthrie's Swiss Army knife. With extra care, he turned the knob, slipped inside, and eased the door shut.

The front office, lit only indirectly by the light coming from the doorway to the warehouse, was barren except for a dark lump near the door. Guthrie knelt and discovered it was a small, black nylon gym bag, zippered open.

"You fucking bastard!" a sudden voice snarled. Guthrie stiffened. The harsh tones were tinged with hysteria. "Let me out of here!"

He relaxed a little. The voice was a woman's, and she hadn't been talking to Guthrie. He peeked around the door jamb until he could view the back room.

The long, narrow, empty warehouse was poorly lit. Half of the tubes in the fluorescent fixtures hanging from the open-beam ceiling were dark or flickering weakly. Out in the center, Travis crouched and peered intently at something cradled in his hands. He looked worse than he did earlier, the bad light twisting his gaunt and wasted features into a grim mask.

"Let me out of here," the woman repeated, trying a wheeling tone.

She sat on a folding metal chair pushed against a support pole about eight feet from Travis. Barbara Sidell, Guthrie realized with a start. Her voice was so hoarse and ragged that he hadn't recognized it. So Egan was right. She had disappeared.

She was just as beautiful as when Guthrie last saw her, even though her clothes were dirty and disheveled, her face smudged, and the light not particularly flattering. Neither was her language when Travis ignored her.

"You sack of shit! You let me out of these or my friends are gonna cook your balls!"

She shook her arms, and for the first time Guthrie saw she was chained to the chair.

"I'll let you out," Travis said tonelessly. "As soon as you meet my friend." He held up the object he'd been cradling.

It was the sculpture.

There was an oddness about the angle as he held it up. The sculpture's face was turned in Guthrie's direction, and Travis was asking Sidell to look at the head's left side. And the way he held it was awkward, as if it were larger than its actual dimensions. Even more curious, an oval of light danced over Sidell's features.

With a gasp, the woman abruptly averted her face and grew stiff in the chair.

"I'm not looking at that thing," she hissed. "No matter how long you keep me here."

There was a clicking sound, then Travis placed the sculpture on the floor. He stood up.

"He wants to meet you. He's very perceptive, and he'll tell you things that will set you free. All he wants in return is a little help."

"I know all about it," she shrilled. "You keep it away from me. You can't make me look."

"How long has it been since you've eaten?" Travis asked, approaching her. "Two days, now? Want some water?" He grabbed her hair and forced her to face him. "I think you'll look. Another two days, maybe three, and you'll look. And then you'll see. He can wait, and so can I. And when you do meet him, you'll be happy. He'll make you happy."

"No!" She writhed in his grip. "I'll never do it! Get away! Get away!" Her cries grew hysterical.

Travis stood over the struggling woman, and laughed. It wasn't a pleasant sound, and the nastiness of it cut right through the woman's hysteria like a dousing of ice water. She must have seen enough meanness in her life to know the real thing when she heard it, and she drooped resignedly in her chains. The laugh rang for a long, terrible moment, and it displayed more vitality than Travis seemed to have in his whole body.

"You stupid slut," he said flatly when the hellish laugh died. "Save us a lot of trouble." The gaunt man scooped up the sculpture, and caressed it as if it were the head of a tender lover. "My friend is anxious to meet you."

"Please don't," Sidell sobbed quietly. "I don't want to die."

"A sacrament isn't death." Travis showed an expression of genuine surprise. "It brings eternal life. It makes you more than yourself. Meet him, and let him set you free."

"Why me?" Sidell sniffled. "Why not one of the others?"

"Their turns will come." He stared blandly at her, then he stepped back and gazed at the sculpture's face, still caressing its brow. It appeared to hold him spellbound. "After all these years of your close association, he wants to meet each of you in person. He's just chosen you to make the introductions."

"I won't do it," she said. "They'll kill me."

"No one can kill the eternal," Travis said absently, still staring at the sculpture. "You will."

"I think not, Travis." Guthrie stepped into the room. He'd brought his gun with him this time and had it leveled.

Travis jerked to his feet and gaped at the intruder.

"Guthrie," breathed the woman.

"Away from her, Travis, or I'll shoot you where you stand."

Travis slowly stepped back, and Guthrie approached.

"Help me, Guthrie," Sidell cooed. "Help me, and I'll give you anything you want. Anything."

"Bastard," Travis grated, recovering from his shock. His limbs shook with fury. "You can't stop me now. It's not right."

"I don't much care. Put the head down and back off."

Travis hesitated, and Guthrie cocked the pistol. Travis must have seen the glint of death in Guthrie's eyes, for he put the head on the floor and shuffled slowly backwards. As Guthrie came forward, his attention was drawn toward the sculpture, its handsome features and striking eyes. Here it was at last. He bent to pick it up, but Sidell's voice stopped him.

"Guthrie, please. Let me out of these." She shook the chains. "He's kept me here for two days. Look. I've soiled myself. I'm bleeding."

Guthrie straightened. "Where are the keys?" he asked Travis. The man reluctantly drew them from his pocket. "Unlock her," Guthrie ordered, and Travis complied. Sidell winced as she stood and rubbed her raw, oozing wrists.

"Thanks," she said.

"Back off, Travis." Guthrie gestured with the gun.

When Travis was ten feet away, Guthrie bent again for the sculpture. As he did, a shadow swooped down on him with a whoosh that ended in a crash. Luckily, Guthrie managed to duck just in time to take the blow on his back instead of his head, but the impact sent a shock through his injured shoulder. He sprawled, half stunned, his gun skittering across the concrete.

Sidell threw the folding chair aside and rushed toward the sculpture. She and Travis reached it at the same instant, and they grappled over it like a harpy battling an angel of death.

Scrabbling aside to keep from being trampled, Guthrie regained his feet and cast around for his gun. It was on the opposite side of the melee. He tried to duck past to retrieve it, but Travis threw Sidell into him, and the three of them went down in an angry tangle. Guthrie barely missed having an eye gouged out by Sidell's coarse thumb just as he brought a quick knee into Travis's groin. The man gasped and sagged against Guthrie, and Sidell wriggled free. Instead of going for the sculpture, she went for Guthrie's gun.

Guthrie shrugged out of Travis's clinging grip, lurched to his feet, and charged Sidell just as she raised the pistol to fire. He got hold of her gun arm with one hand and fended off her claws with the other. Sidell shrieked, and the gun went off, sending a round whining off the concrete walls.

Then Guthrie's hand was on the gun, and he twisted it from her grip just a half second before Travis, a fiendish grin ripped across his skeletal features, slammed into both of them, pitching them backwards onto the floor. The woman shrieked again and fell on top of Guthrie, kicking and clawing. While he fought her off, Travis snatched the sculpture and scurried out the door.

23

GUTHRIE FLUNG ASIDE HIS INHIBITIONS and slugged Barbara Sidell on the jaw. Her struggles stopped abruptly as she flopped across him like a sack of wet cloth. He shoved her off, scrambled to his feet, and seconds later, stumbled into the front office. The outer door was agape, and in the greenish light from the arc lamps over the parking lot outside, Guthrie could see that the gym bag was gone. He dashed through the door.

Inside the Lexus's open door, the steering wheel bar gleamed dully in the off-color light. Guthrie scanned the space between the two rows of buildings and saw Travis running toward the chain link fence at the far end. Travis tried to scale the fence, but the weight of the sculpture in the gym bag hampered him, and Guthrie got to him and dragged him down before he reached the top. Travis spun, but there was no place for him to go.

"Forget it," Guthrie said. "I'm not chasing you halfway across town. I'll shoot you if you run. Give me that bag."

"It's mine!" Travis shrilled. "You can't have it!"

"It's not yours," Guthrie growled, wrenching the bag out of Travis's hands. "It belongs to the Harveys."

"Those scum! They don't care about him. What *he* wants. All they do is use him for themselves."

"Zeroth?"

"You should know." Travis's expression was hostile.

"I'm not one of them," Guthrie said. "But I know about them."

"Then they'll kill you."

"You're probably right."

Travis reached out his hands imploringly.

"Let me keep him," he whined. "Don't give him back to them. All they do is use him to hurt other people."

"And what do you plan? Seems like you had a woman chained up back there."

"That bitch!" Travis spat. "She's hell's whore."

"And God gave you the right to torture her?"

"I wasn't going to hurt her."

"You threatened to starve her if she didn't do what you wanted."

"It was what *he* wanted. She'd have appreciated it after she…."

"Save it, Travis. Just tell me who it was you wanted her to meet."

"I…I don't…." Travis seemed genuinely perplexed. Then his eyes brightened, and a laugh burst from his pale lips. "You really don't know anything, do you? All this running around to get that back for them, and you haven't the faintest idea of what it is. What it means."

"Why don't you enlighten me."

"Oh, no. You're so fucking smart. You've got the head, now you figure it out. And you will." He cackled bitterly.

"Look, I don't know what's happened, but I want to help. You've got to play straight with me. Tell me what you know and I'll…."

"He'll get what he wants," Travis interrupted. He had a glazed look in his eyes and didn't seem to hear Guthrie. "But it'll be without me. He'll get it," his eyes, unnaturally bright, focused on Guthrie, "and he'll take a stupid asshole like you with him, not me."

He jumped Guthrie.

Guthrie was half expecting it, only the speed of the attack surprised him. But a single burst of speed was all Travis had left. The strength was gone from his wasted body. He wrestled futilely for the bag for a moment before Guthrie cuffed him with the flat of the gun, and he fell back whimpering.

"It's mine. Without it I'm nothing."

It was pitiful. The portrait of Travis that Guthrie had developed from studying the man's house and circumstances was one of a strong, directed individual, not this sniveling worm.

"I'm leaving now," Guthrie said. "It's over. Go home, clean yourself up, and eat something. Come over to my place next week. I'm in the book—Clay Guthrie. Like I said, I'll share the reward money with you. Help you get it back together."

"Money won't help me," Travis whined. "He's all I want. All I need."

"You'll feel differently tomorrow," Guthrie promised, and Travis burst into wracking sobs. Guthrie couldn't stand to see it, and he turned to leave.

"You'll never share that money," Travis burbled, then his voice strengthened with petulance. "You'll never even get to spend it. You give the sculpture to them, and they'll kill you." Guthrie walked away. "They'll kill you! Kill you! Kill you!"

The words echoed in Guthrie's head as he walked down the pitted pavement. He didn't doubt them one bit.

When Guthrie reached Travis's Lexus, he retrieved his lock bar. As he turned away from the SUV, Sidell stumbled through the door into the parking lot, rubbing her jaw. When she saw Guthrie, she let him know how she felt about him with a tirade of foul epithets.

"Shut up," Guthrie told her. He'd had about all the trauma he could handle for one night. "You're lucky I came."

She quieted, and Guthrie, keeping his distance, skirted the Lexus and started toward his own car. Sidell followed, but he set the gym bag onto the floor of the front seat and slid behind the wheel without looking at her.

"You can't just leave me here," Sidell said.

"You tried to brain me with a chair and shoot me with my own gun," Guthrie pointed out. "Why shouldn't I?"

"Don't leave me," she pleaded. "I promise I'll be good."

"Yeah, sure," Guthrie said. He closed the door and started the engine.

"Wait, Guthrie! We'll give you anything you want. We'll share the money and power! Beyond your wildest dreams!" She looked at him with a sultry expression that ignored her begrimed state. "You can even have me."

But Guthrie had nothing left to care with. His emotions had been drained dry by the violence in Travis's house and by the scuffle in the warehouse, and he felt dead to it all. Worse, his lack of desire went beyond a tired indifference toward Sidell's tawdry lubricity. His body was cold and his mind detached. It was not absence of desire, he realized, but an utter lack of cravings of any sort. All the hungers and urges of life had evaporated, driven out of him by the incessant gravity dragging through his veins. The single passion that remained in him was greater than physical desire and more base at the same time. It was compulsive instinct. It was the will to live.

Only now, as he realized this, did the truth really sink in. He was, indeed, dead.

But damn if he was going to go out like a cringing dog. Only one thing was important—retrieving his life—and he was going to fight for it with everything he had. If that meant facing the truth about himself as well as discovering the truth of this case, so be it.

"We?"

"Martin," she said. "Martin and me."

"You and Martin." Guthrie's mouth twisted. "And he won't mind me sharing you as well as the money and power?"

"It isn't like that," she said, lowering her lashes.

"Strictly business, eh?"

"That's right. Martin was to get the head, and I was to use it to take care of Prentice."

"Is that who Travis wanted you to meet?"

"What?"

"Someone who scared you."

"Prentice doesn't scare me," she said. Her voice was deliberately indifferent, though the look in her eyes belied her words. Suddenly the trepidation was replaced by understanding, and that in turn by sarcastic humor. "You don't know, do you?"

"I know you're scared of someone, and it wasn't the boogeyman."

Laughter barked from her lips, and just as suddenly she sobered. Her eyes narrowed as scorn drew back her upper lip.

"You're a fucking idiot, Guthrie. Let me tell you something that's absolutely true. If you take that head away from here by yourself, it'll be the last thing you ever do. The next time I see you, you'll look like that." She gestured toward Travis without taking her eyes from Guthrie's. "Play it smart, Clay. Let me go with you, and you'll make it out of this with everything you ever wanted and more."

"What about Prentice and Egan and the rest of them? Let me tell you something about Martin. When I discovered he might have had a hand in the theft, they killed him."

"Martin's dead?"

"That's right."

"It doesn't matter," she shrugged. "Now that we have the head, we can do worse to them."

"He was eaten alive by rats. I can't imagine much worse."

"We'll be safe. They'll be weaker without me and Martin. Just take me with you, and none of the rest matters."

"Sorry. The head goes back to the Harveys."

"Okay," she spat. "Take it to them. But you'd better do it quick. Right now. Don't go anywhere else, don't stop, and whatever you do, don't open that bag. Give it to them, and collect your slimy little fee —if they let you live—and be glad that's all you get." She gave him one final scathing glance, then her expression altered. Now she was a vixen again, caught in a pensive moment. "And while you're going, think of everything that you threw away."

Her eyes gleamed seductively as she lifted her coarse thumb to her lips and nipped coyly at the deformed nail while her other hand caressed the juncture of her thigh and groin

Guthrie turned from her and put the Honda in gear. As he pulled off, he glanced in the rear view mirror. Sidell was close enough for him to discern the mask of scorn and hatred covering her features, but he wasn't watching her. He was seeing beyond her, down the aisle between the two buildings.

Under the glow of the arc lamps, stood Travis. The slump of the wasted man's shoulders indicated about as much defeat as one person could expect in a lifetime.

Guthrie almost stopped, tempted to give the sculpture back, but he caught himself and crushed the last remaining shred of humanness he felt beneath a cold heel. He'd trade Travis's disappointment for his own life, any day.

As Guthrie drove toward the freeway, he didn't, for the slightest instant, consider taking the head straight to the Harveys. Or Egan. Or home, which probably had become as dangerous as a downtown bus stop at midnight. No telling who would be there to threaten him or kill him even though he was already dead.

Instead, he headed toward a place where a weary-looking stranger would be common and go unnoticed—the North Freeway near Intercontinental Airport. By the time he found a moderately priced motel, angry clouds were scudding across the darkening sky, and fat drops spattered his windshield. The storm promised by the close heat and his aching hip had arrived.

He went to his room and put the bag on the bed, tossed his jacket over the chair, cleaned himself up in the bathroom, then went back to the bed and sat down.

"Don't open the bag," Sidell had warned.

Like hell!

He slid open the zipper, drew the head from the bag, and cradled it in his hands. It rested there easily, with a weight less than the mass of metal and stone implied.

He'd never actually held anything so valuable, if he discounted the kilos of cocaine and heroin he'd handled during drug busts. Certainly nothing so rare or ancient. It was in excellent condition, giving no overt indication of its age, but even if its antiquity wasn't obvious, it was apparent. The thing felt old. Very old. Older than the metal from which it was fashioned.

And there was another sensation Guthrie could not immediately identify. It seemed at first to arise from intriguing features so superbly depicted they appeared to be caught in the act of altering expression. The features delineated a man in early old age, highbrowed, benevolent, perceptive, and even wise. Whiskers curled down his cheeks and over his strong chin, but his upper lip was shaven. For a brief moment, disgust flickered so powerfully through Guthrie that he almost dropped the sculpture. It was too much like holding a real human head so recently severed that it still retained a spark of life. But the coldness of the metal reassured him, and closer examination of the technique and finer details kept his grip.

Oddly, the vital quality vanished as soon as he searched for the exact line or curve that imparted it. He drew back and surveyed the whole once more, and the animate property returned. The features were artfully fashioned, but no single element or confluence of particulars quickened the metal. Perhaps the vitality rested in the eyes.

Those very striking eyes.

The white orbs held crystalline brown irises surrounding pupils as dark, deep, and mysterious as those of Master Tereba. The eyes were so starkly contemplative that they held an almost hypnotic quality. Guthrie wondered how ivory, topaz, and black jasper could conspire to explore so insistently into his own mind and heart.

But as with the sculpture's features, scrutiny of the eyes' finer details erased all semblance of life. Though he tried repeatedly to isolate the element that lent vitality to the sculpture, each time, he was forced to return to the whole. It was not the bone and stone perusing him from beneath metal brows, nor was it the angle of those brows or the command of the skeletal structure lurking beneath the metal skin that gave life to the head. Instead, it was the relationship of all the features, the completeness of the expression, and the piercing gaze taken all together that transmitted the sculpture's sense of aliveness.

Guthrie stared at the face for long minutes. He realized he was being compulsive, maybe even obsessive, but the sculpture's animate power drove him on, bringing a slow boil of self-loathing. Now that he was all too aware of the truth of his own emptiness, his own deadness, this inanimate object he held in his hands, this weight of metal and stone, seemed to possess more power of life, more mastery of pure being, than Guthrie had ever had.

He found himself ascribing personality to the head, and he began to understand something of why this sculpture was so important to everyone. It didn't talk, but through subtle shades of its appearance, it spoke like an old acquaintance. Hadn't Travis called it his friend? Guthrie could easily believe it. The head gave off an aura of ancient wisdom while, at the same time, exuding a sense of intimacy that included Guthrie in the circle of solons.

At last, with effort, Guthrie pulled his attention from the face and began examining the rest of the sculpture. On the bottom of the black marble base, an incised inscription that looked vaguely Arabic proclaimed information that remained oblique to Guthrie, though he knew it must contain the words "Katib of Jashyari."

He righted the bust and stared at the face again, thinking of something else that puzzled him. When Travis showed the head to Barbara Sidell, the action had appeared awkward. Guthrie arranged himself in front of the big mirror in the bathroom so that his image gave an approximate view of the head he'd seen when Travis held it up. He held out the head as if Sidell were in front of him and he was showing her its left side. The face was turned toward the mirror, and Guthrie glanced there to see if the thing looked as he remembered it looking in Travis's hands.

It didn't.

Guthrie sat on the bed and stared at the sculpture's left side. There must be something there. Travis showed that angle to Sidell and she'd panicked.

Guthrie almost missed the crack cunningly concealed along the beard line and beneath the locks framing the forehead. The crack ran completely around the face, separating the face from the rest of the head. Guthrie remembered then that before Travis had placed the head on the warehouse floor, there'd been a distinct clicking sound. The face opened up. That's why it looked so strange when Travis held it. Travis hadn't been showing Sidell the head's left exposure. He'd been showing her its interior.

There had to be a catch. Since the face opened to the right, the catch must be on the left side. He found it a moment later—a simple push button disguised as the little nibbit in front of the left ear hole, burnished with the polish of frequent manipulation. He pushed it, heard a click, and the face hinged open a crack. Guthrie pulled it open all the way, exposing the interior of the head. Reflected light danced across the ceiling.

Inside the head glittered a mirror.

24

THE MIRROR WAS CLEAR AND unflawed. Its oval face was about eight inches high and six inches across. Oddly enough, the glass looked to be more than an inch thick. Pretty solid, Guthrie thought. The thickness of the glass also gave an absorbing depth to Guthrie's reflected image, which was crystalline in its clarity, making the glass seem more like a window than a mirror.

A mirror hidden inside the sculpture was interesting enough, but as he sat with the head comfortably cradled in his hands, just as alluring was the fact that unlike most mirrors, which show a reflection slightly smaller in size than the original it mimics, this one reflected a life-size image that perfectly filled the glass oval, giving the illusion that the metal head bore Guthrie's face.

Considering the mirror's size, the illusion was unexplainable for the surface was flat and there were neither a fish-eye effect nor blurring distortion around the edges to indicate magnifying convexity.

Guthrie's examination of the outer edges of the mirror brought him almost immediately back to the center. He thought, for just an instant, that he'd seen a flaw there, out of the periphery of his vision. The mirror had to be old. At least as old as the head, for obviously the sculpture had been fashioned to contain the mirror. And glass that old had to be flawed. But Guthrie's search for cracks, bubbles, or distortions was fruitless.

Maybe his own movement had caught his eye. But he hadn't moved appreciably, so that couldn't be what he'd seen, though for just an instant it seemed....

The face in the mirror really attracted his attention, then. It appeared wan and pale and tired around the eyes, but otherwise it was still the same old face he'd seen when he shaved every morning.

Or was it?

He stared hard at the reflection, and the longer he gazed, the less he liked what he saw. He saw a guy who still had brains and resourcefulness but who'd lost something as indefinable as it was vital. He wasn't poverty stricken, but he owned nothing. He wasn't bad looking, but love had eluded him so thoroughly that he felt nothing. And all his possibilities, buried profoundly and indurately within him, inevitably amounted to nothing.

Nothing, the mirror seemed to say. I can barely hold this image of so much nothingness.

Guthrie wanted to close his eyes and shut out the sight that was scouring at all his inexpressive pain and exhausted fear. His loneliness. At his few barren successes, his many and disturbing failures, and the one desperate success that had been his greatest failure. But he couldn't turn away from the disquieting but riveting image. Why did he continue to stare when all he saw was anguish and torment so empty it seemed that nothing could again fill it? What was it he searched for? What secret in his image could the mirror reveal?

Many torturous minutes passed before he saw what he'd been searching for. Praying for. Yes, there, like a double exposure, like a shadow hovering over the face of a man gone to seed, was another face, and this one was different from its empty twin. This one contained not loss but powerful, if unfulfilled, potential.

Guthrie was so relieved he could have cried. Life wasn't lost. It hadn't died. It showed in a mysterious sparkle in the eyes of the image, light years distant but immediate in its promise of boundless success. It was a clarity reflecting not on endings but only on beginnings.

He had to search deep within the image to find himself and understand that denial of the image was the root of his self-destruction. And just as he could not deny the truth of his potential, he could not deny all the many changes necessary to create himself anew. For too long he'd let the world stifle him, hold him back, and beat him down. Now was the time to free himself. No longer would the world control him. He would control the world. He would devour life as a starving man consumes a feast, completely and with absolute relish. All he need do was seek the truth in his own image and understand that life was a blossom whose inviolable flower could not be plucked because it grew inside the image in a place that could not be touched.

Guthrie's eyes reached out to the image as his heart opened to the melody of freedom, his mind to the lyrics of transformation. But even as he did, something within his veins sang an altogether different refrain that droned with a tightening hum, dragging him back to reality.

It was the thrumming of the leaden wires that strung his body and made him cold, indifferent, and introspective. It was the dirge of his own imminent demise playing discordant tones against the shimmering aria offered by the image.

Guthrie jerked back into himself as if he'd fallen into quicksand and been pulled out just before its suffocating weight covered him completely. He tore his eyes from the image, but almost instantly looked back.

There he was, staring out at himself, haggard and pitiful. And Guthrie wanted to pity, but the image was wrong, and he knew it. The problem he had with it was a recasting of the old question of whether or not a tree falling in a forest makes a sound if there are no living things to hear. No, the answer goes, because sound is the perception of compression waves moving through a medium. Without an ear to translate them into sound, they remain simply compression waves.

Now, here, that question asked whether or not hope could animate the dead. No, Guthrie had to answer. For hope to animate Guthrie, there must be life within him for hope to act on. Without spirit, Guthrie was only a hunk of mobile clay, and hope was just a compression wave dissipating in an arid medium. Any hope the image offered was a lie because the single truth that remained in Guthrie lay like a nasty lump of refuse in the middle of a deserted room, beyond hope for it was beyond forgiveness.

"I'm dead," Guthrie told the image. "You see that, don't you?"

After an instant, it *did* see. A look of failure shadowed the intensity of its eyes, and Guthrie again tore away his gaze, unable to endure the reflection's profound expression of disappointment. Then his eyes quickly returned as a hint of movement barely caught the edge of his vision. He looked away again and back twice more, and the question of energy, mediums, and perception suddenly developed a new dimension. He was forced to ask if a mirror continually reflects an image or whether reflection requires attention.

The question was more than simple semantics. Every time he stared into the glass, he saw that double image of his haggard features and the face of accomplished potential staring out. And when he turned away, his peripheral vision caught the reflection devolving into formless shadows buried more deeply within the glass than its inch of thickness could allow.

A chill worked its way through Guthrie's brain—a chill that didn't show in the eyes staring back at him. He frowned, and the image wrinkled a thoughtful brow. He blinked in confusion, and the image winked slyly. His lips pulled back in a strained, twisted grimace, and the image smiled serenely. Guthrie looked away, and the image devolved, only to reassemble in the instant he returned his attention to the glass.

Guthrie noticed that each time he looked away the act required less effort. At last, he was strong enough to close the face over the mirror and lay the head on the bed. For a moment, he examined the sculpture's features, noticing for the first time the pinched bitterness marring the corners of the mouth and the slight but definite sag of guilt beneath the eyes. Then he turned the head face down on the pillow and stared across the room. He was blank, without thought or feeling, and what he was seeing didn't register for many minutes.

In the far wall was the room's single broad window, the heavy curtains customary to hotels and motels drawn over the glass. How long Guthrie had stared, uncomprehending, at the dull rim of light edging around the curtains he didn't know, but finally, as a flash of lightning outside lit it more brightly, he noticed it with a shock. He was seeing daylight. He glanced at his watch. It read just before seven.

He'd been totally absorbed by the mirror for more than six hours. He also noticed how cold he was. How dead.

After a long, hot shower, he left the head on the bed, locked the room, and went down to the breakfast buffet. The sight of the eggs, bacon, and pancakes, normally mouthwatering, was enough to turn his stomach. The coffee was oily and unpalatable. He gathered a small plate of fruit, drew a glass of orange juice, and went to a table in the corner of the dining room. His hands shook as he forked a chunk of cantaloupe into his mouth, and he wondered if they were shaking from his experience with the mirror or from the knowledge of the mortality creeping through his flesh. Every passing moment was another small but remorseless step taken toward final stiffening darkness.

He finished the fruit and returned to his room.

As soon as he got close, he knew that leaving had been a terrible mistake. The door was open, and parked next to it was a maid's cart. Guthrie went in, not knowing what to expect.

The maid, an Hispanic woman of about thirty-five, was sitting on the edge of the bed, the head in her hands. The face was open, and light reflecting from the mirror lit her features, which bore an expression of concentrated attention as she stared into the glass. She didn't seem to hear Guthrie as he came in. He went to her, but even when he stood right in front of her, she didn't respond to anything but the sight of herself in the mirror.

"Excuse me," Guthrie said, then said it again, louder. She didn't budge, didn't appear to hear him. He shook her shoulder. "Excuse me."

The mirror was small and gave a limited view. As Guthrie craned around to peer over the woman's shoulder, he could see only about a one-quarter crescent of the mirror surface. In the glass was a face that resembled the maid, but at the same time it wasn't her. It was more than her. In person she was frowzy, dumpy, and complacent, but the mirror shed over her the glamour of a queen of the Spanish-language telenovelas. In the glass she was beautiful, svelte, wealthy, and self-possessed.

The maid gave out a brief, surrendering sigh that indicated she'd resigned herself to the future that fate had in store for her. Whatever that fate might be, Guthrie was sure it wasn't as a glamour queen. The glitter he saw in the single eye revealed to his view held no warmth, only a frigid calculation in which ambition, avarice, and lust replaced incentive, charity, and love.

With a swipe, he knocked the head out of her hands. It tumbled across the floor, crashed into a chair, and came to rest still open, mirror down.

Guthrie wasn't afraid the mirror might break. He was concerned about how the maid would respond.

He needn't have worried she would react violently. Instead, as her eyes were torn from the image, she gave a moaning gasp and crumpled off the edge of the bed. Guthrie managed to slow her fall, and he eased her to the floor, where she lay panting and whimpering. When her eyes stopped fluttering, they fastened on the sculpture lying on the floor, face up and face down at the same time. Her whimper ballooned into a throaty moan of desire, and she groped toward the head.

She was stronger than Guthrie expected, but her attention was completely on the sculpture, not him, and he managed to force her to the door.

"Dame lo!" she cried, struggling to remain in the room. "You must give it to me!"

Guthrie shoved her into the hall, levered her behind her cart, stepped back into the room, and slammed the door. He shot the privacy bolt home just before her pass card opened the lock.

"Señor, por favor!" she wailed. "Let me see!" Guthrie heard her slump on the floor outside the door, still crying for one more look in the mirror. At last she was just crying.

He sat on the bed and waited. After ten minutes, he heard a second female voice speaking rapid Spanish in a concerned tone. Another maid had found the first. She got her friend up, and in a little while, the hall was silent.

The struggle with the maid had left Guthrie drained, but he had to get the hell out of here before the management came to investigate. He stood for a moment, contemplating the sculpture where it still lay on the floor, showing all its external aspects at once, yet keeping its true face hidden. Then he picked it up, snapped the face closed, and deposited it into the gym bag. He didn't bother checking out but simply left the key card in the room. As he hurried from the building, he thanked his luck that he didn't encounter the maid or anyone else.

Outside, rain drenched the air, and the low, dismal, thickly oppressive clouds promised no relief from the continual downpour. Occasional lightning flashes rolled distant thunder over the city as more water fell onto the saturating ground. Guthrie splashed through the puddled parking lot, found his car, and left the motel.

He drove carefully through the mid-morning traffic, which was moving more slowly than usual because of the weather. He had a lot to think about. On the one hand there was a contract to fulfill. He had Zeroth's sculpture, and by now they no doubt knew he had it. He had to give it back to them. On the other hand, he'd seen what the damn thing did to the maid in just a few minutes, and what it had done to Travis over the course of ten days. He realized, no matter how improbable it sounded, that Tereba has been telling the truth. The mirror was alive, somehow, or had something living inside it that mesmerized its victims and sapped their wills. No wonder Travis talked to the head. The poor guy probably survived as long as he had only because whatever was in the mirror wanted something from him. Something Guthrie had interrupted.

And when Guthrie looked, the thing did its damnedest to subordinate him, too. It should have been easy—Guthrie's will power was probably no stronger than Travis's. But the mirror couldn't hold him. He'd escaped, and he was beginning to understand why.

Part of it was that he was empty of real desire, and there was nothing for it to hold on to. Tereba had hinted at that much. But there was an insistent itch beneath his belt buckle that reminded him that Tereba's talisman etched on his skin probably had something to do with it, too. He'd thank the old man for that later.

If he lived long enough.

He glanced at the gym bag sitting on the seat next to him. It might be his imagination, but he thought he could feel the damn thing radiating with hatred and thwarted lust. Or was Guthrie only projecting on it fear and desire for a life he felt had slipped out of his control? A life that was beginning to seem like nothing more than a mirage cast in an enchanted mirror.

Control. That was the key. Guthrie was in control right now, but for how long? He could vanish with the sculpture, but Zeroth would surely track him down. Except for Sidell and Hastings, they hadn't known about Travis, and the two Zeroth renegades surely wouldn't have let on that the thief had been their tool, especially since he'd vanished with the goods. And Travis might have gotten away if Guthrie hadn't been lucky in latching onto him. But Zeroth knew Guthrie, and it was just a matter of time before Egan and his large organization caught up. When he did, nothing Guthrie owned would be worth a plugged nickel, including his tenuous hold on life. Zeroth would get the head back just as surely as if Guthrie handed it over gift-wrapped.

And they would realize that Guthrie knew the secret of their mirror. But why shouldn't he know? Everyone else seemed to. Only, he wasn't supposed to know. He was the patsy, the small-time loser chosen for sacrifice in the name of Zeroth's well-being. Or of Zeroth's power, for now Guthrie had no doubt that this hunk of metal, stone, and glass in the gym bag on the seat next to him was a source of the group's ability to subvert its victims and make them ripe for financial and political plunder. It was a tool, no less than Guthrie was.

He wondered how many politicians, lawyers, and corporate executives had partied at the Harveys' in the name of advertising and public relations, only to be given a glimpse of their hosts' most treasured antique—a curious sculpted head with a mirror hidden inside. Certainly a few moments or hours alone with their own hyperbolic images while the thing inside the mirror worked its wiles on their wills would do wonders to make anyone friendly and tractable. After that, compliance would come easily.

Guthrie felt sick. He wanted nothing more than to stop at the first bayou and chuck the thing off the bridge and let the rising, roiling, murky brown waters swallow it. Or maybe take a hammer to the brittle surface. But he didn't. He couldn't be sure that was the right thing to do. But what *was* right?

He thought about Tereba's request that Guthrie bring the head to him before returning it to the Harveys. Guthrie didn't know what the old man would do with the sculpture. He'd said he wanted to discharge the thing's negative energy, and maybe he did. But Tereba was equally mysterious as Zeroth and, in many ways, probably more dangerous. Even so, for some reason, Guthrie trusted Tereba more than anyone.

He had to. The others surely wanted him dead, and even if Tereba had done something to Guthrie that would eventually kill him, only the old man had promised to help him live again.

Guthrie drove in-bound on I-45, heading for the Southwest Freeway interchange, which would take him to Tereba's territory. He'd just crossed the North Loop when he spotted the pastel green van. Vans that color are an uncommon sight, and this one was pacing him, hovering back at a steady two hundred feet.

As Guthrie steered through the long curve the freeway takes just before it reaches the downtown exits, he peered into his rearview mirror and saw a flash of white blazoned on the side of the van. The distance was too great and rain too heavy for him to be able to read the lettering, but the logo was familiar enough.

Rampart.

25

HE KNEW THAT EGAN POSSESSED the resources to mount a surveillance net, and no doubt the driver of the van already had radioed Guthrie's position and heading to other Rampart vehicles. Before long, the Ravens would be circling.

So far, there was no reason for the driver of the van to suspect Guthrie knew he was there, so Guthrie headed for the I-10 ramps, the last interchange on the north side of downtown. He kept to the left, as if preparing to take the ramp onto I-10 East, and slowed to thirty miles per hour. Exiting traffic began to build an impatient line behind him. He could practically hear the drivers gnashing their teeth at the slow fool in front. The Rampart van fell into line about ten vehicles back. Heavy through traffic whizzed past in the lanes to the right.

At the last possible instant before taking the exit, Guthrie punched the gas and twisted the wheel. He tore past the crash barrels protecting the ramp entrance, into the stream of traffic. Horns blared and tires hissed as a Ford Mustang barely missed plowing into him. Traffic behind immediately backed up, forming an impenetrable barrier, trapping the Rampart van in the exit lane. In another few seconds, the van was forced onto the ramp, and Guthrie sped off down the freeway, trying to ignore the obscene and completely deserved gesture the Mustang's driver threw in his direction.

Between here and the south side of downtown there were only two entrances to the freeway, Allen Parkway and Memorial, whose ramps feed into the freeway opposite each other. Guthrie passed them without seeing a Rampart vehicle, but he knew his luck would play out when he reached the interchange for Highway 59, only a mile or so ahead. He arrived at the interchange, hoping that Egan's people would figure he'd continue south on I-45, toward home, and would gather their forces there.

Instead, Guthrie veered off onto the Southwest Freeway, which would lead him to Tereba's. He didn't know if Egan knew where Tereba's door was, but Guthrie had to try for it. He made it as far as the first entrance past the interchange before another Rampart van found him. This driver made no pretext of secrecy but kept close on his tail. Before long, there would be others.

Guthrie glanced at the gym bag on the floor of the passenger seat. He didn't know what the hell he was going to do, but he had to keep the head out of Egan's hands.

Guthrie tried to out-maneuver the van, but the morning traffic, denser on this section of freeway and slowed and clogged by the pounding rain, didn't provide the opportunity. Besides, this driver was ready for Guthrie's tricks, and evasive driving didn't do much good. And Guthrie's little Honda could never out-run a V8, even if the traffic hadn't been running slow. All too quickly, Guthrie found himself halfway from downtown to the West Loop and feeling increasingly nervous. Other Rampart vehicles couldn't be more than minutes away—certainly they'd rendezvous by the time Guthrie got to the Loop. He had to do something and do it quickly.

The Honda couldn't out-run the van or maneuver it in heavy traffic, but maybe there was someplace it could. Greenway Plaza, a huge complex of office buildings and hotels built over a massive three-level underground parking garage, loomed to Guthrie's right. Taking the Buffalo Speedway exit, Guthrie swerved all the way across the feeder, whipped into a parking garage entrance, and was swallowed by the permanent twilight beneath Greenway.

At the bottom of the ramp, Guthrie took a hard right and, in a few seconds, spun down a spiral ramp to the second level, then the third, the van close on his tail. The air was damp, and trails of algae-slimed water streaked the walls and pooled on the floor, but Guthrie barely noticed as he steered around lines of parking spaces and between cement pillars. The Honda could U-turn on a narrow two-lane street, and its low center of gravity and front-wheel drive gave it traction on the wet pavement that the van didn't have. Gradually the van lost ground.

Guthrie wrenched into a hairpin turn in the middle of an aisle and ducked between a pair of parked cars. The van, too unwieldy to follow, was forced to go to the end of the aisle. By the time it was there, the Honda was out of sight, ripping down the length of the adjacent parking area.

Guthrie peered through the gloom for an up-ramp, found one, and a moment later, was on the second level. He couldn't see the van, but he knew it wouldn't take the driver long to realize which direction the Honda had gone. Guthrie quickly made his way around to the far side of the parking garage, found another up-ramp, went to ground level, and burst into the sheeting rain. He oriented himself and saw he was about to enter Richmond Avenue on the opposite side of Greenway Plaza from the freeway. He turned west on Richmond, made the first light on yellow, and glanced in the rearview.

There was no sign of pursuit, but even if the density of the cement above the parking garage prevented the van's driver from immediately radioing for back-up, he would emerge all too soon and sound the alarm that he'd lost Guthrie. They would know he was in the area, and more Rampart vehicles would close in until they found him. It was only a matter of time. He'd probably never make it to Tereba's.

He had to get rid of the sculpture before they caught him. If he managed to get away, he could always come back and retrieve it, but if he didn't, at least they wouldn't get it. But where could he hide it? It had to be somewhere where nobody would accidentally stumble across it. Richmond, west of Greenway, was lined with small businesses behind which were neighborhoods. After Richmond crossed the railroad tracks, less than a mile from where he was, there were just neighborhoods until the Loop. Neighborhoods were too insular to invade with hopes of hiding the head. Guthrie needed some place more public but at the same time secluded. He reached the Loop before he knew what he was going to do.

Steering though a series of quick turns outside the Loop, onto a one-way street between the huge jut of Williams Tower to the right and a trio of dark, cubical office buildings to the left, he swerved to the left curb and stopped beneath a no parking sign. A chain of small, artificial lakes graced the grounds of the three blockish office buildings, and Guthrie grabbed the gym bag, got out of the car, and splashed across the wet grass toward the lake most distant from the structures.

Well before he reached it, he was soaked. The lake was the lowest of the chain, each lake dumping into the next down a short waterfall, each waterfall topped with wide cement stepping stones between which the water sluiced. The water was a deep blue more akin to food dye than to any natural shade. Guthrie had always been amused by the phony color and amazed the ducks and geese swimming around in the lakes didn't wind up as blue as the water.

At the nether end of the lowest lake was a pumping station that sent the water back up to the first lake, and near the head end was a little hillock of an island reached by stepping stones. The path from the stones continued through the sparse growth of trees on the hump of the island to another group of stepping stones on the far side. Here, protected from all eyes by the island and trees, Guthrie knelt on the center stone and peered into the water rushing over the small dam. The water was shallow on the upstream side, but deeper below the dam, and the swirling blue color hid the bottom.

Guthrie carefully lowered the gym bag into the water as far as he could. Bubbles streamed for a few seconds as the bag filled with water, then he let go. The bag sank from sight.

Guthrie ran for his car, then headed toward Richmond Avenue, intending to turn onto Sage. After that, he hoped to zigzag southwest across the next few miles of city until he reached Tereba's lair. The irony wasn't lost on him that, at the Southwest Freeway, Sage changed names to South Rice—he was only about a mile down the road from Travis's house.

A Rampart sedan was waiting like a predator in a parking lot at the intersection of Richmond and Sage. It pounced after him, and by the time Guthrie made the feeder at the Southwest Freeway, three other Rampart vehicles had joined the first. They forced him off the feeder at Westpark, and a mile farther down Westpark, they hemmed him in and crowded him into the empty parking lot of a vacant two story building. He dropped his keys to the floor and shoved them under the mat before getting out and trying to run.

He didn't get far.

None of the men who surrounded him were as personally efficient as the Ravens, but they were effective enough, there were a lot of them, and they didn't seem to mind getting wet if it gave them the chance to rough him up. Inside of a minute, a gasping Guthrie was handcuffed and tossed into the bed of one of the vans. Two men kept him company in the back while the driver steered the van back to the inbound freeway and found an entrance ramp. Neither of the men with Guthrie missed a trick, said an unnecessary word, or blinked back a tear of remorse.

Guthrie wasn't surprised when, fifteen minutes later, the van rolled down the long, palatial drive of Ben Egan's estate. He glanced through the rear windows and saw the iron gates swing shut across the entrance.

After the driver parked, the other two men escorted Guthrie to the front door where Ingram and Stanton waited. The Ravens took Guthrie inside, leaving the flunkies in the downpour.

Just as the door thumped closed, Ingram, with a motion like a striking snake, chopped the side of Guthrie's neck. As Guthrie went down, his stunned vision caught a glimpse of Ingram watching him fall with the eye of a north woods logger who can lay out a tree right where he wants to. Guthrie could still vaguely see Ingram as Stanton's meaty hands found his armpits and dragged him into the interior of the house.

26

GUTHRIE'S BLEARY MIND HALF EXPECTED Ingram and Stanton to take him to Egan's office, but they went a completely different direction into the house. After a few moments, Ingram opened a door, and Stanton dragged Guthrie backwards down a flight of stairs. The heels of Guthrie's soggy tennis shoes thumped uncomfortably from step to step, but at least Stanton wasn't dragging him by the feet.

Even half conscious, Guthrie was surprised at the stairs. Houses in Houston just don't have basements. The combination of wet climate and shifting thick gumbo clay that masquerades for soil in this region is not friendly to holes in the ground, no matter how well shored up. The only holes that could exist, such as beneath Greenway Plaza and much of downtown, were walled by massive shells of concrete that acted as much like boats as they did foundations.

After they reached the bottom and Stanton dragged him around a corner, though, Guthrie realized they weren't entering a basement but a lower story. Since the house was close to Buffalo Bayou, there was enough texture to the terrain for Egan to have a split-level home. Through the picture windows that opened at the back, the drenched gray light revealed a well-manicured lawn with a fringe of forest beyond. In that direction lay Buffalo Bayou, and beyond that Memorial Park.

Then all sight of the backyard disappeared as Stanton hauled Guthrie through a door leading into a large, windowless room beneath the front of the house. Guthrie was unceremoniously dumped into a heavy wooden chair, and Ingram and Stanton handcuffed his wrists to the arm rests before they left, shutting the door behind them.

Guthrie shook his head gingerly to clear out the dusty film glazing over everything. That's when he saw the feet. There were two of them, wearing dark sneakers, casually extended next to him. Guthrie's eyes trailed from the feet, up blue-jean-clad legs, to a shirttail sloppily stuffed into a waistband. The shirt was only half-way buttoned, and on either side were hands cuffed to the chair arms. Farther up was Travis's face, chin down, eyes closed, and mouth slack.

At first, Guthrie thought he was dead, but then the eyes twitched and opened slowly, as if even this dim light was painful.

"I was waiting for you," Travis said, contempt twisting his features. "The great detective. How long you been at it?"

"About a week and a half."

Travis snorted and shook his head in disgust.

"Yeah, well, I was good enough to find you and the head," Guthrie said. "How long you been a criminal?"

"Since I went on sabbatical," Travis admitted, and both of them laughed, though Travis cut his off quickly enough. "Hastings tell you about me?"

"He was too busy covering his own ass and looking for you. Besides, he's dead."

"How?"

"Somebody sicced a bunch of rats on him."

"Poetic justice," Travis gave a bitter smile. "But if it wasn't him, how'd you find me? I thought I covered my trail."

"Your car. I already knew that you'd done the research on the bust, so I was familiar with your name. Then Tony at Armin's said Mark Batten drove a Lexus SUV. That's a pretty expensive car for a delivery driver, and when I did a routine background on Lexus owners, your name popped up."

"Yeah. I bought that to impress the women I was dating. Looks like it backfired on me."

"The wrong reasons have a tendency to do that."

"Well, it doesn't matter, now. They've got him back."

"Not yet. I hid the head."

"If that's true, I hope you hid it where they'll never find it."

"What do they use it for? To control people?"

"How should I know? I never actually saw it before I took it. Until then, it was just another artifact I'd researched."

"You were planning something back there in the warehouse. With Barbara Sidell. That something you don't know about, either?"

Travis's face showed a troubled frown. He hung his head.

"Come on, Travis. You were trying to make her look in the mirror. Why?"

"I'm not telling you anything. If it wasn't for you, I'd still be out there." Travis jerked his head to indicate the world outside this room. "I'd still have the mirror, and I'd be free."

"Bullshit! The second you laid eyes on that mirror, you lost your freedom. And you didn't have Sidell by accident. That thing in there wanted her for a reason, and I think you know what it was."

"What does it matter?"

"It matters to me. It's part of what brought me to this." He rattled his chains.

"What's the difference?" Travis shrugged. "We're not getting out of here alive."

"Then you might as well tell me. Besides, I'm as much a victim in this as you."

When Travis refused to answer, Guthrie tried a different tack.

"At least tell me how you got into this mess."

Travis just shook his head, a sullen expression falling over his features. "You wouldn't believe me, even if I told you."

"Try me," Guthrie said. "Two weeks ago, I wouldn't have, but right now, I might believe anything."

It took a long moment for the bitterness to build up enough in Travis that he had to open his mouth.

"Yeah. Okay. It was Hastings. He convinced me to do his dirty work. I met him about two years ago. At the time, I knew nothing about any of these people. As far as I knew, the Harveys were just some of William Mason's rich clients. Hastings came to my office, told me he had a proposition. He knew I was researching the bust for William, and he wanted me to help him steal it.

"I told him he was insane. I was a college professor, not a thief. Besides, it wasn't principled. He just laughed at me and asked about my fight against antiquities looting from archaeological sites. He told me the head was no different. How did I think the Harveys had gotten hold of it? He said the deed was a phony. I didn't believe him—William isn't like that. Or so I thought. And I'd researched the provenance. I tried to keep out of it. What did I know about burglary? But Hastings was too persuasive. He said he'd pay me five million dollars, but he'd also give me something more precious than money—he'd give me power."

"Like the watchdog?"

"Watchdog?"

"The thing guarding your house."

"Yeah, only he called it a guardian. That was his demonstration of power. He came over to my house and sang this...song, I guess. It had a melody but no real words. Afterwards, he said that no enemy of mine would ever be able to approach the house. I guess it didn't work too well. Not against you, anyway."

"Don't worry about its efficiency," Guthrie told him. "It worked fine on me until I got a little protection of my own."

"That's right," Travis said. "You said you're dead. Walking and talking and dead." There was contempt in his voice, but also a trace of curiosity.

"Is that all Hastings gave you?"

Travis hung his head and shook it sadly.

"Go on," Guthrie urged.

"It's not easy to admit."

"We've all got ugly things in our past."

"He had this woman teach me a different song."

"Barbara Sidell?"

"I couldn't keep my eyes off her, and she knew it. She said that all I had to do was sing this song to any woman, and I'd be irresistible. She was right—I had my pick. I thought that was what I wanted." He gave an ugly snort of self-derision. "I was a cheap buy."

"If it's any consolation, I came cheap myself," Guthrie said. "So you're saying Hastings and Sidell can work some kind of magic?"

"They all can. But Prentice is the top dog. Hastings and Sidell told me some—enough to arouse my curiosity—and I researched the rest of what I know while I was waiting for the chance to take the bust. Prentice, their leader, used to be a music student in Stuttgart in the early '50s. He was studying to be an opera singer. His tutor was a famous German voice coach who was rumored to have given lessons to children of the Nazi elite. One day, the voice coach seemed to be frightened of something.

He gave Prentice a manuscript of music by an obscure sixteenth-century Hungarian composer named Agoston Neci and asked him to keep it for a few days. Neci's primary contribution to music history consisted of a collection of gypsy folk ballads. He was known to have attempted a number of original works, but these were inferior in quality to the ballads. At the time, Prentice didn't see the importance of the manuscript aside from its novelty value, but valuable or not, the tutor asked Prentice to take the manuscript with him and bring it back at the next lesson. When Prentice returned a few days later, he learned the voice coach had been murdered."

"You think he was killed for the manuscript? From what you said, it wasn't that valuable."

"Have you read about Adolph Hitler's obsession with the occult?"

"A little. Enough to know he was interested in collecting supposedly mystical objects. Was the Neci manuscript one of them?"

"Apparently, though it's only mentioned twice in the historical record, and those in obscure sources. But it seems likely that Prentice's tutor came into possession of it during or after the war, and someone who knew about it eventually tracked him down and killed him for it."

"But Prentice had it."

"At first, he didn't know what he had. But after he connected the manuscript with the murder, he really looked at the music. It was odd and completely unlike other music of Neci's time and milieu. The pieces had vague similarities to other musical forms like Gregorian chants and madrigals in that they were written for voice alone. The technical name is organum, which is an early form of polyphony developed in the early Middle Ages. It's made up of one or more voice parts that accompany a principal voice, most often in parallel. In this case, though, there were no words, as such, just meaningless syllables, strange timbres, and unusual phrasings. Later, after Prentice had the titles translated, he discovered they were equally odd—things like 'Portal,' 'Trezka's Lament,' and 'Symphony of the Damned.'"

"You mentioned that Hastings and Sidell sang songs, one that gave you the guardian and one power over women."

"Two from the Neci manuscript, I'd guess. Out of curiosity at the unusual music, Prentice sang one of the simpler solo songs, called 'Embroidery of Shadows.' A woman who had recently rejected his advances was strong in his mind while he was singing, and the following morning she was found dead of suicide."

"The song killed her?"

"Or caused her to kill herself." Travis shrugged. "At least that's what Prentice believed. He began experimenting with the rest of the music and discovered the power inherent in each song. Some are solo works, others are for multiple voices. Over the years, he's gathered a group of singers, and they use the songs to increase their wealth and power."

"Zeroth?"

"That's the name they use to cover their businesses. Prentice is the one, though. He's taught them only a limited number of songs, like the guardian song, but he keeps most to himself."

"So Hastings was going to use the head to control Prentice just as Prentice had used it to control others. But why did he need Sidell?"

"Isn't it obvious? She's Prentice's slut. She's the only one who could catch him unguarded long enough to get him to look in the mirror."

"And you? What was going to be your part?"

"Hastings promised to bring me in and teach me more songs after he took command, and the Neci manuscript, from Prentice. It would have meant power and wealth. I could have owned antiquities instead of just appraising and researching them for others. But on the way, something happened. I don't know what. Instead of taking it straight to him, I went home and examined it. Some of it was professional curiosity, I guess—to actually hold this thing that for me had only existed in photographs and old records. Some of it was just plain curiosity. The bust didn't really seem worth the effort Hastings had gone to to have me steal it. But more than that, it seemed to call to me on a personal level. And then I found the catch and opened it and met my friend."

"Frankly, Travis, I don't think that thing in there is much of a friend to you or anybody."

Travis laughed again, more acidly. "What would you know about it? You haven't even met him."

"I spent all night with him," Guthrie said.

"You saw him?" When Guthrie nodded, Travis stared at Guthrie through slitted lids. "You're lying. You wouldn't be so...."

"So what? Clear? Unpossessed?"

"So unconvinced."

"That's one euphemism for brainwashing."

"It's not like that."

"The hell it isn't. Just because it couldn't get to me doesn't mean it didn't try. I saw a woman who looked in that mirror for less than half an hour, and I had to beat her off to get it away. Does it have that effect on everyone?"

"Apparently not on you. But, that's right—you're dead." Travis turned away. "Well, so am I. I'm just allowed to go on breathing for a few more hours."

"But I don't understand why you kidnapped Sidell and tried to force her to look in the mirror. She didn't care about Hastings. She'd have given you anything you wanted to play ball with her."

"She couldn't make me whole again. Only he could do that. Besides, he doesn't share."

"So you had to make her look, but she wouldn't. What happened to your power over women? Why didn't you sing to her?"

Guthrie couldn't help the dig, but he immediately regretted it. The wasted man shot a sharp look at him and said, "You're an asshole as well as a fool." Then he lapsed into a silence from which Guthrie could not shake him. At last Guthrie quit trying.

The quiet of the next few minutes was broken only by the sound of Guthrie shifting uncomfortably in his chair. His bad hip had taken a beating from all the rough handling he'd had, and the change in weather made it stiff as hell. The storm must be a doozy. At least the hip didn't hurt like it normally did in bad weather. Being dead did have some advantages, but that didn't make him feel better, and he was all too aware of his increasing morbidity—a grim coldness that seemed to emanate from his very bones. He wasn't shivering, and in fact, the air in the room felt unnaturally warm. But despite the heat and his sense of doomed anticipation, there was no cold, nervous sweat under his arms.

He was about to die, but...no sweat.

Guthrie had to laugh, but he wasn't happy. So far, death had been less than comfortable, and it was only growing worse. His flesh was stiffening almost imperceptibly from the confinement, and that was the best of it. Inside, he was completely devoid of emotion, desire, and hope. Life was an empty curiosity that would totally implode the moment he paused to consider anything beyond the physical actions necessary for material survival. For Guthrie, sitting in this chair was like being choked while drowning. If Prentice chose to send him to the place where the dead truly belong, it couldn't be much worse than this. Guthrie just wished he'd hurry up about it before perfect inertia set in.

They must have heard his thoughts because, without warning, the door opened.

27

BEN EGAN ENTERED, FOLLOWED BY Lloyd and Carla Harvey and a tall, stocky, late-middle-aged man with thick, iron-gray hair. The latter wore an expensive dark gray three-piece suit and an air of casual arrogance. Ingram and Stanton trailed the rest like well-heeled attack dogs.

"Hello, Mr. Egan," Guthrie said cautiously, wondering if he'd be slapped down for his temerity. He wasn't, and taking courage, he went on. "Mr. and Mrs. Harvey." Then his eyes fell on the stranger. "And you are, sir?"

"Who I am is not your concern," the man said. His voice carried the rich, easy timbre of a man used to public speaking. Or singing opera. And the way the others deferred to him and the fact that he was here in such intimate and important circumstances made him Zeroth's CEO, Avery Prentice. But if he was, he was very well preserved for a guy who must be in his eighties or nineties.

"What is important," Prentice went on, "is that you have something that belongs to us.

"Not at this time, obviously."

Prentice contemplated Guthrie for a few moments. His eyes seemed to bore right through Guthrie, but after staring into the wells of Tereba's eyes, Guthrie didn't find them so hard to take. Just dangerous.

"Our interrogation of Mr. Travis was quiet thorough," Prentice went on. "He insists that you took the bust from him."

"He's lying."

"You're the liar!" Carla shrilled, her voice cracking. Guthrie stared at her. "You're rotten with lies! I knew it when I saw your hand. You cheap, sleazy...."

"Quiet," said Prentice. He didn't say it loudly, but Carla instantly shut up. When Lloyd tried to take her arm, she angrily brushed him off. She'd definitely lost her cool, and it did Guthrie good to see it.

"Another witness has verified that you had it in your possession."

"Barbara Sidell? What makes you think I didn't give it to her? She wanted it as badly as you do, and she can be extremely persuasive."

Prentice laughed. "Yes. But I think not. She says you drove off with it."

"What if I told you I gave it to someone else? You're eager to get hold of it, why not others?"

The smile on Prentice's face darkened.

"Who?"

"Maybe you know him. An old African-American gentleman?"

"Why would you give the sculpture to him?" Prentice's voice was soft.

"He wants it. And he made an offer I can't refuse."

"So you haven't yet given it to him."

Oops, Guthrie thought as Prentice looked at Egan, who shook his head.

"We monitored access to that part of town as soon as Barbara called. He couldn't have gotten through. Besides, he was coming in from the north, and he ran when he spotted us. I'm sure he had it with him."

"You positive, Egan?" Guthrie asked. "The old guy's a pretty tough bird to pin down. You ever try knocking on his door?"

The expression on Egan's face told Guthrie he'd hit a nerve.

"I'd guess not. In fact, I'll bet you don't even know where his door is."

"You'll tell us, Guthrie," Egan promised. "Right after you tell us where you hid the bust."

"It's too late for evasions," Prentice said to Guthrie. "We have time now only for the truth."

"He won't tell you," Travis spoke up. "No matter what you do. He knows my friend. He told me he's seen him. They're friends, now. He'd rather die."

"There's time for that," Egan assured him.

Prentice laid a hand on Egan's arm. "He's got a point. If he had the bust all this time, wouldn't he have looked at it? Wouldn't you?"

They both carefully inspected Guthrie. Even Lloyd and Carla bent forward. Guthrie blandly stared back.

"He doesn't look like he's seen it."

"Seen what?" Guthrie prompted.

"Our friend," Travis supplied conspiratorially.

"Did you look in the mirror, Guthrie?" Egan asked.

"Not lately. Your boys didn't give me a chance to tidy up before they brought me here. Do I look bad?"

"We're talking about the mirror inside the head," Prentice said, tone impatient.

"There's a mirror inside that thing? Why would anyone put a mirror inside a sculpture?"

"Why, indeed?" asked Prentice.

"Don't fuck with us," Egan rapped. "If you examined the head, you'd have found the mirror, and if you looked into the mirror, you'd know about the entity."

"The what?"

"The entity that lives in the mirror," Egan said, eyes narrowing.

"Entity in the mirror? Inside the sculpture? Sounds nuts to me. But if there is an entity inside the sculpture, why should I give it to you?"

"If there isn't," Prentice asked, "why shouldn't you?" Before Guthrie could come up with an answer for that, Prentice went on. "The sculpture belongs to us, and we want it returned."

"Like I said, I went looking for the old black man. I found him, I gave him the sculpture, and that's all I know. If it's any consolation, he said he'd give it back so I could return it to you. You should let me go so I can go get it from him."

Like hell they were going to let him go.

"You may believe him, but don't expect us to be so foolish. Tell us where he is, and after we've retrieved the bust from him we'll release you."

"This thing is pretty valuable to you. Maybe we can make a deal."

"I'm listening," Prentice said.

"I'll get the head for you in return for freedom for me and Travis. And immunity."

"That can be arranged," Prentice said, expression hopeful. "I want the immunity assured."

"I'll assure...."

"I want the proof now."

"How can I do that?"

"Order Stanton to kill Egan and Ingram."

"You low-life freak!" Carla shrieked, but Guthrie didn't look at her.

And he didn't look at Prentice. Instead, he stared at Egan. Outwardly, Egan remained as inert as a pile of sand, but underneath Guthrie sensed a seething cauldron of rage and hatred. And fear. That fear told Guthrie all he needed to know—there was a possibility, however remote, that Prentice might agree to Guthrie's request.

"You must be joking," Prentice said.

"Do I sound like I'm joking, Mr. Prentice?"

"So, you know who I am." The man appeared thoughtful. "And you want a human sacrifice."

"That shouldn't be too hard for you. I hear you have experience at that sort of thing."

The tension in the air was electric for a long, long moment. Guthrie thought he saw Stanton subtly shift his weight and Ingram follow suit in a motion that was almost completely internal. Guthrie held his breath, waiting for the bloodbath to erupt.

Prentice laughed.

"Interesting, Guthrie," he nodded. "Indeed an interesting proposition. But I think not."

"We'll get the information from you," Egan snarled. "We'll open you up like a can of beans. Be sure of it."

"What are you going to do? Torture me? Use sodium pentathol?" Guthrie was beginning to get concerned. Even a dead man has feelings and limits.

Prentice's eyes narrowed. "Mr. Ingram tells me you're somewhat impervious to pain. And if Travis is correct and you have met the entity, such crude methods wouldn't be adequate. At any rate, we have much more effective means at our disposal."

Prentice signaled to Ingram and Stanton, who dragged Travis's chair off to the side then went to the cabinet at the end of the room, removed four folding chairs, and set them up around Guthrie. Prentice sat in front of Guthrie, Carla behind, and Egan and Lloyd on either side. Ingram and Stanton left the room, snapping off the light as they went.

The room was not in complete darkness. A single spot over the space between Guthrie's chair and the chair directly in front of him threw a circle of illumination over Prentice's face as well as his own.

"Before we hired you, I had Ben run a background check on you. In college, you were in a rock band. Are you still a music lover?"

"Yeah, I like music."

"Any particular genre?"

"Classic rock and prog, old blues, classical. Some jazz."

"Eclectic tastes." Prentice's tone was approving. "Have you ever noticed that certain love songs can be read as prayer? Especially in the blues."

"I've noticed."

"The sacred is often so close to the profane that one can be mistaken for the other."

"I don't know—I never had much trouble distinguishing."

"Hmm...well, you have proved more perceptive than we'd originally given you credit for. But back to music. Would it surprise you to learn that we are all accomplished singers?"

"I heard you sing a cappella."

"Yes, I suppose you have." Prentice shot a glance at Travis. "We have an interesting repertoire of songs. Perhaps you'd like to hear one."

"It wouldn't be called 'Embroidery of Shadows,' would it?"

"No," Prentice chuckled. "That one would have the undesired effect of making you most reticent and uncommunicative."

"And suicidal?"

"Very likely. We'd rather have you loquacious. Our piece titled 'Memories' will be more to the point."

"Sounds nice. Like something out of the forties."

"You're thinking of 'Unforgettable.' And no, it's not nice, as Mr. Travis can tell you. At least not for the one forced to divulge even his most cherished and dangerous secrets. And you do have secrets, don't you, Mr. Guthrie? Still wish to remain silent?"

In answer, Guthrie pressed his lips together. He knew well how to keep secrets. You hid them behind lies and told yourself the lies long enough that they seemed true. He stared stolidly between his knees, into the circle of light illuminating the area between him and Prentice, knowing he was finished whether he talked or not. He was determined not to.

"Very well." Prentice glanced at the others. "Shall we begin?"

They all settled back in their chairs, and for a time nothing happened. Everyone just sat there, or so it seemed to Guthrie.

Then Guthrie heard a low humming sound, nearly inaudible, vibrating the air. Gradually the sound rose in volume, and he could make out the four distinct voices adding tones and timbres that melded so perfectly that Guthrie couldn't tell which throat issued each sound. Before many minutes passed, the sound bathed the air in the room in a grating resonance that raked Guthrie's mind with a nervous intensity and sent him shifting uncomfortably in the confines of his handcuffs.

The vibrations grew more insistent, edging like electric needles into his skin, making his flesh crawl and raising his hair. Like a current, the electric sensation flowed across him and coalesced at the crown of his head, causing a faint but demanding ringing in the top of his brain that echoed chillingly down his spine. The humming began to take on an undulating intonation akin to the sound of breakers on a distant, timeless beach—monotonous, soothing, insistent. Prentice's sonorous voice broke from the others to whisper in an unknown language words whose syllables and accents strode in counterpoint to the already powerful hypnotic effect of the oscillating drone. The sounds seemed to work their way into the back of Guthrie's mind, and he felt the creeping tingling at the crown of his head snake into his brain and become an area of throbbing cold that formed diagonally through his head, from the rear upper left of his skull towards his right cheekbone.

A minute passed as the cord thickened and hardened into a pencil-sized bar of frigid, echoing vibration that shimmered every nerve of Guthrie's body. Prentice's eyes seemed to expand, threatening to totally fill Guthrie's field of vision. Everything else, even the shadows of the room, grew indistinct with ancient distance.

But there was one important fact Prentice couldn't have helped but overlook because it was hidden beneath Guthrie's belt buckle.

The hypnotic vibrations in Guthrie's brain met the oscillations already present within Guthrie—the leaden rhythms that had emanated from behind his navel ever since Master Tereba had marked him with the talisman. Like the merger of two waves of energy whose crests and troughs cancel each other, the mesmeric force met his internal oscillations, was neutralized, and simply vanished.

The humming and chanting reached a peak of intensity, and Guthrie felt as if eternity poised over his head. Prentice's huge orbs stared deeply into his eyes, and the man whispered in tones that begged to be obeyed, "Tell us what you have done with the sculpture."

"No," Guthrie said flatly.

He didn't know if his unexpected refusal simply startled their concentration, if their melody could not stand interruption, or if the single syllable added a destabilizing element to the music, but the effect was instantaneous. The bitterly vibrating bar sizzled into a blinding light and seemed to explode in his skull. The hair stood out on his head, and the energy, released from his brain, jolted with blinding velocity down his arms and blasted from his fingertips into the already charged air.

He wouldn't have been surprised to see St. Elmo's fire branching and fizzing from his hands, but though no pyrotechnics were visible, the effect on the singers was just as entertaining.

The energy grounded through Egan and Lloyd and the metal folding chairs they sat on, and they jerked and moaned with enough pain to edge their voices with hysteria. Carla screamed down Guthrie's neck. Prentice was not hit directly with the charge, but he sat bolt upright in his chair and trembled as violently as if he was being electrocuted. Then he slammed back into his seat, and his chair tumbled over backwards, spilling him awkwardly onto the floor. Guthrie couldn't see Carla, but the instant the loop was broken by Prentice's fall, her scream cut off in a gurgling noise as she retched onto the floor behind Guthrie.

Someone had lost control.

28

THE DOOR BURST OPEN AND Ingram and Stanton flew into the room, snapping on the lights. While Stanton saw to Carla, Ingram rushed to Prentice and helped him to his feet. The older man was shaking, but he recovered quickly enough. Ingram finished brushing him off then shot Guthrie a dangerous look. Egan, though trembling, was able to stand unassisted, but Lloyd and Carla were another matter. The Ravens helped them out of the room. After they were gone, Prentice regarded Guthrie with eyes whose thoughtfulness ill-masked the dull pain in their depths.

"Something's protecting him," Egan said. "The entity?"

"It did nothing to help Travis," Prentice pointed out. "No, it must be the old man."

And it was, Guthrie realized. Or at least, the tattoo he'd engraved on Guthrie's abdomen. Guthrie hoped they wouldn't strip him and see it. If they did, they might simply skin it off, which probably would be an appropriate prelude to torture.

But they didn't seem to think of examining him physically. Instead, Ingram simply reentered and checked the security of Guthrie's bonds, then did the same with Travis.

"You pose an interesting problem," Prentice said to Guthrie. I've never seen 'Memories' fail to elicit the desired response."

"Win some, lose some," Guthrie said.

"I never lose." Prentice gave a smile whose nastiness looked out of place on his patrician face. "I'll just have to perform a song that will be a little more persuasive than 'Memories.'" The smile tightened. "More certain and much less pleasant."

Egan, standing behind Prentice, shuddered, which didn't bode well.

Then Egan and Ingram moved to the door as if they knew what was coming next and didn't want to be around when it did. In a moment, Guthrie was alone with Prentice and Travis.

"You were a guitarist in your college band. And a singer. Do you still sing?"

"I can carry a tune, if that's what you mean."

"Interesting. Travis must have told you something of our little vocal ensemble." Prentice didn't bother to look at the man shackled across the room. "And the Neci Manuscript."

"He told me. Music to conjure the devil by."

"I wouldn't want to do such a foolish thing even if it were possible. If I conjure up anything, I want a power I can control, not a power that will control me. Besides, we're not some sort of cheap Satanists, slaughtering animals, reading entrails, bathing in blood, and praying for intercourse with the devil. Call us sorcerers, if you must. We operate on a principle of acquisition of power. The universe is full of energy that can be amplified, focused, and manipulated in various ways. All one requires is knowledge. With sufficient expertise, one can accomplish many useful tasks such as remote sensing, opening doorways, and control over animals and weak-willed humans."

"Animals? Like rats?"

"You're thinking of Martin."

"Why'd you kill him?"

"He was untrustworthy. I gave him more than he dreamed possible, but he tried to take what belongs to me."

"You're in no position to criticize greed."

"I'm in an excellent position to do anything I want. And I have knowledge of the correct mechanisms and vibrations required to tap powerful resources. You just have to know what you are doing."

"And you do?"

"I don't pretend to know the profound secrets of the universe, but I'm able to manipulate physical reality to some extent. Much as I've taught the rest of my group to do in their own limited ways. Unfortunately, Martin's death has restricted the range of our ensemble. We need his voice, and now we'll have to find a replacement." He peered at Guthrie. "I'll offer you a deal, and it's the best you'll ever have—return the bust and you can take Martin's place in our choir."

"I'm not sure I'd fit in. These others don't like me very much."

"That's no problem," Prentice laughed. "None of them like each other in the least. But we make marvelous music."

"How many do you need? With Hastings gone, there are only five of you. That is, if Barbara Sidell is still in the group."

"She's resting at home. Travis was a bit rough with her, and she strained her voice yelling at him."

Prentice chuckled again, and so did Guthrie, but he kept it inside. Apparently Prentice wasn't aware of Sidell's complicity in the scheme to take over Zeroth, and Guthrie saw no point in revealing that fact. Let Prentice continue to sleep with betrayal.

"You'd never believe that a voice that can utter such horrendous epithets also produces a rich contralto," Prentice continued. "I discovered her singing in a men's club. Totally untrained, but I saw the potential and recruited her. But to answer your question, five is enough for about half the songs. With seven, we can sing everything in the canon except "Symphony of the Damned." That requires thirteen."

"What's it do?"

"I don't know," Prentice admitted. "I've never had thirteen reliable singers assembled at one time. But I'm working toward it. Someday, I hope to have my entire choir." He paused and stared hard at Guthrie. "Interested in becoming a member?"

"No thanks. Too risky."

"I'd say you're at ultimate risk right now."

"I could join your group, and you can promise not to kill me, but you can't stop me from dying."

"Are you bargaining for immortality?" Prentice asked. He sounded like he took the idea seriously, and he did look thirty years younger than his probable age.

"I'll settle for the rest of my normal span. According to that old black man, I'm dying. Right now. And I know he's right. He's promised to cure me, but I have to bring him the head to him first."

"I can't allow that."

"Like I said, he told me he just wanted to examine it for a few moments. He said he'd give it back so I could deliver it to the Harveys. To you."

Prentice was unimpressed.

"Why would he want it for just a few moments? And why should he give it back?"

"He didn't say," Guthrie shrugged. "And I wasn't inclined to try to shake the information out of him."

Prentice studied Guthrie carefully.

"Perhaps your story about your untimely death is merely a ruse and you want to keep the bust for yourself in hopes of gaining control over it."

"I wouldn't know how."

Guthrie could tell it was the right thing to say. Prentice took him for the fool he probably was. How could a poor slob like Guthrie know anything worth knowing, much less how to control the power of the thing in the mirror? To Prentice, Guthrie was like a roach in the kitchen who'd crawled out from under a counter and invited itself to be squashed under heel. Prentice would be only too happy to oblige.

But the bluff wasn't good enough.

Guthrie not only knew where the head was, he now knew at least as much about the thing in the mirror as any of them did. Probably more since none of them dared face it. Prentice was the kind of man who understood power above all else. And he was smart enough to know that knowledge and experience were as powerful as wealth. Guthrie might not have possessed experience, and he might not have known what the thing in the mirror really was or where it came from, but he had personally met the power Zeroth tried to wield as a psychic bludgeon in their battle to scramble to the top of the heap. He'd seen that which only the doomed ever fully saw, and it had not enslaved him. Never mind that he'd escaped because he already was beyond doom or that he had indispensable help from old Tereba. Accidental knowledge is as valuable as that which is ardently sought. Sometimes better. Guthrie had seen the face in the mirror and walked away, and he couldn't keep that strength out of his eyes.

Prentice laughed. It was not an unpleasant sound, and he seemed genuinely amused.

"You surprise me, Guthrie. You have resources I did not anticipate. You accomplish the nearly impossible by recovering the head. You come through practically unscathed, which, considering the power of the entity, is a miracle in itself. And now you bargain with a commodity I cannot resist, though your words may simply be a lie to prolong your life."

"You don't believe me?"

"I'm not sure what to believe when it concerns you, and even so, it's too late for belief." Prentice shrugged. "I suspect it has always been too late. You are protected, and I could never be sure you were telling me everything. I must have the entity, therefore I must be certain that I know everything you know. There's only one way to do that."

"Another song?"

"'Oculus.' Incidentally, I've noticed the process is quite unpleasant for the subject, but it gets me what I want because, for a short time, before your mind breaks, I will be able to see every nuance of your thoughts. I will know everything you know."

Guthrie wondered if his face betrayed the horror he felt. Dead or not, he didn't want someone digging around in his mind. The secrets of his memories were all he had left, and if Prentice took those, he'd be nothing but a shell ready to collapse at the slightest touch. He jerked the handcuffs without conscious thought since he'd already spent an hour trying to get loose.

"Relax, Guthrie. There's nothing you can do, and this won't take long. After that, you'll have nothing further to worry about."

Easy for Prentice to say. He took a seat in front of Guthrie, but Guthrie noticed he didn't bother to draw it close. For a long time, Prentice just sat there with his eyes shut, hands folded loosely in his lap. He almost appeared to be asleep but for a slight tension tightening his throat and the corners of his mouth.

Guthrie glanced across the room. Travis's eyes held only blankness. Hearing a sound, Guthrie looked back at Prentice.

A low undulation was coming from his half-parted lips. As the sound gradually rose in volume, the range of its modulation increased.

Guthrie glanced at Travis again, then back at Prentice. The gradual amplification in volume and range continued, but aside from that, nothing had changed.

Or had it?

The air in the room seemed...thicker. And was Prentice peering at Guthrie from beneath half-closed lids? Guthrie bent forward and stared hard, but the man's eyes appeared to be completely closed.

Even so, Guthrie couldn't shake the uncomfortable feeling that someone was watching him. He shifted his gaze. Travis's eyes were closed now, and his jaw hung slackly, as if he'd passed out or was asleep.

The sensation of being watched built, as if someone lurked just out of Guthrie's range of vision, cataloging his every movement. Guthrie knew the feeling well from his days on the force when he'd gone into areas where the police were feared and hated, where dangerous eyes watched perpetually.

He twisted around to see if Egan or Ingram had entered the room, but the door was shut—he, Travis, and Prentice were the only occupants. Was there a video camera? One could easily have been concealed in the ceiling or the cabinetry on the wall. But, no. This was where Zeroth performed its secret rituals—they wouldn't take a chance that anyone might observe them.

A change in the quality of the sounds that Prentice was making caused Guthrie to listen more carefully. The modulated tones no longer seemed part of the same waveform, as if Prentice had split the highs and lows into two distinct yet parallel tones. Guthrie would never have thought it possible, but Prentice seemed to be singing in two separate voices at once.

Travis moaned quietly as the sound changed, but Guthrie couldn't pay attention. He was too distressed as the sensation of peering, unseen eyes grew, taking on an almost physical pressure. He cringed as the eyes stared next to him, past him, through him, searching. But never on him.

Prentice's two voices suddenly widened the gap, splitting the highs and lows even farther apart and causing a psychic disjuncture to wrench at Guthrie's mind.

And there was something else. Eyes was the wrong word. Guthrie began to perceive the searching awareness as a single, monstrous orb, like a spotlight of attention probing the room. Each time it swept across him, its energy not only increased but took on a quality that compelled as strongly as it repelled. At last, it settled on Travis.

The gaunt man cried out and writhed in his chair, not as if in pain but as though the brilliant focus was too much to bear.

"Not me," Travis shrilled. "I already told you! Not me! Take him! Take him!"

The attention of the big eye moved off Travis and cast back and forth across the room. It grazed over Guthrie and passed on, then came back and focused again on Travis.

"I don't have it!" Travis screamed. "*He* took it! Get away! Get away!"

Travis's screams abruptly subsided into whimpering gasps as the eye's attention left him and circulated around the room. Again and again it swept over Guthrie, and each time he could fleetingly feel its loathsome pressure, but it did not settle on him as it had on Travis. Finally, he realized that the eye couldn't see him. He was invisible to it, and he wondered if he should be glad or worried. Was it because of the talisman, or was he already too far gone for even Tereba to save him?

The disjoined sounds that issued insanely from Prentice's throat spread even farther apart, and as the gap and their strength increased, Guthrie could hear strain pluck at the tones. The eye swung its attention around and around the room, growing more intense and more insistent in its movements but remaining blind to Guthrie's presence. Sweat stood out on Prentice's skin, and his lips drew into thin, grim lines.

Then, abruptly, he quit singing. The horrible attention shed by the eye vanished, and the fissure through which it glared snapped shut. Prentice's eyelids quivered and raised, revealing carefully repressed rage and disappointment. He stood and stepped over to Guthrie, his body exuding an unpleasant, acrid odor.

"Kind of has a sense of inevitability about it, doesn't it?" Guthrie asked.

"Nothing is inevitable," Prentice replied. "Not even death and taxes. But I think you are right, or very nearly so, when you say you cannot be made to talk. We'll simply have to locate where you hid the sculpture without your assistance. It can't be far from where you were captured." Guthrie guessed Prentice was a perfect example of how arrogance can get you everywhere and nowhere at the same time.

Prentice opened the door and called Ingram and Stanton. When they came in and saw Guthrie blinking at them from the chair, they looked startled but quickly hid it.

"Get rid of these two," Prentice ordered. "After dark." He smiled coldly. "We don't want to arouse the neighbors' suspicions and damage Ben's standing in the community."

The Ravens' grim smiles replied that they'd be all too happy to comply. The three went out, leaving Guthrie to contemplate how soon darkness might come.

29

BEING DEAD HAD HELPED GUTHRIE up until now, but he didn't think it would stop the Ravens from finishing him off. There wasn't much he could do, though, except listen to the muffled rolls of thunder from the storm outside while he waited for them to come. It was tough sitting in the hard, straight-back chair all those hours, denied more than the slightest chance to shift position. His hip throbbed in steady rhythm with his heartbeat as his other joints began to jell. Anticipating the final darkness didn't provide much sense of impending relief.

The confinement seemed not to affect Travis as much as it did Guthrie, though they both suffered the same bondage and would soon share the same doom. In a way, they already shared it. Guthrie was dying and Travis had so lost his will to live he was readily accepting his fate. Why then couldn't Guthrie, who was already most of the way there?

Maybe it was because Travis had lost something that he believed in. That something had offered a vista of hope and fulfillment, and he'd completely bound himself to it. But it had been a tenuous something, a power external to Travis and beyond his control. When it was snatched from his grasp, with it went his reason for living.

Guthrie remembered that he, too, had once had a something to believe in—the future, represented by his job and his marriage, the only two things that had really mattered. They had been powerful reasons to keep tramping steep trails and desolate reaches where occasional flashes of insight hinted at something deeper, at a goal whose reward was as mysterious as the journey's beginning, at an imperative that went deeper than vocation or even love.

Somehow, the external motive led to the internal truth if only one looked long enough, but somewhere before that, for some reason, Guthrie had turned away. Blinded himself to himself and forgotten why he ever started, if he ever knew, and in the process, he'd lost what dim sight he'd once had. He found the quest had been supplanted by conventional wisdom, the mysteries smothered by the satisfaction of pedestrian and numbing appetites.

But the material rewards he'd finally accepted as substitutes for his ideals were, if not deeply satisfying, at least less obscure and distant. He could switch on the TV and see them flicker like a golden dream across the screen. He could drive past edifices marking their territories. He could meet people who actually lived the golden dream, though it had never crossed his own threshold.

Was Guthrie somehow at fault that the golden dream proved as elusive as his former unknown goals? Or worse, had he been the evasive one? He didn't like to think about that because the answer might be more familiar than he cared to contemplate. But he now recognized that change had come so gradually and subtly and thoroughly that he hadn't noticed as the quest for the mysteries of life vanished into pat explanations posing as structure and shallow certitudes mimicking security. Both were simpler than the quest for the mysteries of life that demanded impossible solutions, and they provided shuttered relief from the glare of memories and thought.

However he'd arrived at his present state, the results were damning. External goals can be snatched away, but internal goals ignored or rejected wither the soul's vine.

Tereba was right when he said Guthrie was already dead. He began to die years ago, when he lost sight of the path that would have inevitably led him to a place, no matter how mysteriously shrouded from him now, where he could feel real and true and alive. And each farther step he'd taken toward the mirages lying in tangles off the side of the path was another step toward death. He shuddered at how he'd been overrun by a spiritual destitution filled with self-pity and a blind, hypocritical denunciation of all that he wasn't but secretly longed to be.

Real death could not be any worse than the spiritual mortification of his recent life, but now that it was approaching closely enough to see the glitter in its eye, Guthrie desperately wanted one more chance to live and take up the search, even if ultimately there was no destination, no solution.

His mouth and throat were dry, but he was glad he hadn't had a chance to drink much before Rampart had taken him prisoner, otherwise he'd have pissed himself long ago. Small comfort for one of the condemned awaiting execution. And the executioners would be here any moment to take him into the stormy darkness.

Guthrie stretched out his legs and tightened all the muscles in his body. That was about all he could do—flex muscles and tune the leaden wires and feel them sing alongside his nerves like ethereal harp strings beneath practiced fingers. The vibrancy did not debilitate him as it had during the days past. On the contrary, it now seemed a strength. Was it possible to draw on emptiness as a resource, as a reservoir of vitality? Could death be a power instead of a weakness?

Then the Ravens came.

Ingram stood by the door with a 9mm automatic in his hand while Stanton unlocked the cuffs from Travis's wrists then from Guthrie's. Finished, he stepped back and drew his own pistol.

"Get up," Ingram ordered, and the two doomed men rose. Guthrie was surprised that he didn't audibly creak as he stood.

The Ravens backed through the door, motioning for Guthrie and Travis to follow. They trailed the Ravens down the hall, across the room, and out the back door onto a covered patio. Heavy drops pounded the metal awning, and sheets of rain hung the wide, spotlit expanse of backyard beyond. Lightning cracked and briefly illuminated the woods at the rear of the yard.

"Let's go," Ingram said and gestured with his gun toward the yard. He and Stanton picked up heavy flashlights from a white iron patio table as they followed Guthrie and Travis into the deluge.

In seconds, all four were drenched, but Ingram and Stanton ignored everything except the captives and the aims of their guns. Guthrie, for one, was glad for the rain, and he opened his mouth and let the fat drops splash and trickle into his parched throat.

As the group neared the edge of the yard, the Ravens snapped on their flashlights, and the beams cut brilliantly through the diamond-sparkled air. Stanton unlocked a gate in the tall wooden fence dividing the yard from the woods, and Ingram tersely directed Guthrie and Travis through. The trees ahead loomed darkly. Stanton left the gate open, and in a few moments, the four were sloshing down a path masquerading as a small stream. The ground began to roll into a series of ever-deepening gullies that swelled with black, rushing water, colorlessly illuminated by occasional flashes of lightning.

They walked far enough that Guthrie was no longer sure they were on Egan's property. Gradually, over the hiss of the rain, rustle of leaves, and occasional bark of thunder, Guthrie began to sense a steady, subliminally heavy vibration that grew in intensity as they waded. Just as Guthrie thought the gully they followed would become impassable, Stanton swept his light across a slight rise where a muddy path snaked up and out of sight.

"That way," Ingram ordered. Guthrie started up the path, Ingram followed, Travis came next, and Stanton brought up the rear.

At the top of the rise, the path ran through thick brush for twenty yards, dipped, then stopped abruptly. A flash of lightning told Guthrie why. They were standing on a grassy bank above Buffalo Bayou. The normally sluggish stream was now a raging torrent, muddy water clawing nearly as high as the ground where Guthrie stood. The far bank was well over a hundred feet away. Lightning flashes revealed a surface surging and roiling with hidden currents. The steady, heavy vibration Guthrie felt had become the soft rumble of the flood as it coursed down the channel. The tops of small riparian trees thrashed above the surface as the torrent combed through their branches.

Guthrie and Travis faced their captors. Their assassins. The Ravens blocked any exit from the bank, and Guthrie knew it would be futile to try for the water. He'd be shot before he could leap, and anyway, he'd never survive in the overwhelming flood.

Stanton holstered his gun then handed his light to Ingram.

"You wanted to see me kill someone," Stanton said as he came toward Guthrie. "You're gonna get a real close look."

So that was how it was going to be. No telltale bullets for Guthrie. A few quick blows followed by unconsciousness and a toss into the bayou, and there was poor Guthrie, washed up in some treetop downstream. If his body was ever found, he'd just be a statistic on the evening news—local man drowned in bayou.

Guthrie didn't know if they expected him just to accept his fate, or if they thought he'd whimper and plead. Whatever they expected, Guthrie wasn't going down without a fight, no matter how ineffectual. Cornered, Guthrie was filled with desperation, and, shockingly, because it seemed so long since he'd felt anything, that desperation bloomed into a fear-driven rage. It seemed that the worm could still turn. Stanton would kill him, but the bastard would remember how hard it was for the rest of his life.

Guthrie tried to ready himself, but he couldn't hold the rage, and suddenly, all tension fled from him, dissipating as if boiled into a steam that billowed from his spirit. Again he felt void, but it was different than the mean hollowness he'd experienced before. This was not the sour bowl of a hungry belly but the emptiness of a bell, and his head rang with pure, clean tones.

As Stanton threw a fast right jab at Guthrie's face, something clicked in Guthrie's mind. He stepped in with his left foot, twisted his waist to the left, and thrust his left arm up and forward. Stanton's punch grazed harmlessly by Guthrie's upper arm, and Guthrie hammered his right fist down onto the bridge of Stanton's nose. Bone ground beneath the fist, and Stanton fell back, obviously shaken and in pain, but without hesitation, his booted foot whirled toward Guthrie's gut. Guthrie couldn't avoid the blow, so he went with it.

The shock jolted through him, but he managed to hook a hand around Stanton's shin and bring his other elbow down hard on the side of the exposed knee. Stanton grunted as the slick sole of the boot on his supporting foot slipped in the muddy wet grass, and he went down. Guthrie tried another elbow strike, but Stanton was too quick. His free foot slammed Guthrie backwards, pitching him to the ground. Stanton rolled to his feet and pounced.

They grappled, tried to rise, slipped in the mud, and went down again in a tangle of elbows and knees. Guthrie lashed at Stanton's face, but in close quarters, the big man's superior strength and weight gave him all the advantage he needed. Twisting and heaving, he got behind Guthrie and levered a meaty forearm across Guthrie's throat. Muscles clenched, and suddenly Guthrie couldn't breathe.

Guthrie pawed vainly at the arm as fire burned in his chest and ballooned behind his eyeballs. He kicked and writhed but couldn't shake Stanton. They rolled into a water-filled hollow as Guthrie tried to reach his killer's fingers with one hand and groped for purchase with the other. That hand found the branch, little more than a stick, fallen from one of the trees overhead. The bones in Guthrie's neck were grinding painfully when he jabbed the stick backwards, over his shoulder.

Stanton bellowed and loosened his hold on Guthrie, who staggered to his feet and turned. Stanton was holding the place where the stick had gouged a chunk out of his cheek, barely missing his left eye, then he dropped his hand. Blood snaked like living war paint across his twisted grimace of rage and was instantly diluted in the rivulets of water running out of his hair. He flexed his shoulders and swung toward Guthrie.

As he did, Ingram stepped in to help. He tossed Stanton's light to the ground, sending its beam at a crazy angle into the soaked darkness. He must have thought the two of them could finish off Guthrie quicker than one, though in truth Stanton was more than a match for Guthrie. He just hadn't expected Guthrie to fight back, and Guthrie had been lucky. But Stanton was wary of Guthrie now and would bring his superior combat experience to bear instead of wading in wearing galoshes of over-confidence.

Maybe Ingram just didn't want to miss out on all the fun. But he'd forgotten about Travis, whose near catatonic compliance made him already seem like a ghost instead of a living man with his own measure of anger and courage.

As Ingram stepped toward Guthrie, Travis leapt onto his back and slammed downward with his fist, knocking Ingram's gun into the mud.

Travis was even less of a match for the Ravens than Guthrie. In a second Ingram threw him off, and the emaciated man splashed into the mud with a woof. He landed heavily, but when he came up, he came up with Ingram's gun.

His first shot went wide, and he never had time for a second. Stanton whirled, drew, and fired in one blinding motion. Travis jerked, clutching his chest, and Guthrie could see the life evaporate from him. In that instant, all Guthrie's accumulated feelings for Travis, all the antagonism and envy, drained out like tainted blood expressed from a festering wound. Guthrie could feel nothing now but sorrow that Travis's will had not exceeded his ambition and remorse that, for Travis, there would be no second chance.

And then, as Ingram slammed Travis's already sagging frame into the bayou, Guthrie, without thinking or looking where he would fall, flung himself after Travis.

Shots almost too rapidly spaced to distinguish boomed dully in the saturated air, and the water around Guthrie gouted as lead raked the surface. A burning slashed across his shoulder, then raw, primeval force sucked at his feet.

His head went under the churning, muddy current.

30

THE EDDY THAT SUCKED GUTHRIE under probably saved him a face full of lead even if it nearly drowned him. By the time the dragging swirl played out, his lungs were bursting. He kicked free, hoping his underwater acrobatics hadn't so disoriented him that he didn't know which way was up. Fortunately, he broke the surface instead of diving to some deeper, more primal current that might have held him in the bosom of the flood until it emptied into Galveston Bay.

Guthrie sputtered, snapped a mouthful of air, and saw flashlight beams sweep the surface sixty or seventy yards upstream. The water was really moving and had carried Guthrie many times farther than he could easily swim on the single gulp of air he'd taken into the bayou. Travis was nowhere to be seen, and Guthrie knew he was gone for good. Then the lights were gone, too—whether because the Ravens snapped them off or because they were now obscured by bank and foliage, Guthrie couldn't tell. He just knew one thing. He had to get out of the water and the turbulent currents plucking and pulling at him.

He was bobbing down the center of the flood. His only chance was to try to make it out of the main flow to the calmer water near the bank, then pray for an auspicious opportunity to haul himself ashore. Even that would be tough, supposing Guthrie made it as far as the bank. He was having a hard enough time just keeping his face above the surface, and the raking of a submerged tree as the current dragged his legs through its branches reminded him that getting to shore could prove impossible. He might have been more frightened, but there wasn't time or energy for anything that didn't have survival written all over it.

His thoughts flashed ahead, scanning the course of the bayou downstream from where he'd jumped in. In another mile or two, he'd hit the section where the water was sandwiched for a couple of miles between strips of park bordered on one side by Memorial Drive and on the other by Allen Parkway. Along there, trees lined most of the bayou's lower gully, but they were generally small. Even better, the edges of the swollen current would be brushing the grass growing on the manicured banks where they sloped up toward the parkways on either side. There would be his best chance to get out of the water alive.

If he didn't get out by then, he probably never would. Just past the park, the bayou threaded through the north side of downtown, where it was joined by White Oak Bayou, which would be carrying almost as much water as he now wrestled with so ineffectively. The confluence would finish him, and if it didn't, he'd be finished, anyway. Fighting the current and trying to keep his head up was fast using a lot of energy, and he didn't have a hell of a lot of that to begin with. Even if he made it as far as downtown, he'd be too tired to fight any more.

Just as he thought this, he heard the noise.

It rose out of the troubled darkness ahead, at first a barely perceived rushing sound accompanied by a faint vibration in the water. As the flood swept him along, the vibration hummed deeper, and the rushing sound amplified to brutal insistence. By now, he'd realized what it came from. In his mind's-eye survey of the course of the bayou ahead, he'd concentrated on possible landing sites, completely forgetting about the Shepherd Drive bridges where millions of gallons of rushing water cascaded through a forest of metal and concrete pillars and, very likely, trapped flood debris.

Gripped as he was in the middle of the current, unable to get to shore because of the trees on either bank, he reasoned he was probably in the best possible place to ride out the bridge passage. The pillars would be more widely spaced in the center, and there also was a lot less chance of debris. He figured he might survive a collision with a round and relatively smooth pillar, but if he was slammed up against a jagged log jam, he'd be lucky to be impaled immediately.

All he could do was position himself roughly in a sitting posture, with his feet aimed downstream. He tried to keep his feet high as he waved his hands back and forth in the water to stabilize himself and keep his head in air. The insistent rushing sound abruptly became a mute roar, and dense shapes loomed up out of the darkness.

There were two bridges. The northbound one, downstream, was high with widely spaced pillars that afforded a lot of room in the center of the stream, but the roadbed of its lower, older companion was supported by twice the structure.

As Guthrie wafted down the straight quarter-mile stretch preceding the first bridge, the torrent picked up speed, but he barely noticed. He was too busy quailing at the roaring darkness ahead. In daylight, he would have been able to see the water piling up against the horizontal beams supporting the lower roadbed and the furiously swirling rush as it sucked out of sight beneath the pavement. Had Guthrie seen where the currents carried him, though, despair might have paralyzed him, numbing the instincts that make even the dumbest animal grope for life. But he could not see and kept his legs pointed downstream in blind trust.

If he'd been two feet to either side, nothing would have prevented his face from plowing headlong into the rusted steel I-beam that formed the lower edge of the bridge. But a split second before that happened, his feet rammed into the only solid thing that could exist in this watery chaos—one of the many pillars he'd hoped to avoid.

He struck so unexpectedly and with such force that his torso was flung up against the I-beam. Luckily, his bad leg collapsed first as he struck, twisting him as he pitched forward, and he took the impact with his chest and shoulder instead of his head. The pressure of the surging water pinned him for tense seconds against the pillar as he scrabbled for a handhold. Then the raging currents snatched him loose from his mooring and dragged him under the bridge.

Instinct curled him into a ball, knees drawn up to his belly, arms wrapped around his face and over his head. As he somersaulted along in the current, his ears filled with a sound he would never forget. Guthrie knew hell was supposed to be the heat of fire and the stench of brimstone, but if there was a Satanic presence it could do no worse than commission a flooding bayou to compose the cacophony of its domain. Hissings, crashings, snappings, rendings, gratings, thuds, thumps, and the sharp cracks of current-borne debris slapping against the pillars—all were overlaid with the ferocious but magnificently indifferent roar of water and the heady thrumming of the structures of the bridges as they stressed under the enormous pressure. It was a symphony of irresistible power performed on instruments only the gods could play. The music of it might have been massively, impossibly cruel if it felt anything at all. Perhaps this was "Symphony of the Damned."

Guthrie was as awestruck and fascinated as he was afraid. He wanted to close his ears, but there was no way to shut off the appalling din thundering with raw force right into the marrow of his bones. He was caught in the rush, and all he could do was try to protect his head and keep his scream from adding its single, feeble, watery note.

Then Guthrie slammed into another pillar. His shoulders and back took most of the shock, and his stunned body uncurled. As he tumbled helplessly in the current, hours seemed to float by, their existence filled with perfect pandemonium.

He knew he'd passed beyond the bridges, knew he should be trying to climb toward the troubled surface somewhere above him where air beckoned with a growing urgency. A spark of consciousness managed to hold what little breath remained and told him to swim, but it was a gut-level response that controlled his body and started his arms and legs flailing well before his brain could make contact.

Insatiable demand blew the last stale breath out of his lungs, and his next inhale would have convulsively sucked water heavily laced with muck. Instead, his head broke the surface he dreamed he'd never see again, and he gasped in deliciously cool air.

By the time Guthrie regained his breath and sanity, he'd swept another hundred yards, and panic was again blooming in his brain. There were more bridges coming up soon, and one carried a train track above a hatch-work of creosoted beams. He'd been lucky at Shepherd, but his luck would run out at the trestle. He had to get to shore.

With ebbing strength, he struck out for the right bank. To his surprise, he actually made it as the bayou rounded a left-hand bend that elbowed into a basin-like area where the flood's ferocious edge slipped away. Here, the diminished flow allowed him to reach land. Gripping clumps of sodden grass, he dragged himself onto the sopping slope and collapsed, vomiting muddy mucous.

He lay there for a long time after his lungs and guts cleared, completely helpless, arms and legs like lead on the trembling verge of becoming molten. Even so, he couldn't keep his fingers from kneading and digging thankfully though the grass into the stiff, dark clay beneath. He was on top of the earth, not under it. Maybe he was less than completely alive, but he had one more chance to live.

31

AT LAST THOUGHT RETURNED. GUTHRIE'S muscles still ached like hell, but his strength was coming back. He had to do something, he realized, so he did something simple and crawled to the top of the bank.

Before him lay a field of stumps. At least, that was what he first thought as he stared at the blocky dark shapes that squatted in the darkness. Then he realized where he'd come ashore. A couple of hundred feet away was Allen Parkway where Dunlavy Street emptied into it, and between Guthrie and the intersection was an old cemetery. The stumps were gravestones.

Guthrie threaded his way through the cemetery, heading toward Allen Parkway. When he reached the last row of graves, he crouched behind a large tombstone and surveyed the road in front of him. Across the pavement was an apartment complex, and Dunlavy, to its left, led into the Montrose area. Guthrie rose and was just about to vault the low cemetery fence when headlights swathed through the air. He ducked behind the tombstone and waited as the car approached. It came from the direction of River Oaks. Most likely it was an innocent traveler, but there wouldn't be many pleasure cruisers out on a night like this, at this hour, driving down Allen Parkway, a street notorious for flooding during heavy storms.

The car, a dark Mercedes, passed by, going slowly. Night and rain obscured its occupants, but Guthrie was willing to bet it contained a couple of black birds looking for a wet worm.

In half a minute, it rounded a bend and was gone. Guthrie got to his feet, jumped the fence, hurried across the pavement, and disappeared into Montrose.

He didn't have much of a plan, but he didn't have a lot of options, either. He could go home, where a reception committee no doubt awaited him, or he could head for the lake, where he'd hidden the bust, and from there to Master Tereba's. The lake was a long way —miles—and Tereba's even farther, but what choice did he have?

Between Guthrie's present location and the lake lay an alternating pattern of neighborhoods and businesses with a scattering of office buildings, and he zigzagged through the streets like a shadow. When headlights came up a street he was on, he hid behind a bush, tree, or parked car. Innocent people might just think Guthrie was homeless and wandering, but Ingram and Stanton and other Rampart personnel would be out searching for him.

Nor did he want a run-in with the cops. He could give them a plausible enough story for superficial inspection, but a lot of the guys on patrol might take him into custody just to get out of the weather and monotony for an hour or so. And besides, Prentice and company could have reported that he was responsible for some crime, in which case the cops would take him in for sure. Guthrie didn't figure he was being excessively paranoid. Egan, being the head of a major security company with lots of police on the payroll, could all too easily learn that Guthrie was in jail, and there he'd be a sitting duck.

By the time Guthrie was within a mile of the lakes where he'd hidden the head, two hours had passed and the rain had dwindled to a steady drizzle. That bothered Guthrie. The rain was cover for him, and without it, the last half mile would be a no-man's land as he attempted to cross under the freeway and several blocks of open streets that lay between him and the field in front of the lakes.

He was nervous about Egan's people. They'd caught him only a couple of miles away, and they might figure he'd come this direction instead of going home. They had the advantage of numbers; his only advantage was they didn't know exactly where to look for him.

Guthrie hid behind the corner of a small office building and surveyed the intersection where Richmond crossed beneath the West Loop. Although the intersection wasn't particularly crowded, several cars waited for the traffic signals to change. None of them were pastel green, but that meant nothing. He let the traffic signals cycle several times, feeling frustrated. He could sit here the rest of the night, waiting for more rain, or he could take his chances and go across. In the end, he had to opt for chance. He made it into the shadows under the bridge without incident, then there was nothing to do but dash across the open streets toward the field next to the lakes where he'd hidden the head.

He tried not to think what a frightening figure he must have presented to the few drivers stopped at the light, but at least none of them chased after him. He reached the field and, once out in its expanse of dark obscurity, felt relatively secure, a dim shape hidden in shadows.

The lakes lay just ahead, and in two minutes, he stood on the stepping-stone bridge. He squatted, then slipped into the water.

It was deeper than he expected. Up to his armpits. Holding on to the stepping stones, he felt around with his feet.

Nothing.

Panic blossomed in his gut. Had someone seen him drop the bag? Did Zeroth have the head? Maybe that was why he hadn't seen any of them patrolling the area. Maybe they'd already recovered it.

He swung his legs in wide arcs, and on the third swing, his right toes nudged a lump that shifted aside at his touch.

He was working off the wrong stepping stone. He moved over and gently swung his foot in an arc outward from the base of the dam.

There it was!

He took a deep breath and ducked into the black water, groping. Just before the force of the current running over the dam pushed him away, his fingers closed on fabric, and he dragged the bag out of the mud.

Gasping, he floundered to the surface. He'd been swept away from the dam, and the water was deep enough that he couldn't stand. He struck out clumsily for shore, dragging the bag, and when he got there, he lay back, ignoring the drizzle, thinking about his next move.

He had to get to Tereba's, but not only was he exhausted, the shopping center that hid the old man's door was at least five miles away. That was a lot more ground to cover, and Guthrie wasn't too familiar with the area, so he couldn't cut through the neighborhoods like he'd done inside the Loop. He thought about his car. He'd left it not far from here, and maybe Egan hadn't towed it off. Then he abandoned the idea. Even if the car was still there and the keys remained under the floor mat, it was too dangerous. Egan was probably having it watched.

Guthrie would have to make it on foot.

He forced himself up. There was a long way to go, and he wanted to arrive before daylight made him too visible.

He walked nearly a mile through the older neighborhoods bordering the Southwest Freeway, then another mile through an area of office–warehouse buildings along Westpark before he spotted a van with the Rampart logo. Scurrying across a rough asphalt parking lot, he ducked behind the corner of an office building. The occupants of the van didn't see him, and the vehicle cruised on by.

Guthrie crossed Westpark, went through another office–warehouse district, and came out on Harwin, a three-mile-long street bordered by a plethora of wholesalers, cheap clothing and jewelry outlets, junk shops, and retailers, most of whose names contained words like trading, international, and importers. The hodgepodge of buildings gave ample cover, and he made his way up Harwin for about fifteen minutes before he spotted another Rampart vehicle— this one a car. He flung himself behind a low hedge surrounding a four-story office building that looked more respectable than most along this stretch, and the car drove on by.

Guthrie was fast reaching his limit. He needed a few long moments to rest before he completely collapsed. Standing, he scanned the area. From where he stood, it was a long way to the next group of buildings, and the most inviting prospect was the building next to him. He went around it and found an alcove entrance at the back that could be seen only by someone who deliberately drove to the parking lot behind the building. It was a perfect place to rest—secluded, relatively safe, and sheltered.

Inside the alcove, the door was bordered with silver burglar alarm strips. No matter. He wasn't going to try to get in the building. The cement inside the alcove was dry and out of the fading drizzle, which was more comfort than he'd enjoyed for too many hours.

Guthrie lowered the gym bag, thankful to be rid of its weight, and sat down with his spine against the side of the alcove so he'd be hard to spot, even if someone did drive this far back. Being out of the weather didn't warm him significantly, but he felt better just knowing there was even minor improvement in his condition.

Feeling better makes you....

Not yet, he thought. The effort of riding the current and the chill of the miles of damp, cool air through which he'd fled had drained him of the last vestiges of warmth. He wanted desperately to take a long, hot bath to lend him a semblance of life then lie down and sleep. He wanted to lie down right here, but he dared not. If he was going to survive the night he had to make it to Tereba's, and the shopping center was still two or three miles away.

But for the moment, he couldn't seem to make himself abandon the temporary haven of his nook. He sat there, hugging himself, trying to ease the creeping numbness and telling himself to get up and move. After half an hour, a bit of strength returned to his limbs, and he felt somewhat restored. By then, the drizzle had finally dissipated, leaving crystalline air sparkling with lights that cast glinting reflections off everything.

He stood, moved to the alcove entrance, and stared around. From there, he could see down the length of the office building on either side. About sixty feet away on the right was a chain-link fence closing the gap between the building and the parking lot for the adjacent building. Beyond that was a street and an apartment complex. Above everything, a corona of electric light bathed the air with an insincere if persistent glow strong enough to reveal the last, low remnants of storm clouds shredding across the sky.

For some reason, Guthrie suddenly felt more frightened than he had while riding the flood. It was almost as if someone was up there, in the wind-blown, rarefied welter—someone impervious to the fury of the storm, someone who relished the height and distance from the grime and bustle in the streets below. Someone who was looking for him. Guthrie could sense an insistent gaze penetrating the distances and darkness, sweeping and probing the streets for a feeble flicker that would indicate his presence. It was the gaze of a single, monstrous orb beholding the landscape with a blazon of smoldering animosity.

Guthrie cringed involuntarily and was about to huddled back into the alcove when he saw the rat.

32

AT FIRST IT WAS JUST a single whiskered nose inching around the corner beyond the chain-link fence. Then the rest of the rat came into view. It wasn't particularly large. The furry body passed through the chain link and padded down the wet pavement toward the alcove.

The rat spotted Guthrie when it was still a couple of dozen feet away. It stopped but didn't run. Instead, it stood there, staring at him, whiskers twitching. A minute later a second rat appeared on the other side of the fence, and it had a difficult time squeezing through the links. It was a big one. As big as Guthrie had ever seen. It looked more like a small opossum than a rat as it waddled quickly down the pavement and stopped by the first rat. Together they perused Guthrie with tiny glimmers in their beady eyes.

The first rat hadn't elicited much of a response from Guthrie, only a tired wariness. Spotting a rat at night in a port city with a subtropical climate wasn't unusual. Houston probably has more rats than all the rest of Texas combined. Guthrie had killed plenty of them around his home. But he didn't like the fact that the rat didn't run when it saw him, and the second rat brought a knife of tension that sliced through his exhaustion. The way the big fellow squatted there, staring placidly at him, wasn't typical rat behavior. A picture of Martin Hastings, or what was left of him, flashed through Guthrie's mind, and fear hollowed his gut.

Yeah, Houston probably has more rats than the rest of Texas combined, and after the big guy stared at Guthrie for a minute or so, about half of them followed him around the corner.

Guthrie heard them coming. At first he thought the rain was returning as the pitter-patter of thousands of tiny feet made an audible rustle in the washed air. But rain doesn't squeak and snuffle and twitch whiskers. Before Guthrie could do more than gape, the pavement on the other side of the fence was awash with a mottle of gray, black, and brown fur. In moments the rats were a sixty-foot-deep carpet spread just as widely. Then the horde squeezed through the mesh like hairy drops of hideous pestilence. A host of beady button eyes glittered in the glare of the street lamps. It was dark enough that Guthrie couldn't see the multitude of tiny jaws lined with needle-sharp teeth licked with tiny, hungry tongues, but he had no trouble imagining. His temporary haven had become a trap.

Guthrie visualized himself sprinting across that carpet as it came alive, leaping, clinging, climbing, and snapping. He'd crush a few under foot before they brought him down, but down he'd come, most likely before he reached the street. He focused on the two who'd first poked noses into Guthrie's retreat. The gray snout of the big one lifted, nose twitching, sniffing the air, as if it awaited some mysterious pheromone to signal the attack. Its glossy little eyes watched Guthrie with more intelligence than Guthrie cared to imagine a rat possessing. It was a Mahdi rat leading a rodent Jihad against Guthrie's alcove Khartoum. Once this horde got done with Guthrie, he'd be lucky to have remains as intact as Hastings.

It wasn't a pretty picture to contemplate, and Guthrie didn't. Instead, he swung around, took three steps toward the door, and rammed his shoulder against the upper glass panel. A second blow cracked the glass, knocking one side of it out of the rubber seal attaching it to the metal frame and tearing the fringe of burglar alarm strip. The police would come, now. Yes, his mind howled. Please. Anyone. His third blow, fueled by blind panic, took out the other side of the glass. On the second blow the big rat went for Guthrie, and on the third, the mottled carpet billowed into hideous flowing life.

Just as Guthrie dove through the broken door, the big rat leapt onto his back and scrambled into his hair, clawing its way toward his face. The first rat followed the big one up Guthrie's leg and onto his back as he fell inside the building.

Beyond the door lay a narrow hallway, and about fifteen feet up the corridor, a short flight of steps led up to another stretch of hall. Guthrie bolted to his feet and ran.

Before he'd gone ten steps, the first wave of the horde piled up against the door's lower panel, forming a living bridge to the opening above. The rest of the multitude scrambled up and over the knot at the bottom, spilling through the broken panel in a grue-some, hairy waterfall.

There were not more than five steps. Guthrie didn't bother to count, but there couldn't have been more because he took them all in a single bound. The rat on his back clung precariously at the surge and shock of his leap, but the big one had a good grip in his hair and was still scrambling for his face. Guthrie kept it off with his free hand as he raced down the hall toward the too-distant open-ing he could see at the end.

Behind Guthrie, the steps barely slowed the rats' advance. He knew he'd have to find some sort of sanctuary before they caught up with him, for catch him they surely would. He barely made the end of the hall when the leading edge of the wave clawed up his legs, the rest literally nipping at his heels.

The hall opened into the building's foyer in the center of which were two elevators. The elevators' open doors and dark interiors told Guthrie all he needed to know. They were shut down for the night. Given time he could open the panel in the roof of one of the eleva-tors and climb out of reach of the rats, but time wasn't cooperating, and neither was the big rat in Guthrie's hair. It had already scooped flesh out of Guthrie's scalp, ears, and hands, and Guthrie couldn't climb while keeping those insistent teeth away from his eyes.

He raced past the elevators and around the corner. The first door on his left was to the women's restroom. He hit it, praying it wasn't locked. It banged open, and he managed to slam it before more than a dozen rats got inside with him. He dropped the gym bag in front of the door to act as a doorstop and flung himself onto the sink counter, cracking his knee painfully but leaving most of the rats milling around on the floor, unable to climb the slick tile to reach him. Bending forward, he rammed his head, and the rat that raged there, into the mirror. The glass cracked, and his head spun, but there was a satisfying gasping squeak as the rat suddenly let go of his hair and dropped into a wash basin. It lay there jerking as Guthrie got rid of the two remaining on his back in the same fashion. One of them fell off the counter, and Guthrie kicked the other after it.

The big fellow in the wash basin was coming to. It had been stunned but apparently not severely injured. Guthrie remedied that oversight by pushing it into the bottom of the basin with his foot.

The rat hissed and snapped and took chunks out of Guthrie's tennis shoe, but Guthrie ignored the struggles and turned on the water. In a few seconds the water rose over the rat's head. All the malevolent intelligence in the beady little eyes turned off like someone had thrown a switch. Then the rat was just a poor mindless thing struggling to breathe.

Guthrie almost let it go then, remembering his own all-too-recent encounter with the same fate. But the filmy red of his blood clouding the water as it dripped off his head and hands was a powerful reminder of the crazed madness he'd felt as the rat clawed through his hair and tried to blind him with slashing incisors. Guthrie kept the rat down and and pressed the furry body into the basin until bubbles stopped coming out and its muscles quit writhing. Then he let up, kicked the limp body out of the basin onto the floor, and turned off the faucet. Several of its comrades scurried over and sniffed it, but the rest kept trying to leap onto the counter.

Guthrie took off his T-shirt, dangled the cloth over the side of the counter, and let one of the rats climb up to get him. Remorselessly he subjected it to the same fate as its leader. One by one the other rats followed. In ten minutes the restroom floor was littered with wet, furry rags, and Guthrie was the only thing left alive. Inside, that is. He put his ear to the door and could hear the rustle and squeak of the rest of the horde milling around in the lobby.

He returned to the wash basins and ran one full of hot water. Using wads of wet paper towels, he bathed his wounds. He drained the water and ran more. This time he plunged his hands into the water, relishing the feeling of heat soaking into them. It wasn't as good as a bath, but a bit of energy flowed into him.

The water cooled, and he let it out and ran more, then he jumped as he heard a muffled man's voice say, "Jesus Christ!"

A security guard or cop, Guthrie thought. He ran to the door and yelled, "Hey! Help!"

"There's someone in there," said another man's voice. Then louder, "What the hell!"

"Watch it!" yelled the first, and there was a scattering of gunshots and the sound of running feet. Guthrie could still hear the horde outside. Either the rats were going to get Guthrie themselves or they were going to force him to wait for the cops to take him in. Guthrie preferred the latter, though either way he was done for.

But maybe there was a way out.

He went over to the stalls, clambered up onto the partition nearest to the wall adjacent to the elevator shaft and pushed up a ceiling tile. The space between the suspended ceiling and the cement of the floor above was about three feet and interlaced with metal beams, wires, ducts, and pipes. Guthrie peered toward the wall of the elevator shaft, and four feet away was an opening into the shaft.

Guthrie climbed up into the space, dragging the gym bag after him, and sidled along a beam toward the opening, trying not to fall through the tiles into the restroom below. In a moment, he was crouched in the opening, staring into the elevator shaft, which was dimly illuminated by light filtering around the edges of the elevators. The tops of the two elevator cars were right in front of him, just below where he crouched. Being as quiet as possible, he swung across the gap onto the top of the nearest car then gingerly opened the hatch in the roof of the car a bare crack, just enough to see a slice of the foyer beyond the open elevator doors. From his vantage, the tail edge of the carpet of rats was visible, still milling around the corner closest to the restroom door.

He lowered the hatch and went across to the second car and opened the hatch there. The section of foyer floor he could see from here was clear of rats. What's more, he could see the head and shoulders of a man protruding around the corner just outside the open elevator door. The man wore a police uniform and an expression of fascinated disgust. Footsteps approached from the hall behind the cop, who glanced over his shoulder.

"What'd they say?" It was the second voice Guthrie had heard.

"They thought I was kidding," answered the first cop, edging around his partner's shoulder. Apparently he'd been outside on the radio. "They asked if I wanted Sergeant Orkin for backup."

"What the hell are they going to do?" asked the second cop. He didn't sound like he appreciated the joke.

"Beats me. They said to hold tight, and they'd send someone."

"Damn, you ever see so many rats?"

"Never seen anything like it."

"I hope they hurry up. This is making me sick."

"Hey," said the first cop, turning suddenly and switching on his authority like a light. Only then did Guthrie hear the sound of two pairs of footsteps treading quietly down the tile. Both cops disappeared around the corner.

"We're with Rampart Security," said a voice Guthrie recognized instantly as Corbin Ingram's. "We're in charge of the security on this building."

"Let's see some ID," said the first cop, and that was followed by a moment of silence as Ingram and Stanton showed their identification.

Then Ingram said, "What's the problem?"

"Take a look for yourself," said the second cop. Guthrie lowered the trap until it was just the barest crack. Ingram's head edged around the corner. He didn't appear to be surprised by the horde of rats. If anything, he looked hungry, like a predator closing on prey. He withdrew his head.

"What are they doing?"

"They're not doing anything," the first cop replied, his tone implying he thought it was a nutty question.

"Some guy's trapped in the ladies' john," the other cop amplified.

"There's someone in the ladies' room?" Ingram asked.

"Yeah. We heard him yell."

"Maybe we should check," Ingram said.

"I think we should get out of the building," the first cop said.

"We've got back-up coming. They'll be here in a few minutes."

"Yeah," said the second cop. "I'm not going out there with all those rats."

"I'm afraid you'll have to," Ingram replied. The cracks of two gunshots was followed by two clattering thuds. One of the cops, still twitching, fell partially within Guthrie's view. The side of his head was shattered and bleeding. A second later he moved as Stanton, gripping him by the feet, quickly dragged him out into the foyer past Guthrie's range of vision. Ingram followed with the other cop. The sound of the rats increased in excitement as the killers dumped the cops then quickly retreated. Right into Guthrie's elevator.

"Give them a minute to get distracted," Ingram said. "Then we can get by them."

"You think that's him in the ladies' room?" Stanton asked.

"Its him," Ingram said. "I can smell his fear."

Guthrie was only thankful Ingram was a Raven, not a bloodhound, or he might have followed the scent straight upward and seen Guthrie peering through the crack, too afraid to close the hatch because of the sound it might make.

"Most of them are drawn off, now," Stanton said a moment later, and Ingram nodded. They dashed out of the elevator. As soon as the sound of their hurrying feet diminished, Guthrie flung back the hatch, dropped down into the elevator, and darted around the corner into the hall. The one brief glimpse of the writhing furry mounds covering the police officers was all he needed to give wings to his feet. He sprinted along the hall, leapt down the steps, ducked through the now-open broken door, and was out in the cool night.

Without slowing, he ran between the police car and the midnight blue Mercedes parked just behind it then down the length of the building. He just reached the corner, when headlights flared behind him, and the Mercedes plunged down the parking lot, tires squealing.

Guthrie threw himself behind a low decorative hedge. The bottom was sparse, and the cover it provided wouldn't have fooled anyone in the daytime. Had they seen him? He wasn't sure. No doubt they were as anxious as he was to leave the rats and the dead cops behind. Maybe their haste would make them careless, though Guthrie didn't bet on it. They'd gambled the lives of two cops that they'd find him in the women's restroom, and they'd lost. Now they'd be anxious to redeem themselves, and they had to know he was close. Guthrie thought of the dead cops whose bodies the Ravens had used to draw off the rats, and suppressed a shudder that merged with a moment of panic as headlights blazed over the hedge.

But the Ravens passed on. The dark, combined with their haste, made his slight cover sufficiently opaque to their eyes. A discreet peek showed the Mercedes slewing out of the parking lot and racing off down the street. Ingram and Stanton weren't taking any chances on being in the neighborhood when the police started to hunt for the cop killers who'd left two of their own to a horde of hungry rats. After a couple of blocks, the car's taillights disappeared around a building.

Guthrie climbed from behind the bushes and glanced down the street. Flashing red and blue lights danced on distant buildings and sirens echoed in the pensive air.

He didn't want to be around, either. He turned and ran for the nearest shadow.

33

WITHIN HALF AN HOUR, GUTHRIE came to the edge of a golf course. The gently undulating murkiness beyond the fence invited him into its obscurity, and the open space felt good after the claustrophobic maze of buildings, apartments, and houses through which he'd been wandering ever since he emerged from the flood. He almost felt free, almost felt as if hope could buoy his leaden spirit. Then he sensed the big eye again, sweeping across the landscape like a prison spotlight searching for an escapee.

Searching for him.

Guthrie sank onto the wet grass, hardly daring to breathe or even think. It knew he was out here. It could taste the breath of his passage and was trying to focus on his location so it could highlight him in its glare and bellow with a siren voice for assassins to come on wings of black silence.

But the eye passed over Guthrie and kept going as if he was no more to it than the grass of the fairway. He rose and moved on.

Guthrie didn't see the man until he'd crossed the first two fairways, and then it was too late. The man was about fifty yards away and coming fast.

"Hey, bubba!" the man called out. "Wait up!" The voice dripped with false camaraderie, and here and now that made it dangerous. Besides, Guthrie had a natural antipathy for people who called him bubba.

The big eye stopped sweeping and fastened on the slouching figure. That really bothered Guthrie. Apparently the big eye couldn't find Guthrie on its own, but if it tapped into the living consciousness of the approaching man, as it had through the rat horde, it might be able to see through his eyes.

Guthrie's circumspection vanished. He dashed up the slight rise of a green, skirted a sand trap, then ran headlong across the mowed grass. Footsteps swished through the wet rough behind him then pounded on the turf as the man followed Guthrie over the green, down the incline on the other side, and across the adjoining fairway.

Guthrie didn't waste energy or equilibrium trying to look back, though he wasn't sure what he hoped to accomplish by running. He was dead tired. His bad leg limped, and the bagged weight of the sculpture dragged him down like a sea anchor. The man would catch up well before Guthrie reached the far side of the golf course. Guthrie realized he wasn't thinking, only reacting by taking flight, but he didn't have a hell of a lot of choice. He was too weak to fight, and the man might be armed. Running was futile, but it was all Guthrie could do.

Then the running was over. As Guthrie stumbled down the long, gentle incline of a fairway, he could hear the man's wheezing breath too close behind and gaining. In the middle of the fairway, Guthrie stopped. He couldn't run any farther, and he didn't want the man to take him from behind. He turned and faced his pursuer.

The man stopped, too, and now he was close enough for Guthrie to take in his appearance. He was about Guthrie's height and build, though he outweighed Guthrie by twenty pounds, centered loosely around his gut. He was dirty and tattered, with a scruff of grizzled beard and wild, greasy hair. He wasn't as decrepit as the drunken bum who begged at the traffic circle near Guthrie's home, but the two were generic siblings. Even at ten feet he stank. His eyes were dark pools covered with flat scum. The nasty sliver of a knife gleamed in his right hand.

The bum wiped saliva from around his mouth with the back of his left hand then gestured with the knife toward the gym bag dragging at Guthrie's aching arm.

"Whatcha got?" he snarled.

Guthrie hung back, and the man jerked the knife and took a step forward.

"Don' gimme no trouble." The way he said it implied that whatever Guthrie did would be trouble. The bum probably didn't need that much of an excuse to carry out anything impulse might suggest. He was here to kill, not rob, and he came toward Guthrie, knife threatening.

Guthrie raised the gym bag. The head was the only weapon he possessed, though the bum's snort indicated he didn't think much of it.

"The distinction between those who burn and those who rot demonstrates that it is preferable to burn. Don't you think, Guthrie?"

The grizzled face twisted with surprise as great as Guthrie's own as the words came out of its mouth. The bum's eyes went slack for a second, then he shook his head to rid himself of whatever was going on inside it. Whether it worked or not remained a mystery, because he sprang at Guthrie, slashing with the knife.

Guthrie jumped back, and the bum slashed again. Guthrie swung the gym bag and caught him a glancing blow on the jaw. He staggered back then came on fast. The next slash of the knife went for Guthrie's gut. Guthrie managed to twist aside, and the blade ripped only air. He tried to whip the bag toward the man's head, but the angle was wrong and the distance too short. The weight of the bag fell ineffectively against the bum's shoulder.

Before the bum could counter, Guthrie leapt back, out of knife range. The two men circled warily. Guthrie knew he'd have to keep the bum back at least five feet. At that distance, his make-shift mace was moderately effective, but inside that radius, it was a cumbersome disadvantage.

The bum feinted once, twice, then turned the third feint into a real attack. As the gym bag swished by his head, he got inside the circle of safety, knife glittering. Guthrie let the bag's downward and backward swing help him back pedal, and as the bag swung up again, he aimed it at the outstretched knife arm. The weight struck the bum's arm down to the side, and Guthrie stepped in and smashed the man's face with the heel of his hand.

The bum went over backwards, surprise parting the scummy glaze of his eyes, but as he fell, his flailing arm tore the gym bag from Guthrie's grip, and it thudded to the ground. The bum shook his head groggily, and he opened his eyes to see the bag lying on the grass. He grinned and started up, knife raised. Guthrie aimed a kick at the knife hand and missed. Then the man was on his feet, and Guthrie didn't have time to mourn the loss of his weapon as the bum charged.

Guthrie side-stepped, snatched the snaking knife arm, and levered the man over his outstretched leg. The blade slashed a burning arc across Guthrie's chest as the man pivoted past Guthrie and over his own center of gravity, pulling Guthrie after him. All Guthrie could think about was keeping the blade out of his vitals as they fell, and he twisted the knife away from him as they went down. There was a heavy gasp, and a fetid odor of rotten teeth, cheap wine, and what might have been chemical solvent hit Guthrie's face like a physical blow.

The bum was on top, his free hand on Guthrie's neck. Guthrie tied to pry the fingers loose, but the grip was like a vise. Guthrie felt his air passage constrict as he concentrated on keeping the blade out of his side. With both his hands he twisted the bum's wrist, grinding the bones audibly. The bum gave a reeking groan, part pain, part rage. His grip opened and the knife fell out, but he wasted no time trying to recover it as his free hand joined its brother at Guthrie's throat.

Guthrie groped for the knife as darkness swirled into his vision. His fingers closed on the hilt, but he was too weak to stab through the bum's clothes. As the world closed in, all Guthrie could see were the bum's two forearms, brown saliva bubbling over the stained beard, and above that a broken-toothed grimace. Guthrie stabbed weakly into the center of that grimace. The man, gasping and choking, jerked away, hands coming off Guthrie's throat.

Guthrie heaved in air, but the respite was brief as the bum, blood spilling over his lips, leapt back onto him. Almost unthinkingly, Guthrie raised the blade, and the bum's rush did what Guthrie hadn't the strength to do. As the man fell onto Guthrie, the blade rammed into his chest, just below the sternum. He howled and let go of Guthrie, and somehow, desperation gave Guthrie the strength to stab him again.

This time the bum jerked off Guthrie, tearing the hilt from Guthrie's hand. Guthrie was up in an instant, but the bum didn't follow. The knife protruding from his chest would never let him follow again. For more nightmarish seconds than Guthrie cared to count the bum writhed in agony and tried to pull out the knife, but his fingers kept slipping on the blood-slimed wooden handle. Finally, he fell back, coughing thick blood.

Guthrie watched in shock as the twisting subsided, the moaning cough weakened, and life drained out of the man like air leaking from a punctured tire. The man beckoned Guthrie close with a weakly raised forefinger. Still leery, Guthrie pinned the bum's arms to the ground as he leaned into the cloud of his halitosis.

"When I was dying of thirst," the bum's mouth said, almost whispering, "I did not dream of oceans or gallons of ice water. What I saw in front of me like a vision of glory and liberation was a ripe, juicy apple. Bring the bust to me, Guthrie, and I will give you an orchard."

"Solution is better than dissolution," Guthrie replied hoarsely.

The bum's mouth grimaced into a sarcastic grin that vanished abruptly as the big eye removed its attention from him. His body convulsed twice, more blood rattled from his throat, then the stench of his breath sucked in and stopped. Guthrie stood and backed away, staring at the body. It lay there on the grass like a discarded sack of offal.

The man died as meanly as he'd lived. Guthrie wasn't sorry it had been the man instead of him, he was just sorry it had to be anyone. He turned away, retrieved the gym bag, then, after a moment's hesitation, pulled the knife from the cooling flesh. He wiped the blade as clean as he could on the wet grass, and afterwards, there was nothing left to do but continue his trek.

He didn't have much farther to go, which was good, for he was weak as a baby. Most of the distance, he simply stumbled on out of sheer stubborn fixation, a black haze threatening to completely overwhelm him. The only thought he held was a prayer that he not meet any further attack. He was too exhausted. The next confrontation would be his last.

Miraculously he made it to the shopping center without being stopped by a cop, though he must have seemed a gruesome sight to early morning passersby, shambling along like a monster from a bad horror movie. He was torn and dirty, and blood, his own and the bum's, stained the ragged remains of his T-shirt. Dawn was just reddening the sky when he staggered into the alleyway behind the shopping center.

"The door will be there when you need it," Mary had said. "Have faith."

Guthrie was beyond faith, but the elusive door was his only hope.

He'd gone only about fifty feet when Craig Stanton emerged from behind one of the dumpsters. Light from the street lamps glinted off the gun in his hand.

Guthrie half expected it, but there wasn't anything he could have done to avoid it. His shoulders sagged with defeat. What did it matter? He literally could feel rigor mortis setting in. He was spent, and his heavy limbs waned into immobility with every step. If he didn't get to Tereba's, he'd die, and now he was going to die getting there.

Stanton must have been watching the way Guthrie limped and dragged his way down the alley and the defeated slump of his shoulders, because a caustic chuckle escaped from the shadow masking his face.

"You look like a fucking derelict," Stanton sneered. "But, hell, you come from that side of town, don't you?"

Now he was in the light, and Guthrie could see the red, puffy lump that was his nose. Stanton reached up and touched the clotted gash on the side of his face where Guthrie had gouged him with the stick, and the laugh stopped. He opened his jacket and slipped the automatic back into the holster beneath his armpit.

Guthrie could almost hear him thinking how much more satisfying it would be to finish off Guthrie the way he'd planned on the bank of the storm-swollen bayou—up close and personal. Payback for the way Guthrie had hurt and humiliated him in front of his boss and then gotten away.

A few quick steps brought Stanton close, and Guthrie drew the bum's knife and held it out, hand shaking. With a contemptuous snort, Stanton slapped the blade from Guthrie's hand, and it went skittering under the dumpster. Then Stanton wrapped the thick fingers of his left hand around Guthrie's neck, and jerked. Guthrie flopped like a limp rag in the big man's grip as Stanton drew him close enough for Guthrie to feel the heat of his breath. Guthrie blinked.

"You got mud in your ear," he gasped.

"And you've got blood in yours," Stanton sneered. His eyes glittered darkly in the illumination from the streetlights, filled with arrogance and oppressive strength completely devoid of compassion.

"Egan said you didn't know where the old man was."

"Obviously we know close enough," Stanton said. "We had it narrowed down to this shopping center or the next one down the street."

"Where's Ingram?"

"He's watching at the one down the street. We had a hundred dollar bet. Looks like he loses." Stanton chuckled. "You know what? I'm glad. I wanted to be the one to find you. We got unfinished business."

"I'm surprised he still trusts you," Guthrie said with as much élan as he could muster, which wasn't much. Stanton cuffed him on the side of his head, hard enough to make his ears ring.

"We'll see after I take him this." Stanton twisted the gym bag out of Guthrie's grip and set it on the pavement. "Even Prentice will notice. And now, Guthrie, say good-bye."

Sneering, the big man drew back a rigid right hand to chop Guthrie's exposed neck.

Guthrie decided that if there was anything he hated worse than being dead, it was watching some arrogant bastard kill him. He closed his eyes.

Suddenly, with a violent flurry, Guthrie was flung to the ground. He rolled, came to rest against the dumpster, and opened his eyes to see Li Wu facing Stanton.

Cursing, Stanton tried to draw his automatic, but Wu closed the gap in a leap that was almost instantaneous. As the gun came out, it flew from Stanton's hand, hit the wooden fence, and fell to the pavement.

Stanton didn't waste his breath on more cursing but counterattacked. The battle was blindingly fast—too fast for Guthrie's exhausted mind to follow—and vicious as hell. Stanton put up a good fight, but as powerful and trained as he was, Wu's body flowed like liquid lightning around his angular movements. He got in a couple of good blows and threw Wu to the pavement once, but it was all over in two minutes. Stanton overestimated a hammer fist to Wu's head, and Wu's hand, fingers rigid, snapped forward like a cobra striking and rammed up to the knuckles into Stanton's throat.

For one brief instant, Stanton's eyes blasted rage at Wu, then astonishment sucked away everything but one final flickering awareness of life. He swayed for a second, fingers raking feebly at his torn, pulsing throat, then even that final spark was gone. With a spasm, Stanton went stiff, then slack. He toppled and splashed into a greasy puddle.

Guthrie groped to the gym bag and tried to get to his feet, slipped, and then he was up, the weight of the bag pulling him nearly double. He could see the red door in the wall down the alley, and he directed his shuffling feet toward it. It was all he could see, all he could hope for, all he had left. But damn if it seemed closer, despite the enormous effort it took to drag each foot one step forward.

Suddenly he was lying on the cold asphalt. A short rest, he told himself. Just a short rest, and then I'll try again.

Everything went black as the pavement.

34

GUTHRIE WOKE TO FIND HIMSELF in an unfamiliar bed, covered by a white sheet. At least the sheet wasn't drawn over his head, so he must not be completely dead yet.

Wu sat in a chair across the room, but he rose and came over to the bed when he saw Guthrie was conscious.

"How do you feel?" Wu asked as Guthrie groggily levered himself into a sitting position. Guthrie lifted the sheet and looked down at his body. He was naked. And clean. The many scratches, cuts, and bites on his body had been treated, the larger ones with bandages.

"Not good," Guthrie admitted. "But better than last night."

"Nearly two days have passed," Wu amended.

"That long?"

"Master Tereba told us not to disturb you. He said you would need the rest." A faint smile lifted the corner of Wu's mouth, but the smile faded in an instant as Guthrie's gaze fell to the floor near the foot of the bed.

The gym bag sat there.

"You didn't take it? I thought Master Tereba wanted it."

"You must deliver it personally," came a voice from the doorway. Guthrie glanced up and saw Cindy and Mary staring at him with big, serious eyes. He pulled up the sheet, but still they hovered outside the door.

"Don't tell me that you're too modest to come in," Guthrie tried lightly, but their faces remained grim.

"We dare not," Mary said.

Guthrie looked back at Wu.

"Why didn't Master Tereba come for it, himself?"

"Since you arrived, he has been preparing," Wu said. "Bring that." He gestured toward the gym bag without looking at it. "We will take you to him."

He passed a bundle of fresh clothes to Guthrie then shooed the girls from the door. The clothes were Guthrie's own, so Wu must have gotten them from Guthrie's house. Had he encountered Rampart people there? Guthrie would ask later, but for now he simply put on the clothes, picked up the gym bag, and went into the hall.

Wu and the girls met him there and led him past a couple of more bedrooms, through the kitchen where he again saw the impossible landscape outside the window, then through two living areas to an open archway. Beyond the archway was an empty room that was completely bare and seemed to have no obvious purpose. It was about fifteen feet to a side, with white stuccoed walls that radiated a sense of austerity. The only feature was a wood-paneled door in the far wall. Wu gestured toward the door.

"He waits for you there."

"What's in there?"

"We don't know what lies beyond the door," Wu said. "We're forbidden to open the door or even to enter this room." He indicated the space in front of them.

"You mean you've never sneaked a peek?"

"When Master Tereba speaks, the wise man heeds, but when Master Tereba commands, even fools obey."

"You are the only person besides the Master who has ever entered," Cindy said.

"I'm not sure that's an honor," Guthrie said.

"It is the wish of Master Tereba," Wu said.

"Okay." Guthrie took a deep breath. "Will you be here when I get back?"

"We can only wait," Wu replied.

Guthrie went across the room and tried the door, and it swung open. He stood on the threshold and stared into a small decorative garden enclosed by an ancient, plastered stone wall patched with moss and draped with thick ivy. He stepped into it, and the door closed behind him.

The small garden was illuminated by a low but warm sun that spread a diffuse glow over the plants and the stone wall. The foliage was heavy with dew, and the atmosphere held a subtle but pervasive perfume, though none of the plants were in bloom. His feet left beaded prints on the smooth flagstones.

There was peace here in this enclosure, peace as replete as it was pliable, virtuous as it was seductive. Guthrie was suddenly crushed with an exhaustion that went deeper than his exertions. He wanted to sit on one of the three low stone benches scattered along the foot of the stone wall and just let himself exist here in the cool, fragrant, serene air for a space of time, let himself forget the weight of the gym bag tugging at his arm and the responsibility and danger it held.

But the weight was there, and Guthrie had to find Tereba to get rid of it. He glanced around the garden once more, then shook his head. Wu and the girls were mistaken. The garden may have been redolent with the old man's presence, but Tereba wasn't here. Guthrie reluctantly opened the door, went back into the house, and closed the door to the peaceful garden.

He turned from the garden door to confront Wu and the girls and saw that the door leading from the white stuccoed room to the rest of the house had been closed. That's odd, he thought, remembering clearly that the doorway had been a wide, open arch without a door when he'd come through a few moments earlier. Now it was a nearly square gap edged with stone blocks and capped with a massive lintel that must have weighed a ton or two. The gap was somewhat wider and lower than an average doorway and closed with a heavy door of roughly finished wood planks that looked very old. A single calligraphic symbol embossed on a bronze-like metal plaque adorned the door dead center.

That couldn't have been the door Guthrie had passed through to enter the room and then the garden. The fact that it was there now wasn't so much a shock as it was an unmistakable beckoning, telling Guthrie to come on in. Guthrie knew Tereba was there, on the other side of that door, waiting for him. He slipped the catch, pushed open the ancient, heavy panel, and went through.

As the door thumped closed behind Guthrie, he sensed that there was something very different about this room, if room it was. Convention center was more accurate—vast, hazy, and glowing with golden light.

The atmosphere was intense with energy tangible enough to breathe. The stone floor, or at least as much of the floor that Guthrie could see, was broken at irregular intervals by thick columns that appeared to be hewn whole from living rock. Each column held a pair of iron sconces in which flickered two fat white candles, and each sconce also held a heavy incense stick billowing smoke and pungent aroma, adding to the illusion of palpable force suffusing the room.

The smoke and the dimness of the light restricted visibility, and Guthrie's sight could not penetrate to the limits of the apparently huge hall. Although the stone columns testified to solidity, a wave of vertigo gripped Guthrie, and he was forced to step back and lean against the door he'd just come through. It and the stretches of stone wall on either side seemed to be the only real things in the hazy vistas of this enormous space.

Leaning there, Guthrie stared into the columned obscurity. Master Tereba was out there somewhere, waiting for him. He could feel the old man almost as if he was calling, but Guthrie was too terrified to leave the safety of the doorway. Out there, in the dim, endless, smoky distance, he would surely lose his way. The nebulous roil of smoke and flickering shadow, the columns so beguilingly solid yet so obliquely treacherous, the vastness of the unending emptiness that lurked like a presence, all threatened to swallow him in a limbo more utter than death.

His aching hand made him realize how painfully tight his grip was on the door latch. He let go with deliberate effort and stood without support. He had to force himself to move, to find Tereba. He could hear him calling. The old man's voice did not sound in Guthrie's ears but somewhere deep inside his mind. Seek me, the voice urged. Discover me in the depths of your fear.

Yeah, Guthrie admitted. I'm scared. Too scared to venture out into the middle of a replete emptiness devoid of reference points. He peered to either side. The walls for as far as he could see, which was only about fifty feet in each direction, were dry, raw, light-brown stone that showed no tool marks. He looked up, but the ceiling was obscured by the dark and smoke inhabiting the vaults above the flinching reach of the candlelight.

Follow the wall, Guthrie reasoned, and you won't get lost. Brushing his fingertips against the stone, he started off toward the right. It seemed a convenient direction. His mind argued that if he just went on in one direction he would eventually circumnavigate the room and return to his starting point, but the charged atmosphere was reacting peculiarly on another, less easily defined part of him, and that other part ridiculed his reason. Instead, he'd go for a short distance and see what he could see. If nothing happened, he'd retrace his steps and try the other direction.

Guthrie walked, wondering at the presence of an immense cavern located inside a shopping center that was at least two hundred miles from the nearest rock capable of holding a cave. After about a hundred and fifty paces, the wall had not deviated from its apparently straight course, and Guthrie found no sign of anything except what he'd already seen.

He stopped and stared out into the haze of the infinite room. He was seeing different pillars than he had when he'd begun walking, but they looked no different, and the space appeared much the same as it had from the door. Guthrie decide it was time to go back. He retraced his steps to the door. But there was no door. Though he was certain he'd gone far enough, all he saw was an unbroken stretch of rock wall.

Guthrie continued on for another hundred feet, but still the door eluded him. Fighting down panic, he went on. Nothing. He turned and went back.

No door.

Guthrie went onward another hundred paces, searching for the exit, but it had vanished.

Guthrie stared out into the infinite room, at the columns, the smoke, the distances so vast the sound of his feet on the stone floor had not once teased an echo from them. The weight of the head dragged at his deadened arm like an encumbrance of sin.

Skirting the periphery was getting him nowhere. Guthrie had to take hold of himself. He had to go out, into the smoke.

35

AFTER FIFTY PACES, THE STONE wall vanished in the swirling golden haze. Guthrie seriously wondered if he should turn back, but he suspected he'd already lost his way. Even now, the wall was but memory and the presence of a door leading to the outer world an elusive idea whose validity could be surmised but never proven. Certainties in this cavernous realm were reduced to the half-dozen stone pillars he could see at any given moment and the relatively smooth stone floor on which he walked.

Time attenuated into uncertainty. He kept walking long after he finally lost count of his footsteps, though after more indeterminate time passed, the feel of his leg muscles indicated he must have covered a couple of miles or more. By then, he'd become thoroughly disoriented, with absolutely no way to tell if he kept on a straight track, described a circular course, or wandered like a staggering drunk.

Curiously, the farther he walked, the less apprehensive he became. Maybe his lack of fear was because he had forced himself to take that first step, forced himself out into the unknown, out where he seemed little more than a disembodied spirit floating in the ether. But even so, there remained something integral about him, something that eternal space and infinite time could not alter.

As the haze swirled around him, the possibility of impending death yielded to the idea that ultimately his present state seemed no different than life itself, where the past, present, and future are equally shrouded in the unknown. Death was suddenly less important. Guthrie did not want to die, but if he did, would it really matter? He would still go onward through the fog, just as he had always done, seeking occasions of light, each illuminating a single pillar of solid truth.

Abruptly a shadow condensed out of the fog, startling Guthrie from his reverie. He stopped, wary but not frightened. The shadow became a figure wrapped in gray robes that could have been woven from the very fabric of the smoky air. It was Tereba.

"I found you," Guthrie said.

"You found me." The voice was no less melodious than ever, but the matter-of-fact tone lacked the undercurrent of Tereba's usual humor. Guthrie had found the old man, but no reassurances lay in the discovery.

"I wasn't sure I was going the right way," he ventured.

"Any way you chose would have brought you to me." Tereba smiled, and the powerful emptiness of his eyes made the smile appear sharp-toothed. "Even if you had only followed the wall."

"I was afraid."

"The dead need have no fear," Tereba replied. "Perhaps you are not as dead as you believe."

"I want to live," Guthrie admitted.

"Do you? Really? Are you ready to act on your desire? To do so you must act on yourself. Strength of will is required if you are to assume responsibility for those elements of life over which you are granted control."

"I'm ready."

The old man smiled even more starkly than before.

"You are ready to face the fear and uncertainty living brings?"

"I'm here." Guthrie held out the gym bag. "Here's the head."

The old man did not take the bag but continued to stare into Guthrie's eyes. His gaze was uncomfortable, not because it frightened or embarrassed Guthrie but because it read beyond fear and embarrassment.

"But what about joy and beauty, Mr. Guthrie? What about hope and love? You must embrace these as well."

"Somehow those are a little harder to get hold of and keep."

"Is not fear as transitory as joy? Is not bitter desperation simply the other face of benevolence?"

Guthrie could not answer with more than a perplexed shrug.

"Do you trust me, Mr. Guthrie?"

"I trust you'll do whatever you wish, Master Tereba."

"Open the bag and remove the head."

Guthrie took out the sculpture and dropped the bag to the stone floor.

"You want me to open it up?" Guthrie asked. "You must know what's inside."

"I know better than anyone. Open it."

Guthrie thumbed the catch, and the sculpture's face hinged to the side, revealing the glass. Guthrie regarded the image he saw there.

"You do not fear to look in the mirror?"

"No, but I fear what looks back."

"You fear yourself?"

"Even a true reflection wouldn't be me," Guthrie said. "But that thing in there isn't even a reflection. Prentice and the others called it an entity. They think it's alive. Travis believed that, too."

"And you?"

"I might have believed it once, but now I'm not so sure a force has to be alive to be animate or even to be sentient. Look at me."

"You begin to grasp the truth," the old man soothed. "You are correct when you say the image in the mirror is not you, and you are also correct in thinking it is not alive. Just as we are representatives of life, it represents the antithesis of life."

"It's dead? Like me?"

"No, never like you," the old man said gently. "Most people mistake death as the antithesis of life, but that is not the case at all. Death is simply the reverse of birth. Exit for entrance. Life has a converse, but it is not death."

"What is it?"

"How can we who live know for certain life's antipode? We can only know that life consumes to expand in fullness, but its antithesis consumes to maximize emptiness. Life is fertile and reproduces itself in myriad diversity; its antithesis is barren and reproduces itself in exclusive conformity. Life is the inertia of motion; its antithesis is the inertia of rest."

"And the mirror?"

"As you said, mirrors reflect. This mirror does more than reflect. It is as much window as mirror. A window to a room with an inhabitant who would like to leave."

"And you want to keep it there, locked in its room."

"No, Mr. Guthrie. I want to help it leave. I just don't want it to go where it wants to go. It wants to live in the world. It wants to devour the world."

"But?"

"I'm going to send it back where it came from," Tereba finished. "With your help."

"Are you going to break the mirror?" Guthrie managed a smile. "That would bring seven years of bad luck."

"More than seven," Tereba replied, not returning the smile. "Breaking the mirror would only release the inhabitant into the world. True, it would be without a body and thus without instrumentality, but its corrupting influence would feed off the suffering it would foster. It would be like an ineradicable psychic epidemic upon the countryside, growing ever stronger and widespread until it infects the whole world. No, we must use other means to send it home."

"Here," Guthrie held the head out to Tereba, completely confident of the old man's abilities and power. "What can I do?"

"Please," Tereba said, quickly averting his face. "Only the dead may look upon Aswad Mar with impunity."

"Aswad Mar?" Guthrie asked, pressing the glass to his chest. He was shocked that even this old man, so replete with mysterious power, was afraid of the mirror.

"The name of the inhabitant of the mirror. A demon."

"With jaws that bite and claws that snatch?" Guthrie paraphrased, and this time the old man chuckled.

"More frightening than torn and consumed flesh." Tereba grew serious. "This is not some rough, bestial belly, but insatiable gluttony that expands eternally in capacity as well as appetite. It is a powerful demon, but it is a foolish one as well, for it constantly transforms its own desires into a prison at once larger and more confining. Aswad Mar is a parasite of the spirit, Mr. Guthrie, as you know well, for you have seen its face."

"Yes, I've seen its face," Guthrie said. "I'm dead, and it couldn't possess me, but that didn't matter because I saw I was already possessed. By something else." He hung his head. "I don't think I really understood until Stanton killed Travis—the man who stole the head. He had so much I wanted, and when he died, I could see that my envy was like a living thing."

"You come to understandings of the pervasive and subtle reach of this demonic power. A little of it resides in us all."

"Not in you, Master Tereba."

"In me. I am here because of it. Now it's time for us to help each other exorcise this demon that has taken control of our lives."

"How?"

"Look in the mirror. Call Aswad Mar as only the dead who lust for life can call it."

Guthrie cradled the head in the familiar position and gazed into the glass. There was Aswad Mar, staring back at him, mimicking Guthrie.

No, not exactly. It was more. It was what Guthrie yearned to attain, what he dreamed behind a sleep that even dim memory could not penetrate. It was the Guthrie he could become if only he continued to stare into the glass, if only he listened carefully and gave more. If he only united with the image.

He could not unite. Somewhere between Guthrie and the face in the glass was discontinuity. Guthrie could feel the force of suggestion coming from the image, but it failed to find a grip within him, as if there were no handholds, as if his spirit was as hollow as the head, as smooth as the mirror's flawless glass.

Guthrie knew it was because he was dead inside, and maybe Aswad Mar knew it as well. But such was the demon's force of will, its unbounded confidence in its own power to consume, that it stubbornly kept probing, seeking to possess Guthrie, to find the vital meat of Guthrie's spirit. It could not conceive of eyes that saw but failed to be enthralled.

Guthrie did not resist. Resistance would have been futile, or worse. Resistance was what it fed on. But Guthrie did not resist, partly because there was no need, but mostly because resistance was a drive he no longer possessed. He didn't want Aswad Mar to enter; he didn't want it to leave. He simply did not want. Inside he was void. And the void was as intangible to Aswad Mar as the smoke in the infinite room was to Guthrie. It could no more grasp and possess Guthrie's spirit than Guthrie could the candlelight flickering through the smoke.

Then Guthrie felt a brush of breath on his neck as Tereba whispered in his ear with a voice as soft as gossamer, as powerful as steel cable.

"Live again, Mr. Guthrie. Face the demon and live again."

Live again, Guthrie thought bitterly. As if I have ever lived once that I can do it again.

All the hatred, anger, and bitterness that Guthrie once felt and that had gradually abandoned him returned in a sudden raging flood. What the hell did the old man know? He didn't know what it was like living with what Guthrie had to live with.

The stars of greed in the eyes of the image in the mirror went nova. Guthrie, even through the haze of his own anger, saw the change in Aswad Mar's expression, and that was enough to wash away his own rage. What had the demon perceived?

For long moments Guthrie studied the look in Aswad Mar's eyes, striving to see the source of its perception. But there were only emptiness and appetite and attention. Then Guthrie realized with a shock that while the emptiness and appetite, and even the attention, belonged to Aswad Mar, the focus of its attention could lie in only one place—within Guthrie. He stared at it, and it stared back, and he saw in its eyes that it sensed not simply vulnerability but something to consume. But how? Guthrie was dead. He was not vulnerable; he had nothing to consume.

He must have spoken aloud, because Tereba's voice sounded in his ear.

"Perhaps something yet lives inside you."

"Nothing," Guthrie moaned, not wanting to detect the thing he knew was in him. "Nothing's there."

"What is it?"

"I don't know," he cried. "I don't want to know."

But recognition was at him like a scavenger at a corpse, and being dead, he could not escape.

"What?" Tereba's voice came urgently. "What is it?"

What?

Guthrie tried not to look, and at first he did not see it because he'd so long blinded himself to its presence. But it was within him, inescapable, and he could no longer turn a blind eye. And then, though he did not want to see it, there it was—just one little thing wriggling into the shadows like a shriveled, ugly worm.

But if Guthrie had never really seen the worm, he'd always known it was there, thriving beneath the welter of anger and condemnation that had been his life for longer than he cared to remember. It was a creature of darkness, living in the hidden corners of his mind, burrowing through the residue of memories he'd carefully curated in his consciousness. With his mind cleared of everything, though, its wriggling brought it no escape but only advertised its presence. And now that he did see it, how could he fail to recognized it? He was as riddled and brittle with its passages as termite-eaten wood.

In a perverse way, Tereba was right. Guthrie was not quite as dead as he thought. The worm was his guilt, and his guilt was still very much alive. Of all things that had been in Guthrie, it was the last to die, the hardest to kill. And in the dark emptiness of Guthrie's spiritual decay, it had ventured far enough from its haunts that it had been caught in the open by Aswad Mar's ravening eye.

It was nothing but a worm, but it was all Aswad Mar needed to gain entrance. Aswad Mar sent slithering barbed feelers through the worm holes of Guthrie's mind, seeking the source of the energy. Guthrie felt no pain, only horror and disgust as the demon groped swinishly deeper, insinuating tendrils throughout his mind, pulling more of its avarice into him.

Aswad Mar touched the worm, and its desire opened like a pit. This worm, so apparently insignificant, was everything the demon coveted, for it was desire itself, overwhelming desire to become other than itself. The surface of the mirror remained placid, but beneath the surface, the image of Guthrie's face faded and his eyes diminished into twin points of incendiary lust enclosed in ebon emptiness. The worm was irresistible bait.

And Guthrie's emptiness promised a comfortable new home that would allow Aswad Mar access to the world.

Probing and gouging with snarling insistence for the ultimate source of the essential vitality it ached to consume, the demon clawed its way out of the mirror, through Guthrie's eyes, and into his mind.

36

GUTHRIE'S MOUTH DISTENDED IN A scream that remained silent as he was riveted by the blast of terrible force invading his sight. His vision eclipsed in an umbra of ravening voracity that tore his gut with bile and acid, and in seconds, his consciousness resonated with a gluttony whose pit could open wide enough to swallow all of creation then churn inward upon itself, gasping, pounding, bellowing for more.

In that moment Guthrie knew not only the massive urgency of Aswad Mar's hunger, but the raw bowels of its cunning. It had a plan to escape from the mirror and unleash itself on the world. The demon needed a man it controlled instead of men who controlled it. Not just any man, but Avery Prentice.

Aswad Mar wanted Prentice because Prentice possessed wealth, power, and an organization already at his disposal—an organization the demon itself helped build and control. It also recognized in the man's compulsive desire for control a kinship with its own being. Prentice would be easier than most to subsume, and afterwards, the world would belong to Aswad Mar.

The demon also had another reason, more compelling and personal. It wanted Prentice because Prentice had dared to enslave it, starve it, leash it, and make it perform like a trained animal, all for Prentice's personal aggrandizement. Prentice had used Aswad Mar to build an empire, and then he called that empire his own and himself master. It was not his. It belonged to Aswad Mar, and the demon would prove to Prentice just who was master.

But Prentice would never voluntarily look into the mirror. His personal power and a caution born of many years of wielding that power had made him wary, and he would not easily be tricked.

There was one person, though, who could get close enough to him and know him at his most vulnerable. That person was his consort, Barbara Sidell. She could trick him into looking the demon full in the face.

Sidell couldn't do it alone, though. She didn't have the means to free the head. One of the others would have to help her, and Hastings was the obvious choice. The Harveys hadn't actually possessed the combination to the cabinet, and neither had Egan. And while Egan could find the right person to steal the bust, he was too loyal to Prentice. Hastings's loyalty, on the other hand, was severely compromised by his growing jealousy of Egan's superior position in the Zeroth hierarchy. It was just the sort of emotional leverage Aswad Mar needed.

And Aswad Mar was more than ready. Just two decades ago, it had been helplessly trapped in the mirror, as it had been for more than a millennium. But years of constant exposure to greedy and powerful people in the service of Zeroth had vastly increased its potential. It had always had the knowledge that would allow it to depart the mirror and inhabit a living host, and now, at last, it had the strength. Once it possessed a body, it would be free.

The process of influencing Hastings took time despite the demon's growing power, for Prentice had been very careful. The safe in which the head had been stored had a Faraday cage built into the lead, silver, and gold layered inside its case-hardened steel and bullet-proof glass. The construction effectively banked the demon's force and confined it to the cabinet, keeping the Harveys' home free from contamination. And when Prentice opened the cabinet for Zeroth's nefarious purposes and the head was exposed to unsuspecting victims, a recorded organum played quietly in the background to protect Zeroth members from the demon's influence.

So the demon had waited, had been forced to wait, knowing that the subtle nudging it gave Hastings would eventually blossom into action. If it had to endure months, or even years of waiting, so be it—it already had endured a millennium and more, and there was little else it could do.

And then Hastings finally succumbed, and John Travis came along, took the head from the protective cabinet, and given the demon the chance it needed. An even better chance than it had with Hastings, in fact, because Aswad Mar had seen into Hastings and knew that the man had another protective cabinet waiting when Travis delivered the head.

But it didn't matter, because a new and superior plan had found its way into the demon's mind. Until the head was safely locked away, Prentice would be suspicious and careful of anyone he came into contact with, even Sidell, and he probably could resist any attempt to trick him into looking at the mirror. But if Sidell brought Travis and the bust, he would look at Travis, and if the demon was inside Travis instead of the mirror, one look was all it would take. Aswad Mar could eventually completely subjugate Prentice then transfer, leaving Travis a lifeless shell.

Travis had been pitifully easy to control, and Sidell's own greed had betrayed her when Travis called her on the phone. She thought she was going to collect the head, but instead, Travis overpowered and bound her. Travis then tried to make her look into the mirror to make her tractable, not knowing that tractability wasn't her strong suit. And she knew a protective organum. Even when Travis gagged her, she could still hum. The demon was patient, though. It knew that eventually hunger and thirst would make her vulnerable, and as soon as it had her bound to its will, it would fully occupy Travis. Then the three of them would visit Prentice.

But now Travis was gone, and Aswad Mar's plan to use him as its Trojan horse had gone awry. No matter. Guthrie was as good a messenger. Better. He was empty already—a ready-made suit into which the demon could step immediately. And with the empty head and a single phone call, Guthrie could gain direct access to Prentice. The demon could operate from Guthrie as well as from Travis, so the plan was still in force—only the temporary housing had changed. Guthrie would deliver the head to Prentice, and while Prentice wouldn't look at it, he would look at Guthrie. And when he did, everything he owned, everything he was, would belong to Aswad Mar.

But first the demon had to control Guthrie, and to do that, it had to find and consume the final spark of Guthrie's spirit, the spark animating that wriggling worm of guilt.

Suddenly, horribly, the demon was completely inside Guthrie, chasing the guilt that was the sole remainder of Guthrie's essence. All Aswad Mar's hunger, that maw of desire that owned no belly and so could never be filled, was limned in intimate, awful detail.

Guthrie's flayed mind lay exposed to the barren, grasping core of the demon need—a naked singularity that gorged on spirit instead of matter.

For a split second, the demon's wordless yowl of triumph slammed through Guthrie like thunder through an empty room.

Everything! Everything!

Guthrie could not fight the demon. Yes, he thought. Everything. Give it everything. If all he had were the memories, give it those. He didn't want them, anyway.

So he gave it his memories—the true memories that lay beneath the lies he'd told himself so often these past two years that they'd begun to masquerade as truth. The evil memories that he knew, deep inside, he could no longer disguise within the crucible of his own emptiness.

Feed, he cried in his mind as the layers of his self deceit peeled free, completely exposing the worm of guilt that became, suddenly, the caterpillar of truth. Feed! he screamed as Aswad Mar sucked at the flesh of the corrupt truth Guthrie had so long denied. Feed, he moaned, as he gave it his violent petulance when Alice would not submit to his bullying. And he gave it his foul humor as he slammed out of the house, jumped into his car, and screeched out of the driveway. And he gave it the sound of his car wheels crushing the life out of Carrie. He hadn't meant to kill the poor thing, but once he realized what he'd done, he'd been filled with a savage satisfaction that Alice would suffer for refusing to submit to his temper. Then he gave it his carefully hidden glee at Alice's mourning and the ugly suspicions that flourished within him as her behavior hardened and grew more distant. He gave it the rage he had hidden just as carefully as his glee when he followed that night, months later, to the motel where she spent two hours alone in a room with Art, the partner he had trusted with his life, and to whom, he discovered, he'd lost his wife.

And he gave it the shove, that unplanned but indomitable moment when opportunity thrust up a vulgar head in the form of a madman dressed in jockey shorts and a machine gun. The man with the machine gun was mad, all right, but he was too drugged to move well, and Guthrie, weapon at the ready, could have taken him out easily enough as he and Art burst through the door. But that nasty little opportunity diverted his attention away from the madman and reached out with Guthrie's free hand and shoved, and Art stumbled toward the gunman. Art hadn't a chance. Before he could recover and bring his weapon up, the madman filled his head with emptiness. For that split second, as Art's head disappeared, Guthrie felt the emptiness in his own heart fill with the same savage satisfaction that Alice would suffer again and even more deeply than before. And then the satisfaction was seared, in an instant and forever, by the bullet that crippled Guthrie.

Now, two years later, even more crippling was the memory of Art's brains, hot, wet, and clotted on Guthrie's face. Worse, it had all been for nothing. Art was gone, and Alice had immediately understood the truth, just as she had understood about Carrie. Then she, too, was gone as if she had never been, leaving only emptiness, memories of his corruption, and an isolation that was all the more damning because he'd already damned himself.

If Aswad Mar wanted what Guthrie had, it was welcome to it. Let it take the guilty memories and leave him alone, as Alice had, in his vacant house.

Dimly, Guthrie was aware of fingers closing like claws on the tendons of his forearms. He felt no pain, but his fingers opened spasmodically, and the head clanged to the floor and rolled out of his range of vision.

"Hold it," Tereba whispered hoarsely in Guthrie's ear, voice weak and distant. "You must hold it by yourself." Then Tereba was gone, and Guthrie was completely alone with the demon.

Suddenly, Aswad Mar understood that suck as it might, it could never completely consume Guthrie's guilt. The demon fed on desire, not abandoned need, and Guthrie's guilt, his consuming memories, had not fed it but only deepened its hunger. Now there was nothing for the demon to hold, nothing to devour, nothing but the forlorn wisps of everything Guthrie had lost, everything that had abandoned him, and everything he had forsaken.

Worse, it was trapped in the solitary cell of Guthrie's mind as inexorably as it had been in the mirror. Not only was Guthrie a cell as lifeless as the mirror had been, he was far more transitory—the mirror, hidden in the sculpture, had outlasted centuries, but Guthrie was all too mortal. And Guthrie was himself trapped in this chartless, exitless cavern of smoke and distance.

Aswad Mar's wail of thwarted fury slashed the echoes of its triumph to tattered shreds. It tried to flee back to the mirror, but the head that had been its home for so long was gone, lying somewhere unseen on the stone floor.

Despair gripped the demon. Confused, it spun inside Guthrie, seeking escape from this prison it once thought so tempting. But the cold metal head was an unreachable haven, and escape was no longer possible. Aswad Mar rampaged through Guthrie's mind, and Guthrie gripped his head and howled at the madness of the wild thing trapped and trampling his thoughts into dark corners.

"Drive it out," said a voice, but Guthrie didn't hear until it came again with greater insistence.

"Drive it out, and it will return to its own realm."

"I can't," Guthrie gasped.

"It's yours now. If you don't send it back, it will die with you."

"It's too strong. I can't think."

"You can't fight it with strength or thought," the voice said. "Find the way. It's there, inside you."

"No," Guthrie cried, and collapsed to his knees, clutching his head as if fingers could trap the demon thrashing inside and rip it out. "I can't." He fell over onto his side.

Right in front of him was the bronze head, lying on its left ear, facing him, not three feet away. The face was closed, mirror unseen and unseeable, and its eyes appeared to watch the conflict inside Guthrie's skull with calm detachment.

"You had no right!" Guthrie raged. "It's all your fault!"

The placid eyes stared back dumbly, but Guthrie knew it was a lie, anyway. It wasn't the head's fault, or the demon's, or even Alice's. He'd done it to himself. He'd let frustration turn to anger, anger to bitterness, and bitterness to despair. And despair had brought the weakness of a vindictive hate that had lashed out to destroy everything he loved, everything that connected him with other people and with reasons to go on living. Hopelessness had been just a breath away, and hopelessness is a place where hunger thrives but can never be satisfied.

That thought was like a seed germinating in the dark detritus trampled beneath Aswad Mar's own futility. If Guthrie couldn't wrest the demon from himself, still he might be able to rid himself of it. Tereba said Aswad Mar was the antithesis of life. Guthrie would have to use the antithesis of hopelessness, for hopelessness had led Guthrie on his long slide into the demon's territory. In that moment, Guthrie knew he would have to open himself to hope, even in the face of despair and uncertainty.

But could he ever again have hope? He'd done terrible, dastardly deeds to satisfy his own selfishness—deeds that had irreparably destroyed the hopes and lives of others. Carrie was dead, Art was dead, and Alice had fled from him in disgust. He no longer blamed them, though, for he saw that his own fear had given birth to a sense of self-preservation that had been as futile as it was rigid. In the mad guise of protecting himself, he'd been driven to destroy all who had loved and trusted him. And now they were gone, all gone, and he knew it was his fault and no one else's. He could never regain their love and trust, could never bring them back to life. As Tereba once said, some transformations are irreversible.

In that moment, Guthrie knew utter and deep regret, and at its core a truth that went beyond guilt or desire or forgiveness or even love. It brought the knowledge that his own evil acts were as much a part of him as the good, and they would never go away or be forgotten. But despite all the losses those evil acts had bred, Tereba's words reminded him that he still retained a single power. He may not be able to return to that which had irrevocably been altered, but he could go on to something he could not yet fathom. Transformation would not expiate the evil, but that wasn't the point. The point was accepting that he had to keep on moving so that he would not be buried by the weight of his own corruption. Or by his goodness.

And eternity was the key. Eternity was as full as Aswad Mar was empty. Eternity could not be consumed, though the demon consumed for an eternity, and in it, Guthrie was all things good as well as all things evil.

What was it that the old man said? That Guthrie would have to embrace joy and beauty, hope and love, as well as fear and uncertainty? And to do any of that, Guthrie had to accept who and what he was—not blindly or unreservedly and not petulantly or snivelingly, but simply. Just as he had to accept Art and Alice and the gunman who'd crippled him. Accept himself because there was no other. He was no other, nor would he ever be.

Could Guthrie do that after so much bitterness, pain, violence, and hate? He didn't know, but he could try. He would try. He had to try because, despite everything that happened to him and everything he had done, he still wanted to live. And that was all he had. All there was.

As these thoughts echoed through Guthrie, Aswad Mar's thrashing increased in intensity, but at the same time, it shrank in volume and retreated into the base of Guthrie's skull, as if trying to conceal itself somewhere among Guthrie's primordial instincts.

Guthrie laughed. The demon's antic cringing was too ridiculous not to laugh. So Guthrie laughed. It wasn't sarcastic laughter, or humorous, or even joyous. It was just a little thing that said tomorrow might come, even for the dead.

In that instant, Tereba hit Guthrie across the back with a blow that drove all the air out of his lungs with a choking, gasping yell. The force of the blow jolted him to the verge of unconsciousness, and for a timeless moment that stretched into eternity, he seemed not to be lying on cold stone but was suspended in the golden haze filling the space above the floor. He was weightless, formless, and without thought. Only perception remained. At last, even that washed away as the golden glow flared in pellucid fusion, and Guthrie's sense of self vibrated into vanishing echoes.

37

CONSCIOUSNESS RETURNED LIKE DROPS OF clean spring rain melting the snows of winter. Guthrie opened his eyes, cognizant at first only of the flickering candlelight. Gradually, as sensation returned to the rest of his body, he grew aware of weight pressing on him.

It was Tereba, collapsed across Guthrie's chest.

Guthrie gently levered himself from beneath the old man and rolled him over. As he did, Tereba's eyes opened a crack, and his teeth showed in a thin smile.

"It is over. Aswad Mar is back in its own realm. And you, Mr. Guthrie," he breathed deeply, "you live again."

Guthrie helped the old man to his feet. The wiry body beneath the robes felt as frail as an insect wing.

"Where's the entrance?" Guthrie asked.

"This cavern has many entrances," Tereba said. "The one you seek is that way. Straight ahead." He pointed with a gesture so subdued it was symbolic and gave a barely audible sigh. "Take the straight path."

Guthrie got an arm beneath the bent old shoulders, but Tereba stopped him before they could move away from the spot.

"Don't forget the sculpture," he reminded Guthrie in his distant voice. "You are bound to return it to the rightful owners. Isn't that what you said?"

"I guess I did."

Tereba managed to stand alone while Guthrie went over to the head. It lay on its side, closed. He picked it up and regarded the face for a moment. The metal features and stone eyes seemed completely inert. Almost unconsciously, his thumb sought the catch that would open the head and reveal the mirror.

"Are you certain you wish to take that chance?" came Tereba's voice from close behind him. "You are no longer invulnerable to its influence."

Guthrie didn't look at the old man but just replied, "The risk is greater if I don't check."

He popped the catch, opened the head, and stared into the mirror. The face that stared back was alive. Haggard and worn, but alive. And it was his own face. Only his own.

Guthrie closed the head and put it into the gym bag. Then he supported Tereba with his free arm, and together they moved in the direction the old man indicated.

Guthrie's journey through the smoke had seemed like miles, and he worried about how far away the door might be. He needn't have. The stone wall appeared in a hundred paces, and the door was right there, directly in front of them.

"Not so far, really." Tereba smiled faintly.

Guthrie pulled open the heavy wooden panel and got Tereba into the white stuccoed room.

"We will go into the garden for a moment," Tereba said.

Guthrie found the request reasonable since the door to the garden was the only one visible aside from the one they'd just come through, and he wasn't anxious to reenter the cavernous place they'd left.

The air in the garden was cool and damp. The darkness overhead was spangled with stars, but a tinge of red showing in the distance over the stone wall indicated that dawn was not far off. Tereba took in a lungful of the wonderfully fragrant and peaceful air then let it out in a long, almost mournful sigh.

"Are you all right?" Guthrie asked.

"I am tired," the old man admitted. "And I...I...." He seemed at a loss for words, but Guthrie knew what he meant.

"You've been heavily involved in this case for a long time," he told the old man. "Now it's over. Call it postpartum depression."

The old man gave Guthrie a piercing look then nodded and gestured toward the door.

"Let us go back inside."

Guthrie took him in again and wasn't surprised to see the heavy door to the enormous room replaced by the open archway. Cindy was standing there alone, but as she caught sight of Guthrie and Tereba, she turned and called out. By the time Guthrie closed the door, Mary and Wu had joined her. The man wore a stoical expression, but the girls showed fear as Guthrie staggered across the floor, bearing almost all of Tereba's weight. Even so, he noticed they didn't dare enter the stuccoed room. Guthrie took the old man through the archway.

"Be careful," Guthrie warned. "He's weak as a baby."

Tereba turned sharp eyes on Guthrie.

"Strong enough," the old man hissed, "to have delivered you."

Cindy and Mary anxiously took the old man and, supporting him on either side, disappeared into the depths of the house.

"Your work is finished," Wu said solemnly.

"Not yet," Guthrie said. "I've still got to give this," he hefted the gym bag, "to the Harveys."

Wu gave the gym bag a wary look, but Guthrie shook his head.

"It's over. The demon is gone."

Wu suddenly looked as if as much weight lifted from his shoulders as Guthrie felt had lifted from his own.

"You have performed a great service for Master Tereba."

"Then maybe we're even."

Wu smiled and escorted Guthrie away from the stuccoed room. Tereba didn't have a phone. Guthrie suspected a call to the Harveys would be long distance, anyway. He decided to go home and make the Harveys come to him.

It was early evening as he emerged into the alley behind the shopping center. Houston time, that is. The sky was clear and cloudless, the air calm and cool. Wu followed him through the door. Guthrie was surprised to see his Honda parked against the wall.

"I found it and brought it here," Wu explained. "Two men were watching it. They'll be out of the hospital soon." He smiled faintly, then noticed Guthrie's sidelong glance toward the end of the alley.

"No hospital can help Stanton."

Guthrie shuddered, remembering the hatred and death in Stanton's eyes, as Wu handed him two items. The first was his key ring.

"It was under the floor mat," Wu explained.

The second was a 9mm automatic.

"Stanton's. You might need it. After all, your personal fighting skills aren't all they should be." He smiled again.

"Maybe you could give me lessons sometime," Guthrie said.

"I'd be pleased. We can begin as soon as you've recovered."

The inside of Guthrie's car was in shambles. The Rampart men had been crude in their search for the bust. They'd even broken off the rearview mirror. Guthrie put the gym bag on the passenger seat and headed for home.

When he reached his street, he drove slowly toward his house, scanning for signs of Rampart vehicles or Ingram's Mercedes. Neither were evident, but when he pulled into his driveway and stopped, he wasn't about to take chances. He cocked Stanton's automatic then took the sculpture out of the gym bag. Cradling the head in his left arm, he pressed the muzzle of the automatic right between its eyes. He got out of the car and walked toward the front door.

He was halfway there, when Ingram stepped out of the shadows of the bushes at the front of the house, gun drawn and aimed at Guthrie's face.

"As you can see, I've recovered the sculpture," Guthrie said.

"Good work, I have to admit," Ingram replied. "But you could have saved yourself a lot of trouble."

"If I had, I wouldn't have had the pleasure of seeing Stanton die. Recognize the gun?"

Ingram didn't react, but Guthrie could tell the words hurt him.

"You cheap piece of shit," Ingram hissed.

"Don't get abusive. You've earned your share of dirty names."

"I'm going to earn a whole lot more than that when I take that," Ingram nodded toward the sculpture, "to Mr. Egan."

"That's not going to happen. The Harveys get it. Not you, not Egan, not even Prentice. After all," he smiled wryly, "they're the ones with the deed."

"I only regret I can't take my time with you." Ingram tensed ever so slightly.

"Shoot, and I'll blow this thing to pieces," Guthrie ground out. "How will Egan feel about you, then? Or Prentice? Not too good, I suspect. Maybe Prentice'll use that big eye of his on you."

Ingram shuddered but his weapon didn't falter.

"You can be stupid or smart," Guthrie said. "Use your gun, and it's all over for everyone. Drop your gun, and Zeroth gets the head back in one piece. And we both keep ours."

Grudgingly Ingram lowered his gun.

"Put it down there." Guthrie indicated the front step. When Ingram complied, Guthrie told him to back off. For the first time, he removed the muzzle of Stanton's automatic from the sculpture's face and aimed it at Ingram's heart.

"I want to waste you, Ingram. You're a murderous sack of shit and you deserve to die. But I think I'll enjoy it more thinking about you slinking back to Prentice and telling him a stupid klutz like me beat you at your own game. Then tell him to send the Harveys over here to collect this. And they better bring the money Egan promised —in cash—or I'll put bullets in both of them as well as this."

"The next time I see you," Ingram grated, "I'll take you down."

"Better make that a real long time. I've got your gun and Stanton's gun, and I saw you use them on those cops you fed to the rats. I'll bet HPD would love to have them for ballistics checks. And the finger-prints on them. I can see the headlines now—high-ranking security personnel murder police officers investigating break-in. Wouldn't go over too well with Egan and Prentice. Too much profile."

Ingram's fists clenched, and fury twisted his lips.

"I'll find a way, Guthrie. One day, I'll find a way."

"Fly off, Mr. Raven, back to your boss. Time to eat crow."

Ingram left, striding down the front walk with stiff, deliberate steps. At the street, he reached into his jacket, and Guthrie shoved the muzzle of Stanton's gun against the sculpture, waiting for Ingram to turn and fire. But Ingram simply made a flipping motion with his wrist and raised his hand to his ear. The hand held a cell phone. Guthrie couldn't hear what he said, but it couldn't have been much, for almost immediately he pocketed the phone.

Thirty seconds later, the midnight blue Mercedes rolled almost noiselessly down the street and stopped by Ingram. As the Raven got in, Guthrie could see the car was driven by the big, hatchet-faced Mexican, Cuchilla. Then the car rolled off and was lost in the darkness. When it was gone, Guthrie retrieved the gym bag from the car and put the head inside.

As he returned to the front door, he picked up Ingram's gun, being careful not to leave his own prints on the metal. He wondered why Ingram met him outside instead of ambushing him in the house, but as he pulled open the screen, he saw the diagram on the front door and understood. Except that it was painted instead of carved, it appeared to be identical to the image on Master Tereba's red door.

Watchdog, he thought, staring at the diagram. Old Tereba gave me a watchdog.

He twisted the key, went into the house, and closed the door. Inside, he set the gym bag and guns on the coffee table, then lowered himself onto the sofa and contemplated the bag.

He felt clean for the first time in years. He relished the feeling for nearly half an hour before tires crunched shell in the driveway, followed by the sound of two car doors slamming and quick footsteps tracing up to the front door.

"Come in," he called in answer to the brief knock, not bothering to rise but picking up Stanton's gun. Carla came in, followed by Lloyd. Guthrie pointed the gun at the bag.

"It's in there." He couldn't help needling them a little. "Want to look at it?"

He reached toward the bag as if he were about to unzip it and take out a proud trophy, but Carla quickly said, "No!" as she and Lloyd visibly shrank.

"I think you should," Guthrie insisted. "If you are going to pay me twenty thousand...." He let it hang and changed tack. "You are going to pay me in cash, aren't you?"

Lloyd's face reddened with anger.

"We can't afford to dishonor a contract," he snapped.

"Not this one," Guthrie affirmed.

Lloyd tugged a fat legal-size envelope from his inside jacket pocket and tossed it to Guthrie.

"We hope you're going to keep quiet about this affair," Carla said.

"My mouth is sealed," Guthrie promised. "As long as you and Prentice and the rest leave me alone. And that includes Egan and his people at Rampart."

"Agreed," Carla spat, and Lloyd reached for the bag.

"Hold it," Guthrie ordered. "If you're paying me all this cash, don't you think you should make certain of the merchandise? Think of how foolish you'll feel if you deliver a chunk of rock to Prentice instead of the head."

Lloyd stopped and glanced at his wife. "He's right, Carla."

"Do you want to look at it?" she retorted.

He obviously didn't, but Guthrie had dealt a hand he couldn't ignore. One of them had to check the bag.

Lloyd regarded Guthrie with suspicion. "You know we don't dare look in there."

Suddenly Guthrie was weary of the game. He was tired of these people and their grubby greed. But that wasn't what really bothered him, he realized. What he couldn't wipe away was the memory of the total defeat radiating from Travis as Guthrie drove away from him just a few dark nights ago. Nor could he forget Stanton's bullet tearing the life from Travis's lanky, wasted frame or Ingram pitching him into the muddy, swollen bayou. Guthrie had made it out of the flood, but Travis never would, his body tumbling and drifting in the deeper currents until it reached the Gulf of Mexico and its journey's end. It must be there by now, food for fish and crabs.

Guthrie stared at Lloyd's six-foot-two of arrogance in python boots and Carla's sick chic and wished he hadn't taken the head to Tereba but instead contrived to give these two their own good look at the face of hell. Yeah, he'd let them get good and sucked in, then he'd take the thing away from them just like he'd taken it away from Travis and the motel maid.

That would be fitting. The Harveys and the rest of Zeroth had used the mirror to entrap and manipulate others in order to gain wealth and power. Maybe it would only be fair to give them a taste of their own medicine. When poor slobs like Guthrie or the maid or Travis stared into the glass, they saw visions of wealth, power, and fulfillment. These two already possessed those. Guthrie wondered what they might see, what the demon would promise.

He shrugged mentally. Even if he stood right there and watched, he'd never know. The mirror was for individual viewing. It charmed the beholder with a personal vision that probably could never be fully apprehended by another. Each person lives alone in an interior and solitary world. Each person's thoughts and dreams and schemes are mostly secret from others. And some, like the dreams and visions revealed by the demon of the mirror, often are secret even from the dreamer.

Guthrie was tired of the game. Dead tired. All he wanted right now was for these two sad samples of humanity to get the hell out of his house as quickly as possible. They were only two, but they represented a crowd of trouble. And here they were, practically panting with lust to get back their scrofulous meal ticket so they could enslave the wills of who knows how many more in their quest to scramble to the top of the heap.

But Guthrie had knocked their pins right out from under them, and they didn't even know it. Cheap, sleazy Guthrie. That they would discover the truth all too soon gave him no satisfaction. He just wanted them out so he could take a good, long, hot bath and wash their stench down the drain.

So he let Lloyd off the hook by saying, "It's closed. You can't see the mirror."

Lloyd received this information with visible relief, which he tried to conceal as he pulled back the zipper and gingerly peered inside just enough to ascertain the object was indeed the bust.

"It's it," he said to Carla's unasked question. She eyed Guthrie thoughtfully while Lloyd zipped the bag.

Lloyd grasped the handles, but Guthrie couldn't resist one more dig. It might be his last opportunity.

"Don't I get to count this?" Then he reminded them, "I let you examine the merchandise."

Lloyd's face seethed with ill-suppressed anger, and Carla's face went white as her lips pressed into a razor-thin line. She stared at Guthrie like he was insane. Guthrie deliberately ignored them as he opened the envelope and thumbed through the bills. There were four packets of fifty crisp, hundred-dollar notes fresh from the bank.

"Okay," he said, carelessly tossing the envelope onto the coffee table. "Like you said, you can't afford to welsh."

"Is that all?" Cold indifference replaced Carla's lividity.

"You can tell Egan I'm declining his offer of employment. Now...." He let the sentence hang as he gestured toward the door."

Lloyd, not used to being ceremoniously dismissed by his inferiors, stomped out of the house carrying the bag. Carla, quiet and thoughtful, followed. At the door she glanced back at Guthrie for a moment, but he couldn't discern any meaning behind the glassy surface of her stare. Maybe she wanted to read his palm again.

Then she was gone, too, and a moment later, the Jaguar backed out of the driveway and snarled off down the street. He knew that after a hot bath, a good meal, and a sound sleep he'd be ready to face life again, but right now he wasn't feeling so generous. He shut the door and locked it against the world.

38

THE MORNING WAS HUMID AND hot as the sun burned off the moisture that had soaked into the ground. Guthrie could have groused at the mugginess, but he felt too good. The case was over and the Harveys and their crappy friends were off his back. Plus, he possessed twenty-seven thousand dollars in cash. And he hadn't yet checked the bank account or Travis's savings deposit box.

But no matter how much money was in them, he had something better. Master Tereba had made him alive again. Hell, he felt more alive than he had in five years.

He ate a light breakfast, and while he sat at his desk and drank his first cup of coffee in a week, the phone chirped.

"Yeah?" he answered it.

"You are quite a resourceful man, Mr. Guthrie."

"Well, if it isn't Mr. Prentice," Guthrie replied amiably. "What induced you to call at this early hour?"

"You are mistaken. The hour is late, indeed."

"I hope I'm not going to be subjected to veiled threats over the phone. I've had a rough couple of weeks, and I'm in no mood."

"I can readily understand your mood. I'm not so pleased, myself."

"Understandable. It's tough losing an old friend. But then, it was about as trustworthy as the rest of your cronies."

Prentice chuckled and said, "Their lack of trustworthiness is precisely why I chose them."

"Doesn't it bother you not to have any real friends?"

"I require a chorus, not friends."

"Maybe you don't need friends, but I do, and I've got them. In fact, I helped one of them send the little demon in the mirror back to the hell it came from."

"So that's what happened. I wondered. I admit it disturbs me to lose such a valuable resource."

"Yeah, I suppose I'd be bothered, too, in your position."

"It would seem my position is a good deal more secure than yours," Prentice replied. "I know your home is protected, and perhaps I can't get to you there, but you have to emerge sometime. I'll be waiting."

"Wait all you want, Prentice, but maybe you better not do much more than wait."

"Veiled threats, Guthrie? I thought you were in no mood."

"I'll make it clear, then. You have a lot more to lose than I do."

"And how is that?"

"I've gathered a lot of information on Zeroth. Enough to cause a big stink. Enough to link it to scandal, corruption, and murder. Imagine how the politicians, contractors, and corporate execs you've controlled with the mirror and by other means are going to feel about your little power hungry group when they receive a full dossier on its activities."

"No one would believe it."

"Even if they don't believe nine pars of it, they'll believe the tenth they're personally involved in. They'll tear you apart like a horde of hungry rats. I'm sure you can imagine what that's like.

"I suppose you are able to support your contentions with proof."

"Enough. Especially in the case of the murders. Egan was pushing his boys hard to get me, and they killed a couple of cops. I've got their guns, and one, at least, has fingerprints. The cops don't take lightly to the murder of one of their own. I know because I was a cop once. Remember? And I've still got friends on the force. Think of the repercussions in the police department when they learn the top enforcers of Rampart Security murdered cops investigating a break-in and fed their bodies to a horde of rats. Your influence might be able to get them to ignore a lot, but they won't ignore that. Especially with an eyewitness who's ready to testify."

"What do you want?"

"Not a damn thing, Prentice. Just leave me alone. I don't want to see or hear of you. If you decide to kill me, fine. Just be prepared to have a full report disseminated to all interested parties immediately afterwards. Oh, and don't forget a certain elderly black gentleman who seems to have a stake in my continuing health and well being. And if you have any lingering doubts about the wisdom of leaving me alone, let me tell you this: I faced the entity in the mirror, I saw what was there, and I turned away. I even know the entity's true name. Names are power, aren't they, Mr. Prentice?"

"As I said before," Prentice's voice was quiet, "you have proved to be quite resourceful."

"When Egan first approached me, I didn't have much to look forward to. I was down and out and good as dead. I just didn't know it. But I learned something, thanks to all the shit you put me through. I learned that life is too precious to piss away on games invented by assholes like you. You might have time to play around with other people's lives, but this is the only life I have, and I'll do anything to keep you from meddling in it. Anything."

Prentice was silent for a moment, then said in a low voice, "I see I'll have to acquiesce to your demands. For now. Perhaps, though, my day will come."

The line clicked dryly, and Guthrie lay the phone on the desk. Yeah, he thought, maybe it will. But not today. He picked up the phone, went out to his car, and drove to the alley behind the shopping center.

Guthrie wasn't sure if he'd find the door in the alley. That occurrence seemed chancy. But he figured the old man might be expecting him. The door was there, all right, gleaming red. Guthrie stepped inside.

Tereba sat behind the counter, appearing frailer than on their first meeting but a hell of a lot better than when Guthrie had half-carried him out of the cavern. The withered cheeks seemed fuller, and the deep black eyes twinkled when he glanced up as Guthrie entered. He smiled just like a spider who's seen a juicy bug hum into its web.

"Hello, Mr. Guthrie. My, those are some nasty marks you have there. May I see?"

"Rat bites. This," Guthrie said, exposing the gash on his shoulder, "was a bullet. And this," pulling up his shirt, "was a knife."

"As I told you, your skin would be in danger."

"Yeah, well I just hope I don't get tetanus or rabies."

"Tsk, tsk," the old man shook his head. "You don't have these diseases." He spread his hands. "Only the living can get them."

"I'm alive now."

"So you are," the old man nodded. "And what has become of the bust?"

"It's done. I gave them the sculpture, and they paid me. The contract is filled." He chuckled. "Prentice called to express how upset he was to lose Aswad Mar and threaten me."

"What did you tell him."

"I explained that I had a substantial dossier on Zeroth that would be released if I met a sudden demise. I also have the pistols the Ravens used to kill the two cops. Then I invoked you as my protector. I hope I wasn't wrong."

"Certainly not. And the kuei over your power center should afford a certain degree of protection of, shall we say, inimical forces that Zeroth might bring to bear on you."

"Okay. I was pretty pissed about the tattoo at the time, but it helped me get through all that. "Now," he looked the old man in the eye, "what's it all about, really? Where'd that thing in the mirror come from?"

"That's far too long a story to tell right now, and I'm too tired."

"What about you? How did you get involved?"

"That's part of the story. For now, let's just say that I'm trying to bring a little order to the world despite the proliferation of entropy, chaos, and whim."

"That doesn't tell me a heck of a lot about you."

"Who is Tereba?" The dark old face grinned. "He's just an old man who collects poetic aphorisms and quaint diagrams."

"And uses tools?"

"A hammer can smash a thumb as well as pound a nail."

Guthrie thought about tools. He thought about himself, but he also remembered a defeated man standing alone beneath a midnight street lamp. Guthrie knew about aloneness.

"I am sorry about Travis," the old man said. "He associated himself with those whose only interest was manipulation, and when he attempted to seize power, he was himself seized."

"Some consolation."

"Perhaps you are saddened because you see something of yourself in him, and you mourn its passing from your life."

"I'm alive, Master Tereba. More alive than before. If I regret anything, it's not facing the demon of guilt earlier. I did terrible things, but at least now I can learn to live with them. But it's not quite like I thought it would be."

"And how was that?"

"I thought there would be peace. I thought there was a place where there was an end and everything would be all right. But I realize now that there is no end, and it's never all right, and we have to accept who we are because that's all we have. Life just keeps moving, but at least that means we have chances to make changes for the better. Maybe that's enough."

"I think you're right," the old man said, his eyes dropping for a moment. "It is better to learn wisdom late than never at all."

"I don't feel particularly wise."

"I was referring to myself," Tereba replied a bit testily. "And now...." He pulled out a drawer, rummaged in it, and held out his hand to Guthrie. "These are for you."

Lying in Tereba's incredibly smooth palm were a key and a slip of paper. Guthrie took them and looked at the paper. The name of a bank was typed on it, followed by a series of numbers. Underneath that was a line, and beneath that the name of another bank and a second, shorter number.

"What's this?"

"The first is the number to a bank account in your name. Your payment for your services as a detective, paid through a legal firm and correctly reported as income."

Guthrie wondered how much was in the account, but he didn't ask. He'd check when he got home.

"And this?" He turned the key in his fingers.

"It is the key to a safe deposit box located at the second bank. The box number is below the bank's name. It belonged to Mr. Travis. It is full of cash. His ill-gotten gains from his employment with Hastings."

"I can't take that."

"Suit yourself, though I suspect if you don't, it eventually will find its way into the hands of Zeroth as soon as they learn its whereabouts."

"Maybe I'll take it, after all," Guthrie acquiesced, pocketing the key and paper. "Thanks."

"No," Tereba said. "Thank you." He seemed sincere, but Guthrie could never be sure about the old man. His eyes were just too deep and his smile too mischievous and joyous and implacable, all at the same time. Wearing that same smile, he ushered Guthrie to the door.

"What happens to Travis's watchdog?" Guthrie asked, wondering if the house on South Rice would be infected for eternity. "Will you take care of it?"

"No need. Such things do not outlive their owners," Tereba said, reaching for the door latch. "By the way, Mr. Guthrie," he said as he pulled the panel open. "There is one question I would like you to answer."

"What's that?"

"You are the only person ever to have known Aswad Mar intimately and survived unscathed. What was the demon like?"

Guthrie paused on the threshold. How could he answer? Did he want to? He gave the old man a steady look and a wry smile.

"It had my face."

The old man's own smile deepened.

"Good-bye, Mr. Guthrie."

"Good-bye, Master Tereba."

The old man closed the door, and Guthrie walked to his car and got in. Only after he started the engine did he glance toward the red door. An unbroken stretch of cement-block wall met his eye.

He put the car in gear and drove home.

For the further adventures of Clay Guthrie, check out these titles.

THE DEAD DETECTIVE

Teetering on the edge of the gutter, ex-cop Clay Guthrie is offered a way out of his bitter isolation. All he has to do is locate a stolen sculpture. The task seems simple enough until Guthrie finds himself enmeshed in a series of surreal events that push him to the breaking point. His disturbingly dangerous employers threaten him with pain and death if he fails, and the mysterious old man who is their antagonist forces Guthrie to act on his behalf, warning that worse horrors will greet his success. The only way Guthrie can survive is to find the sculpture and help the old man destroy the terrible power that lives within it. But first, he must endure a series of trials that test his endurance and drive him into the core of his own corruption.

LANDSCAPE WITH BEAST

"Who better to send into a grave situation to find out what lies buried there than one who has known death? Such as you." With those words, mysterious old Tereba sends Guthrie on the trail of a missing artist. Having to deal with a witch from an ancient lineage and the ultimate hunter seeking the ultimate prey didn't bother him, but the doorway to another world was a different matter. Out there an unknowable predator waited, and it wanted nothing more than to lay waste to everything in its path. But Guthrie couldn't refuse. He knew that anythingTereba directed his way would be as interesting and important as it might be dangerous, and those were lures he couldn't resist. Besides, when he set a trap for his nemesis, the bait wasn't the only thing that disappeared into the unknown along with the artist. Now Guthrie's client had vanished, too.

THE TEXAS TROLL UNLIMITED

When a frightened railroad employee tells Clay Guthrie that a monster in a boxcar ate his co-worker, Guthrie finds himself drawn into a web of corrupt and warped ambition and wanton violence. Traveling to far West Texas in search of the monster, Guthrie and the trainman encounter an organization whose goal is the total destruction of social order and whose weapon is an abomination from the past. Waging a guerrilla war against their enemies beneath the harsh Texas sun, they quickly discover that the nights hold a mortal danger more terrible than their human enemies. With the fate of civilization in the balance, they must eliminate the humans who stand in their way before they can root out and confront a canny and clever inhuman foe.

DARKNESS INSATIABLE

Clay Guthrie is sent by his mysterious employer to track down a missing man, but finding the objet of his search in an unnatural place and in an impossible condition provides no easy answers. Far worse, he encounters a town the grip of an unknown, unseeable, and malevolent force that thrives on turmoil and destruction and has left the utter annihilation of three other towns in its wake. What will it take to learn the cause and remedy it before it's too late? And who—or what—will get in the way?

Non-Fiction from Phosphene Publishing Company

A SMALL WAR AT CLOSE QUARTERS

Vic Hinterlang

A young state tax attorney decides to follow his dream of becoming an international photojournalist, moving in 1987 with his new bride to El Salvador to cover its civil war. With the help of a few contacts, he becomes part of the freelance photographer ecosystem in Central America, going out daily to cover newsworthy events in El Salvador's "low intensity conflict." During his time there, his professional and personal concerns evolve along with the course of the war, culminating in an intersection that directly challenges his commitment to his dream. *A Small War At Close Range* is not only a fascinating up-close look at the conflict in El Salvador, it also highlights a stultifying bureaucracy almost as tough to navigate as the country's rugged terrain as well as the challenges of adjusting to the often dangerous working environment that journalists there faced.

THE WELLSPRING: AN INQUIRY INTO THE NATURE OF CHI

Christopher Dow

Since prehistoric times, peoples the world over have believed in a creative force that inspires life. Throughout history it has been known by many names: mana, prana, ka, and chi, to name only a few. Much has been written about this energy and the ways in which it can be strengthened to enhance life and well-being as well as to provide the basis for many of the Eastern martial arts, particularly tai chi chuan. But if chi is real, why is there so little scientific evidence for its existence or for the physiological structures that generate and channel it throughout the body? Moreover, what is the exact nature of chi, and how can it interact with physical reality in the sometimes esoteric ways that are reported? *The Wellspring* draws together, for the first time, two significant but disparate lines of scientific research that not only identify the physiological structures that produce and channel chi but that point to the true nature of this mysterious power.

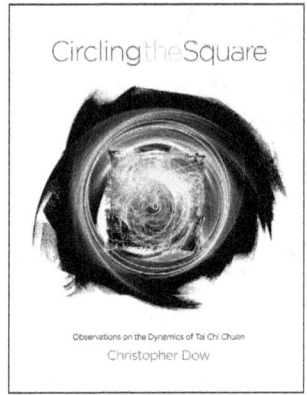

CIRCLING THE SQUARE: OBSERVATIONS ON THE DYNAMICS OF TAI CHI CHUAN

Christopher Dow

Tai chi chuan is many things: a martial art, a superlative exercise, a mode of meditation, and a method to build internal vitality, strength, and power and to improve health. But what exactly is tai chi? How does it function? What makes it work? In *Circling the Square*, Christopher Dow draws on a variety of fields to examine this fascinating movement art, beginning with an analysis of its basic physical structure. From there, he delves into how chi, the energy behind tai chi's legendary power, is generated and then manifested through the movements of the tai chi form to create a gestalt that is greater than the sum of its parts. Along the way, he evaluates the distinct characteristics of the Thirteen Postures, breathing techniques, the concept and physiology of the tai chi bow, power emission, and a number of other topics of interest to the serious student of tai chi. The lessons of Circling the Square can apply to any tai chi style, and the book will appeal to anyone— beginner and more experienced practitioner alike—who wishes to deepen their understanding of this fascinating and timeless martial art.

ELEMENTS OF POWER

Christopher Dow

Tai Chi Chuan is an art that adheres to natural laws, and its operating principles and practices can be found in myriad objects, activities, scientific fundamentals, and engineering applications.
In *Elements of Power*, Christoper Dow explores a number of the fascinating connections that can be drawn between Tai Chi and the physical world around us, opening new dimensions to the art. The lessons of Elements of Power can apply to any Tai Chi form, and the book will appeal to anyone—beginner and more experienced practitioner alike—who wishes a deeper understanding of this fascinating and timeless martial art.

Phosphene Publishing Company
publishes books and DVDs relating to literature,
history, the paranormal, film, spirituality, and the
martial arts.

For other great titles, visit
phosphenepublishing.com